TO SAVE AN EMPIRE

A Novel of Ottoman History

ALLAN R. GALL

Published by: Allan R. Gall

ISBN: 978-0-692-08755-8

PROLOGUE

The Ottoman Empire was a hereditary autocracy based on the lineage of Osman I, who ruled a relatively small principality in western Anatolia at the end of the thirteenth century. His descendants made it an empire, capturing the seat of the Byzantine Empire, Constantinople, and extending their suzerainty west as far as Vienna and east as far as Russia, Persia, Afghanistan, Yemen, and Morocco. The Mediterranean Sea and the Black Sea were Ottoman seas. The sultan's rule extended into three continents. At the height of Ottoman power in the sixteenth century under Sultan Süleyman, called "The Magnificent" by the West and "The Lawgiver" by the Turks, the Ottoman Empire was the world's military superpower and the apex of the world's sumptuousness. The sultan of the Ottoman Empire claimed the title "Caliph of Islam."

When the chief protagonist of this novel ascends the throne as Sultan Abdülhamit II in 1876, the empire's land mass is moderately reduced, but its power is greatly reduced. Europe has ascended, and the Ottomans are turned westward for cultural, political, and military currency.

Maps and a glossary of Turkish words are found at the back of the book. The maps are provided to help the reader visualize the relative geographic locations of sites and events that are mentioned in the novel. Where place names have changed such that a reader would not be able to find them on a modern map, I have indicated their current name.

ONE

"The time has come," Hüseyin announced, addressing his guest, Mithat. It was just past midnight, May 30, 1876.

Mithat had waited for this moment, the moment when they would launch an event that could change the future of their country. He would have said the words himself, but as a guest in Hüseyin's home, he deferred to him. "Yes, let's go," Mithat responded, his voice reflecting his relief and resolve. Tonight they would carry out Mithat's plan. He had convinced the Council of Ministers and the Council of State, of which he was president, that tonight's action was necessary; and he asked Hüseyin, who was minister of war, to be his partner. The soldiers would do as Hüseyin ordered.

Hüseyin rose and called to a servant, "Have Agim meet us at the dock."

Hüseyin was of moderate height and build, but his military bearing and uniform gave him the appearance of a taller man. Mithat was tall and also stood erect. They left the room, stepped out of their indoor slippers—Mithat into his European-style shoes and Hüseyin into his polished military boots—and walked down the steps to the dock under the house.

Only when he stepped into the small *kayık* rowboat with which they would cross the Bosphorus did Mithat feel anxious. The steady rain—unexpectedly cold for the end of May— made him shiver, and he gripped the sides of the *kayık* tightly as he sat down on the forward bench.

The strong Bosphorus current dictated the point on the opposite shore that a small *kayık* could reach, based on the strength, number, and skill of the rowers. Mithat suggested they use two oarsmen, but Hüseyin insisted on using only his most trusted personal servant.

"Agim's rowed me across the Bosphorus many times. I didn't tell him our purpose, and, if asked, he'll know nothing," Hüseyin said, but, of course, he knew that under torture every man knew something.

Agim edged the *kayık* out of the dock, pulled hard on the oars, and sent them out from under the house, onto the black waters, into the rain, and on to their mission to save the Ottoman Empire.

Already, Mithat felt the effect of the unforeseeable. He was not dressed for the unseasonably cold rain. The dampness triggered involuntary shivers, as though he were afraid. The rage of the current was apparent even in the starless dark through which Agim forced the *kayık*. The Bosphorus was no man's friend. As fast as the current flowed on the surface, it flowed faster in the opposite direction below.

Many died in the Bosphorus. Everyone knew the stories of harem girls and women tied in rock-weighted sacks and thrown into the Bosphorus with no one to ask what their offense had been or why forgiveness had been left to Allah. Even the strongest swimmers succumbed to the Bosphorus. Drownings were regularly reported in summers when hubris led young men out into the current from the indentations of shoreline that protected swimmers. Mithat gripped the sides of the *kayık* tightly and looked away from the water, hoping to see the opposite shore. He could not.

But from the shore they had just left, Mithat could still see light from one of the windows of Hüseyin's house, a *yalı* on the Asian side of the Bosphorus in the seaside village of Kandilli.

Light from a single window came from the upper floor that extended out above the water, drawing Mithat's eyes to the *yalı*'s dark outline. The image hovered over the water, a one-eyed vulture, watching, waiting for the little *kayık* to make an error, to give up the lives it cradled.

After what seemed twice as long as he knew it had been, Mithat made out the welcome beam of the lighthouse and the shadow of the opposite shore. They were approaching slightly up-current from a dock, so that Agim had only to ease off the oars for the *kayık* to deliver them to their destination. Agim was a master. They were wet and cold, but the first step of the plan had gone perfectly.

"Where are the carriages?" Hüseyin's voice revealed a trace of anxiety. "Agim, see if they're at the next dock. I was very clear that we'd be landing at this dock," he added, as though to absolve himself.

They waited in silence in the dock's passenger shelter. They needed one carriage to take Hüseyin to the palace, where the guards would do as he ordered. Mithat would take the second carriage to the Ministry of War, and on the agreed-upon signal, he would announce the change in government to the officers and the troops in the barracks. There would be no opportunity for opposition.

Mithat was the driving force behind what they were about to do. Sultan Abdülaziz was no longer carrying out his responsibilities as head of state. He was closeted with a seventeen-year old odalisque and was squandering the empire's wealth in a sumptuous palace inhabited by thousands of functionaries, women, children, and slaves.

Mithat chafed at the anachronism that was his country, an empire with the bureaucratic and military trappings of a modern state, but one that remained a medieval theocracy headed by an autocrat. The sultan was also the Caliph, the acknowledge figurehead of the faithful, and he appointed the Sheikh Ul-Islam. But, ironically, among the powers of the Sheikh Ul-Islam was the power to depose the sultan who appointed him. Mithat reflected on this irony with amusement. It allowed him to bring down Sultan Abdülaziz with the stroke of Sheikh Ul-Islam Hasan Hayrullah's pen. His *fetva* of deposition was with Hüseyin Pasha and read:

> If the Chief of the Faithful gives proof of mental derangement … and if his continuance in power becomes injurious to the nation, may he be deposed? Answer: The Sharia says, yes. Signed: Allah's humble servant, Hasan Hayrullah, to whom may Allah grant his indulgence.

Mithat's thoughts were interrupted by the sound of horses' hooves and carriage wheels on the cobbled street. Running toward the carriages, Mithat shouted to Hüseyin, "May Allah be with you. I'll wait for your signal."

"And with you, my brother. I've sent word that you're coming with orders from me," Hüseyin responded.

"With the help of Allah, we will serve our country."

"I commend you to Allah."

The rain and cold did not relent, and the black streets revealed nothing of what lay ahead. Yet in the carriage, Mithat was warmed by the comfort of steps taken as planned, of fitting in a puzzle piece that made selecting the next one obvious. Tonight was only the first of many steps needed to prevent the collapse of the empire. But on tonight's base, he would build a stairway; he would climb it; and he would pull the nation up behind him.

******

Prior to tonight, Mithat had met with Murat, the nephew of Sultan Abdülaziz and the next in line, to get his measure, to confirm Murat's reputation as progressive and informed on the state of the empire and on its relations with other countries, principally Britain, France, Austria-Hungary, and Russia— countries that exercised power—indeed, called themselves "the Powers." Mithat did not state the purpose of his visit, but he knew that Murat would know. It was said that one in every six residents worked as a spy for the government or one of the European embassies. But custom prevented Murat from asking the obvious, Mithat from stating it, and both of them from confronting its consequences.

Murat passed the test. He understood constitutional government and the potential for democracy to unite the heterogeneous population of the empire and make it strong against the forces threatening to tear it apart. He raised no questions about the impact of such a government on the authority of the sultan. Murat came across as a bit high strung, nervous, but he would do. Mithat would ask only that Murat serve the interests of his country.

Mithat had been to Britain, where he studied the British system. And after returning to Istanbul, he shared his proposed constitution for the empire with the British Ambassador, Sir Henry Elliot, and secured assurances of Britain's support. He envisioned the sultan/Caliph as a constitutional monarch, a functional head of state to entertain foreign visitors and provide the faithful with an object of pride and pageantry, a guardian for the relics of the Prophet, and a name to be invoked at the Friday Noon Prayer. Real power would lie with the civil servants, the parliament, and the civil courts.

Even the *ulema*, the religious leaders and scholars, and the *softas*, the students of the advanced religious schools, understood and expressed support for constitutional government. Mithat described it to them as a legal framework grounded in the Muslim principle of consultation. He reminded them that the codification of the Sharia, Muslim Holy Law, had been established by checking and re-checking the stories of the acts and sayings of the Prophet to verify the credibility of teller and tale, to establish the veracity of witnesses. The Sheikh-Ul-Islam made rulings only after conferring with the *ulema*. Had not the Prophet advised his followers to consult one another? A Muslim leader held regular public audiences to listen to and take the petitions of the governed, a tradition predating Islam. Under the constitution, a council of the people, the parliament, would enact laws. And in the manner of the Sharia, these laws would be applicable to all, from the sultan to his poorest subject. To Mithat's surprise, the *softas* even issued a statement that declared autocracy to be contrary to the Sharia. This, after a thousand years of autocratic rule! He could not have asked for a more perfect coming together of events and public support for his vision, and he was exhilarated as his carriage moved through the empty night streets. Everything he had hoped for and worked to achieve seemed about to be realized.

The Ministry of War was dark. The guards, standing in shelters at either side of the main door, snapped to attention. "I bring you Mithat Pasha, president of the Council of State," announced the driver of the carriage.

"I'm here representing Hüseyin Pasha," Mithat announced. "Rouse the commander of the barracks."

Mithat waited inside the Ministry of War in Hüseyin's office. The commander of the barracks arrived and saluted him. "Good morning, sir," he said.

"Good morning," Mithat responded. "I bring you greetings and orders from Hüseyin Pasha. Soon, we will hear a gunshot, the signal that Hüseyin has presented the fetva of deposition to Sultan Abdülaziz and will arrive shortly with Murat, whom we will announce as Sultan Murat V. Rouse the troops and prepare them to salute the new sultan."

"Yes, sir."

******

At the dock, Hüseyin stepped into the second carriage and addressed the driver, a soldier he knew well, "Greetings, Ismail. Take me to the barracks across from Dolmabahçe Palace." His first task was to alert the soldiers guarding the palace. If there were any commotion inside the palace, he wanted no confusion about their duty, no over-reaction.

At the palace barracks, Ismail announced Hüseyin Pasha to the startled guards who roused their commander. The commander's unsurprised demeanor told Hüseyin that only the timing of their mission was unknown. It was impossible to get a *fetva* without the news getting out. Hüseyin took the commander and four soldiers with him across the street to the Dolmabahçe Palace entrance. The palace guards ushered them in and called for the chief eunuch of the harem, an obese black man whom Hüseyin addressed, "Show the sultan this *fetva*. If he comes peacefully, he'll not be harmed. I'll wait here."

"Yes, sir, I will bring him to you."

This was not Hüseyin's first time to enter the reception hall of Dolmabahçe Palace, but he was struck again by its opulence.

A giant baccarat crystal chandelier, said to be the largest in the world, hung in the center of the hall. Gold leaf covered the ceiling. Marble, alabaster, and mahogany were everywhere. Here, hundreds of slaves ate the finest lamb and pastries, wore clothing from imported cloth, and were warmed by European coal stoves. Lived and died here in this great palace built with the blood, tax, and sweat of the empire. And his soldiers? They shivered in the cold, gave thanks to their sultan for bread and water, and died for his honor.

Feeling the cold through his damp clothes, Hüseyin was angry. For centuries, deposed sultans had been executed. Hüseyin wished that practice still held. He shifted his weight with impatience, shivered, and muttered a silent curse. The door to the harem opened. The chief eunuch was followed by Sultan Abdülaziz, wearing a strambouline jacket thrown over his night-shirt and a fez lightly resting on un-brushed hair. He carried a sword loosely in his right hand, as though to defend himself—an absurd pretense, Hüseyin thought.

"Have you come to kill me?" Abdülaziz asked in a barely audible voice.

Hüseyin thought that his answer should be "yes," but he said, "No. If you come peacefully, no one will harm you."

"What will happen to me?" Abdülaziz asked in a pitiful, frightened voice.

"You will live your remaining days with your wives and children and some of your servants." Hüseyin felt disgust at having to state this truth. The man's head should be placed on a hook outside the Topkapı Palace gate as had once been the fate of common criminals. Had he not robbed the empire and prostrated it before its enemies as no army had been able to do?

"Allah is merciful. I will go peacefully," Abdülaziz said in an inflectionless voice, soft with defeat. He closed his eyes as though unwilling to witness what was happening.

"Allah is most merciful," Hüseyin echoed.

Hüseyin stepped out of the palace and fired one shot into the air, the signal to Mithat that step one was accomplished. He walked briskly, almost at a run away from the palace. The whole business disgusted him, and it was over, a past he was glad to brush off like threads of lint on his uniform. He was eager to get on with what lay ahead. Despite his doubts, it was now the future, and he rushed for it, shouting to the carriage driver, "Ismail! To the *konak* of Murat. I have just deposed the sultan. We live in awful times. Allah be with us."

"May Allah bless you, my commander. The country needs you."

"With Allah's help, the future will be better for the country and for our children."

Hüseyin's words were obligatory optimism. Mithat's plan might improve the state of the empire moderately and briefly, but Hüseyin feared it was not radical enough. It would not remove the hands of the Russians, British, French and other Western governments from the Ottoman treasury, crush their lust for its lands, or halt their meddling in every sphere of the empire's religious and civil life. Nor would it alter their prejudice against Muslims.

Arriving at Murat's *konak*, Hüseyin found Murat genuinely surprised to learn that his uncle had been deposed and asked in a barely audible voice, "Why are you here?" Murat was a small-framed man and stood slightly stooped as though leaning forward to hear. His face lacked distinguishable cheek-bones and bore a long, sharply hooked nose above a dark mustache that curved down at the ends over a thin mouth and a small chin. He stood before Hüseyin in a robe and slippers, resembling nothing of a sultan.

"I'm here to take you to the Ministry of War, where I will introduce you to the officers and soldiers as Sultan Murat V. The cannons from the ironclads will announce your accession to the nation." Hüseyin had not met Murat before, and he was surprised that Murat exhibited none of the confidence and poise Hüseyin had expected to see, based on Murat's reputation as a learned man, comfortable in Western social circles.

"I will come with you," Murat said, but with no inflection in his voice—almost, Hüseyin felt, as though he did not comprehend what was happening. He was about to become sultan and showed no emotion whatever. What kind of man was this?

In the carriage Murat began to shake, as though in fear. His eyes searched the dark out one side of the carriage, then the other, until fixing on Hüseyin's gun and sword. Hüseyin could think of nothing to say to the man who was about to become sultan, a task for which he appeared unfit.

How had the empire come to this? The tradition of a new sultan assassinating potential rivals had been rejected in the early seventeenth century as barbaric. Instead, sons of sultans were confined to a restricted area of the harem where they received a limited education but almost no experience of the world outside. They simply waited in chronological order for a turn at being sultan, preserved like fruit in a jar.

Now, sultans-in-waiting were treated better. They left the harem on reaching adulthood, but remained without a purpose, without duties that would prepare them for the power and responsibility of being sultan. Mithat and the reformers before him may have thought that this system allowed them, the bureaucrats, to exercise power, but Hüseyin knew that the people looked to the sultan, not to public officials, for leadership. And they looked to the military to protect the nation. Military strength was the hallmark of the Ottoman Empire, and the only measure the outside world respected.

Hüseyin squared himself to his most rigid military posture and forced himself to look directly at Murat, searching for any sign that this man could lead the empire. But he saw nothing and turned his gaze away, almost relieved. The empire would be led. But not by Murat.

At the Ministry of War, Mithat greeted them enthusiastically and congratulated Hüseyin.

"May Allah protect us, Mithat. Believe me. This man is unfit," Hüseyin said.

"What do you mean? I met with him. He's well educated," Mithat answered in surprise.

"And, I think, devoid of what you and I know it takes to lead the empire. For the sake of the country, I hope I'm wrong," Hüseyin said reflectively.

They each took Murat by an arm and led him up the steps of the Ministry to be introduced to and saluted by the troops. Standing on the steps, Murat continued to shake.

Dawn was on the horizon. Everything was on schedule. Hüseyin raised his pistol and fired the signal for the ironclads. Murat jerked and screamed as though the shot had hit him, and Hüseyin grabbed and held him. "It was nothing, my sovereign. I shot in the air," he said.

But with the boom of the first cannon, Murat bolted and ran into the Ministry of War. Mithat followed close behind.

Hüseyin dismissed the troops and joined Mithat inside. "What do we do with him?" he asked, looking at Murat, who was cowering in a corner of the room.

"I'll take him to the palace. The doctors there will have something to calm him. Maybe it's just a shock that will wear off quickly."

"I'll wait for word. May Allah be your helper."

"May He help us all," Mithat responded. Suddenly, the bright future he had seen for his country but moments before looked uncertain.

******

Hüseyin ordered the barracks commander to ride with Mithat and Murat in the carriage to Dolmabahçe Palace. On hearing the orders, Murat stood up, walked calmly beside the commander, and climbed into the carriage.

Hüseyin waited until they were out of sight before re-entering the ministry, passing between the armed sentries, who snapped to attention and saluted him. Both were young men of heavy bones and set jaws, with whom he could go to war confident that they would die for their country, their commander, their fellow soldiers. These were the men the Ottoman army had marched to Yemen, Vienna, Iran, Baghdad, Jerusalem, Mecca, Medina, Egypt, and North Africa—men beside whom he had fought.

The nation had many such men, and he, Hüseyin Avni Pasha, was their chief. That was his official title, *Serasker*, chief soldier. In the civilian administration, he was minister of war and served on the Council of Ministers. But he was honored to have the title of *Serasker*, an historic identity that the times called for him to make real again. The times called, not for a sultan, a grand vizier, or even a reformist dynamo, like Mithat, who was betting the empire's future on a European legal instrument, a constitution. The times called for a *serasker*.

His office had a high ceiling and long, narrow windows arched at the top along the east wall from which he now looked out onto the Bosphorus, specifically at the fleet of two ironclads that had sounded the transition from Sultan Abdülaziz to Sultan Murat V. The Ottoman armada, destroyed by the Western Powers at Navarino in support of Greek independence, had once made the Mediterranean an Ottoman Sea. Now, despite Abdülaziz's heavy investment in ships, Hüseyin considered the navy useful for little more than ceremonial duties and for the illusion of actual power that its presence represented for the people of Istanbul.

To protect its people of multiple ethnicities and religions from external threats, shield them from the fratricidal butchery incited by foreign vultures eyeing the empire's carcass, and ultimately govern them in a manner that would engender their loyalty, the empire needed a best-in-the-world army. A new sultan? A constitution? Salve on a gangrenous wound.

Hüseyin sat down behind his desk and called for tea, which a soldier had anticipated from habit and delivered immediately. Hüseyin raised the glass of hot tea between his callused thumb and forefinger, gripping it at its very top lip. The clear glasses in which tea was served were colloquially called "narrow-waisted," having an hourglass shape that suggested the perfectly-formed body of a young woman. He held the glass up against the light from the windows to admire the tea's color. It was perfect: reddish brown, not too dark, not too light. Just the way he liked it with two lumps of sugar that would already have been stirred in for him.

Tea was a British byproduct of the Crimean War. Many in Istanbul had resented the British soldiers wandering the streets after the war as though the city was theirs. But Hüseyin knew that without them, many thousands more Turkish soldiers would have died, and the empire would have lost the war. He and other Turks had adopted the British custom of having tea.

Coffee remained the drink of choice of upper-class Turks, but it was expensive. Tea could be the drink of the people, and he thought of himself as a man of the people, a man who would lead the people.

Among their enemies, no soldier was equal to the Turkish soldier. But today that was not enough. Maybe it never had been. In 1453, Sultan Mehmet the Conqueror did not lay siege to Constantinople with soldiers alone. He brought to its walls the newest armament money could buy, enormous cannon made in Hungary. Money could buy military power. If he could get control of the empire's treasury, Hüseyin was confident that he could build an army no country would dare challenge. A well-armed, well-trained Ottoman army. Exhilarating to contemplate.

His first priority would be the Balkans. He had to bring the fighting between the Christians and Muslims there to an end. He had to stop the Russians and the Austrians from inciting internal massacres to justify their interference. He could only do this with feared ground-forces. Historically, when the peoples of the world knew that the Ottoman army could march from Istanbul to Vienna and from Damascus to Tripoli at will, there was peace.

TWO

The cannon salute from the ironclads coincided with the morning call to prayer. As the faithful hurried to the mosques, the low-hanging clouds dripped their last onto the roofs and cobble stones to reveal a city washed clean for the new sultan.

Converging from multiple streets on their way to local mosques, Muslims whispered exchanges about the news. "Have you heard? Abdülaziz has been overthrown. The foreign powers are surely behind it."

"The foreign powers?"

"Abdülaziz didn't pay them what he owed. They want their money."

"I hear Dolmabahçe Palace has the largest European chandelier ever made."

"Live in luxury, die in luxury."

"Will he be killed?"

"Who knows? May Allah save him."

"Yes, may He, indeed."

******

In the Greek Christian quarter, they also knew the meaning of the cannon fire. Their lives would be affected as profoundly as those of their Muslim compatriots, and they faced the morning with similar questions, anxieties, and hopes.

"The new sultan must be Murat. He was next in line. They say he's a Western-oriented person."

"Yes, I hear he reads Western literature and newspapers."

"Reportedly, he's fond of cognac too. He should get on well with the French legation."

"The streets will be filled with people cheering the accession. Will you participate?"

"Oh, yes. We should show support, even though nothing will change for the better."

"What's for the better? A progressive sultan could make things worse for us."

"What do you mean?"

"All this talk of equal treatment. But would you want to appear before a Muslim judge? Send your sons to fight Christians under the banner of the Prophet?"

"Of course not."

"And how would your import business fare without our favorable tax rate?"

"I'd move to Greece, Alexandria. Maybe to America."

"Exactly. We'll show support for the new sultan, but we'll be realistic about equality."

"Yes, support the new sultan with no illusions. May God protect us."

"Surely He will."

******

In the Jewish quarter, Dr. Daniel de Fonseca and his wife, Hannah, sat up in bed at the sound of the cannons. "What was that?" Hannah asked.

"We have a new sultan. I heard yesterday that the Sheikh Ul-Islam issued a *fetva* authorizing Abdülaziz's deposition."

"Is that a good thing?" Hannah asked.

"I hope so. The empire is threatened. A new sultan is the minimum it needs."

"Something needs to be done about the refugees from the Balkans. Yesterday, a beggar came to the door. Her daughter had been branded with a Christian cross. It's hard to imagine the suffering, the cruelty." Her voice trailed off as the image returned.

"The sultan's head won't rest on the welfare of the refugees. There are no articles about them in the *London Times* or *Le Petit Journal* in Paris."

"What about us? Will anything change for us?" she asked.

"I don't think so. The fate of the sultan is tied to the bond debt, the welfare of the Christians in the Balkans, and the Russians' desire for territory."

"But if the empire collapses, could we be blamed?" Hannah asked, raising the question made obvious by history and her own experience of helping Jewish refugees.

"Blaming us would not benefit anyone," he said, but he knew that in a time of crisis, harm to innocents, to Jews, was common. It was remarkable, he thought, that the Europeans referred to the empire as "the sick man of Europe," and yet in their own interests they were keeping the patient alive, each afraid that the other might benefit more than they, should the patient die.

"I hope you're right."

"Yahweh will provide. We have been welcome here for hundreds of years."

"That's true," she said, but she took little comfort in it. The survival of the community was, of course, the purview of Yahweh over millennia, but hers was the welfare of those she knew in the present.

******

British Ambassador Elliot also woke at the sound of the cannons. He expected this. Everyone knew of the *fetva*.

"Apparently, we have a new sultan," he said to his wife. "I'll be sending a cable to London. Nice to give the Queen and Prime Minister Disraeli good news for a change. Maybe Gladstone will be quiet for a few hours. Maybe the papers will publish something about the empire other than gruesome cartoons showing Turks as butchers of Christian babies."

"Do you know the new sultan?"

"I've met him. Seems a good enough chap. Reasonably well educated. Reads French literature, I understand, if one assumes that to be a virtue. At least he's not a Russophile. But the hope is that real power will be in the hands of Mithat Pasha, who is expected to be appointed grand vizier."

"What's he like?"

"A devoted public servant. He's served as governor in several provinces. The local people praise him. And I've heard no accusation that he takes bribes or even the small gratuities that officials everywhere take for granted. If the empire had a dozen men like him, it would be healthy."

"So, how's he proposing to fix things?"

"He'll have the sultan publish a constitution he's drafted. He showed it to me. It calls for an elected parliament with an upper and lower house. It's a start." Ambassador Elliot wanted to feel optimistic. He liked Mithat, and he thought Mithat's plan reasonable. He also knew the obstacles and feared that Mithat was as likely to fail as to succeed.

THREE

In her village near Panagiurishte, Danube Province, as first morning light shone through the single window of her small timber house, Ayşe heard women screaming, wailing. Gunshots. Men and women groaning in pain. Pleas for help and mercy. Prayers to Allah in final exhalations. Supplicant voices, gagging in the struggle for breath, cut off in death.

Men become beasts swarmed among the huts of Ayşe's village. They ran untamed and random from home to home, cursing in anger and hatred. As she and her husband sat up on the mattress nightly rolled out for their bed, two men broke down their door. One shot her husband as he stood, and one grabbed her nine-year-old son, startled awake from beside them, and shot him close on, his small body knocked backwards, his open eyes unseeing.

Her ten-year-old daughter, Gül, stood up and screamed, grabbing for her mother who was pleading for mercy and praying to Allah for their lives, praying to Allah to make this a dream. Surely, Allah would not permit this! Surely she would wake up in the comforting smell of her husband, in the pleasure of her young son and daughter sleeping next to them.

The intruders kicked the bodies of her husband and son to confirm that they were dead. They grabbed her screaming, terrified daughter from her arms and tossed her aside.

Blasphemies new to her filled Ayşe's ears as her nightgown was ripped away and her body was beaten into submission. She saw. Yet, she did not. She felt the repeated violations. Once, twice, three times? She lost sensation among the pains of slaps

21

and fists to her face, stomach, arms, and legs. The pain of rape and the pain of despair, of feeling her life destroyed.

And yet, she summoned the strength to beg for them not to harm her daughter, to do what they wanted to her, if they would spare her precious little girl. In her imploring, she opened the one eye not swollen shut and saw that the man on top of her was a neighbor from a near-by village.

"Bitch," he said as he punched her hard. "I'll kill you. It would be a favor to you." But he was spent. "Let's get out of here," he said to the other man.

"What about the girl?"

"Leave her. She can be branded."

Gül was crying, curled in the corner. Her head buried against her legs. Her eyes closed as tightly as she could make them, and her hands pressed against her ears. Two men with a branding iron entered and grabbed Gül. She screamed when the hot iron met her upper arm, a scream that even Heaven could hear.

The men threw Gül towards her mother, fled the scene, and vanished into the hills and forests, bearing their anger, shame, and guilt.

Ayşe gathered a blanket around her and another around Gül, hugging the screaming child, comforting her, losing the pain of her own injuries in the pain of her daughter, the child who would give her reason to live and with the help of Allah give her grandsons and great grandsons and great, great grandsons to avenge what she would never forget, never forgive, never remember without wrath for revenge.

At that moment a woman appeared in the door. "You need to leave. I'll help you. They'll be coming back to burn down the village." Ayşe recognized the woman but did not know her name.

22

She was a Christian from a neighboring village. A poor peasant woman like herself. What was she doing here, and why was she offering to help them?

Gül was crying uncontrollably. The wound was bright red in the shape of a Christian cross and smelled of burned flesh, bits of which clung to the edge of the wound. It was horrid in sight, in meaning, in purpose.

"Hold your daughter. I have a clean cloth. We must cover the wound."

Ayşe looked at her, confused by this Christian woman's offer of help. She would have resisted, except that they were helpless. Gül clung to her mother while the woman bound the wound, tearing strips from a blouse to tie the bandage. Ayşe said nothing, felt numb to everything.

"Dress well. You may be walking for many days. Other women with their children and a few old men are gathered outside the village."

"I can't leave my husband's and son's bodies here," Ayşe said, barely audible, bewildered, unsure.

"I will ask the imam in Panagiurishte to bury them properly. I make you that promise." The woman's voice was strong on this point. She forced the words out, knowing that she could not do what she promised, but knowing that this woman and her daughter had to leave the village quickly. The bodies, she knew, would be burned with the houses and leave only ashes to give the lie that there had ever been a village here, had ever been Muslim neighbors among them. The death and violence of this day sickened her. She lied to save this woman and her child that God might forgive what had happened here, might find it in His mercy to deliver her from the hell of this day and accept her into the communion of Heaven. God could forgive, but man would not. There would be retribution. She expected to be killed, to see her husband and children killed. But even if she lived, this day was the end of her life. "Get ready to go. I'll be back with bread and cheese," she said as she left.

Ayşe looked at the bodies of her husband and son. She grieved silently, relieved that they could not see her as she was—beaten, filthy, untouchable, unrecognizable as the wife and mother she had been to them. Her husband and son faced the peace and mercy of Allah. What she faced she could not imagine. She felt she should be dead. But Allah had spared her for Gül, for grandsons and great grandsons and great, great grandsons to bring hellfire down on the heads of these men, their sons, their grandsons, and their great, great grandsons. That thought would give her strength to face pain and hunger and to save Gül.

Ayşe's mind told her to move. The pain dared her to do it. She held onto her sobbing daughter, her reason to stand, to walk, to live. Gently, Ayşe helped Gül pull on the few clothes she had and wrapped her in a blanket. She did the same for herself. She stared at the still bodies of her husband and son, resisting the urge to touch them, hug them, kiss them. Because she knew that if she did, she would lose all control and be emotionally too empty to do what she had to do—save her daughter and avenge their deaths.

"Here, take this," the Christian woman said as she re-entered the hut, handing Ayşe a small bundle of bread and cheese wrapped in a clean scarf.

Ayşe and Gül walked away from the village, from the life they had known. They walked toward Istanbul, the seat of the empire, to seek the protection of the sultan. They walked for weeks, sleeping in *hans*, free roadside inns for travelers, in fields, in mosques, in homes along the way. Pain, hunger, and thirst travelled with them from behind their eyes to the soles of their feet. Disease and exhaustion felled some of their fellow travelers. But most survived on the beneficence of the earth and the compassion of many. Who could witness these wretched souls and not be moved to save his own? Along the way, doctors of faiths professed and lived— Jewish, Muslim, Christian— attended Gül's wound.

******

The sound of the cannons that announced the new sultan awoke Ayşe from the nightmare of that last day in her village four weeks earlier. She bolted upright in a sweat. Every sharp sound could be the shot that killed her son, a sound different from the shot that killed her husband, the sounds of the men on top of her, cursing, punching, slapping. When a sound startled her awake, it was always that sound.

It was dark. Ayşe heard voices and remembered that they were in the women's section of the Süleymaniye Mosque. The section was elevated, and wood grating concealed the women from the men below. Few women came to Morning Prayer. This mosque, like every other large mosque in the city, had a soup kitchen and an infirmary. The mosques sheltered the thousands of Muslim refugees arriving most recently from the Danube Province, but earlier from Moldova and Herzegovina, and decades earlier from the Morea, which had become Greece.

Ayşe gave no thought to the cannons that had awakened her. They were part of the grand world of empire and the machinations at work to keep it alive, a world separate from the small one in which she kept herself and her daughter alive. Her world was the mosque, the soup kitchen, and begging in the streets. Early morning, as the faithful returned home from Morning Prayer, was a lucrative time for begging. The hearts of some were filled with gratitude, some with piety, and others with guilt.

Ayşe and Gül hurried along the narrow street to reach a larger, tree-lined avenue where the more affluent would pass—some coming from the relief of sin, others launching a day of it. The streets were wet from the night's rain, and they arrived at the cobblestone avenue where it turned slightly downhill. Carriages slowed here.

The first carriage she saw was among the finest in Istanbul, an open, two-wheel carriage pulled by a large, spirited horse—an eye-catching animal that held Ayşe's gaze long enough that she was slow to see the erect man in military uniform inside the carriage. A military pasha!

Ayşe grabbed Gül by the wrist and shoved her sleeve up to expose the branded cross, pulling her into the path of the horse to force it to stop. "Pasha, my pasha! For the love of Allah have mercy upon us! Do you see what they did? Pasha! May Allah bless you in your kindness!"

But she was late in her movement. The horse was too close. She slipped on the wet stones and fell as Ismail was reining in the horse and braking the carriage. The horse reared up to avoid Ayşe and Gül.

"Ismail! See if they're hurt. Allah, Allah, what have we come to?" Hüseyin shouted.

Getting down from the carriage, Ismail saw that Ayşe and Gül were between the horse's front and rear legs, seemingly unharmed. He held the horse's reins and stroked its head. "Are you okay? Come out. The horse won't move."

Ayşe and Gül crawled out from under the horse. "Thank you, thank you. Thanks be to Allah," Ayşe said as she stepped toward Hüseyin in the carriage. "Look at my daughter! See what the infidels did to her? Pasha, if you love Allah, have mercy on us. We have nothing. They killed my husband and son. And they did this to my daughter. Pasha, if you can spare alms, may Allah bless you. I will give you my grandsons to fight, my great grandsons, my great, great grandsons, but you must slaughter them all. Allah have mercy on you, my pasha."

Hüseyin leaned down from the carriage and gave Ayşe a *kuruş*, a large sum for a beggar. "Auntie, I do what I can. We have killed many."

"May Allah bless you. Thank you. Thank you. May Allah give you sons."

It was bad enough that the reports from the field were so depressing, Hüseyin thought. But to have the weakness of the empire's security, for which he was responsible, thrown into his face on the streets of Istanbul was too much.

He knew about the massacre, rape, and mayhem perpetrated by the Christians on Muslim villagers near Panagiurishte. The Russians had deliberately incited people with false propaganda. They pretended to be defenders of the Christians, but the Christians were in no danger except to the extent they listened to and acted on the advice of Russian provocateurs.

Everyone knew what the Russians were up to. They wanted vassal states in the Balkans for access to the Adriatic. And they wanted the Black Sea as a Russian Sea. For this, peasants gave their lives. Christians killed Muslims. And then, Muslims killed Christians, because he, Hüseyin Avni, *serasker*, did not have adequate numbers of professional soldiers to conduct a proper, measured response. What forces he had available were keeping order in Serbia. So he authorized the irregular volunteers, known as "the crazies," who were little more than unpaid bandits and vigilantes, to restore order and mete out justice. Probably some of the guilty Christians died, but a great many more innocent Christians were raped, maimed, and murdered. Property was looted and burned. To the local irregulars, order meant revenge. After the fact, Hüseyin had some of the offending irregulars hanged as examples, but it was impossible to feel that justice had been served.

Naturally, the deaths of the Christians set off the European press, which had not reported the attacks on Muslims or on his execution of offending Muslim irregulars. Every article in the European press screamed of the "Bulgarian massacres" of Christians. If he had the soldiers he needed, the Russians would not have provoked this violence. But he didn't. The Russians knew it. And the people suffered.

He had to get control of the treasury, empty the palace, and subordinate the bureaucracy to the service of the country. The case for a military takeover was obvious.

FOUR

At Dolmabahçe Palace, Murat shook incessantly and cast his eyes about as if cornered by an angry mob. Sometimes he responded incoherently. Sometimes not at all.

The entire city waited for a glimpse of the new sultan. Even the storks on the chimneys, the cats in the doorways, and the dogs in the streets appeared to be on alert for a sighting. They waited for him to glide up the Golden Horn in the royal *kayık* to the Eyüp Mosque for the ceremony of investiture, the girding of the sword of Osman, the father of the Ottoman dynasty dating from the late thirteenth century. They waited to celebrate him as the 33rd sultan, the Shadow of Allah on Earth.

Chief among those waiting was Mithat, unable to leave Dolmabahçe Palace until the situation was resolved — either Murat's restoration to emotional health, or confirmation that he was beyond hope. Mithat's task was to mitigate the perils of a headless empire, to postpone, defer, and re-direct everything that could be.

Mithat had come to Istanbul at age eleven with his father, a judge in the religious court, who got him a job as a clerk in the offices of the Imperial Council. He was a diligent worker and seven years later was transferred to a position in the Office of the Grand Vizier, where he came under the influence of a small group of bureaucratic elite. They were responsible for reforms they called the *tanzimat*, reforms to modernize the administration of the country and bring equal treatment to all subjects, regardless of religion or ethnic origin.

Everything seemed possible, and Mithat was among the most energetic and outspoken of the young men advocating for reforms. But he was arrogant and impatient, which resulted in successive postings to the offices of several provincial governors, a punishment he quickly embraced, as it became clear to him that the provinces, not Istanbul, would determine the future of the empire. The reforms had to have positive effects on the lives of the people in the provinces, where he learned how the empire was governed, taxed, and farmed. How the people lived and the workings of local and national commerce. Within a few months of his first provincial assignment, he would remember discussions with his colleagues in the Office of the Grand Vizier as ignorant.

Either as reward or punishment—he was not sure which— he was appointed as an inspector and sent to investigate reports of corruption in the provinces—usually the behavior of the governors and tax collectors. They were the sultan's appointees and rarely gained their positions through merit. Some appointments to undesirable outposts were punishment. As one governor joked over *rakı*, undesirable governorships were the nineteenth century alternative to beheadings and strangulations. Not quite as decisive, but most officials slept better at night— both those who might have ordered the killings and those who might have been the victims.

Mithat's task as an inspector was not difficult. Most high officials felt protected by virtue of their remoteness from Istanbul. Who in Istanbul would know what they were doing? And they had the arrogance of the powerful, feeling entitled to whatever they could get. Consequently, Mithat found they did little to hide their misdeeds.

With a reputation as a reformer, Mithat went to Europe, a rite of passage to gain respect as knowledgeable about the modern world. But he felt out of his element. The empire could not be reformed from Europe, and he welcomed the opportunity to return home as governor of the Danube, one of the sultan's most troublesome provinces. As governor, he had sufficient independence and authority to demonstrate that, properly governed, the people could prosper as citizens of the empire. Mithat's vision was to give the people a stake in the empire through self-governance. He established advisory councils of Christians, Muslims, and Jews at the provincial, district, and city levels. The councils' primary function was to set the values of goods and property, the basis on which taxes were assessed. This eliminated the potential for bribes to tax collectors. The Danube Province became so prosperous that tax income exceeded expenses, despite his ambitious construction of schools, hospitals, roads, bridges, banks, and orphanages.

In the councils, diverse peoples came together for a common purpose—something they otherwise never did. And Mithat's public schools, trade schools, orphanages, and hospitals were open to everyone. He organized Christian/Muslim patrols to secure communities from bandits.

Mithat attended many council meetings. He could be found in a market, in a bank, at a construction site, and in a village. He was not deterred by two assassination attempts.

Mithat introduced agricultural banks that loaned money to farmers at low interest rates, which undercut the usury of the money-lenders in the markets. He built roads and bridges to move produce to the markets. He abolished forced labor on public construction projects, such as roads and bridges, and paid the workers.

In 1864, he was recalled to Istanbul for a review of provincial governance and to help write a provincial reform law. He knew what the language of the law needed to be. He could have written it in a day. But his opinion was accorded no more value than the opinions of persons with no experience in the provinces. He expressed his frustration with the slow process and his low opinion of the comments of some of his colleagues. He was relieved when he was sent back to the provinces, this time as governor of Baghdad.

The city of Baghdad was an historic, multicultural mix of Arabs, Turks, Persians, Assyrians, Armenians, Greeks, Jews, Mongolians, and Europeans. It retained extensive scars from the Mongol invasion of 1259 and was primarily known as a site of banishment for discredited or unwanted Ottoman military and civilian leaders. The province was home to Arab sheikhs who were notorious in their independence, were perpetually in rebellion against Istanbul, and refused military service, while living off raids of merchant and pilgrim caravans.

Mithat set out to demonstrate that the state was not the enemy. He revised the tax system; distributed land to peasants; drained swamps; and restored historic dams, irrigation canals, water wheels, and water pumps to revitalize agriculture. He installed lighting and built fountains in the city of Baghdad. He paid the troops on time, which raised their morale. They challenged the local Arab tribes and ended their raids on caravans.

Now, at age 54 and after 43 three years of service to his country, he was sitting in the sultan's palace, impatient. He was not the sultan, not even the grand vizier, but by force of personality and will, he held the reins of the empire at this critical juncture in history.

He turned to the map of the world on his office wall. The Ottoman Empire remained a force in three continents, and the Treaty of Paris that followed the empire's victory in the Crimean War committed Russia, France, and Britain to honor the empire's borders, but they could be trusted to honor the treaty only to the extent that its terms served their interests. Queen Victoria needed the Ottoman Empire as a buffer against Russian designs on territory and access to the Mediterranean. She needed unimpeded access to the Suez Canal for her interests in India and East Africa. France's and Italy's interests also would be at risk if Russian ships patrolled the Mediterranean. For their part, Germany and Austria-Hungary created the League of Three Emperors with Tsar Alexander II to maintain the status quo in the Balkans and to keep each other's ambitions in check.

Foreign predators and internal corruption threatened his country. But Mithat saw that this condition, ironically, could spur the empire's rejuvenation. Neither the people nor a new sultan could ignore the danger. He would rally them to transform the medieval Ottoman Empire into a modern country. It was possible. He would not be deterred.

"Dr. Fonseca is here." The eunuch's voice interrupted Mithat's thoughts.

"Send him in."

Dr. Fonseca, a Jewish doctor, was the fourth doctor that day to see Murat and report on his condition. "What's your assessment?" Mithat asked, with a note of impatience. He needed a compliant sultan on the throne quickly. The Russians were outraged at the loss of their puppet, Sultan Abdülaziz. Ambassador Ignatiev was throwing money at spies and officials.

"He appears to suffer from emotional instability. It's not an illness we know how to treat."

"Can nothing be done?" Mithat's tone was urgent.

"In my experience, there is no available treatment." Dr. Fonseca shifted his weight, wishing he had something encouraging to say.

"Have you seen anyone like this before?"

"Yes. And I have seen patients become functional again. But it's rare, and the cause of the improvement is as much a mystery as the onset of the condition."

"What about in Europe? Is there someone there who knows how to cure this condition?" Mithat asked, with a note of desperation.

"You could send for Dr. Leidesdorff in Vienna. He's considered the best in this field. Maybe there's a new treatment."

The skepticism in his voice came through, but Mithat ignored it. "Thank you. I'll send for him immediately. I appreciate your frank opinion. Would you stay for coffee?"

"No thank you. I must get back to the hospital and make calls on patients at their homes. I regret that I was not able to be of help to you. Everyone is aware of the work you are doing for the country. May Allah help you."

"May He help us all. Again, thank you for coming."

The first day following the deposition of Abdülaziz had been a Friday, the day when the sultan attended public prayer services, usually in Hagia Sophia, the mosque that had once been a Byzantine cathedral. Every Friday, the sultan became the visible symbol of the Ottoman Empire, and the ritual proclaimed the sultan as Caliph to the Muslims of the world and as a man who humbled himself before Allah, as they did. Murat's failure to follow this centuries' old tradition prompted rumors among beggars, merchants, and foreign diplomats alike. Each ethnic neighborhood of the city had its own speculations. Had Murat been killed? Was there a plot to take over the government? By the Russians? The British? Was Murat refusing to endorse a constitution? Who was in charge?

Mithat was in charge, and he would act. Abdülhamit, Murat's younger brother, was the next in line. If Murat did not prove capable of assuming the sultanate soon, Mithat would confer with the Council of Ministers about Abdülhamit.

FIVE

Abdülhamit was 34 years old and the great grandson of Sultan Abdülhamit I, during whose reign the seriousness of the empire's military and economic decline was first recognized; the grandson of sultan Mahmut II, lionized for destroying the corrupt and ineffective Janissaries and modernizing the Ottoman military; the son of Sultan Abdulmecit, initially a reformer who later squandered the empire's wealth on palaces; the nephew of Sultan Abdülaziz, deposed for indifference and debauchery; and the younger brother of Sultan Murat V.

As a small boy, Abdülhamit spent many hours in the room of the harem where his mother, Tir-i Müjgan, lay ill. She was a Circassian peasant girl who had been purchased as a slave—the fate of many Circassian girls, known for their beauty. She was stricken with tuberculosis before she was taken from her village in the Caucasus Mountains. Before her diet changed from yogurt and bread to meat and vegetables. Before she was groomed to please the sultan, caught the eye of Abdülhamit's father, birthed an heir to the throne, and became a potential *valide sultan*. Before coughing blood and struggling to breathe. Before being shunned by the sultan for her illness and confined to a small room with a single window, her son for company, her doctors for naught.

Tir-i Müjgan died when Abdülhamit was seven. His memories were of her in bed, coughing and spitting up blood. Of doctors coming regularly but bringing no relief for his mother's suffering. Of feeling afraid for his mother and for himself. He knew his mother was dying. No one said the word. But he sensed what death was before he knew what it meant. She would leave. What would happen when his mother died? Would he die too?

35

Abdülhamit grew up with death lurking and feared it. Death could come from nowhere and no one. In the early centuries of the empire, a new sultan would have his brothers assassinated. One could understand such a death, administer it, and, if fate so determined, succumb to it. But Abdülhamit watched his mother die and saw no executioner against whom to fight or from whom to flee.

As sultan, he would grow to know death, as his ancestors had, as one of the instruments of power. An instrument that could be blunted with spies and counter spies, food tasters, preemptive moves, counter strikes, drugs, and paranoia. An instrument he would use, even though he dreaded doing so.

As a nineteenth century sultan-in-waiting, Abdülhamit was given a limited education under the tutelage of Lala, a black eunuch. He learned a history of the Ottoman Empire—part apocryphal, part real, a story of successive heroic sultans. Osman, who brought the Turkish tribes together under one banner; Bayazit The Thunderbolt, whose lightning strikes took the Ottoman army as far as the Danube to the west and to the Euphrates in the east; Mehmet II, who conquered Istanbul at age 21; Selim The Grim, who conquered Syria, Egypt and Arabia, giving Ottoman sultans dominion over the holy cities of Mecca and Medina and the title, "Servant and Protector of the Holy Places"; Süleyman, known at home as "The Lawgiver" for his codification of administrative, social, and religious practices, and abroad as "The Magnificent" for the opulence of his court; and Abdülhamit's own grandfather, Mahmut II, "The Reformer."

He studied Arabic and Persian. As a sign of education, an Ottoman's Turkish was replete with Arabic and Persian words and grammatical constructions. Ottoman Turkish was written in the Arabic script. Men of education made their points in conversation with allusions to classical Persian poets and to the characters that populated their most famous poems. Ottomans quoted from Omar Kayyam's *Rubaiyat*, Ferdowsi's *Shahnameh*, Rumi's *Mesnevi*, and Nizami's *Layla and Majnun*. They knew the writings of the Arab historian and philosopher Ibn Khaldun and of the Persian theologian Al-Ghazali. They quoted from the Quran in Arabic.

He had a mind for mathematics and for patterns, shapes, and symmetry. He learned to play the piano well enough to play popular western tunes, and he became an excellent carpenter, making furniture inlaid with designs of mother-of-pearl and silver. He was an excellent marksman with a pistol and kept one on his person at all times. He was a skilled rider and had a stable of the finest Arabian horses.

Abdülhamit had a keen interest in world affairs. Being Ottoman in the nineteenth century was to aspire to be a peer on the European stage, and Istanbul's elite followed French culture and fashion. But speaking a foreign language, especially a Christian one, was considered demeaning for a sultan. It was for others to understand him, not for him to understand them. So Abdülhamit studied French by sitting in on the lessons of his sisters.

Abdülhamit had little prospect of becoming sultan. His brother, Murat, only two years older, was next in line to their uncle, Sultan Abdülaziz, who became sultan at age 31, when Abdülhamit was 19. Abdülhamit was a young man prepared for office but with none to hold. Sultans-in-waiting had once been given territories to govern. They led armies into battle. They held regular audiences for the people. They managed men and money. They built and destroyed. They mastered force and persuasion. The skills of a sovereign. Whatever skills Abdülhamit might have were unknown, uncultivated, and untested.

In the early hours of May 30, 1876, Abdülhamit awoke with the sound of the cannons announcing the deposition of his uncle and the accession of his brother.

"My sovereign. Are you awake, sir?" came the low voice of his attending eunuch from the other side of the door.

"Yes, you may come in."

"The cannons, sir. Your brother is sultan. In the market, people have talked of nothing else for weeks. They say it's the work of Mithat Pasha."

"What do they say about Mithat Pasha?"

"That he is ambitious but incorruptible. He does not take bribes. They say he wants to remake the empire into a country modeled on Europe."

"And how would he do that?" Abdülhamit asked with genuine interest.

"Through something he calls a constitution, but the people do not know what that is or how it would help the empire."

"Thank you. Find out about this constitution and everything that Mithat and Murat do in the coming days. I will go into the city to see what I can learn, as well."

In fact, Abdülhamit was familiar with the concept of a constitution. He and Murat had accompanied their uncle, Sultan Abdülaziz, to France, Britain, and Austria in 1867. On that trip, Abdülhamit listened, politely asked questions, and found people eager to tell him about industry and trade, social life and customs, and the functioning of constitutional government—the powers and limitations of monarchs, the election of the people's representatives, the role of the press, the role of political parties, and examples of how decisions were reached. They spoke of their superior form of government.

He was surprised to learn that Louis Napoleon III and Queen Victoria could be influenced by speeches in parliament, gossip in the street, editorials and cartoons in the newspapers. In particular, he was shocked that European monarchs lived with the prospect of assassination as an accepted companion of power. Wasn't the purpose of power to eliminate uncertainties, particularly the specter of untimely death?

With Abdülaziz gone, only Murat was between him and the sultanate. Questions of power and governance were no longer theoretical. Objectively, he could not assume that anything for him would change. And yet, two years earlier, a visiting sheikh from Sidon had said, "Within two years, you will be sultan."

"What do you mean?" Abdülhamit asked, taken aback. They had been talking about relations with the Druze minority and the state of security from bandits in the Lebanon Mountains.

"I'm sorry. I spoke out of turn. I must ask your leave. Thank you for your hospitality. I will send you coffee from Yemen," the sheikh said, bowing slightly, before turning and leaving.

The exchange troubled Abdülhamit. Did he want to be sultan? Sitting at the top would make him a target. Every disgruntled subject could plot his death over the most trivial matter. How easily Abdülaziz had been brought down. Surely Murat would see it advantageous to have Abdülaziz dead. Maybe also his younger brother?

If the sheikh's prediction was correct, becoming sultan was preordained, his *kismet*. He was not ambitious and had reservations about being sultan, but he would prepare himself. He would learn everything he could from sources he trusted and from the gossip his eunuch brought him. He loved gossip. Even as a young boy in the harem, he learned that rumors, lies, and exaggerations could be manipulated to advantage. There was much to do.

He dressed quickly and stood before the large mirror in the bedroom. He was relatively short and small-boned. His cheek-bones and chin were not prominent, and his forehead was too big for the rest of his face. He hid it partially with a fez that was too big. He wore a collarless stramboline jacket, buttoned up to his neck with tails well below his hips. The jacket and his trousers were slightly too big as well, as though handed down from an older brother. He had a large hooked nose and dark features that he knew fed the lie that he was the bastard child of an Armenian mistress. But his full dark mustache was perfect for a Turkish sultan. His close-set, dark brown eyes, attended by bushy black eyebrows, did not project the loving, paternal look he knew the people wanted to see in their sovereign. Nevertheless, he saw the stern look needed of a man responsible for the lives of millions, responsible to convey fear in the hearts of the nation's enemies. These eyes would not laugh or cry. Would never reveal his thoughts or miss a detail in the faces of others. In the mirror, he saw himself as he was—not a handsome man, not the reflection of a regal personage, but a man who would accept his *kismet*. He beheld a sultan.

After the death of his mother, Rahime Piristû, his father's fourth wife, was made responsible for his upbringing. But by choice, he spent more time with Pertevniyal, the mother of his uncle, Abdülaziz. Pertevniyal was a peasant girl whom his grandfather had seen carrying laundry on her head in the street, and she retained a peasant's blunt and colorful language.

"Those dogs who advised your father and now your uncle on reforms are all swine-eating infidels," she told him. "The Prophet, may he rest in peace, damn them to hell. How is it that the empire's unbelievers are more prosperous than the faithful Muslims who pray to Allah five times each day? It's the fault of these so-called reformers who pretend to be Muslims, but kiss the asses of the foreign merchants, drink what is forbidden, and speak in public with unveiled wenches.

"Your uncle is captive to these sniveling whelps. Allah did not send the Prophet, may he rest in peace, to have His followers bowing toward Moscow, London, and Paris. Your grandfather Mahmut knew how to make change. He riddled the bodies of those apostate janissaries with a thousand bullets and burned their bones. Those stinking converts did nothing for their country but milk it of every sinecure and lick the juice of its finest fruit from their fingers."

Abdülhamit remembered how she had smiled and whispered to him, "But these things are just between us, Hamit. Do not speak of them with anyone. The eunuchs plot against me, because I'm kind to the young girls. I buy them Paris fashions and perfumes. And why not? They were sold and bought for their beauty. In Paris, there are no women more beautiful. What is the harm in my gifts to them, except that the eunuchs covet control and weep for their lack of balls at the sight of beautiful women? If they had their way, they would have my son killed just to end my reign as *valide sultan*."

Pertevniyal invited Abdülhamit into her secretive world of potions, sorcery, and spirits that she used to cast spells on those she did not like. He visited her regularly and had done so a few weeks earlier, when she embraced him warmly and kissed him twice on each cheek. "Welcome, my son. What a pleasure to have you visit." She always addressed Abdülhamit as her son, a customary greeting used by adults for young boys, but in this case, she meant it sincerely, as she was closer to him than to her own son, Sultan Abdülaziz.

"You look well, Mother," he responded. "May Allah grant you health and long life."

"When we're young, we want a long life. When we're old, we don't want death, but we wish to die before we want it."

Her voice and manner were anxious. Abdülhamit knew something was wrong. "My dearest Mother, you're young. Your son is sultan. What's troubling you?"

"Rumors. Everyone is talking. The foreign devils are making demands. The swine-eating bureaucrats are bowing to them. The British merchants are pretending to be our friends, while selling our future to the highest bidder. My son and the grand vizier trust the Russians, but their trust is ill-placed. These foreign dogs wrap themselves around your legs as though out of affection, but they only wish to be in the best position to bite your balls when it suits them. I tell my son he must stand up to them, and he says he will. But he's weak."

"The empire has many strong men. Your son is not alone."

"You mean those bureaucrats? They want to make the Ottoman Empire into Europe. May Allah protect us from such a fate," she said with disgust.

"What rumors are you hearing, Mother?"

"What I hear are rumors of rumors. They don't let me out of the palace. They're afraid of me—all of them—these dishonest eunuchs and palace functionaries. Everyone's afraid that I'll hear something, say something. I need to know what's happening. Will you help me?"

"Of course, Mother. Whatever you wish."

"A young Belgian woman who came here from Paris to make the fittings for dresses I purchased has a shop in Pera. The European dandies hang out there. Get to know her. Every breeze between the Black and Marmara Seas brings gossip to her shop."

******

Flora Cordier, the Belgian shopkeeper, sold imported goods popular with the Europeans: soft leather gloves, candles, fragrant soaps, perfume, cologne, balms, and other toiletries. Following Pertevniyal's suggestion, Abdülhamit went to her shop, introduced himself, and purchased gloves to prolong the engagement, despite being ill at ease. He had no experience in talking with a woman who was not a slave, a concubine, or a relative and who did not lower her eyes when speaking to him. But she was warm and unassuming, and this gave him confidence.

He observed her seeming indifference to the conversations among the young men in her store, while surely taking in every word. He imagined that she might share what she knew, not as a spy might, as though the information were privileged, but as a friend might report the news of the neighborhood and market as though known to everyone, even when it wasn't.

He did not follow up on that meeting until today, two weeks later. Today, he was a confident man, the equal of the young dandies in Flora's shop, and he would speak with her. But not in the shop. He sent a messenger to invite her to his home for dinner and to say that, should she honor him with her presence, he would send a carriage for her at 1900 hours.

The messenger brought back the answer. Flora Cordier would await his carriage.

SIX

Flora Cordier grew up in the village of Strepy-Bracquegnies in the province of Hainaut, a French-speaking area of Belgium. Her father died when she was a small girl. She thought she remembered him, but her image of him was from a photograph. In the evenings, she sat at the kitchen table to do her homework, read, and watched her mother cook.

After dinner, they sewed together. Her mother worked in a local bakery, but the pay was not enough. So, she repaired clothing, made alterations, and designed and sewed dresses that she sold on market day. She resisted having Flora help her at first, but she saw that Flora came to it naturally. And it was something to do together.

"Am I pretty?" Flora asked one evening as her mother was at the kitchen stove. Her mother, looking over her shoulder, stared at her, as though this were a question she had never considered. Her daughter was indeed beautiful, but her mother, an exceptionally beautiful woman, knew its limitations and traps. "You'll get by," she said with a trace of smile that was proud, but guarded.

Flora grew up with her mother's practical directness to life. On graduating from lyceum, she went to Paris, where an aunt found her a job in one of the best fashion houses. The manager of the fashion house quickly recognized Flora's skill in fitting clients. So, when a large order came from the *valide sultan* that required a seamstress to accompany the shipment and see to the proper fittings, he sent Flora.

The railroad that would later run from Paris to Istanbul was not yet completed, but after transferring among conveyances, she arrived at the temporary station in Sirkeci, Istanbul, where she was met by servants and carriages to take her and the *valide sultan's* trunks of clothes, jewelry, and toiletries to Dolmabahçe Palace. She alighted, feeling that she had arrived in the orient as a little girl in her village might have hopped from stone to stone to cross a creek, jumping from Strepy-Bracquegnies to Paris and to Istanbul.

Istanbul was inhabited by a babble of languages and the technicolor of ethnic clothing and peoples. By the cries of street venders and beggars, the calls to prayer for Muslims and the chimes of bells for Christians. By the aromas of man and beast, of fish and flower, of baker and butcher. By the breezes off the Marmara, the Golden Horn, and the Bosphorus. By the architecture of the Romans and Greeks; of the Ottoman architect, Sinan; and of the workaday labyrinth of houses squeezed into unplanned streets.

Riding to Dolmabahçe Palace along the Bosphorus, Flora stared at this singular flow of water. A large canal ran through her village, transporting goods and people on barges and boats. Paris had the Seine. But the Bosphorus was a sea masquerading as a river, a massive body of water squeezed between the two continents. Fate had brought Flora to the Bosphorus, to the end of Europe, and to the beginning of Asia.

Flora was forewarned that the *valide sultan* was a harridan. Everyone in Paris knew the story of how, during Napoleon III and Empress Eugenie's state visit to Istanbul, Pertevniyal had slapped Empress Eugenie's face when she entered the harem. Pertevniyal thought it an affront for a Christian woman to be in the harem. But Flora had no occasion to meet Pertevniyal.

The fittings were arranged and scheduled by the *kızlar ağa* in a special room. The young women were excited about their new finery and thanked Flora as they admired themselves in the full-length mirror.

Her success resulted in a cable from Paris, instructing her to remain in Istanbul. The *valide sultan* had put in another order that would be arriving in a few weeks. By the time she finished fitting and adjusting the second shipment, Flora had been in Istanbul for three months, when a cable arrived, notifying her that her mother had died and left her a small inheritance that she could receive through the Imperial Ottoman Bank.

The news shook Flora. She had made her farewell with Strepy-Bracquegnies, but she had not parted from her mother. She wrote to her every week, sharing what she saw and did. At every fitting, every stitch of adjusted hem, tucked in waist or shortened sleeve, her mother's voice was with her, explaining each stitch and guiding her fingers to make the cutting and sewing perfect. She could not block out the voice. Nor did she want to. The voice was loving. Her mother had never scolded her, never even looked at her with disapproval.

What took her to the storefront on the Grand Rue de Pera three days later was the purposeless wandering of a grieving mind. She had been on the street many times before. It was the European quarter's most prominent commercial street with storefronts displaying the latest European fashions, furniture, silver, and china. The small store was closed, its single window draped shut with rough cotton cloth tacked to the window's frame.

"The store is closed, Mademoiselle," said a man seated on a stool outside the adjacent store. He stood up on addressing her. "Are you in need of something?" He was a middle-aged man with greying hair, a well-trimmed mustache, and a kindly smile.

"No. I was just curious. I didn't remember that it was closed the last time I passed here."

"That's right. I closed it this morning."

"It was your shop?" she asked.

"I own the building. The shop was run by a man more interested in the pleasures of life than in business. The purpose of making money is to enjoy life. Fools try to reverse the order. Excuse me for being rude. My name is Cristo."

Flora was aware that Cristo was measuring her—partly in the lustful manner that she knew well and was practiced in discouraging, but mostly exuding curiosity, the addiction of Istanbul. Everyone wanted to know who everyone was, why they were there, what they were doing, and whether and what kind of a connection with them might be advantageous. She relaxed.

"My name is Flora," she said, bowing her head slightly in courtesy.

"Ah, yes, you came from the Paris fashion house to fit the gowns that the *valide sultan* ordered. It's the talk of the city how much money the *valide* spends." Cristo's tone was warm. He was pleased to have solved the mystery of who she was.

Flora was only slightly taken aback that he recognized who she was. She was becoming an Istanbulite herself. "I didn't know everyone was talking about the *valide*'s purchases."

"Everyone talks about everything that anyone knows and speculates about what they don't."

"This shop that's closed. It sold soap and candles, isn't that right?"

"Yes, mostly."

"You spoke of the previous owner as foolish. If one were careful, would there be profit in the store?" She knew something of business. She sometimes helped out in the bakery where her mother worked. She was good at mathematics and interested in the baker's bookkeeping. He showed her how he kept records and explained the importance of records to profit.

"I believe so, yes. Do you have experience in business?" Cristo studied Flora's face and saw that she was serious.

"Some. Will you be looking for a new proprietor for the store?" Her question was spontaneous and surprised her as she asked it.

Cristo understood her meaning. "You're interested?"

"Perhaps. If the terms were favorable," she said in a confident tone, as though she knew what terms would be favorable.

"Would you wish to open the same type of shop or a different type?"

Cristo's tone was warm and inviting. She felt comfortable to continue even though she was not sure that she wanted Cristo to believe she was interested in the shop. "The same, I think. Its customers will come here when looking for the items it carried, don't you think?" she responded, as though she had made a decision.

"Yes, you understand the situation well. The young Europeans promenade the Grande Rue, so there is opportunity to entice them into your shop." The word "entice" had slipped out naturally, reflecting that he saw in front of him a beautiful young woman whose presence would be important to the success of the store. "And these young men have money," he continued.

Flora could see through the crack between the cloth and window-frame that at least some of the goods remained in the store. "The inventory of the shop. Who owns it?"

"I do. I kept it in lieu of the back rent I was owed." Cristo understood that this woman did know something about business.

Flora had expected to return to Paris, but her modest inheritance allowed her to consider a change of course. And there was this shop. Everything was rushing, demanding a decision, pressuring her to be smart about her next move. "Could I see the shop?"

"But of course." Cristo calculated that the lost rent was less than the inventory's value. He could let her have the inventory for his cost, or he could charge her what it had likely cost the previous owner. If only he knew how much money she had.

Cristo opened the door and motioned for her to enter, which, as she did, brought her next to him. He followed her fragrance and the outline of her dress that hid the movement of her hips but not from his imagination. At this moment, he could only think that he wanted this woman next to his store. In his mind, all things were possible.

Cristo started to close the door. "No, leave the door open, please. I need the light," Flora said, feeling a little uneasy. She was suddenly aware of being alone—in the store, in the city, in the Ottoman Empire, in this small shop owned by a middle-aged stranger whose interests might overlap with hers. But might not.

The displays of soap, perfume, and candles were as she remembered. Although the shop was small, there was room for a number of customers to gather. Customers passed time by sharing the news and gossip of the city. The longer they stayed, the more likely they were to buy something. Yes, she could picture this small shop as her future.

"There's also a closet in the back with shelves to store extra inventory," he said as he passed next to her, motioning for her to follow.

But the space was close. He was close. Too close. She could smell the sweat on his clothes and cigarette smoke and tea on his breath. She shifted her weight and took a step away while making a broad gesture as if the sweep of her arm had been the purpose of her movement. "It has enough space for customers to feel comfortable," she said.

Cristo hoped she would step next to him. Perhaps an opportunity for a casual touch. But he understood the meaning of her gesture, and collected himself. He would not jeopardize a business deal over a clumsy attempt at seduction. Maybe later. Business first. "If you're interested in the shop, we can have tea while I look at my records," he said in a business-like manner that freed Flora to see Cristo as a final stepping stone from Strepy-Bracquegnies to Istanbul.

"I'd like that," she said confidently.

Cristo decided to help Flora. It was in his financial interest, and she would be there in the store next to his. He was a middle-aged man with a wife and four children. Some men of means in Istanbul kept mistresses, but it was expensive. So he did as most of the men of his station did and frequented the city's street of prostitution. He always went to the same house and asked for the same woman, who went by the name of Maria. She was like a mistress, but much less expensive. And she pretended to enjoy seeing him. Cristo was a practical man. He might dream of a mistress like Flora, but Maria provided what he needed.

Over tea and some bargaining, he agreed to a price for the merchandise that was only a little more than he had in it. And he agreed to a rent that was the same as he previously received. He offered a fair deal. The vision of Flora next door portended possibilities more alluring than reality might deliver. But allure was enough. No one could predict reality.

That had been three years earlier. Flora's small shop was a success, and she was now known in the city, not as the representative of a Paris fashion house catering to the *valide sultan,* but as the proprietor of a popular shop on the Grande Rue de Pera, a shop where young European men were known to share news from Europe, the latest speculations about the future of the Ottoman Empire, the cost of bribes and goods, and the rumored personal vices and virtues of everyone. Flora's reputation as a source of this information brought the carriage of Abdülhamit to her door.

SEVEN

Abdülhamit walked back and forth and in circles, casting glances out the window. He had sent his carriage to pick up Flora Cordier from her shop in Pera only a short while before. He knew it would not return this quickly, but he looked out at a blossoming cherry tree, as though that was his purpose in going to the window.

Why was he eager to see her? She was attractive but not strikingly pretty like the young Circassian girls available to him. Was it sexual interest? No. His physical needs were satisfied. His role was to respond to stimulus, not to desire it.

His pretext for inviting her to his home was Pertevniyal's suggestion that Flora overheard things in her shop that might be useful for him to know. But he expected nothing more than the usual prejudices against Muslims and Turks that Europeans expressed so casually and frequently among themselves as to be accepted truth. He told himself that, as if doing so would make him less eager to see her.

He stepped outside, where the dusk air was cool, and walked among the spring flowers in his garden. It took his mind off Flora. But within minutes, he returned indoors. If he were outside when she arrived, it could appear that he was eager to see her. "I'll wait for Mademoiselle Cordier in the living room," he said to the eunuch, Ahmet, as he passed him in the entrance.

"Shall I advise you when the carriage arrives?" The eunuch was unsure of the protocol for this evening, and it was reflected in the caution of his voice. No foreigner had been invited to Abdülhamit's residence before. And a foreign woman?

"No. That won't be necessary. It will be enough for you to knock before showing her in." Abdülhamit did not want Ahmet to think he felt the need to prepare himself for Flora's entrance. She was just a merchant, a source of information. Nothing more.

Abdülhamit continued into the house, wondering whether he should be standing or sitting when she arrived and how he would address her. His step-mother Rahime Piristû had taught him etiquette—Eastern and Western—and he knew what was expected in known situations. But this was not a social occasion that fit a mode of etiquette in which he had been trained.

The palace, the embassies, and many merchants and religious leaders had spies who reported what they heard and what they imagined might be worth money to someone—a straightforward relationship of payment for information with no need to disarm someone to reveal what they may not have intended. But the conversation he was about to have with Flora Cordier was not like those exchanges. Would she be offended that he wanted information from her without paying her for it? Could he believe what she told him?

"Mademoiselle is here," Ahmet announced.

Abdülhamit stood up to greet Flora, whose entrance into the room surprised him, as though he had not been expecting her, and he hesitated for a moment before saying, "Welcome, Mademoiselle. It's a pleasure to see you. Thank you for coming."

She was more attractive than he remembered. Her make-up was perfectly applied—the lips red and lined exactly with her lips' natural shape, her cheeks rouged lightly toward the bones, her blue eyes enhanced by minimal shading and a hint of coloring to the eyelids and eyebrows. She wore a hat with a brim that turned down in the front and with a band that held a single feather, as though a statement that this bird needed no further plumage to enhance its beauty.

"I'm pleased to be here. Thank you for inviting me," Flora responded, nodding her head ever so slightly. In seeing him, she was reminded of how very ordinary Abdülhamit looked, the same impression that she had when he came to her shop a few weeks earlier and tried to appear as though shopping were routine for him. Once again his clothes did not fit him properly — slightly too big — and her instinct was to tuck at the seams and put in pins to tailor his clothes.

Abdülhamit hesitated. The words "I'm pleased to be here" hit him. Of course, it was what etiquette required, but she made this casual phrase sound as though the words expressed her genuine feeling.

"Please, make yourself comfortable," he said, gesturing awkwardly to a stuffed armchair opposite the one he would occupy. As she moved, Abdülhamit's eyes scanned from her auburn hair to the high lace collar of her dress, to its ruffled sleeves that tapered to lace cuffs at her delicate wrists and gloved hands, to the narrow waist accentuated by a broad leather belt, to the unrevealed hips beneath the burst of cloth that hung almost to the floor and revealed a few inches of tapered ankles.

Flora surveyed the modest size and appointments of the room, surprised and comforted. The floor was mostly covered by one large carpet with a floral design that suggested it was Persian. A painting of Abdülhamit's grandfather, Mahmut II, a venerated figure whose portrait hung in many public places and shops, hung on one wall.

"Your grandfather," she said, pointing to the portrait, "is fondly remembered as the sultan who saved the empire by reforming the military."

"Is that what the Europeans say?" Abdülhamit asked, surprised at Flora's comment. He did not expect her to know anything of Ottoman history.

"The Turks say the same thing, as I'm sure you know." Flora sensed that Abdülhamit was sensitive about what Europeans thought. Why had he invited her? Was it a mistake to have come?

"Yes, my grandfather was bold, but careful. He did not act until he was assured of success." Abdülhamit stared at the portrait of his grandfather to keep his eyes off Flora and to consider how to take over the conversation. He felt on the defensive. He brought Flora here to find out what she knew. He could not spend the evening talking about his grandfather. "How long have you been in Istanbul?" he asked, as though he did not know the answer.

"Almost three years. I feel this is my home now."

"You came from Belgium," Abdülhamit said, still seeking a way to direct the conversation.

"Yes, that's where I was born."

"How is it that you opened the shop on the Grande Rue?" Another question in his search for a comfort level.

"It happened by chance, really." She related the story of how she had come to open the shop and mentioned Cristo's help.

"You do your own purchasing with the wholesalers?" Abdülhamit knew little of the wholesale district, but he knew it would be difficult for a woman to be accepted as a business equal.

"Yes. Initially, with Cristo's help. He introduced me to men he knew. He asked them to treat me fairly, and he advised me on negotiating prices."

"They did not object to doing business with a woman?" Abdülhamit asked, leaning toward her with his brow furrowed in surprise.

"They're businessmen. I entered their world with the money to buy their goods. There are a few wholesalers, older gentlemen, with whom I've become comfortable to accept their offer of tea or coffee, exchange the news of the day, and listen to their complaints." Flora shifted in her chair.

"Complaints?" asked Abdülhamit in a tone of genuine wonder.

"The wholesalers are Greek, mostly. A few Armenians. They're Christians, so they experience some unique conditions in doing business here."

"The Christians have special concessions for business that give them lower import duties than Muslim citizens pay. Of what could they complain?"

"The import duty is only one of the costs. To have the goods released from the customs house, they have to pay the duty and also the man who signs the document that says they paid the duty. Then they pay the man who signs a paper that authorizes the goods to be turned over to them, the man who unlocks the customs warehouse, the man who finds the goods in the warehouse and delivers them, and the man who signs the paper that says they picked up the goods."

Flora again shifted in her chair. She could see from the expression on Abdülhamit's face that this information was new to him, and this surprised her.

"Do *you* have to pay these men?" Abdülhamit asked with a tone of genuine bewilderment.

"I don't pay them directly, but the cost of the goods I buy includes these payments that the wholesalers have had to make." In saying this, she felt embarrassed for her host. Here was a potential sultan, and he did not know what was common knowledge, even among people who did not engage in commerce. She wondered what else he did not know and why he had asked her to come.

Ahmet entered the room and asked Abdülhamit if he would like dinner served, to which he nodded. Ahmet brought

56

in a small table and two chairs, and Abdülhamit took Flora's hand to help her up from where she was sitting. Lowering his head to reach her hand gave him another chance to admire her ankles.

Abdülhamit had three houses. This one was his farmhouse in Kâğıthane, a valley at the head of the Golden Horn. He did not like excess, often eating meals of rice pilav and yogurt. But he had a guest, and it was spring. He asked the cook to prepare the wild asparagus that grew on his property, to make a salad from fresh greens and spring onions in the garden, and to prepare *menemen*, sautéed vegetables with fresh eggs from his chickens. And they drank *ayran*, made from yogurt prepared from the milk of his cows and water from the spring of Kâğıthane. Dinner was followed by rice pudding and Turkish coffee.

"How is your coffee?" he asked.

"The coffee is excellent. It smells and tastes like the best coffee from Yemen."

"It is, indeed, coffee from Yemen. A trader from Lebanon sends it to me. You have an exceptional sense of taste." Abdülhamit was wondering how to bring the conversation back to the concerns of his Christian subjects, but he did not want to offend his guest.

"I'm afraid I must be going. I have some accounting to attend to before I open the shop tomorrow," Flora said, feeling that the time was right for her to leave.

"You have no accountant? I can find you one and guarantee his honesty," Abdülhamit said hurriedly in the hope of delaying her departure.

"That's very kind. But I enjoy doing the accounting, and I would not feel the business were mine, if someone else did it. I would just be working in a shop."

Abdülhamit saw her to his carriage and watched as it disappeared. Pertevniyal had been right. Flora Cordier was knowledgeable in ways that he was not. He knew he had barely scratched the surface of what he could learn from her.

He went to bed, thinking of Flora, and called for Mela. Mela was a woman in her early forties who had been his concubine since he was 14. She remained one of the women in the modest harem of six women in his Kâğıthane residence. She was the oldest of the women, originally brought from Croatia as a young girl to Abdülhamit's father's harem. But his father had not fancied her. Not pretty in youth, she had matured into a tall and attractive woman with a soft body that was voluptuous naked and always took Abdülhamit back to that night when he was 14 and she was a woman.

Mela entered his bedroom, dropped the robe that covered her, and slipped under the light quilt where, to her surprise, she found Abdülhamit naked and erect. In the ritual of their years together she would find him on his back in a nightgown and playfully remove it while stimulating his erection with her fingers and kisses. But tonight, she mounted him swiftly, and moved into the rocking sway that went from slow and easy to rapid and hard while holding herself on her elbows at just the height that allowed her breasts to brush his chest as she moved—touch that may have given him pleasure but which she performed for her own.

Abdülhamit lay released of sexual tension but troubled. Yes, Flora had information he could use, but he knew that this was not why he wanted to see her again. What he wanted was to kiss those red lips, to hold those slender ankles in his palms and explore the mysteries they suggested, to slide his fingers over calves and thighs. He wanted to see the neck behind the lace, the arms beneath the sleeves, the hips and breasts exposed, and wrap himself among them and over them and into them until he was spent as he was now. He knew it was a dangerous longing that could threaten her potential as a source of information. But desire knows no master.

EIGHT

In Dolmabahçe Palace, Mithat awoke from a light sleep well before dawn. He was exhilarated. He was about to break his country's medieval shell and create a new strength based on a modern political system that would bind its peoples together in mutual self-interest and a common future. He sat up in bed, swung his legs around, and slid his feet into the slippers on the floor. He stood and held out his hands with his palms up, raised his face upward, and said, "In the name of Allah."

He performed this ritual every morning. It was a declaration to live and work in the name of Allah, a commitment to be selfless in his engagements of the day, an emotional purification of the heart and spirit in preparation for the Morning Prayer.

He walked across the room to a washstand with a pitcher of water and began his ablutions, the physical cleansing of the body for presentation to Allah—each cleansing action repeated three times, washing first the right and then the left hand between the fingers and up to the wrist; rinsing his mouth and rubbing his teeth with a *misvak* twig; rinsing his nostrils; washing his face and arms; running his wet hands through his hair, around his ears and the back of his neck; washing his right, then his left foot between his toes and to the top of his ankles.

In the background he heard the call to prayer, "Allah is the greatest. Great One, I confess there is no deity but Allah. I avow Muhammed to be His prophet. Come to prayer. Come to salvation. Save our souls. Allah is the greatest." He unrolled his prayer carpet, pointing it toward Mecca, stood at the end of it, and began his ritual prayer recitation: "There is no god but Allah, and Muhammed is His prophet."

He recited the opening verse of the Quran:

> In the name of Allah, the most merciful. All praise is
> due to Allah, Lord of the worlds. The most merciful.
> Sovereign of the Day of Recompense. It is You we
> worship, and You we ask for help. Guide us to the
> straight path. The path of those upon whom you have
> bestowed favor, not of those who have evoked Your
> anger or of those who are astray.

The Morning Prayer requires performing twice the four
ritual prayer movements of standing, kneeling, bowing, and
prostrating to Allah and concludes by turning the head to the
right and left and reciting, "Peace and Allah's blessing be upon
you," to acknowledge the importance of others, those around
you, those with whom you might interact in the course of the
day, even if no one is next to you at the time of prayer.

On many days, Mithat missed the other four prayer times,
except for the Noon Prayer on Fridays. But he never missed the
Morning Prayer, the act that prepared him to work selflessly
and to treat others with respect. He was confident that this was
acceptable to Allah. Everyone knew men who prayed five times
a day while cheating their customers, demanding bribes, and
beating their wives. What meaning could Allah give to their
prayers? Mithat had grown up in a Sufi, Alevi tradition, which
stressed ethics of behavior over ritualistic fidelity.

He dressed in a starched white shirt with a standing collar,
a black bow tie, slacks, a suit jacket with wide lapels and four
buttons that hung well below his hips, dark socks, patent leather
shoes, and a red fez. Standing in front of the mirror, he gave his
fez a final adjustment and observed that his beard and mustache
were now almost entirely white.

This was the moment for which he had lived. None of the famous reformers before him had his vision or this opportunity. And yet, Murat, who was to have been the sultan who would make Mithat's dream possible, was turning it into a nightmare. How could this have happened? Had he missed clues? Murat appeared to be the perfect figurehead sultan. He appeared to support reform and to be content to be the face of change.

"The foreign ambassadors, your honor, wish to pay their respects and present their credentials to the new sultan," said the principal secretary of the palace as Mithat approached his office.

"Send a message that Murat is ill at this time. They will receive an invitation to present their credentials as soon as his health permits." Mithat knew that he could not stall the ambassadors for many days. In its already vulnerable state, the empire could not be seen as headless. And then there was his colleague, Hüseyin Avni. He had pledged his support for a constitutional monarchy, but Mithat suspected that if he could not show positive results soon, Hüseyin might lose patience.

As if on cue, the principal secretary returned moments later to announce, "Your honor, the *serasker* is here. He wishes to see you."

"Show him in." Mithat's immediate reaction was dismay, but he caught himself. Better to face Hüseyin than to wonder what he was plotting.

"Welcome, my brother. It's good to see you," Mithat said, addressing Hüseyin and embracing him warmly as they mutually kissed the air on each side of their faces. It was a cultural requirement, but not without sincerity. He respected Hüseyin; he needed him; and he would work with him.

"Good to see you, my brother. Who can sleep? In war, the enemy never sleeps. The enemies are circling, Mithat." Hüseyin spoke with a tone of authority honed over 30 years of having his orders obeyed.

"Everything is in place to carry out what the Council of Ministers authorized me to do. Please join me for tea and breakfast." Mithat used the phrase "authorized me" instead of "us" deliberately. "Us" would have been the polite and expected term to have used. But he wanted to be clear that he alone was responsible to the Council of Ministers and to send a message that his plan was not up for debate.

"Thank you. I would love some tea, and I have not had breakfast. What's Murat's condition?" Hüseyin asked in a demanding tone that hinted of annoyance at Mithat's use of "me."

"The local doctors seem unsure. Apparently, the disorder has been known to disappear as quickly as it comes on. I've sent for a Dr. Leidesdorff in Vienna. I was advised that he has expertise in Murat's condition. He should arrive tomorrow."

"I had a disturbing encounter yesterday. A beggar woman and her young daughter ran into the street as my carriage approached. She's one of the refugees from the Danube Province," Hüseyin said, changing the subject.

"We know what happened there."

"But seeing one of the victims makes it personal. Her daughter's arm was horribly scarred— disfigured flesh in the shape of a cross," Hüseyin said.

Mithat hesitated. The refugees were an emotional issue for him, as well. "That's the purpose of a constitution. To bring an end to religious hatred." Mithat watched Hüseyin's demeanor. He showed no evidence of being convinced.

A servant entered and set out a platter of bread, jam, feta cheese, olives, fruit, sugar, and glasses of tea.

Hüseyin picked up the conversation. "The violence occurs because I do not have the forces I need to protect the people from themselves and from external meddling. I need more men, better armed, and paid on time. That costs money, Mithat. It has nothing to do with representative government."

"I'm aware of your needs, brother. If we have fair and honest tax collection, the empire's resources will provide for a well-armed military. But for now, we need financial help from Europe. A constitution will solidify European support, and that will give us time to build a government that works for the people." This time Mithat used "us." He needed Hüseyin.

Hüseyin took the small pincers resting on the sugar bowl, put two cubes in his glass, and stirred it with the small spoon on the tea saucer. As always, he lifted the glass, admired the color of the tea against the light from the window, and watched as the last of the swirling sugar crystals disappeared into the liquid. "I hope your faith in the power of representative government proves well placed, my brother, but only military strength can buy the time you say is needed." Hüseyin reached for a slice of bread from the plate Mithat extended toward him. He studied Mithat's face and body language as he ate. Mithat needed him. Did he need Mithat?

"I understand that," Mithat said, watching for a reaction in Hüseyin's face. He took a sip of tea, spread jam on a slice of bread, and stabbed an olive with his fork. "The declaration of accession that I've prepared for Murat commits him to significant reductions in palace expenses."

"That's a start," Hüseyin said with approval.

"The most important thing is the welfare of the people. When the Christians, Muslims, and Jews prosper, they get along. We'll have a constitution, a parliamentary government. We'll be a modern country."

"This is not Britain, my friend," Hüseyin responded with a derisive tone that stung Mithat.

"Nor is this the thirteenth century," Mithat countered. "Our children will live in the twentieth century. We have to build a country suitable for them."

"The empire was built on military superiority. Everyone respected that, and it will be what nations respect in the next century, as well." Hüseyin's tone was not confrontational, just resolute.

"I'm not naïve. But to protect our borders, we must show the Europeans that we are modernizing in every area, not just the military, although I believe we can do well by our soldiers at the same time. For that, we need to take control of the treasury, and we will."

"You have my support," Hüseyin said, more as a declaration to himself than to Mithat. He would give Mithat his chance. But if the plan did not appear to be working, he would not be a bystander. There were other models of government. Napoleon III came to mind. Even in Europe the people responded to power and authority. Mithat wanted to impress the Europeans with reforms, but he, Hüseyin, would appeal to their commercial interests. For the empire to become a military power again, he would have to buy ships, weapons, and training from the Europeans. The Europeans' strength was in being merchants first and soldiers second. He would be a soldier first to preserve an Ottoman state in which his grandsons could be merchants.

NINE

In Feriye Palace, where the deposed Sultan Abdülaziz and his family were living, Pertivniyal's wail was heard throughout the building. "NO! NO! My son! What's happened to my son?! Allah! Allah, have mercy on me. Allah! Have mercy on my son, my poor son! What's happened to him?"

She was screaming and crying as she looked upon her son, Abdülaziz, through a window in the room where the deposed sultan had confined himself. He was collapsed forward in his chair, a pair of scissors on the floor and a pool of blood below each of his motionless arms. The chair faced away from the door, and the eunuch and guards stationed outside it burst into the room. They looked at the slumped body but did not touch him. No one dared touch a sultan, except for his barber, his mother and children, and the women whose touches were intended to excite the sexual interest that might one day make them the *valide sultan*. They looked at his vacant eyes, his motionless body, the blood and scissors on the floor, and his bloody, wounded wrists. But not one of them dared to say, "He's dead."

"Quick, find Dr. Capoleone," said the chief eunuch.

"I've killed my son," wailed Pertevniyal. "I've killed my son. Allah have mercy on me. I've killed my son." Why had she given him the scissors? He said he wanted scissors to trim his beard. It was an odd request. Trimming his beard was his barber's task, as it was to preserve every hair that was trimmed. It was also a clever request. If he had asked for a knife, she would not have given him one. But a pair of scissors to trim his beard? It was possible. He had refused to see anyone since being deposed. Perhaps he wished even to avoid seeing his barber.

Yes, she had seen that he was unhappy, but wanting to die? She felt crushed with guilt. It had been her decision to separate him from the young Circassian girl who had become his only source of pleasure. She was in the final days of pregnancy, and Pertevniyal had her confined to bed until the baby's birth. Only she could do this. She assured Abdülaziz that this was necessary for the girl's well-being and that of the child, and he agreed, expressing concern for their health.

Pertevniyal had observed many pregnancies and births. She knew this one would not end well. Had Abdülaziz also foreseen this? Would that have been the final blow? To be deposed and then to face losing the person who mattered so much to him that he allowed his devotion to her to be the cause of his deposition? Why had she, his own mother, not sensed his emotional trauma and seen that he was suicidal? Despite a life-long interest in the occult, magic potions, and sorcery, at this moment, when she felt the most in need of help, Pertevniyal had no potion, no power, no prayer to save her son. "My son! My son! What have I done? Allah! Allah, I cannot bear it! I've killed my son!"

Dr. Capoleone and another doctor resident in the palace arrived in minutes. They observed the motionless body, the blood, the scissors, the wounds in the wrists. They did not touch the sultan. "Send word to Mithat Pasha," ordered Dr. Capoleone, addressing the chief eunuch. "And take the *valide sultan* away. I will send something to calm her. No one is to enter the room except doctors sent to verify the cause of death."

******

Secluded in a small room of the harem, the young Circassian girl had a high fever. She was terrified of her impending childbirth. She was a child, herself. She lay in a bed attended by a doctor and servants, casting her eyes about for help. But in prescient certitude that she would soon face Allah, she prayed for the speedy relief of death, for her soul, and for that of her child. She did not ask for Abdülaziz.

******

In Dolmabahçe, Mithat was dumbstruck at the news. Only five days had passed since he had deposed Abdülaziz and nothing was going as planned. He was not a man easily discouraged. He had thrown himself into many a disaster, persuaded enemies to see common interests and diverse peoples to accept the empire as home. But for the moment, even he was without a response.

"Tell them I will be there shortly. They must not move the body," he said carefully, as he considered how this news would affect his plans for the empire. He would personally inform Murat. Murat's reaction would tell him if there was any hope that he could be sultan. A sultan had to be resilient in the face of bad news, particularly now, when the empire was weak. Although Mithat believed that the time for an autocratic sultan had passed, the empire's face to the outside world still needed to be that of a man of strong character. Only behind such a head of state would Mithat have the time and authority to change the structure of the state to one where the sultan was bound by the power of a parliament, the will of the people.

"My uncle is dead," was all that Murat said in a barely audible voice. And then he began trembling, covering his eyes with his hands as he sat shaking.

"He was not assassinated," Mithat said, thinking that this statement might be what Murat needed to hear. But Murat slipped out of his chair and was curled in a ball on the rug, reinforcing Mithat's conviction that he was no sultan. "Have the doctors give him whatever they have," he said dismissively to the attending eunuch, as he turned and walked quickly from the room.

Arriving at Feriye Palace, Mithat sent word to have the best-known doctors in the city, including foreign physicians attached to European embassies, called to the palace to view the sultan's body and give their opinions on the cause of death. In the end, a report stating the cause of death as suicide was signed by 22 doctors.

Mithat's thoroughness in assuring that Abdülaziz's cause of death was documented beyond reproach was characteristic of how he conducted himself in all matters, but in this case, was also something he did to protect himself from criticism. Any doubt about the cause of death could generate internal and external conspirators to implicate him, Mithat. They could say that he saw the continued presence of Abdülaziz as a threat to his plan for a constitution, particularly if, as it appeared, Murat proved unable to assume the duties of sultan. The documentation had to be above suspicion.

Mithat went to Feriye Palace, where the body remained unmoved, awaiting his order that it be prepared for burial. Islamic doctrine required burial before sundown. Mithat stood alone in the room next to the body. In his youth, Abdülaziz had been a lover of poetry and Western classical music, which he also composed. He was an artist and archer of some gift with a muscular body and authoritative posture befitting a sultan. Considered progressive and Western-oriented, he was the first sultan to visit Europe. He had been a partner in the reform movement with Mithat's mentors, Fuat Pasha and Ali Pasha, giving them broad freedom to implement reforms. But then Fuat and Ali died; Abdülaziz became a puppet of the Russians, the harem, and alcohol; and he indebted the nation to buy warships and provide the residents of the palace the finest of everything available in the Ottoman Empire and Europe. A spectacular fall from worthy leader to shrunken corpse, genuinely mourned only by his mother.

In death, Abdülaziz would be the same as the lowliest of his subjects. His body would be bathed once or three times — any odd number, a requirement of Islam — as purification for presentation to its Maker. Then the body would be shrouded in plain, white cotton cloth for burial. The grave would be dug perpendicular to Mecca and the body laid on its right side, facing Mecca, its head and chin suspended by balls of soil, hand-formed from the dirt removed in digging the grave.

Mourners would offer collective prayers that asked forgiveness for the deceased, sprinkle three handfuls of soil into the grave, and recite verses from the Quran on belonging to and returning to Allah, on being made from earth and returned to earth, and on being raised again from the earth on the Day of Judgment. All souls meet Allah stripped of position and pretense.

Mithat had attended many burials and recited the collective prayers and Quranic verses over the bodies of people he knew well, barely knew, and never met. It was one of the duties of a provincial governor. But this death was different. If he had not deposed Abdülaziz, would he not be alive? And yet, was not the life and death of every man in the hands of Allah?

Mithat was a religious man. In his passion to transform his country, he assumed that Allah would give him the time he needed to do that. But in this moment, he had to confront the reality that he, like the once powerful Abdülaziz, was, in fact, everyman in the sight of Allah. In death, he would know all things. In life, however, he lived with the conviction that what he did and how he did it mattered. The death of Abdülaziz and the prospect of his own death changed nothing. He would make a difference.

Back at Dolmabahçe, Mithat called for the principal secretary. "Send word to the ministers. I would like them to honor me with their presence at my home at 11:00 a.m. on Thursday."

Then he called for a carriage to take him home. He had remained at Dolmabahçe since the sultan's deposition, monitoring Murat's condition, conferring with doctors about the prospects for his recovery, and managing the affairs of state vested in the sultanate. But nothing was resolved. How long could he wait before approaching the Sheikh Ul-Islam to depose another sultan? An early move against Murat would increase suspicion about Abdülaziz's death. He would return home and resume the routine of his life, eat meals in the company of his family, walk in the garden, sip coffee in view of the Bosphorus. He needed time. Time for Murat possibly to heal, time for a death to be forgotten, time to craft a backup plan.

TEN

Abdülaziz's death gave everyone cause to speculate on the next surprise, including Abdülhamit, for whom it was an excuse to invite Flora to return. He would ask her what the Europeans were saying.

"No one says, 'I believe this or I believe that.' They exchange what they've heard others say." Flora said in response to his question about the views of the patrons of her shop on Abdülaziz's death.

"They have no opinion on whether Abdülaziz committed suicide?"

Abdülhamit seemed confused by her answer, and Flora realized that he had no experience in the common discourse with which she was so familiar, completely unschooled in the social exchanges among people in the most important section of the capital of his empire. Of what else might he be ignorant? She did not consider this question with any feeling of superiority or pity, simply surprise and interest. She felt drawn to him—the seductive appeal that he needed her, that she could help a man who had the chance to be one of the most powerful men on earth.

"They have opinions, of course," she began carefully, wanting to be truthful without revealing her surprise that she needed to explain what she had said. "And they express them. But mostly they share the opinions voiced by others of higher station and those commonly expressed in the marketplace."

"What do they report hearing?" Abdülhamit asked, without averting his warm gaze from his guest, a look that put Flora at ease to share everything she knew.

"They say that 22 doctors who viewed the body signed a statement that his death was suicide, but that a few of the doctors, particularly the doctor from the British Embassy, privately expressed that there was room for doubt."

"But the cut wrists, the scissors, the blood? What could be the basis for doubt?"

"The amount of blood on the floor was not as much as expected."

Abdülhamit was surprised by her answer. He had not heard this view expressed. "Any other reason for doubt?"

"They question whether a spiritually broken man would have the resolve against pain to cut one wrist and then switch the scissors to the hand of the wounded wrist, and cut the second."

"I heard that he attempted to jump from a window a few days earlier," Abdülhamit interjected to show that he also was privy to news.

"Abdülaziz was known to be distraught, but his half-hearted attempt to jump out of a window was considered nothing more than a plea for sympathy."

"If it was not suicide, who could have killed him?" Abdülhamit asked, feeling embarrassed that he had not considered the possibility of assassination.

"Everyone knows that Mithat Pasha and Hüseyin Pasha were behind Abdülaziz's deposition. As long as he remained alive, he was a threat to their plans."

"So they might have had Abdülaziz killed? Is that what people say?"

"Yes, that's one of the rumors."

"And what are the others?"

Flora hesitated. Did Abdülhamit really not make the obvious connection? "People know that Murat may be unfit, so if Abdülaziz cannot be brought back to the throne, you will become sultan." Flora felt that she should be uncomfortable. She was telling him that some people were suggesting that he might have been behind Abdülaziz's death. But Abdülhamit's warm smile implied that he was eliciting her partnership. This man who might become sultan needed her. And she was available. For whatever he wanted. It was not a feeling she had experienced before, and it surprised her by its presence and by her body's welcoming of it.

Abdülhamit was not surprised to hear of rumors linking him to Abdülaziz's death. Over tea or coffee, in the daylight of shared sweat in crowded places, and in the darkness of bedrooms, people talked and speculated on what they knew and on what they wanted others to think they knew. No probability would be overlooked, no suspect unaccused, no innocent found without guilt. "How would I have killed him?" he asked without lessening the warmth in his eyes.

"Not personally, of course. You would command someone to do it." Flora shifted her position slightly. Her legs, as required by decorum, were closed at the knees with her feet together, but she moved her toes ever so perceptively apart, drawing Abdülhamit's gaze to her ankles.

Abdülhamit had no experience in seducing a woman. They came to him when requested. He did not take them. They gave themselves. But in this moment, he was consumed with the thought of ravaging Flora. He wanted to slowly remove her clothing and see the bareness that he imagined as he stared at her. Her breasts, waist, thighs, and ankles leaped out at him from beneath her clothes. But he was terrified. He had never removed a single article of a woman's clothing. Could he command her to come to his bed naked and present herself as did his concubines, solely as the means for his satisfaction? No, he did not want that. He wanted to expose her slowly. But he felt inept, at a loss for how to approach her, what to do with his hands. What if she were offended, screamed, or ran? What if she laughed at him?

"Could you marry me?" Abdülhamit's question was more stated than asked. An off-hand remark, as though he were speaking with a close friend and asking whether a third party might marry him.

"Why not?" The answer was matter of fact, and the ease with which the words came out surprised Flora. Should she not qualify her answer, make it a theoretical statement, rather than an acceptance of the proposal? She had just agreed to marry this man. Why? If she had responded even nominally to the many flirtations extended to her, she could easily have been married. But she had not wanted to be married—at least not to any of the men she met. No one had been bold enough to awaken her imagination, to make her consider what life, other than the one she had, would be appealing. But to marry an Ottoman prince? Possibly a mistake, but too enticing to reject.

The answer released Abdülhamit from his chair. He rose lightly as though relieved of a great weight. His eyes glowed with pleasure, and his smile was broad to the point of self-consciousness. He put out his hand and took hers, which he kissed, thinking that even through her glove it was the warmest flesh he had known. "I'll make arrangements," he said.

******

In the harem section of the house, Mela was aware that Flora was a guest on this night, and she remembered Abdülhamit's eagerness to have her after Flora left on her previous visit. She expected the same tonight.

She waited to be called by Ahmet, the white eunuch who was the steward of the household. He was an elderly man from the same Croatian-speaking Adriatic province as she was. They spoke the same language, though never in the hearing of Abdülhamit, who might have suspected them of treachery. They shared a bond of slavery, of lives dramatically changed in youth by sexual desire—she as a means to fulfill that desire, and he as a means to restrict access to its fulfillment. But they never spoke of sex, despite the centrality of how it had defined their lives.

Mela prepared herself with Abdülhamit's favorite perfume out of the ingrained sense of duty that servitude imposes. She stood in front of the mirror. Could Abdülhamit's obvious infatuation with this Belgian shop-keeper on Grand Rue de Pera, a street Mela had never visited, affect her life? Probably not. The mirror said that her face was unwrinkled, her body firm and trim. But what would be her fate when Abdülhamit no longer called for her?

She found herself eager for a night that held no surprise as pleasure-provider to the sultan-in-waiting, a man no one expected to ever be more than that. She was trained to assure that he received pleasure, that he was aroused and satiated. But tonight would be different. Tonight he would not have her. She would have him.

When Ahmet knocked on her door, she surprised him by opening it and stepping out immediately in her slippers and robe, already prepared to the last detail—almost. As she walked down the hall behind the eunuch, her finger moved to execute her plan, to excite herself just to the brink but not completely. She entered Abdülhamit's bedroom, dropped her robe, pulled back the light sheet under which he lay erect, plunged herself upon him fast and deep for only the short time it took to fulfill her personal desire. Then, in a single, agile movement, she rolled off of him and swung her legs around to where her feet found her slippers, pulled on her robe, and walked quickly out the door, past the shocked eunuch and back to her quarters. She lay back onto her bed and placed her finger where, smiling, she found no semen.

She lay in peace, her mind drifting to that moment when she had been torn from the arms of her mother, forever denied a life with her family, a life of having family. She would have been poor. She would have raised children among hardships. She might have witnessed one or more of them die before age five. She struggled to remember life in her village and imagine what hers might have been. Here, she lived in luxury, wanting for nothing, except freedom and control over her body. That was it. That was why tonight had been important. In however limited a manner, she had been the master of her body, had given herself pleasure, rather than giving it to a master. She left the sultan-to-be without satisfaction. It was a monumental thing for a concubine even to imagine!

She listened to the silence, listened for sounds of impending retribution. The master had been left unfulfilled. Would he call her back? Might he have her tied in a sack with rocks and thrown into the Bosphorus? She did not think so. She had been his first and continuing source of womanly comfort for 20 years. More importantly, she knew him as a weak person. His fantasies might be drawn from the mythic exploits of historic sultans, but in reality, his most optimistic prospect was to be appointed sultan as a last resort at a time when the Ottoman Empire was disregarded by its enemies and dependent on allies of conflicting interests.

She had given Abdülhamit pleasure when he was still a boy and all through his becoming a man. She knew him to be of modest appetites in all things and without the stomach for violence. Even in pleasure, he sought the vicarious reward of a fully clothed Belgian woman. What would happen when the pleasure was real? Mela rested her hands on her stomach. She would sleep in the knowledge that Abdülhamit would call for her again. What her life might have been she could not know. But she knew what it was, and she accepted its limits. She was at peace with herself, and she was determined to respect herself. She heard Ahmet call for one of the young girls and drifted off to sleep, smiling.

ELEVEN

A young man in a dark wool coat, such as were issued to junior naval officers, sat on the single bench of a small park that consisted of three plane trees with a narrow flowerbed of tulips defining its perimeter. The park was at an intersection of streets, on one of which Mithat's *konak* stood about 100 yards distant. The man was watching the action on Mithat's street where ministers were arriving, each greeted and assisted out of his carriage by a military guard before disappearing behind the wall that enclosed the *konak*.

The young man's name was Çerkes Hasan. He was the brother of the Circassian girl who died giving birth to Abdülaziz's child. His sister had been his ticket into the palace of Abdülaziz, where he served as an aide-de-camp. He had few duties and ample time to engage in his passion, pistol-shooting. His marksmanship was well known in the palace, where his swagger was resented and his brooding nature feared. Now that Abdülaziz and his sister were gone, he had no protectors and no sympathizers. He received orders from *Serasker* Hüseyin Avni to report to the garrison in Baghdad. He had no intention of going.

His coat was heavy for the season and carried the additional weight of six loaded pistols and a newly sharpened, stout dagger that could be driven through several layers of clothing, flesh, and bones. He removed a pipe and a small bag of Indian hemp from one pocket and began tamping the pipe. He had been waiting at the park since before dawn, and this would be his third pipe of hemp. He felt steeled for what he planned to do. The hemp was a door to the next dimension, which could be his future or his past or a world he imagined but could not see. The smoke clouded reality, enticed him to imagine a heroic future that would be revealed with the next deep inhalation. In the world of the smoke, *Serasker* Hüseyin Avni would be a corpse, and he, Çerkes Hasan, would be a hero.

******

Inside his *konak*, Mithat welcomed each of the ministers as they arrived. "Greetings, my brother. Thank you for coming."

Mithat had called this meeting and was the host. In attending, the ministers accepted his leadership. Hüseyin was the last to arrive. Mithat waited for him just inside the gate and greeted him with extra warmth in the strength of the arm he threw around his shoulders, and he was genuinely moved by Hüseyin's equally warm reciprocation. "Thank you for coming. Everyone respects you and will listen to you. I, too, look forward to your counsel," Mithat said as he released Hüseyin from his grasp but held onto his arm.

"I gave you my word, the word of a soldier. It's what I am, Mithat. You are the statesman, and I am the soldier. We need each other. As I promised, I will give you more time, and I will not surprise you, my friend."

The ministers were gathered around the French-style table in Mithat's formal dining room, a room that the family never used but that was required of him as a pasha and an important personage in the empire's power structure. A French chandelier hung from the center of the room, the large windows of which had velvet drapes.

"Thank you for coming," he began. "You know of Murat's condition. I waited until Dr. Leidesdorff of Vienna could render his opinion, and he has. He believes Murat's condition to be the advanced effects of alcoholism, which attacks both the physical body and the nervous system."

"And what is the cure?" asked the minister of marine.

"Dr. Leidesdorff offered little hope. If the afflicted person gives up spirits completely and forever, he might recover," Mithat reported.

"We could have him confined and not permit him access to alcohol," suggested the minister of justice.

"How do you confine the head of state?" asked the grand vizier. "It seems impractical in the extreme."

"No one can deny the sultan what he requests," observed the minister of foreign affairs.

"Hüseyin Pasha, what about having soldiers posted to keep alcohol out of his quarters?" asked the minister of justice.

"As our colleague observed, no one can deny a sultan's request, not even soldiers. They are his soldiers. They pledge their lives to serve him," responded Hüseyin.

"The Russians are massing soldiers on our western and eastern borders," interjected Mithat to redirect the discussion to a plan of action. "In my opinion we must put in place quickly a constitution that guarantees equal treatment for all citizens. This is the only way to discredit the Russian pretext of invading to protect our Christian subjects, and it requires that the sultan be seen to back this decision. Additionally, there's our debt to our Western allies. The world needs to see a credible head of state for us to negotiate these issues."

"What are you thinking?" asked the grand vizier.

"With your support, I will speak with Abdülhamit. We should know his views. We may need an alternative sultan to be invested quickly."

"It seems like a prudent thing to do. Is there any objection to our colleague meeting with Abdülhamit?" asked the grand vizier. Several of the ministers chimed in their support, and no one raised an objection.

Mithat commenced briefing them on the draft constitution, but he had scarcely begun when he was interrupted by a yell from outside. "No, you cannot enter!" followed by a shot, a scream of pain, two more shots that appeared to be right outside the door, the shouting of several men, more shots, more shouting.

Çerkes Hasan burst through the door of the dining room, brandishing a pistol in his right hand and the dagger in his left. His eyes flashed with drug-induced intensity. His mouth spewed obscenities, screamed for Hüseyin Avni, for the eternal damnation of all present, and for the greatness of Allah.

The room was a cage and everyone in it a bird. He fired his pistol repeatedly and randomly, his eyes searching the room for Hüseyin Avni. The pistol emptied. He threw it across the room, drew out another, and fired it as Hüseyin Avni lunged at him from the right side. The bullet stopped Hüseyin where he was, clutching his gut. But as Hasan raised his arm for another shot, Kayserili Ahmet, the minister of marine, threw himself across Hasan's body, knocking the arm with the pistol down so that the shot went harmlessly into the floor. Hasan's left arm, however, which gripped the dagger in its fist, was free, and he stabbed Kayserili in the back and pushed him away in time to face Kayserili's aide-de-camp, whom he shot at close range. The same fate met a servant of Mithat's who was yelling for Hasan to stop, for the love of Allah.

Ministers took cover under the table, behind curtains, and with Mithat in a small closet. As Hasan was distracted by the aide-de-camp and servant, Hüseyin Avni, badly wounded, crawled toward the staircase that led to a balcony overlooking the room. He was in great physical pain, but thinking clearly. He did not want to be shot cowering under a table. He was cursing that for even a moment he had thought this empire could be ruled by idealists and bureaucrats of good will. If he survived this day, every resident from Vienna to the Magreb would know his will and make it their own.

Hasan saw him and skirted several overturned chairs to reach the staircase, emptying his pistol in the direction behind him before he reached Hüseyin, who was struggling to crawl up the staircase. Hasan drove his dagger deep into the back of Hüseyin's neck as he fell on top of him and left it there, as he felt the body beneath him giving up its life.

Turning back to face anyone who might be coming toward him, Hasan fired a third pistol he'd pulled from his coat, and one bullet found the chandelier, compounding darkness upon the chaos of men shouting for the madman to be assaulted and praying not to be seen. Amidst this confusion of yelling and pistol shots, soldiers rushed into the room. Hasan ducked behind the large bannister post at the bottom of the stairs, returning fire and hitting several of the soldiers before a shot grazed his shoulder, causing him to drop his gun and raise his arms in surrender.

The fuel of drugs and adrenaline oozed with the blood from Hasan's wound, leaving a pathetic shell of the man who had assumed unto himself the value once accorded him by the sultan as the brother of a beloved concubine. Now, Hasan was without even the valor to die fighting. He would be quickly tried, hung, and buried. Allah might forgive him, but man would not.

Mithat rushed to the side of Hüseyin Avni, falling on his knees, checking for a pulse. "Hüseyin, Hüseyin," he whispered to the body that responded only with its absolute stillness, the dagger vertical in its neck.

Mithat, seated on the stairs beside Hüseyin's body, watched as soldiers looked after the wounded and yelled for doctors. Two meters away, his most trusted servant was not moving, nor was the minister of foreign affairs. The bodies of two soldiers and one other servant lay nearby.

TWELVE

Abdülhamit sat alone in his small study in the solid wood chair at the desk inlaid with mother-of-pearl, both of which he had crafted himself. He ran his hands along the smooth arms of the chair, remembering the many hours and multiple processes required to turn a log into this beautiful shape that pleased his hands and eyes daily.

He began working in the carpentry shop as a young boy, and from the beginning, he took satisfaction from the work. The furniture he made was among the finest produced in the palace atelier. He still went there on occasion to pick up wherever he had left off in the making of individual pieces. He particularly liked making chairs and desks, taking pride in being a skilled craftsman. It was a rewarding way to spend his time as sultan-in-waiting. Sawing and waiting, sanding and waiting.

But now the waiting appeared to be over. He might, indeed, become sultan, and he was about to marry Flora and experience love and happiness, which in his imagination promised even greater satisfaction than being sultan.

As a prince, he was outside the rules that applied to other young men, whose parents would be concerned about the social and economic status of a potential bride's family, as her parents would be of his. For a prince or a sultan, however, the background of the girl or of her family was irrelevant. Young girls came as slaves purchased in the market, as gifts from prominent officials, and as booty, selected solely on the basis of their beauty and youth. In the harem, they learned what palace life required of them: personal hygiene, sensual arts for pleasing the master, and education in Muslim rituals and beliefs. They were trained in musical instruments for the pleasure of the master and to ward off their personal enemies: boredom, hopelessness, anger.

No marriage could boost a prince or sultan's social status, and no wife's pedigree could improve on the character or abilities of their children. The sons of the House of Osman were assumed to be born with the capacity to rule, regardless of the mother's blood lines. Abdülhamit's decision to marry Flora was in the manner of a prince selecting a slave. He did not consider her background or any of its implications for their marriage. She captivated him. He wanted her.

After the death of his mother, only Pertevniyal, the mother of Abdülaziz, could penetrate his emotional wall, and she, only briefly and infrequently. He did not feel the need for love. But now, love was present, and though it was not familiar to him, he accepted and welcomed it.

On the following day, Abdülhamit and Flora were facing each other in his study, where he had greeted her in the formal manner, kissing her on both cheeks and bowing slightly. She stepped back only minimally and looked directly into his eyes, which disarmed him. So that when he said, "I must ask you to become a Muslim," the statement came out less resolute than he intended, and he feared that she might hear it as a question, as a choice.

But surely she realized she would have to become a Muslim in order to marry an Ottoman prince. He felt he should not have to tell her. Perhaps she had already accepted Islam. All that was necessary was to make the declaration, "I bear witness that there is no deity except Allah, and Muhammad is His messenger," which could be done even in private, since only Allah needed to hear it.

In fact, Flora had given more thought to becoming a Muslim than she had given to the question of marriage. For reasons she could not articulate, changing religion was more profound than changing status from single to married—even to an Ottoman prince. She had been baptized as a Christian but was not devout. She and her mother attended services only on religious holidays and for weddings and funerals, a practice she continued in Paris and here in Istanbul.

But as she considered what she believed, she did not find her beliefs to be in conflict with Islam. None of the Islamic articles of faith were contrary to her beliefs or in conflict with her lifestyle. She believed in God, as Muslims did by the name of Allah. She could accept that Muhammad was a prophet. She could accept that the Quran, like the Bible, was a book from God and that angels and life after death existed. These were the required beliefs of Islam. As for the practices required of a Muslim—to declare belief, to pray five times daily, to fast, to give alms, and to perform the pilgrimage—her years in Istanbul confirmed that she could be as faithful in these matters as the majority of Muslims she knew. The fundamental character of the Christian God in which she believed was not in conflict with the Muslim concept of Allah. The Almighty was loving and forgiving. Believers of both faiths might condemn even minor transgressions of religious prescripts by their co-religionists, but they worshiped the Almighty to be forgiven of their own lapses.

Flora smiled as she looked at Abdülhamit, holding his hand, noticing again that he was not a handsome man. But his voice was warm in tone, and he vocalized the words as an appeal rather than a command. "I must ask you to become a Muslim," sounded to her like a hand extended to prevent a fall, and it was easy for her to answer, "Yes, I will become a Muslim."

Abdülhamit's sense of relief was profound. He again smiled so broadly that it seemed unnatural to him, as though he had committed a social faux pas. "I will call you Nigar, a Muslim name. It's Persian and means 'beautiful woman', 'beloved'. You are a beautiful woman and you are my beloved."

"I'm happy to be your beloved," Flora said, but hesitantly, knowing that she was about to raise subjects that could be unacceptable to him. "My love," she began, surprised at how natural that expression felt and sounded, "I hope you will not ask me to close my shop." She spoke directly and warmly, continuing to look in his eyes as though she were his equal. No woman, other than his surrogate mothers, Rahime Piristû and Pertevniyal, looked at him directly. Even in the dim light of his bedroom, his concubines did not attempt to make an emotional connection. No conversation or visual communication that would presage an exchange between equals, between two souls seeking affinity. On the rare occasion when a woman might speak to him, she did so with her head bowed, looking at the floor. But Flora's eyes were only centimeters from his as she made her appeal about a post-marriage condition that he had not anticipated. Continue to be a shopkeeper as his wife?

"But you'll want for nothing as my wife. You'll no longer need to be a shopkeeper," he responded, perplexed, not understanding why she would even consider this.

"I'm sorry, my love. It's my window to the world—not only mine but yours. I cannot watch the world from behind balcony latticework or experience it through your eyes alone," she said without blinking or moving her head in the least from the focus on his eyes.

"But I may become sultan. A sultan's wife cannot be a shopkeeper." Abdülhamit's voice was incredulous, and the statement sounded like a question.

"We grew up differently, my love. In your world, you provide for your wives and children and have no expectation that they might help you in any way. But I feel responsible to help you prepare to become sultan, to become a great sultan. I can do that as a shopkeeper and as a wife, not as a concubine. Perhaps I'll close my shop after I've adjusted to whatever our life becomes. But when and if to close the shop is a decision I must keep as my own."

Abdülhamit broke the silence that was not long, but seemed so. "Almost two years ago a holy man predicted I would become sultan. Everyone speaks of Murat's ill health."

"Yes, I know. But becoming sultan is not inevitable or in your control. If it happens, I will close my shop. But I want to focus on our life now, on being a shopkeeper *and* your wife. I will be happy in that. Can you be also?"

Abdülhamit heard the question, but he did not answer. Happiness was a new toy that he was afraid to show off for fear it would be taken away by a jealous older brother. The prospect of becoming sultan was also new. Maybe he could be happy *and* sultan. "I am happy," he said at last. "You make me happy, my love, my Nigar."

"My love," was not a phrase he had ever uttered before. The women of his harem were not there for him to love or even to love him. In speaking it, the phrase took him by surprise in how natural it felt.

Abdülhamit reached out to her, and Flora took his face in her hands, holding his lips only centimeters from hers as she stated her last condition in a near whisper: "I hope you understand that I will not live in your harem, my love. You must keep them in a house separate from us. When you wish to be with me, I will be in the house in which you choose for us to live."

Abdülhamit had not given a thought to the relationship between Flora and his existing harem, which in its number reflected Abdülhamit's modest appetites. He did not feel the need for more women, either physically or egotistically, and ambitious notables had little incentive to thrust gifts of young slave girls on a prince unlikely to become sultan. But Abdülhamit was in love and responded unhesitatingly, "It will be as you wish, my love," and he reached out to her as she was leaning toward him.

Flora stretched up to kiss him on the mouth, which grabbed him in its unsuspected power. He pulled her to him. Fully clothed and holding a fully clothed woman, he melted into the unexpected warmth and passion he felt as the shape of her body revealed itself to his and drove in both of them a desire to be one, a desire that was more intense than when a naked young odalisque slipped under his quilt.

******

Abdülhamit and Flora's impending wedding was an aberration. Princes and sultans did not have marriage ceremonies. The first four women to bear a son to the sultan were recognized as his wives without a marriage ceremony. If a sultan wished for the son of another woman to be recognized as a future claimant to the throne, one of the original four had to be divorced, since Islam only permitted four wives.

Flora had attended weddings between the children of prominent Ottoman families in Istanbul. She knew the traditions. The mother of the groom scrutinized the prospective bride and asked her mother for the hand of her daughter. The bride's father gave his approval of the groom and received gifts as an expression of the groom's seriousness. The bride's family negotiated a bride price to protect their daughter in the event of divorce or the death of the groom. The families exchanged gifts and threw a multi-day celebration of banquets and music for family, neighbors, dignitaries, and friends.

Flora was happy to be outside most of these customs. But there were two informal ceremonies that she wanted. The first was to prepare herself at a public bath on the day of her wedding. And the second was to have her hands decorated with *henna*. Customarily, these events would take place in the company of the women of the bride's and the groom's families. They were occasions for relaxed camaraderie, story-telling, and mirth. Flora had participated in these events for a Turkish friend once and had warm memories of this time together with Turkish women.

Abdülhamit was surprised by these requests—even more so when she explained that she wanted to experience these rituals together with the women of his harem, none of whom she had met, seen, or sought any information about.

"Are you sure this is what you want?" he asked in complete surprise and bewilderment. "I've agreed that these women will not live in the same house where you live. Why would you want to spend time with them before our wedding?"

Flora had thought about the emotional and psychological aspects for her and for the harem women so far as she felt able to do so. The one thing she felt would be important to her, if she were they, would be to meet the woman who would be marrying the man with whom they had spent intimate nights but might never again, the man who was their master and could give them away or cast them out without cause or question. In their place, she would want to take the measure of this woman. Not as a competitor, but as a human being.

Flora wanted to convey to them that she would not use whatever influence she might come to have on Abdülhamit to cause them harm, that she had no ill feelings toward them, only sympathy for their fates. They had been dealt a life they had not sought and over which they, unlike she, had no control. She wanted to reach out to them as a woman with womanly feelings, needs, and empathy, so that they would perceive that they were safe, which was the least and most she could offer them.

As she contemplated becoming the wife of an Ottoman prince, likely of the Ottoman sultan, she felt her aloneness in this foreign world, where she spoke and understood the language well, but not perfectly, where she knew most of the customs well enough so as not to give offense, and where her status as a foreigner gave her privileges and limitations—assumed to be more educated than she was and more ignorant than she was. Alone.

Although it was a "women's day" at the public bath in the neighborhood of Abdülhamit's home on the day of Flora's preparations, Abdülhamit paid to have the bath closed to the public and reserved for Flora and the women of his harem. The baths were one of the few venues where the women of every nationality spent time together. They might be known as Turkish baths, but the residents of every ethnic community, including the Europeans, bathed there. The baths were where she had learned the Turkish words for most male and female body parts, Turkish proverbs relating to the relationships between men and women, and risqué tales with nuances that particularly pleased her when she understood them well enough to laugh spontaneously, rather than because everyone else was laughing.

The baths were locales reflective of the class and character of the neighborhoods where they were located. People attended the public bath of their neighborhood without regard to religious or ethnic affiliation. The purpose was physical cleanliness, not godliness, not ethnic separateness, not linguistic commonality. Just a chance to shed the smell and grunge of humanness, to be free of dirt and filth, of sorrow and, perhaps, of guilt. For women, a chance to escape the male world, to be free of expectations and drudgery, to loiter even when there was work to do. To laugh without accountability.

The introductions occurred in the *hararat*, the hot room, where Flora joined the other women after undressing in a separate room, wrapping herself in a *peştemal*, a light cotton towel, and stepping into wooden clogs with a single strap. The women of the harem were seated on two of the marble benches around the sides of the room, each also wrapped in a *peştemal*.

"Hello, I'm Flora," she said with a slight nod of her head. "I'm pleased to meet you." Should she have introduced herself as Nigar? She thought not. The name still seemed an intimate secret, a term of endearment, more than a name, and it would require explanation. She smiled warmly and was relieved when they returned her smile.

"My name is Mela, and they are Elif, Emine, Halide, Suheyla, and Esen," Mela said, gesturing toward each of the young women as she said her name, as though she were introducing her daughters.

Flora was surprised by how very young Suheyla and Esen were. They could not have been more than 16. Elif might have been 18 and Emine and Halide, early 20's. She judged Mela to be 40 with a body that was still alluring and must have been exceptional in her youth. Elif had mischievous eyes and was turning plump in a way that Flora imagined Abdülhamit might find attractive. *Elif* is the first letter of the Arabic alphabet used to write Ottoman Turkish and is formed by a single vertical line that calligraphers spend years perfecting as a serpentine statement of grace in stationary movement—a slender and elegant form that parents imagined for daughters. An *elif* from the hand of a master calligrapher pulls the reader's gaze into the first word of the first sentence and pronounces the skill of the scribe.

Flora met all their eyes sequentially and said, "Pleased to meet you," wondering what to say next when Mela dismissed the need for further talk by slipping off her *peştemal* and stretching out naked on her back on the heated marble surface in the center of the *hararat*, called the *göbektaşı*, a large, round platform in the middle of the room that was the source of the heat. It was a deliberate move. The *peştemal* could have been left where each of them had wrapped theirs, above their breasts, could have been lowered to expose their breasts, or could be dropped to the floor, the least common action.

Mela was not the future mother-in-law inspecting the merchandise, although she was not indifferent to Flora's body, despite wanting to be. She knew what she thought of Flora's body would not affect Abdülhamit's decision about Flora, her, or the girls, for whom she felt some responsibility. What might affect their future was what Flora thought of them. Could she ignore, forget, or care nothing for women with whom she had spent time naked in the hamam on the day of her wedding? Women she had seen as herself—mortals with physical imperfections. Flesh and blood that laughed, expressed embarrassment, and touched her without malice. This might be the last time Mela could exercise control, and she would not squander it.

Each of the other women and Flora followed Mela's lead, moving in sequence around the *göbektaşı*, dropping their *peştemals* and stretching out on the marble surface as though in practiced choreography, ending the sequence as a seven-pointed star of bodies, their heads to the center and their feet stretched to the edge of the marble *göbektaşı*. Flora relaxed in the heat of the room, comfortable being naked in the company of these women, whose lives were defined by nakedness on demand. So it seemed right to be naked with them as she stared up at the domed ceiling, watching the light shafts coming through the small windows at the top. It was her favorite part of the bath experience, lying on the *göbektaşı*, sweating and admiring the majesty of a large dome seemingly held in place by nothing but the steam that clouded the shafts of light from its small windows, wisps that formed and reformed into the images of one's imagination.

"Have you been to a public bath before?" Mela asked.

"Oh, yes," Flora answered, welcoming the question, since she felt the need to say something. "I've been many times. Lying on the *göbektaşı* is what I like best. What's your favorite thing?"

"My favorite part is being scrubbed and massaged. It makes me feel pampered and clean," Mela responded.

The exchange opened up the conversation. Mela flipped onto her stomach, as did the other women so as to be facing each other as they talked about the sweating, scrubbing, soaping, and perfuming of the bath experience. It introduced laughter and camaraderie that Flora hoped would transmit her intended message that she would do nothing to cause them harm. Surely, they were as unable to grasp her life as she was theirs, but the acceptance of each other was based on not attempting to do that—just being together without judgment, sharing the pleasure of becoming clean, of feeling desirable for oneself and not as the object of someone else's desire.

Flora felt she could lie there for hours, soaking in the heat, feeling her body release every hint of tension or grime, but the young girl attendants arrived to begin the real cleansing. First at the basins, where they were soaped, rinsed, and shampooed. Then back to stretching out on the *göbektaşı*, where the attendants applied the paste used to remove private body hair and scrubbed every inch of them with a coarse cloth that removed not only any dirt but even the epidermal skin to which it might have been attached. Soaped, sudsed, and massaged their bodies beyond any urge to resist. Then the final rinsing with warm water from the basins around the side of the room and on to the cooling room, where they drank tea and commenced to decorate their hands with *henna*.

For Flora, the process, not the result, was important. The process of sitting with these women, touching each other's hands, placing small carved stones on the hands to create designs, drawing decorative lines on the hands, palms, and fingers. This tactile ritual was a bond that she wanted with these women—for them and for her. Of all the pre-wedding rituals, it was the most relaxed context in which to joke and laugh together over nothing.

"I know you came here from Paris," Mela said, "and did dress fittings for the women in Abdülaziz's harem." It was a bit of a know-your-place remark, but Mela was careful not to sound disrespectful. "We hear so many rumors about the *valide sultan*, Pertevniyal. What's she really like?"

"Actually, I never met her. The dresses she ordered were for the other women in the harem. She treated them as her daughters, and they spoke appreciatively of her for it."

By the time their hands had been elaborately decorated, the bond among the women made it easy for Flora to ask them if they would braid her hair.

"But you're a modern woman," Mela protested. "You could get your hair done in the finest hair salon in Pera, as the brides of all the prominent families do now."

"I'm not the daughter of a prominent Ottoman family, so I cannot be the bride of one. I choose to be a traditional Turkish bride, and I would be honored if you would fashion my hair in one long braid in the traditional manner. Will you do that for me?"

For the first time, Mela looked directly into Flora's eyes. She feared what this imminent wedding might portend for her and the young girls, but in Flora's eyes she saw nothing that supported her fear. "It will be our pleasure to braid your hair," she responded.

What else could she say? But what surprised Mela was that she felt sincere in saying it. She felt the same as she might have for the sister she had been separated from as a young girl and had not seen since. In Flora's eyes, she saw an ally, a woman to whom she could appeal for help if that proved necessary. Twenty years of sharing her body with Abdülhamit might well mean nothing to him, but she felt it would mean something to Flora.

To prepare for this day, Flora had gone to a wedding shop where she purchased the clothes she brought with her—clothes she knew to be common for a traditional bride: a white shirt and white baggy pants, red leather boots, a pearl necklace and earrings, and a tiara of multi-colored cut glass that held in place a completely transparent red veil of ultra-fine thread. Of course, her wedding would not really be in any respect traditional. Flora was not pretending that it would be. But it would be her only wedding, so it was her prerogative, she felt, to make it as she wished, to make it an historic wedding between a once-upon-a-time prince and a fairytale princess in a real time empire.

And that was how she stepped out of the carriage to be met by Abdülhamit, who was waiting at his summer home in Tarabya with the imam who would marry them.

Abdülhamit did not hide his surprise and happiness at seeing her dressed as a traditional bride. Even in baggy trousers, she was gorgeous. Maybe it was the tiara, which made her look truly like a princess. Maybe it was the sparkling fresh look on her face that surprised him. She looked delighted to be marrying him. He felt like the sixteenth century sultan, Süleyman the Magnificent, with Roxelana, the most famous couple in the history of the Ottoman Empire. He felt handsome, worthy, and capable to be not only sultan but a great sultan. Capable to lead armies, to promulgate the laws of his country, to stare down the Powers and restore the Ottoman Empire to greatness. Without speaking, but once again self-consciously smiling broadly, he took her hand and led her into the house, into the parlor, and before the imam.

The ceremony was short. They signed the marriage contract and pronounced three times each that they accepted its terms, and the imam recited a verse from the Quran that declared blessings on the Prophet Muhammad. As part of a wedding, the groom would scatter coins to the people attending. Abdülhamit, superstitious by nature, had, in fact, sent generous alms to several mosque soup kitchens.

But now, it was just the two of them in this summer house attended by two servants. Abdülhamit took Flora by her ungloved, hennaed hand, which pleased him, though he did not know why, as though she were feeding him pleasure in a secretive manner. They had a simple meal followed by strawberries from his garden and Turkish coffee. They said little as they ate, each self-conscious in his or her separate way.

Abdülhamit's proposal and her immediate acceptance of it had come as such a surprise that she had not fully accepted it as real until now. Tonight she accepted that she loved him and was prepared to be his wife, his Nigar.

Abdülhamit had been denied no physical pleasure he imagined or wanted since he was 14. Still, this experience felt new, and he was anxious. But in the bedroom, his apprehension dissipated. She kissed him. First tenderly, and then passionately. The fire of lips on lips freed Abdülhamit from the expectations and rituals of all previous sexual encounters. They helped each other remove their clothes and slipped under the coverlet on the bed, where, as though on a winter's journey afoot, they had stumbled upon a campfire.

Flora lay beside the sleeping Abdülhamit. Her marriage was consummated. Her husband was not a handsome, muscular young man, as she had thought to marry. He was a middle-aged man who was only tolerably good looking and physically unremarkable. Yet, she loved him. She was a princess in the Ottoman Empire, likely to become the wife of the sultan, perhaps the mother of a future sultan. But that was not what she thought about. Abdülhamit was her husband, not a prince, not a sultan, just a man who needed her, and to the extent he would allow, she would be his helpmate—even in saving the empire.

******

Tarabya was a district of villas and gardened estates along the Bosphorus north of the city. Many of the Ottoman elite, prosperous non-Muslim Ottoman citizens, and expatriates, including most of the foreign ambassadors, had homes here, many of which were used only in summer, when Tarabya became a bustling mini-metropolis of people strolling along the Bosphorus and overseeing the care of manicured tulip and rose gardens.

On this first morning after the wedding, Abdülhamit, a man of habit, awoke early and slipped out of the bedroom. It was pre-dawn, and he set about conducting his ablutions for the Morning

Prayer. As he washed, he reflected on his marriage as a statement that he was a man like other men, choosing a wife, rather than conferring the status of wife onto the first four women to bear him sons. If he became sultan, he would attempt to know the lives of ordinary men. Ordinary men said the Morning Prayer. The Caliph of the Muslim world said the Morning Prayer.

To his surprise and pleasure, Flora had also risen early and was waiting for him when he arrived at the dining room, where they took a simple breakfast of soft-boiled eggs, yogurt, toast, and tea. "Will this be our home?" Flora asked.

"At least for the summer. You'll like it here. The gardens are beautiful. The air is fresh."

Flora felt a tinge of apprehension. The city and her shop in Pera were distant. Even in the comfort of one of Abdülhamit's carriages, the journey would be tiring on a daily basis. Yes, Abdülhamit had agreed that she could continue operating her shop, but could he be setting her up to abandon it of her own volition?

"Today, I'll go with you to the city," Abdülhamit continued. "You'll open your shop, of course. And I'll spend time with acquaintances at the bourse. They'll know the latest gossip, and I can check on my investments."

His tone was matter-of-fact, his voice warm, his demeanor loving. Flora felt reassured. "I'll be ready in half an hour," she said.

On the way to her shop, Flora made a plan. At least for the summer, she would open a second shop in Tarabya. Many of her customers lived in Tarabya over the summer months. Curiosity about her would promote sales. And she would keep the shop in Pera, as well, but hire someone to run it.

******

In Pera, she found Cristo, sitting on his stool outside his shop. "Good morning, Cristo," she said. "I hope you're well. It's a lovely day."

"Thank you very much, Madam. I hope you are well also. It is indeed a lovely day. As I'm sure you would expect, every breeze in the city whispers that you have become the wife of Prince Abdülhamit. Congratulations. I'm happy for you."

Flora watched his face carefully, wondering what he really thought, seeing his face as a window to what the city was thinking. The marriage could affect her business. Would the young men still congregate in her store? Her response to their flirtations was always cautious—never a rude rejection, never a hint of encouragement. A demure smile, a quick parry to the business at hand: a new perfume just arrived from Paris, the herbs in a particular soap, the price of a lotion, the credibility of a rumor's source. The young men came not for reward but for the game that would have been spoiled for all, if she had rewarded any one of them.

And they came because it was a trusted environment in which to share the latest news. She was a Belgian woman, whom they knew to be one of them. Would they feel equally comfortable talking in her presence now that she was the wife of Abdülhamit?

Cristo's face revealed nothing. He seemed genuine in wishing her happiness. "Yes, I guess you could say I have become a princess. Thank you for your good wishes. We're living in Tarabya, at least for now, and I would like to open a shop there. Do you know anyone who owns a storefront I could rent?"

"What about your shop here?"

"I'd like to find someone to manage it for me. A Christian woman would be best. The young men need to feel free to talk with each other. They trust that a Christian woman will not be in the employ of the palace as a spy."

"I have a niece. She experienced a tragedy and is not likely to marry. She needs a new life. In your shop, where I'm next door to watch out for her, I think my sister would agree. Leave it to me. As for Tarabya, I have a summer home there, myself, and I know many merchants. I'll make inquiries. But you must promise to come to Pera regularly to check on the shop here, so that we can have tea."

"Of course. I'll check on my shop, and I'll have tea with my friend Cristo." She had never directly addressed him as friend before. But, of course, he was her friend. They shared tea and gossip every day. Could a prince's wife have a friend?

"I'll look forward to every visit. You know, of course, the rumors about Murat's health. People say it's only a matter of time before Abdülhamit becomes sultan." His voice was sad, and he recognized that he had expressed this news as though it were not good.

"Yes, I've heard that Murat is not well. But many doctors are engaged to cure him." Flora heard in her own voice the solemnity of Cristo's. Did she not want Abdülhamit to become sultan?

THIRTEEN

In Istanbul, everyone was captured by the idea of change, yet feared becoming the victim of it. Would the empire's decomposing corpus yield fertile soil, or only more decay?

In Dolmabahçe Palace, Mithat searched for answers, options. He decided to delay speaking with Abdülhamit. The death of Hüseyin Avni reinforced his sense of the fragility of his country's condition and his need for allies. He sent for Namık Kemal, the only member of the exiles in Europe, who called themselves the Young Ottomans, with whom Mithat had formed a friendship. Like himself, Namık was an idealist who believed in the common people. Namık was known and respected in the empire and in Europe, but feared by the palace as an intellectual of forceful and influential rhetoric, the cause for multiple exiles over his career.

"Welcome my brother. Wonderful to see you," Mithat said, grabbing Namık's hand firmly and embracing him warmly.

"Thank you. Wonderful to see you, as well, my brother. It's been a long time."

"We need you now more than ever."

"Nothing could keep me in Europe once I heard you'd deposed Abdülaziz. I'm humbled that you feel you need me."

Over coffee, Mithat filled in the details since Abdülaziz's deposition. "I fear we have to abandon the prospect of Murat as sultan," he said in conclusion, as he shrugged his shoulders in a gesture of helplessness.

"So, you will turn to Abdülhamit?" Namık questioned in a tone of surprise.

"Yes. The Council of Ministers has given its approval for me to speak with him."

"We never thought of him." Namık observed. "It was always Murat we saw as the potential leader of reforms. What do you know about Abdülhamit?"

"Not much. None of the ministers know him. I will wait for Murat to recover as long as I feel I dare to do so, but then I will make the case to the Sheikh Ul-Islam that the empire's future is at stake—specifically that Islam would be harmed by a Caliph who is unable even to attend the Friday Prayer. The Sheik Ul-Islam cannot ignore that." Mithat raised his gaze to the window, where he watched a strong wind throw wisps of dark clouds across the sky, promising a storm and taking his thoughts with it to the squall of events that could wipe out everything he had spent his life working for. "We're heavily in debt to our allies, and now we're behind on our payments," Mithat continued.

"Because of the high interest Ottoman bonds pay, everyone in Europe buys them. I bought them myself, and I have done well too. But surely our European allies, particularly the British, would not be so quick to abandon us?" Namık asked, more as a statement of his own belief than as a question.

"We need European public opinion on our side. The Russian troops remain on their side of the border only because they think the British and French might come to our aid."

"I came back to be of service. What can I do?" Namık asked.

"You must resume publishing your newspaper. In the modern world, the message is important."

"I've already spoken with several writers and businessmen. The presses we used before my last exile remain as we left them. I'll have a paper in your hands within a week."

"Wonderful. We need a voice for freedom," Mithat said with enthusiasm. This was the first positive news he had heard since deposing Abdülaziz.

"I've decided to give my paper, *Freedom*, a new name. People think of freedom as a revolt against the rules of religion, a creed of anarchy and atheism," Namık pronounced as though making a speech in Hyde Park.

"It's true. And we have citizens of many religions and Muslims of several sects. If we want them to be loyal citizens, they must feel free to practice their religion," Mithat said, warming up to the oratorical nature of their discourse.

"Exactly. I'll call my new paper *Warning*. Its mission will be to educate the people about what we face, to portray a sense of urgency, and to call on them to participate, rather than to be led. That is the future."

"I like it. You're right. The people, Muslims *and* Christians, need to be warned about the dangers. If Russia invades, everyone will suffer. And if the empire's economy collapses, no one will be spared." Mithat's voice trailed off, as he considered the truly grave situation they faced.

Namık sensed Mithat's shift in mood and tried to change the conversation to his joy in returning to Istanbul, breathing in the fresh sea breezes, eating his favorite foods, and sharing coffee and *rakı* with friends. He thanked Mithat again for deposing Abdülaziz. "I feel completely invigorated by being home again," he concluded.

"What's needed is what you have written of so eloquently — loyalty to the fatherland," Mithat continued reflectively. "We need to build a government that inspires the people to be loyal to the empire, rather than to their ethnic and religious community, their *millet*."

"Yes, intellectually, the people don't know patriotism, but they experience it in their loyalty to their *millet*. We need to make them feel patriotism for their country," Namık enthused.

"For hundreds of years the subjects of the empire were loyal to the sultan, because he provided food, shelter, and safety. My mission is to rebuild the public's trust in their government. Yours must be to build a belief in nationhood, the fatherland, patriotism," Mithat said.

"I craft my words as powerfully as I can. But you have credibility. People know that you've acted, not just talked. You need to become grand vizier."

"It's not enough. We need a whole new structure, a constitution that guarantees human rights. The people want the right to be who they are—Muslims, Christians, Jews, Armenians, Arabs, Laz, Kurds. It's not too much for them to ask. It's not too much for us to ask that they also be Ottomans," Mithat emphasized.

"Can we make this happen?"

"If we do not, the empire is lost."

FOURTEEN

"Bonjour, votre altesse," called Yorgo Zarifi, in French as Abdülhamit entered the bourse. Members of the upper classes in Istanbul, even those whose French was minimal, used common French expressions as a nod to the Francophile culture of the city. "I have good news for you," Yorgo continued in Turkish.

Yorgo was a Greek banker and financial advisor who managed Abdülhamit's personal wealth. Yorgo was known to everyone, had a tuned ear locally and internationally, and was admired in the Greek community for his charity to the Greek Orthodox Church and his approachability by those in need. He loaned his own and other people's money, including that of Abdülhamit, at high interest rates, accepting that some people might be unable to pay in full but that the arc of payment overall would be favorable. Retribution against those who failed to pay was not in his interest or nature. Courtesies—some personal and some of potential financial value—could always be expected. Negative measures were never good for business.

Wealth that arrived as a river brought resentment. Wealth accumulated from a thousand rivulets allowed believable modesty and admiration, even from those who were the sources of his wealth. The times were exceptional, and the exceptional profited.

"Good morning to you also, sir," Abdülhamit responded as he approached. "It is indeed a glorious morning. Blessings and good health be upon you and your family."

Abdülhamit's ebullient manner, normally so subdued as to project melancholy, took Yorgo by surprise. "Blessings and good health to you also, *votre altesse*. The entire city is talking about your marriage. May Allah favor you and give you sons."

"Thank you. What news in the financial world?" Abdülhamit had a keen interest in finance, was curious about how the market worked, and was conservative in every aspect of money.

"Your wealth increases daily. Some of your money is now in German and British banks."

Abdülhamit never inquired of Yogo about what guided his money transactions, and Yorgo did not volunteer such information except when he could report a correct prediction that had made both of them richer.

"There's no shortcut to riches in banking," Yorgo continued in a self-protective mode, "but if you're careful and patient, the money grows remarkably well over a life-time, and if one lives long, he lives well, as do his children."

"You've done well by me. I'm grateful."

"Thank you, *votre altesse*. I am your humble servant, and it's my pleasure to serve you as well as I'm able. It's the guiding principle of my work—doing well for myself by doing well for others, thanks be to Allah." Like most members of the non-Muslim communities in Istanbul, Yorgo conducted much of his business in Turkish, and used common Turkish expressions, such as, "Thanks be to Allah." Sometimes, even when speaking in French.

"You've heard the rumors about Murat's ill health, I'm sure," Abdülhamit said, looking at him more intently than Yorgo could ever remember him doing before. "Will this affect the value of our money?"

"Potentially, of course. I'm following it closely. The market believes that Murat will be replaced soon. Everyone looks to you to be the next sultan. The empire has many resources, *votre altesse*. In wise and strong hands, it will surely prosper."

Yorgo knew that some Greeks were delighted to see the empire in economic difficulty. The dream of recapturing Istanbul and reestablishing the Byzantine Empire was ever a topic of idle moments in Fener, the Greek quarter of the city. But Yorgo knew, as everyone did, that if the Russians marched into Istanbul, they would not hand it over to the Greeks.

"Greetings, *votre altesse*, and to you, also, my friend," came another voice from across the bourse. It was Assani, Abdülhamit's Armenian investment broker. The three of them exchanged pleasantries and Yorgo excused himself.

Assani was a stock and commodities broker, a real estate investor, a currency and precious metals trader, a man with a sharp eye for revenue in many spheres and as tough in his dealings as was required to turn a profit and maintain the trust of those with whom he negotiated. He had contacts through family and friends in most of the major cities of the empire, in Europe, and in America. These contacts were key sources of information that helped him profitably trade stocks and commodities. And he reciprocated to their benefit, as well.

"What news do you have of my investments?" Abdülhamit asked with uncharacteristic directness.

"British steel and woolen manufactures are up. American silver and cotton are up," Assani began. "German industrials, French fashions and furniture, even Italian stained glass is up. And we have done particularly well with rice from Persia. People consider it a sign of status to eat and serve Persian rice. We anticipated this in time to make a good profit."

"You know your work. It's a virtue we need in this country."

"You're very kind, *votre altesse*. Thank you," Assani responded, noting the difference in Abdülhamit's manner. Never before had he spoken of the needs of the country.

"What investments do I have in Turkish-owned companies or locally produced commodities?" Abdülhmit asked.

In the many years Assani had invested Abdülhamit's money, this question had never come up. Abdülhamit never proposed a single investment or hinted that he would favor investing in a particular business or commodity. "Of course, you do. Sorry that I neglected to mention them. We have invested in grain. After the terrible drought, agriculture has rebounded in Anatolia, and we have done well with wheat. Bread feeds everyone. We have done well with sheep and wool with the recovery from the drought also. And silk. More money in the pockets of the merchants and pashas here, and in Europe, is always good for the silk trade. The silk mills in Bursa run 24-hours-a-day. And tobacco has been especially profitable. The British and French soldiers in the Crimean War became fond of Turkish tobacco. Now the Americans are importing it to use in their cigarettes, as well."

"I hear from many sources that the economy of the empire is weak, but why? What needs to be done?" asked Abdülhamit in a tone of genuine interest and concern.

An unexpected question. Assani hesitated, unsure how candid he should be. Abdülhamit trusted him, a trust he had earned and wished to keep. "I know personal finance, not the finances of nations. A man cannot spend more than he earns and survive. But sometimes a ruler may need to spend more than the nation can afford, if, in the short term, it's essential for the survival of his subjects and of the nation."

Abdülhamit understood that Assani was skirting the issue of the profligacy of his father and uncle. And he appreciated that this did not need to be said. If he became sultan, he would bring an end to the excesses of the palace. "And what do you hear in the Armenian community?" Abdülhamit asked, probing for a candid tidbit, as though inquiring about the health of his family.

"The talk is of the Russians massing troops on the borders. You know, of course, about the negotiations for the purchase of rifles from America that have been on-going for several years. I'm told that these rifles could decide the outcome of a war with Russia. Negotiations over their sale are in the hands of the Azerian family, here and in America. The elder Azerian is a good friend of mine. We will make money *and* help the empire."

FIFTEEN

At the Süleymaniye Mosque compound where Ayşe and Gül lived, Ayşe made friends with Fatma. Fatma, one of the oldest residents of the compound, had spent 50 years there. At the age of 12, she escaped from the village where her parents and everyone else died at the hands of Cossack marauders in the Caucasus Mountains. She and two other young girls lived only because they had been sent into the hills to collect firewood. They made their way to Istanbul in the company of neighboring villagers, who felt it was too dangerous to stay in the Caucasus Mountains.

Fatma knew what a refugee needed to know. She knew remedies for physical, emotional, and spiritual ailments. She knew folk healers, doctors, pharmacists, dentists, and merchants who had once been refugees. She was a reminder of what they had left, and they offered help. But Fatma was careful not to abuse anyone's kindness or generosity. She asked only on behalf of the most destitute and for the minimum required. For herself, rarely.

Today, Ayşe needed her. "I'm carrying the baby of the men who murdered my son and husband," Ayşe sobbed, burying her head among the folds of the scarf Fatma had around her neck and head.

"Are you sure it's not your husband's?" Fatma had suspected Ayşe's condition.

"No. I'm quite sure. My husband—may you live a long life—was a kind man. Many women in the village complained of being pressured by their husbands to have more children. But my husband and I agreed not to. We were joined together a few nights before that horrible night, but we were always careful.

I used a wad of cotton with herbs and vinegar and I washed everything out with vinegar immediately afterwards," Ayşe responded, looking at the ground in embarrassment.

"Have you ended a pregnancy before?" Fatma asked.

"No."

"But you must have known women in the village who did," Fatma said in a matter-of-fact tone, not passing judgment.

"Of course. It was common. Many husbands did not approve, so the women did it in secret."

"I know a Rumanian gypsy. She'll give you choices, but she'll charge you. The amount depends on the method you choose. I can give you money."

"No. I've saved money since the day we arrived. You told me the best spots for begging. Thanks be to Allah, I have money. I only waited until I could leave Gül. Will you look out for her while I'm gone?"

"Of course."

"And if something happens to me..." Ayşe's voice trailed off, and she hid her face in her hands.

"I will pray for your safe return. Allah is merciful. I have sent many women to the gypsy, and she has never failed me. But I swear on the Quran, if something were to happen to you, your daughter will be safe with me. I'm old, but I know many people in this city. I would find a family for her, a family that would treat her as their own and not as a servant. When do you wish to go?"

"Tomorrow."

*****

Ayşe left before the morning call to prayer, slipping carefully away from Gül's warm body, which was always pressed against hers. She walked briskly, passing among the few street sweepers still active and among the faithful hurrying to the mosques for Morning Prayer.

What if it was her husband's child? Perhaps a boy who could avenge his father's death, who could sire sons and grandsons and great grandsons to do the same? For a moment, she slowed her stride. Among the refugees, some were miscarrying and some were dying in childbirth. And many babies were dying within a few days and months. She re-quickened her steps.

The gypsy camp was easy to see from some distance away. Children were playing among the tents, and smoke circled from fires that had heated morning tea and bread. "I'd like to see Raluca," Ayşe said to the first woman she saw.

"There are several Raluca's here."

"I understand she may have some herbs, some potions, maybe a procedure," Ayşe said, hesitantly.

"You want Raluca, the doctor. We call her doctor, because she helps the sick and the mentally ill and does more good than those in the city who call themselves doctors," the woman said. "You'll find her in the big tent. Third one on the right, the one with the poles and ropes in front where the herbs are drying. May Allah help you." The woman looked her over knowingly.

"Welcome. Please, come in. How may I help you?" Raluca asked, as Ayşe stepped before the opening of the tent. She spoke Turkish with a distinct Rumanian accent. The tent was large and had a raised platform on one side that did not appear to be used for sleeping. Otherwise, the tent looked like any other poor person's home—with bedrolls and pillows along the sides, a trunk, and a few pots and pans. Raluca wore a dress patterned in red, orange, and purple with embroidery of gold thread in multiple configurations. She wore nothing on her head, and she had a broad and warm smile that made Ayşe feel welcome and took away her fear at being there.

"Fatma said you may be able to help me. I was raped and I don't want this baby," Ayşe said holding her abdomen. "I don't know what to do."

"Please sit down. Denise!" Raluca called to her daughter outside the tent. "Bring us some tea!" Raluca took Ayşe's hand and guided her to sit on one of the bed rolls and put a pillow at her back. "First, we'll have tea. How is Fatma? She's a soul of mercy for all."

They finished their tea, and Raluca explained the choices and the cost of each. One choice was punching. Raluca's brother did this. She assured Ayşe that her brother was very skilled in exactly where to punch, so that it would be effective without a great many blows. But the description took Ayşe terrifyingly back to the brutal punching of the rapists, and she could not bear the image of a man standing over her with his fist raised, even if the harm he would do her was measured and precise. There was poison which usually worked, but it made women sick. Some women remained sick for a long time. There were herbs that sometimes worked, but often did not. Finally, there was the wire. This always worked, but there was a danger from bleeding. When she had a cut, did the wound stop bleeding quickly? She would have to stay the night, maybe longer. "We'll have another glass of tea while you think about it. Denise! Tea."

Ayşe decided on the wire. Raluca prepared a narghile with hashish and instructed Ayşe to breathe deeply and hold the smoke in as long as she could. She also gave her opium syrup. After several hours, Raluca decided that Ayşe was sufficiently drugged to bear the pain.

Four women held her. Ayşe knew pain, and it did not frighten her. But the actual pain was unbearable. She passed out, and when she awoke, the pain was inside her, around her, over her, omnisciently present as though it were the only thing left in the universe. She heard herself moaning as the voice of another person from a world unattached to her. Raluca held her head and gave her more opium syrup. "We were successful," she whispered, "but you'll need to stay here until the bleeding stops."

In the city, Gül cried. Fatma worried. Two days later Ayşe walked slowly into the mosque compound and was almost knocked to the ground by her screaming daughter.

SIXTEEN

Early in July, Redif Pasha, the minister of war who had replaced Hüssein Avni, brought the news to Mithat in his office at the Council of State. Serbia and Montenegro had declared war against the Ottoman Empire, and Austria was set to invade Herzegovina and Bosnia.

"I've ordered our troops in the neighboring provinces to join those in Serbia, Montenegro, Herzegovina, and Bosnia. I believe we can prevail so long as Russia stays out of the fight," Redif reported.

"Keep me informed. Is there anything I can do?"

"I need money for the troops. They fight in the name of Allah and for their sultan. Still, it would boost morale if we could pay them," Redif pleaded.

"I'll speak with the minister of finance. May Allah be with you and with our troops."

"Thank you. And with you as well, sir."

Even before Mithat could send word for him, the minister of finance arrived to report that the Ottoman Empire was no longer able to pay any of the interest due on the Ottoman bonds sold throughout Europe.

"We can pay nothing?" Mithat asked in a tone of moderate incredulity. The news was not unexpected. The empire had failed to make regular payments on its debt for most of a year. He had used this argument as the primary cudgel to convince the Council of State and the Council of Ministers on Abdülaziz's deposition. Mithat wanted a new government for many reasons. Getting control of the empire's finances was among them.

"I gave the little that was left in the treasury to the ministry of war for the troops, who will give thanks for even the most minimal support. The bankers of Europe are less easily satisfied," responded the minister.

Throughout his career, Mithat had singularly focused on how the empire might administer the affairs of state honestly and fairly and on the structure of government needed to make such rule expected and common. But he had failed to focus on the empire's finances.

In his vision, reforming the finances of the empire would flow naturally from democratization. The citizens of a representative government would be allies against wasteful spending. But how could he not have foreseen that a failed economy would sabotage everything he wanted to put in place? Mithat was familiar with the empire's many streams of revenue, and he knew the amounts as percentages that were collected for commercial transactions as fixed fees and as taxes. Goods transported along the major east-west and north-south trade routes were taxed. Both the production and consumption of goods were taxed. Mining rights and mineral tonnage were taxed. The sale of every kind of good from the most everyday necessity to precious metals and stones, property, animals, land, and food was taxed. The government levied poll taxes on households in the cities, the towns, and the villages. Even nomads did not escape the tax collectors. Anything officially recorded had a fee: birth, marriage, divorce, place of residence, licenses. A special tax was levied on non-Muslim males in lieu of military service.

What Mithat did not know was the total that the empire collected from each income source or in aggregate. No one did. The empire did not have a central office to collect income and distribute money based on predetermined allocations, a national budget. Each government entity had income sources assigned to it, but no administrative department spent based on knowing how much was available to spend. Mithat felt foolish, incompetent.

The minister of finance waited in the awkward silence. "I'm sorry to bring you such bad news," he said at last. "Is there anything you wish me to do?"

"No, thank you. I appreciate your position," Mithat said, but he was thinking that there were many things he would want the minister to do—stamp out corruption among the tax collectors, eliminate procurement kick-backs to senior officials for everything from supplies to battleships; eradicate bribes for lower fees or a turned eye; abolish the nepotism that swelled the state's payroll. But he continued, "Have you reported this to the Council of Ministers?"

"I go there from here."

"Good. Tell them that I will be cutting the palace's spending as much as I have power to do so, and I urge the ministers to do likewise. May Allah be with you."

"And with you."

Mithat sat back in his chair, called for coffee, and picked up the day's edition of *Warning*. The paper was a daily comfort to Mithat, a reminder that he was not alone, but in the company of other committed and intelligent men trying to save the empire. Namık's editorial was on the concept of citizenship. It was a concise and well-reasoned argument for the self-interest of the residents of the empire to share an equal status and work for the success of their government and country. Mithat wanted to believe it was possible. He needed an infusion of hope and sent for Namık Kemal.

Over coffee, they shared their reactions to the news of the default and how it might affect European public opinion and the prospect of European help in a war with Russia.

"At least the British press has something other than what they call the 'Bulgarian massacres' to write about," Namık mused.

Mithat observed that Namık's mood was uncharacteristically dour. "Our default makes change even more urgent—perhaps more radical change than I had planned. Murat cannot govern. We always talked about reform as a new order, but within the existing structure. Maybe we need to be bolder. Could we have a government without a sultan/Caliph?"

Mithat watched Namık's face. He saw that he had overstepped. Namık was a political progressive but a religious conservative. If Namık was not ready for radical change, certainly the people were not. He changed the subject. "I have little control over the empire's purse, but I've pledged to make cuts where I can. You can help. You can campaign against bribes and kick-backs. If the people in the street start to complain about these things, maybe officials will be shamed. Public opinion *does* matter, even here."

They drank another coffee, spoke about mundane and lofty matters, and said their goodbyes.

Mithat paced. What significant expenditures could he control? Armaments. He sent a message for the minister of war to return.

The conversation with Redif was short. Mithat reminded him of the large contract with Providence Ironworks in the United States for Peabody-Martini rifles and informed him that he would be asking the senior Mr. Azerian to renegotiate the payment schedule, to stretch it out.

Redif objected that this would mean extending the delivery schedule, to which Mithat responded that this was preferable to receiving no rifles, which would be the consequence of not meeting contractually agreed upon payments. Mithat tried to end the meeting on a cordial note, but their goodbyes were of forced politeness.

In Britain, the financial impact of the default diminished the pensions and savings of ordinary people, as the bonds took on their true value, paper. The reaction was outrage. The press replaced its relentless cartoons of Turks skewering Christian babies with images of Turks driving British citizens into debtors' prison. Money trumped blood.

******

The news of the default reached Abdülhamit from several sources, but Assani, his Armenian investor, was the first. He arrived at the door of Abdülhamit's *konak* in Tarabya with the horse of his carriage lathered and his driver stressed. Speed on Istanbul streets could cost you a carriage, a good horse, or worse. But Assani was composed. He had anticipated the default and acted accordingly. Nevertheless, he felt the need to personally inform Abdülhamit of the actions he had taken. He could not do so beforehand without raising questions. Clients expected foresight, not foreknowledge. Sources expected secrecy.

"You sold my stocks in Providence Ironworks?" Abdülhamit asked, surprised.

"Yes, their contract for the Peabody-Martini rifles will be affected, I'm sure, and the stock will lose value. We made a good profit on the sale."

"But the empire needs those rifles. Surely, that contract will be honored?" Abdülhamit felt ashamed that he was learning this from Assani. Men like Assani had access to information that allowed them to be proactive, while he remained an observer. As sultan, he could not lead the empire without the kind of information these men had. Clearly, information, particularly information not known to others, was important to power, to making decisions. When he became sultan, information would be his priority. Nothing would be too trivial for him to know.

"I've spoken with the elder Azerian. He expects to be asked to renegotiate the payment and delivery schedule. I will buy Providence Ironworks stock again at the lower price just before the new contract is signed. The army will get its rifles, and if they prove as good in battle as expected, the empire will buy many of them over many years. I will take my leave now, *votre altesse.* I must attend to reinvesting the money we've made. Allah be with you."

Assani left Abdülhamit's *konak* energized. Trouble was opportunity. He would invest in the supplies that the empire would need for its forces if there were war with Russia. Even before he heard of the Russian troop movements to the empire's western and eastern fronts, he noticed Russia's interest in lead and invested in it. Subsequently, Russia began buying lead as fast as it could be mined in Anatolia. Troops needed bullets. Russia planned to attack.

He did not welcome war. War threatened death, even for investors. Nothing could be predicted with certainty. Trusted sources might have misinformation or erroneous intelligence. Even victory could be loss. Twenty years earlier, new to his trade, Assani had watched the empire's victory in the Crimean War destroy its economy and his with it. He saw the collapse of the Ottoman Empire as a likely disaster for him and his family. His children attended the best schools. His sons would not be sent to war. He enjoyed wealth and status, and he hoped he would not have to use it to buy his family a new life somewhere else.

******

The news of the default disturbed Abdülhamit and sent him on his favorite horse into the hills behind his *konak*. Riding was a passion and a skill. He had spent many of his idle hours as prince-in-waiting in becoming an expert horseman. As a young man on a striking white Arabian, he easily imagined himself leading an army to the walls of Vienna.

He sent word to Mr. Johnson that he would be riding. Mr. Johnson lived on the estate adjacent to Abdülhamit's in Tarabya. He was an Englishman, a businessman, and an avid horseman and hiker. They often rode or walked together in the wooded hills above their estates. Mr. Johnson was one of the few people, Muslim or Christian, with whom Abdülhamit had a conversational relationship.

Mr. Johnson owned several retail stores in Pera and imported British wool fabric, tailored woolen garments, and used clothing from Britain, Germany, and France. He exported Turkish wool, tobacco, and the "oriental" products sold in European department stores. Everyone assumed he spied for the British Embassy, but he assured Abdülhamit that he did not.

Today, Abdülhamit had a special interest in talking with Mr. Johnson. He wanted to know what people like Mithat knew. It was clear to him from what happened to his uncle that remaining in the seat of power required that the sovereign keep one step ahead of his servants. He did not want to be a figurehead sultan and respond to advice out of ignorance, or, worse yet, be perceived to be doing so.

Mr. Johnson was a man of whom Abdülhamit could ask questions without feeling inferior or ill-educated. Mithat's intent to turn the empire into a constitutional monarchy modeled on Britain was no secret. What were the implications of this if he became sultan? "Can the queen dismiss the prime minister?" was his first question.

"No, she cannot. The prime minister is elected by the majority party in the House of Commons. Those same delegates decide when they want a new prime minister."

"And she cannot pass laws or demand that they be passed, isn't that right?"

"Yes. Parliament passes laws, and she must abide by them, just as any other citizen."

"So, what are her powers?" Abdülhamit asked, feeling more confused than enlightened.

"She does not so much exercise power as influence. Her opinion matters, even when it's not obeyed." Mr. Johnson went on at some length about the "prerogatives" that gave the queen powers she never exercised, about her close advisory relationship with the prime minister and the Privy Council, and about her representational duties as head of state.

Abdülhamit had many questions, most of them about the queen's ability to have her will carried out. Mr. Johnson gave a few examples, but acknowledged that exercising power was not the role of the queen. Although Abdülhamit had grave doubts about the British model for the Ottoman Empire and for him, he was reassured by the lack of precision in the exercise of power.

On the other hand, he was surprised that the queen needed to fear assassination. It was this fear that made him hesitant to become sultan. The specter of Azrael, the Angel of Death, had been with him since the days when he sat, listening and watching, at the foot of his tuberculosis-afflicted mother as she coughed up blood. Azrael appeared regularly in his nightmares. Would becoming sultan lure Azrael in the form of assassination?

*****

Flora, now Nigar, heard the news of the default from Cristo over tea, which, as was their custom, they took on low, backless stools on the sidewalk in front of his shop before they opened in the morning. The tea was delivered by a boy who moved unceasingly among the streets and shops. He carried a brass tray suspended by three arched ribs with a ringed loop at the top through which he put two fingers for carrying the tray and against the outside of which he pressed his thumb to keep the tray steady. The boy could move at a near run with a tray full of tea glasses and demi-tasse Turkish coffee cups without spilling a drop and was as dependable and depended upon as the many imported clocks from the previous century that delineated prayer times in the hundreds of mosques of Istanbul. Istanbulites were tolerant of many unreliable features of life and the absence of some physical comforts in this crowded city of sewerless neighborhoods, but unfailing tea and coffee service was expected and supplied. Tea and coffee were sipped slowly, as befit the taking of a simple pleasure in lives with few of them.

This was to be Nigar's last day in Pera before opening her new shop in Tarabya, for which Cristo helped her find a space in a building owned by a cousin of his. His niece would manage the shop in Pera.

"Don't worry," Cristo said. "I'll be right next door to help if she has any difficulty or questions. Your shop will be in good hands."

The easy thing would have been to give up the shop in Pera. But keeping the shop was about being independent, about being the daughter of her mother, self-reliant. And it was about hedging her future. Nothing was a given in Istanbul in the summer of 1876. The report of the default portended unpredictable change. "What will the default mean for the empire?" she asked, though she was thinking of what it might mean for Abdülhamit.

"The British will wring their hands. The Russians will salivate. And European journalists will pronounce the 'sick man of Europe' dead." Cristo paused and took a sip of his tea. "But the residents of this great city know that dead men rise and that despair for the present is essential to hope for the future. We will survive, Madam, with the help of God," Cristo pronounced, raising his glass to his lips, as though the joy of sipping tea at this moment was the only pleasure he could count on, and the only one he needed.

SEVENTEEN

Conversation at the shop was lively. Nigar was eager to see the carriage arrive to take her back to Tarabya. She had much to share with Abdülhamit. There could be no doubt now that he would become sultan and that the default would restrict what he could do and empower those who wanted to tear the empire apart. He would need help. Would he allow her to be one of the helpers?

"All the talk was of the default," she reported. "Most of the young men from Britain lost savings or know people who did. They said the London papers have anti-Turkish cartoons. They think this will prompt Russia to declare war and prevent their government from fighting with the empire."

"Do they speak of Murat?"

"Yes, everyone reports that the doctors have been unable to help him and that you will soon be sultan," she said, looking at him with a whimsical smile of approval.

"What do they say of Mithat and his constitution?"

"They speak of him and the constitution favorably, but they disagree on whether it is more important to address the economy or the constitution first. Someone said there is talk of setting up a debt commission managed by European bankers." She knew that Abdülhamit had scant knowledge of the finances of the empire. He would have authority to do anything and capacity to do little. She wanted to ask him what he thought should be done, but she did not want him to think she was questioning if he knew what to do.

After dinner, they walked, catching the day's last light and the moon's first on tended rose gardens, magnolia trees, and weathered wooden *yalıs*. On the *kayıks*, sailboats, and steamers.

On the wide expanse of the Bosphorus here that presaged the dark waters of the Black Sea a short distance beyond. They were among many who walked in Tarabya that summer, many who recognized and acknowledged them, who spoke of them, though rarely to them or they to others, and many who speculated on the empire's and their own uncertain future and the role Abdülhamit might play in it.

The shore of the Bosphorus featured many forms of entertainment: fire-eaters, acrobats, jugglers, musicians and dancers. One evening, they attended a *Karagöz* puppet show that performed a skit popular that summer. The show lampooned Abdülaziz as a dissolute brought down by the clever Mithat Pasha and murdered by unknowns, whom the audience might easily conjecture to be those who might profit from his demise—a happy ending that prompted cheers from the audience. Abdülhamit had no memories of his uncle that were special or fond. And yet, hearing his uncle mocked, jarred him. One day a sultan could be exulted as the Shadow of Allah on Earth, Sovereign of the Orient and the Occident, and the next be mocked on a shadow puppet stage—amusement for the same people who had venerated him, even as his body barely had begun to decompose. He vowed that if he became sultan, no one would dare laugh at his expense.

In every corner of the city that summer, facts and fabrications were repeated without distinction. Nigar and Abdülhamit sometimes shared a laugh over the absurdity of some of the speculations. But at other times, they silently and separately mused on the potential truth of the rumors. The empire *could* become unable to pay even itself, much less its debtors. Maybe there really *was* a European banking channel through which the empire's revenue was being secreted out of the country. *Maybe* some of the pashas *were* in on it. There *could* be a secret agreement among the Western Powers and Russia to divide up the empire and leave nothing at all for the Turks. The Persians and the Arab Sheikhs *could* be in on it. There *could* be a secret plan to turn the empire into a vassal state of Britain, similar to that of India. Istanbul *could* become the capital of Byzantium once again. No scenario was outside the realm of speculation or without those who declared its truth and offered evidence thereof.

Nevertheless, Abdülhamit and Nigar enjoyed a glorious summer. For the first and only time in his life, Abdülhamit was comfortable in public, among the people, with his Nigar, and out of character from the person he had been. Comfortable talking about everything and nothing. They switched between Turkish and French, sometimes using mixed language sentences for deliberate comic, dramatic, or affectionate effect. Some phrases of intimacy seemed more expressive in one language, some in the other. Sometimes they expressed a sentiment first in one language and then in the other—sometimes for emphasis, sometimes for amusement. They were lovers.

Nigar understood their bond. Abdülhamit needed her, enjoyed her company—talking with her. She enjoyed sharing what she knew with him. She was surprised only by his moderation in all things. He was not sexually demanding. Their physical bonding had occasional spark without consistent fire, as though a relationship of decades, instead of weeks, a relationship of contentment with nothing to prove. He followed her lead more than he took initiative in what they did outside of those things that were the rituals of their days.

The empire may have been in crisis, but they were in love. He never said, "I love you." She never expected that from him. But when he looked at her, she knew. And when she looked at him, he knew. Silence created a magic the spoken word could only dissipate.

Their existence at Tarabya was simple. They shared the *konak* in which they lived with the eunuch, Ahmet, a secretary, and Abdülhamit's personal Greek physician, Dr. Mavroyeni. A cook and a gardener came to the *konak* by day. Dr. Mavroyeni's job was to keep Abdülhamit apprised of Murat's health. What the doctors were saying and prescribing. What the palace staff reported regarding Murat's intellectual engagement and his ability to sign required documents.

Dr. Mavroyeni reported the diagnosis of alcoholism made by Dr. Leidesdorff of Vienna. "Alcohol provides pleasure, so addiction comes easily, unnoticed. The addict loses control and then loses the ability to function," he reported.

"Murat liked cognac and champagne. Foreign drinks. I only drink *rakı*," Abdülhamit responded defensively.

"Their addictive qualities are the same. I'm your doctor. I feel it my duty to advise you to stop drinking *rakı*."

Abdülhamit was disciplined in most things. Chain smoking, coffee, and a fondness for *rakı* were the exceptions. But he trusted Mavroyeni, and the truth of what he said was obvious in his brother's dissipation. He gave up *rakı*. He wanted to be sultan.

EIGHTEEN

Mithat Pasha woke early from a fitful sleep, interrupted by nightmares in which Russian troops marched into Istanbul, in which thousands of creditors looted the city, and in which Europeans and Russians sat at a table bargaining over pieces of the empire. He could wait no longer. He needed a capable and willing sultan who could approve decisions, take responsibility for the empire's actions, and be accountable for its fate. Abdülhamit would have to be made sultan. He called for Minister of War Redif. "What's the latest news from the front?" he asked.

"Our troops won an important battle at Alexinatz against the Serbian rebels. I received a report from one of my most reliable spies this morning that Prince Milan of Serbia will accept a peace deal if he learns that the Russians will not send troops to help him. According to other spies, that message from Russia is imminent."

"I'm told that British Ambassador Elliot reminded Russian Ambassador Ignatiev yesterday that Russia is obligated by the Treaty of Paris to honor our borders," Mithat reported.

"The Russians have violated treaties before," Redif observed. "And the Russians surely are counting on the current anti-Turkish sentiment in Britain to keep her from being our ally."

"Britain needs a sign from us. I've decided to advise the Council of Ministers that Murat must be deposed. You could support my position by pointing out that his deposition is necessary to the security of the state."

Redif knew that Mithat was using him. He was taken aback by the baldness of it and felt he should object. But what would he object to? That Mithat was asking for his help to save the empire? "With the help of Allah, I will make the case as well as I can," he said. "Will Abdülhamit stand up to Ignatiev?"

"He must. Allah be with you."

"And with you."

Mithat pondered the likely discussion in the Council of Ministers as he waited for the grand vizier, for whom he had sent. The ministers would be concerned about how the outside world would view such a rapid change. It was August and Murat had been sultan for not even 90 days. But it would be even worse if the outside world became aware of Murat's true condition. The ministers would also be unhappy; they knew Murat personally. He had been a public presence in the pasha social scene. They liked and respected him and wished him to be sultan. Mithat had once shared this feeling, but this was not a time for sentiment.

When Grand Vizier Mehmet Rüşdi was shown into his study, Mithat rushed through the formal greetings and said, "I think it is imperative that you ask the Council of Ministers to request a *fetva* for Murat's deposition. His health shows no improvement. We have no choice but to invest Abdülhamit."

"It's been such a short time. How well do you know Abdülhamit?"

"Personally, not at all. But he is known to be a modest man who lives unpretentiously. That's certainly a positive. As a young man, he went to Europe with Abdülaziz, and, reportedly, showed interest in parliamentary democracy. I heard that he spoke with the British businessman, Mr. Johnson, just the other day about the powers of the queen, so he is not ignorant of a constitutional monarchy. Allegedly, he speaks French reasonably well, and he just married a Belgian woman. So, he appears to be open to Western influences and ideas. In any case, is there another option? I don't think we can wait any longer."

"I'll convene the Council tomorrow morning. You have my vote. I hope you're right about Abdülhamit and that we will not live to regret this decision. Will the Sheik-Ul-Islam agree?"

"He'll follow the council's decision. He needs a mentally competent Caliph, as much as we need a functioning sultan."

******

From the first day after the deposition of Abdülaziz, Murat's condition was like the face of a beautiful woman behind a delicate veil, its allure of modesty more irresistible than a barren face. Officially, nothing was revealed about his condition, and yet the veil of secrecy was transparent. No one could resist envisioning features of his condition or speculating on the length of his tenure—manna for an empire starving for news that might keep it alive.

Everyone knew that the pretense of Murat as sultan could not continue. The Powers might call the empire sick, pretend to want it well, and plot to dismember it, but they knew the danger—even for them—if its dissolution occurred in the context of chaos. In his illness, Murat's specter hovered over the city even more oppressively than the most despotic and powerful of the historic sultans.

Mithat attended to every detail. The Council of Ministers and the Council of State unanimously signed a pronouncement to depose Murat and invest Abdülhamit as sultan. He had Murat's chief physician in Dolmabahche Palace prepare a declaration of Murat's mental incompetence and had it signed by him and five other physicians, four of whom were Europeans attached to the embassies of Britain, France, Germany, and Austria-Hungary. Mithat's message to the Powers was that he could heal "the sick man of Europe."

Mithat went to see Sheikh Ul-Islam Hasan Hayrullah, who was not surprised by the visit. He knew of Murat's condition, and the absence of a functioning Caliph weighed on him. But so too did the prospect of issuing another *fetva* before even a year had passed, the minimum time required by tradition, and he expressed this concern to Mithat.

"I accept that tradition is a guide we must respect," Mithat responded cautiously, "but your obligation is to the Faith and the Believers. The Caliph must be capable to administer your interpretations of the Sharia."

"What will happen to Murat?"

"He'll live under guard for his own safety in Çırağan Palace."

"And if he should recover from his illness?"

"He would be entitled to be reinvested as sultan."

"Do the doctors give any hope for this?"

"None, at this time."

The *fetva* was short:

> If the Commander of the Faithful is suffering from mental illness and if the exercise of his function is thereby rendered impracticable, can he be deposed? Answer: The Sharia says, yes.

With the *fetva* in his briefcase, Mithat stepped into his carriage and directed the driver to take him to Abdülhamit's konak in Tarabya. He had what he wanted. And yet, he could not enjoy his success. Rumors persisted that Abdülaziz had been killed to anoint Murat. Rumors of ambitious people unjustly tossing Murat aside would surely follow—the subject of satire and ridicule in *Karagöz* puppet shows for public entertainment, as well. No matter how transparent his every move, people imagined secrets, whispered conspiracies. The forces of power and vulnerability were locked in a standoff. Every move he made could be fatal or healing—for himself, his beloved empire, or both.

******

In his *konak* in Tarabya, Abdülhamit waited. The message that Mithat wished to see him arrived just after word of the *fetva* deposing Murat. Mithat would be coming to offer him the sultanate. His eunuch, Ahmet, told him of the reports in the market of dissention between Grand Vizier Mehmet Rüşdi, who was reluctant to take any action, and Minister of War Redif Pasha, who pressed to overthrow Murat.

To his surprise, the reports did not put Mithat in the primary role of seeking Murat's ouster. It seemed out of character. Mithat knew Murat's condition better than anyone. He should have been at the center of advocacy to oust Murat. Mithat was no bystander. He brought back Namık Kemal and other Young Ottoman revolutionaries specifically to spread the idea of a constitution. That was it. The constitution. That was Mithat's real passion. He was not concerned with who was sultan.

Everyone knew that Mithat had conferred with British Ambassador Elliot on a draft of his constitution. The whole city was talking about the constitution as the next stage in the series of reforms implemented over almost 40 years by Mithat's predecessors and mentors. It would be difficult to oppose a constitution. The result of opposition was plain to see. Abdülaziz ended up deposed and dead—probably at the hands of the reformers. Murat went mad as soon as he was made sultan. Too coincidental. Starting tomorrow, he would engage an official food taster.

As for the restrictions a constitution might impose on his authority, apparently Queen Victoria influenced events, laws, policies, and wars, while retaining a measure of immunity from enmity when events turned badly. Maybe the constitution could, in fact, be used as a tool to keep the empire together, he mused, and to assure, as well, that his death would be of natural causes. But Mithat, on the other hand, might be too ambitious to trust.

"I have with me a *fetva* from Sheikh Ul-Islam Hasan Hayrullah, declaring Murat to be unfit to serve as sultan," Mithat said upon arriving. He opened his briefcase and handed the *fetva* to Abdülhamit. "The Council of State and the Council of Ministers have asked me to express their desire that you be sultan," he continued.

"And if Murat recovers? Could he be reinstated?" Abdülhamit asked, much to Mithat's surprise.

"It would be permissible."

"If he requested to be sultan, who would decide if he were mentally fit?"

"Doctors would be consulted, of course, but there's no precedent."

"If I accept, those who may become discontent over any matter could threaten to return Murat to power in order to pressure me—even to blackmail the country. It would suit the interests of many to have a mentally weak sultan. These *fetvas* of incompetence appear to be easily obtained."

Abdülhamit's tone and look was accusatory. Mithat shifted uncomfortably. He had not expected Abdülhamit to express any reservation about becoming sultan. "The Sheikh Ul-Islam does not issue a *fetva* to depose a sultan lightly. He must be convinced that it is essential for the welfare of the people and of Islam," Mithat responded.

"Murat's malady came on suddenly. Could it not disappear equally without warning?"

"I cannot say, but the doctors express no hope. More importantly, there would be no support to reinstate him if, under your leadership, the empire were prospering. Your subjects of all faiths pray for the blessing of the next life, but in the experience of this life, they look to their sultan."

"The people did not rise up against Abdülaziz. He was brought down by you and the ministers."

"He brought himself down by failing to carry out his duties," Mithat said defensively.

"I understand that you have convinced the ministers that the empire should have a constitution and an elected parliament. The people won't have recourse to a *fetva* to disband the parliament when it passes laws they do not like. Nor will you or the ministers," Abdülhamit pronounced to demonstrate his knowledge and to goad Mithat.

"The people will have the opportunity to elect new members to parliament," Mithat responded.

"But no election deposed Abdülaziz or Murat," Abdülhamit said, staying on the offensive.

"The sultan will not be elected under the constitution. That will remain handed down through the lineage of the House of Osman. And the sultan will retain significant authority. He will be the head of state." Mithat's defensive tone revealed his discomfort.

"When I was in Europe, I spoke with many people about the functions of parliament. A parliament would encourage the people to be loyal citizens, would it not?"

Mithat was taken aback. Abdülhamit had seemingly switched positions. Was he endorsing representative government? "Your grandfather is revered for his reforms. If you issue a constitution, our country will be a peer of Britain and France, and your legacy will be honored."

"I will serve my country," Abdülhamit stated, looking at Mithat as though Mithat should express gratitude.

"The country will be well served, my sovereign," was all Mithat could think to say, but he left the meeting agitated. He had hoped for reassurance that Abdülhamit would be the sultan they needed. Instead, Abdülhamit's reference to Murat's potential reinstatement as sultan and to blackmail presaged a despot's fear. Worst of all, his characterization of Abdülaziz's and Murat's depositions as events that he, Mithat, had engineered, was a personal attack that added suspicion and intrigue onto what Mithat saw as acts of patriotism. And Abdülhamit's enthusiasm for a constitution, a document he had not read, sounded insincere. If Abdülhamit issued the constitution, would he abide by it? But Mithat could see no alternative. The empire needed a functioning sultan before the hot-heads within and the Powers without stoked fires that would leave only charred remnants for them to divide.

******

The news that her husband would be sultan reached Nigar in Pera, where she had gone to have tea with Cristo on the pretext of checking on her shop there. "I promised Abdülhamit that I would cease to be a shopkeeper when he became sultan. At the time, I think I wanted to believe it would not happen, but I was sincere in what I said. I will sell you the inventory, if your niece wishes to continue the business in either or both of my shops," she said, her voice revealing none of the emotions she was feeling.

"And what will you do? Move to the palace?"

"No. I will not live in the palace harem. Abdülhamit knows that. Nothing will be the same for him or for me. *Kismet*, as the Turks say."

"We Greeks use the same word. So much happens for which there is no explanation that we accept it as our *kismet*, whether we are Muslim or Christian. In Istanbul, we Greeks have become half Turkish, but don't tell anyone I said that," Cristo responded with a chuckle.

Nigar smiled and sipped her tea, savoring the pleasure of tea with Cristo, the warmth of the sun finding its way among the buildings along the Rue, and the satisfaction she had known as a shopkeeper: exchanges of pleasantries and gossip with customers, a living earned by her own business acumen, and the affirmation that young men came to the shop because she was there, even though nothing other than the lightest of flirtations ever occurred. The shop had been her domain in this Francophile corner of Istanbul. Now, she could not see her future.

"Abdülhamit will not be angry?" Cristo asked.

"No. I'm not rejecting him. I'm rejecting life in his harem. He knows that. Anyway, he's not an angry person. He's kind and generous," she said, reflecting the truth of what she had experienced with him. But she did not share with Cristo what was nagging at her, which was his apparent indifference to her and their life together. They had passed the summer in love. How could he turn his back on that?

"If you change your mind, I'll help you open a new shop. This city is a repository of history, but it lives for the future. From tomorrow, the talk will be of Sultan Abdülhamit II and of his every move and pronouncement. No one will speak of the woman who ran this shop or be interested in what she is doing." Cristo paused, aware of how cruel his words were. "Sorry, I didn't mean it that way. I'll care. I meant the gossipers."

"I know you care, but you speak the truth. This part of my life is over, and I do not wish for anyone to feel sorry for me. You're kind to offer to help. I will return and have tea with you," she said and smiled warmly at him.

She knew she had been naïve in marrying Abdülhamit, but she had her rationale. At the time, his investiture as sultan was far from certain. And there was the example of Süleyman the Magnificent, who loved Roxelana above all others, was true to her, confided in her, consulted with her. Love was supposed to prevail.

She decided to ask Abdülhamit for permission to live in the house in Kağıthane. It was remote from the city, and she loved the gardens and animals. Abdülhamit had been proud of his flowers and vegetables and of the sheep, cattle, and horses. He might miss them and come to see her there. One thing of which she felt confident was that he would never look at her and say, "I divorce thee," three times, by which he could officially discard her. But he also would no longer be her husband. He would be sultan. And she would not live in his harem.

******

Routinely, Abdülhamit came out to meet her when he heard the carriage arrive. Today, he did not. She found him engrossed in papers at his desk, and although they exchanged the spoken and physical familiarities to which they were accustomed, a subtle awkwardness intruded.

"You will be sultan." she said.

"Yes, Mithat Pasha showed me the *fetva* deposing Murat."

"And you accepted."

"Yes, with some reluctance. I don't like having Murat available for dissidents to see as an alternative, whether or not he recovers his health. Foreign enemies might also exploit this. But I accepted as my duty to the country," he said, as though announcing that he would be taking a walk in the garden.

"The country is fortunate. What I hear in my shop are predictions of disaster for the empire. You have the opportunity to change their perception. Every ethnic and religious community, every foreign power, knows that the collapse of the empire would benefit no one. They'll give you a chance," she said with eyes that implored him to ask for her help, ask her to be his partner—not from the harem, but next to him.

As if reading her mind, Abdülhamit asked, "My Nigar, will you come with me to the palace?"

"Only if you do not require that I live in the harem. I accepted Islam, and I have no regrets. But I cannot be a traditional Muslim wife. I do not believe that Allah requires this of me." In saying this, Nigar realized it was the first time she had attempted to articulate even to herself what she believed as a Muslim woman.

In the silence that followed, Nigar waited for the words she wanted to hear, words that would invite her to come to the palace but not live in the harem. She wanted him to be daring, to propose a new order, in which she could continue as his one and only love and they would live together in their own quarters within a palace without a harem, a new era, in which she would be by his side, share his joys, bear his burdens. But Abdülhamit's eyes did not meet hers and were not capable of seeing what she wanted. The concept of a lover, a partner in all aspects of life, was beyond his desire or imagination.

"The harem quarters are beautiful and furnished with the finest of everything from Europe. Why would you not want to live there?" he asked.

"It's not the physical harem I reject. I cannot be one of the members of your harem. I'm sorry, my love. I would not be happy."

"The members of my harem are entitled to join me in Dolmabahçe. If you cannot accept to live there, you may live wherever you wish. You will want for nothing."

"I'm closing my shops, as I promised. I would like to live in the house in Kağıthane."

"It shall be so."

Much that needed to be said, that needed to be acknowledged and confronted, went unsaid in their last evening together in the *konak* in Tarabya. They enjoyed a simple meal, followed by Turkish coffee and cigarettes, but skipped their routine of walking along the Bosphorus, and remained, instead, on the paths among the flowerbeds in the *konak*'s extensive garden. They retired early, and Nigar sensed that Abdülhamit was tense and unlikely to sleep much, if at all. If she whispered that she would go with him to the palace, maybe he would sleep. Maybe they could make love. But she could not say that, and she fell asleep in the discomfort but resolve of her decision.

She awoke well before the morning call to prayer. Abdülhamit was already gone. She lay in bed and waited for the sun to rise. Today, she would begin another unplanned phase of life to complement the several serendipitous lives she had already lived: life as a shy young girl who learned to sew and asked her mother if she were pretty; life as a skilled seamstress in a Paris fashion house; life as a confident young woman who opened a shop on the Grand Rue de Pera; life as an attractive woman who married Prince Abdülhamit and imagined being his one love.

She cried for her losses. Cried for the father she never knew; for the mother she loved dearly and missed daily; for the loss of her business, which had defined her; and for the loss of her lover, her husband, her partner in the secrets of the city—information mostly of common knowledge but a kind of aphrodisiac that bound them to each other.

But nothing could be reversed. This beautiful woman of past lives lay quiet in the bed from which Abdülhamit had departed and turned her thoughts to what she would now become. She would not be the angry, abandoned wife. She would not be one wife among several. She would not be the occasional source of physical relief for the sultan. She would find her own niche in this capital of intrigue, power, dissolution, and love.

NINETEEN

In the predawn of August 31, 1876, Abdülhamit, in his 34th year, prepared to be proclaimed the 34th sultan of the Ottoman Empire. An empire that once had lain upon the earth as the finest of Turkish carpets, woven with hundreds of knots per square centimeter and displaying intricate geometric patterns in warm and beautiful colors of complementary natural dyes, but which now lay exposed as thread-bare with loosely woven and ill-tied knots, course designs, and the garish colors of chemicals. And yet, despite neglect and abuse, its fabric continued to hold, providing shelter to Muslim victims of torture, rape, murder, and plunder from the Morea, the Crimea, the Caucasus, and the Balkans; shelter for Jews expelled from Spain, Portugal, and the Morea; shelter to Sunni, Shiite, and Alevi Muslims who suffered each other as heretics; shelter to Bulgarian, Greek, Armenian, Russian, Protestant, and Catholic Christians who distrusted each other and competed for souls. Most of the people under its protection were poor. They did not need or aspire to own a fine carpet. They wished merely for even the coarsest coverlet to shield them from cold, the hardships of their lives, each other, and, occasionally, from their protectors.

Abdülhamit had slept little, eager to step onto this tattered rug as its sultan and restore it to its rightful state as a beautiful and lush carpet. He mounted his white Arabian, a classic horse befitting the occasion. In the saddle, passing along the spectator-lined streets, he projected the image of his fantasy, a proud sultan of a feared empire, prepared to lead hundreds of thousands of men from early spring to early winter against the infidels of Europe and Russia, the heretics of Persia, or the subjects of suspect loyalties from Baghdad to Beirut, Mecca to Sana, and Cairo to Rabat. His route to the historic home of the sultans and seat of government, Topkapı Palace, took him down the Grand Rue de Pera. He gave no thought to the irony of riding to his coronation as sultan of the Ottoman Empire via the Grand Rue, the Istanbul cradle of all that was not Ottoman, but that the Ottomans admired and sought to emulate. A street where the Europeans plotted for the remnants of greatness over which he was about to preside. A place where everyone was jockeying to control the forces of impending change that fate would reveal in forms none of the players could orchestrate or predict.

Out of obligation and a genuine expression of hope that the summer's malaise of a leaderless country had come to an end, the crowd cheered as he passed, although Abdülhamit did not physically acknowledge the crowd. The cries of "Long live our *Padishah*, Shadow of Allah on Earth" reached his ears but did not resonate in his heart. Were the people sincere? The unexpectedness of Murat's incapacity to be sultan had thrown a shadow over this day that was reflected in the dour gaze Abdülhamit fixed just above the heads of the onlookers, as though he feared that the faces of the people might reflect his own doubt.

He concentrated on the horse beneath him and the horizon ahead and took little notice of his surroundings, not looking in the direction of the shop where he had gone on the advice of Pertevniyal to meet Flora, blocking out his thoughts of the summer he had passed in love and of the woman who loved him, the woman he named Nigar. That was his life before he became sultan. He could not go back. His country needed him.

Astride his white Arabian, sensing its muscle and spirit, Abdülhamit was in command, guiding the horse via rein on neck, calves on mid-section. He, not Murat, was sultan. He, not Mithat, would determine the future of the empire. He, not the Europeans, would preserve the empire. In the Western embassies and shops of the Grand Rue de Pera they might speak of the "sick man of Europe," but Abdülhamit's experience gave him a determination against illness that they could not appreciate. As a small child, watching his mother die, he had been helpless. Now he was not.

His father and uncle were seduced by luxury and emptied the treasury. That would not happen to him. He would impose austerity and repay the debt. The Europeans might speak of protecting Christian subjects, but their first love was money. Personally, he still found the simplest meals to be the most satisfying: rice pilav, yogurt, a skewer of kebab, fresh fruit, fresh vegetables, rice pudding, Turkish coffee. The flavor of simple dishes could not disguise the taste of poison.

His father relied too heavily on the British; his uncle fell under the influence of the Russians. He would pit the British and Russians against each other and be the pawn of neither. He would need to be informed even of their thoughts. Many spies were in the employ of the government, but he would have more.

The pashas told him that the treasury was empty. Was the treasury empty because they, as much as his father and uncle, helped themselves to it? Did he dare to believe that they worked for the good of the country and would also be loyal to him as their sultan? Surely they were motivated by love of position and privilege. Most of the pashas lived in houses furnished in the latest European fashion and sent their children to foreign schools. Apparently, they saw their country well served by becoming a vassal of Europe, a status that also served their personal interests. He would have spies on the pashas.

Entering Topkapı Palace's walled compound of buildings and open spaces was comforting to Abdülhamit. As a small boy, he had wandered its courtyards and gardens, sat under the trees, cooled himself at the fountains. As a young prince, he had lessons here. He rode through the arched doorway of the main gate between the peaked towers joined by a turreted wall that permitted passage on horseback, and as he did so, he thought this palace a more fitting place from which to rule than Dolmabahçe Palace with its nineteenth century glitter. This place felt secure, secretive, and rooted timelessly in the empire's history, a thoroughly Ottoman edifice removed from the world that threatened it. Floor after floor, wall after wall, and ceiling after ceiling covered in the finest Turkish tiles from İznik. Tiles in shades of blue and green floral and geometric patterns on white with splashes of red and black—a feast for the eyes, a nod to heaven for the spirit.

Abdülhamit dismounted at the Chamber of the Sacred Relics in the third courtyard of Topkapı Palace. The Sacred Relics of the Prophet Muhammed manifested the sultan's status as Caliph to the Muslim world. In the office of Caliph, the secular and religious worlds over which the Ottoman sultans reigned became one. Among the relics preserved, the most important were the Prophet's robe and standard, the standard behind which armies had established the Muslim world and terrified the Christian world. Amid the relics and the sayings of the Prophet and passages from the Quran that hung from the walls, the Sheikh Ul-Islam pronounced him Commander of the Faithful, Lord of Two Continents and Two Seas, and Guardian of the Holy Cities: Sultan Abdülhamit II.

From the Chamber of the Sacred Relics, Abdülhamit walked the short distance to the Audience Chamber and took his place on the Golden Throne that Selim I had brought home as booty from his conquest of Persia. Seated here, Ottoman sultans for hundreds of years received the supplications of their subjects, declared war, promulgated laws, awarded sinecures, sentenced the accused, forgave the contrite, and ruled on the loftiest matters of state and the most prosaic concerns of individual subjects. The Golden Throne was a reminder that his ancestors were feared, that to be sultan was to be measured against an epic standard. He felt simultaneously powerful and inadequate. He was sultan of the late nineteenth century Ottoman Empire, not that of hundreds of years earlier when the empire was feared and envied by Europe.

Particularly at this moment when the empire was weak, the empire needed a strong ruler. He would be one. The people wanted safety, food, and shelter. He could provide that. And when the representatives of the non-Muslim communities bowed to pay their respects, Abdülhamit assured them of his concern for the welfare of *all* his subjects and of his commitment to the prosperity of the country. This was what he truly wanted. He would make it so.

******

One week later, Nigar stood among the crowd gathered along the northern shore of the Golden Horn to watch the approach of the Imperial *Kayık* as it carried Abdülhamit to the venerated Eyüp Mosque, built by Mehmet the Conqueror in honor of a companion of the Prophet who had died in the first Muslim siege of Constantinople in the seventh century. In this sacred venue, Abdülhamid would gird the Sword of Osman, founder of the Ottoman dynasty, in the last of the rituals to become sultan.

The crowd on the shore was large and included many who came from distant parts of the empire dressed in the finery of every culture—a jumble of assorted head-gear over a rainbow of clothing. Everyone knew each other's origins based on what they wore. They knew their religion, their language, and the personal and communal characteristics attributed to them. But on this day, shouting "Long live our Padishah," they presented a unified front of adulation and well-wishing for their new leader. Nigar was pleased and joined in. Yet in doing so, she could not help but wonder at the task facing Abdülhamit. How would he evoke loyalty to the empire from these disparate peoples? Outwardly, they appeared to have nothing in common, except that they were Abdülhamit's subjects.

The *kayık* was elegant in its graceful and slender shape, nine feet by ninety feet, its sharp bow extenuated by a sword-like ornamental accessory that jutted out in front of it, as though directing a cavalry charge. Thirteen pairs of oarsmen filled the bulk of the vessel, and its stern carried an open pavilion, where Abdülhamit II sat in a large, French-style armchair, as though it were a throne.

From the shore where Nigar watched, Abdülhamit did not strike an impressive image. He was not a large man and was not imposing, even when met close up. Perhaps her perception reflected her knowledge of how little he knew, even of the city in which he would reside, much less of the empire over which he would reign, or of the world in which the Powers would look for an excuse to reduce his domain to insignificance. To succeed, he would need advisors of exceptional ability and absolute loyalty. She could have been one. But not from the harem. She saw

Abdülhamit change from the moment he knew he would become sultan. He leaped eagerly and instantly into the traditional role of sultan. She would have been isolated in the harem and unable to help him, even if he sought it. She had no regret, only the fear of a lover watching the object of her affection going off to war. She watched the *kayık* make its way up the Golden Horn and applauded with the crowd. And although she mourned inside, her cheering was genuine. She wished him well, and she wished prosperity and peace upon her chosen homeland.

"May Allah protect him! May He protect us all!" cried someone in the crowd to rejoinders of "Amen" from many, including Nigar, who, in that moment, accepted, as a Muslim, that Allah would determine Abdülhamit's fate, her fate, and the fate of the Ottoman Empire. The burden was lifted from her. She did not need to help Abdülhamit. She would find a new life.

"If you love Allah, please, *Hanımefendi*, will you help us?" asked the woman who pushed her daughter's sleeve up to expose the ugly, cross-shaped scar. The woman was only one of many beggars using the occasion to appeal to the obligation of Muslims and Christians alike to give alms to the poor.

The woman's appeal interrupted Nigar's thoughts; her stomach tightened at the sight of the scar. "May Allah bless you and your daughter, Auntie," she replied, reaching into the small purse she clutched and retrieving one of the coins she had brought with her in anticipation of the many beggars who patrolled public events. "How was your daughter injured?" she asked, feeling that giving a coin with no personal outreach was a gesture too cold for the heat of the wound.

The question took Ayşe by surprise. She raised her head to look at the woman, who appeared to be a Christian. She hesitated. "Foreign devils, Mademoiselle. They killed my husband and my son. I live only for my grandsons to take revenge with the help of Allah."

"You're from the Danube Province?"

Ayşe felt uncomfortable. She was turning to move to the next person in the crowd when she saw Nigar reach into her purse again. "Yes, Mademoiselle."

Nigar left her hand in her purse. "Where do you live?" It was an unnecessary question. Everyone knew the refugees sheltered and ate in the mosque compounds. Nigar knew this. But something about the permanent damage to this little girl that would stigmatize her for life demanded Nigar's attention.

"We live in Süleymaniye Mosque, Mademoiselle. We live by the grace of Allah and those who worship Him." Ayşe's eyes did not leave Nigar's hand that remained in her purse.

"May Allah care for and protect you, Auntie," Nigar said and handed her another coin. Nigar watched Ayşe and Gül move on, successfully soliciting money from many in the crowd cheering the new sultan. These tens of thousands of homeless, destitute refugees were the sultan's subjects, and he was responsible for them. But she knew that their welfare would be left to the grit of their desperation, the alms of strangers, and the conscience of religious institutions. She resolved to visit Süleymaniye. The plight of these people might be a thread with which she could stitch together her new life as a Muslim named Nigar.

TWENTY

"A new era," said British Ambassador Elliot as he sat up in bed, seemingly steeling himself for unknown challenges.

"You mean the new sultan?" asked his wife.

"Yes. I've asked for a meeting with him. I have the unenviable task of informing him that Britain is convening a conference of the Powers to discuss our response to the Bulgarian massacres. It will be held here in Istanbul, and I have to tell him that the Ottoman Empire will not be invited to have an official representative at the conference—only observers. A nice 'welcome to the throne', don't you think?"

"Yes, but the massacres were months ago. Why call for a conference now?"

"The conference is an attempt to preempt a Russian invasion. The Russian propagandists are spreading disinformation everywhere among the Christian populations. Our consul in Erzurum reports that they are issuing Russian passports to Armenians and using a compliant Armenian press in the eastern cities to spread fear and pro-Russian propaganda."

"I thought the Armenians in Eastern Turkey distrusted the Russians, particularly the Russian Orthodox Church?"

"The Armenians want to be on the winning side, and they see that the sultan has too few regular troops—particularly in the east—and the troops he has do not have adequate boots and clothing for winter. And no one knows what the Kurdish 'irregulars' will do."

"If the Russians invade, will we fight with the Turks?"

"I certainly hope so. A Russian victory could open the Mediterranean Sea to Russian ships. Britain cannot let that happen."

"Could the Ottoman Empire collapse?"

"Napoleon and Tsar Alexander once agreed to divide up the world, including the Ottoman Empire. But not so many years later, the French burned Moscow and Russia invaded Paris, while almost seventy years later the Ottoman Empire remains intact. It's enough to make one believe that Allah is protecting it."

"Well, we've done our part in preserving the Ottoman Empire, haven't we?"

"True. We haven't seen the demise of the Turks' empire as beneficial to the health of our own."

"Isn't it strange that Britain, a Christian country, fights to preserve the Muslim world?"

"Perhaps. But, of course, Britain has not sided with the Turks *because* they are Muslims. We've supported them in spite of that, which is only admirable if you discount self-interest."

"But most educated Englishmen respect Islam, and the educated Muslims I've met respect Christianity."

"Yes, we respect each other. But underlying our relations is the fact that Christians feel superior to Muslims, and Muslims feel superior to Christians. The true Christian position should be that all men are equal in the sight of God, which would require a neutral foreign policy, instead of the existing façade of a secular one," he said, pausing to contemplate his undiplomatic slip. "Sorry, I must sound like an atheist," he concluded, looking mildly repentant.

"Maybe like a hardened diplomat, dear," his wife said with a wink and a warm smile.

Ambassador Elliot returned the smile. He valued their early morning talks during which she mostly asked questions that, in answering, prepared him for the day, got the wheels spinning. In the early days of their marriage, their morning banter sometimes led to intimacy that had him scrambling to get to work. But now, he was an ambassador, and they had been married a long time. He continued, "Yes, of course. The diplomat must see the subtleties. The French claim to be defenders of the Catholics and the Russians of the Orthodox. So, Britain, not to be outdone, defends the rights of the Protestants, Jews, and Druze. It's amazing, really, the use of religion as a justification for imperialism."

"Now you've slipped from the diplomat to the cynic, dear," his wife said as a prelude to changing the subject. "And this proposed conference, how will it dissuade the Russians from war?"

"They'll have to get something out of it. We all will. The conference will divide up the empire into spheres of responsibility and influence. Russia will be given some of what she wants, plus a message that going to war for more will mean war with the Powers."

"So, how much of this does the new sultan already know?"

"I suspect that he knows a great deal. But, of course, he'll not admit knowing or not knowing. It's all protocol. He has to hear it from me. He has to pretend he's hearing it for the first time, and his response may have no relation to what he's thinking or planning to do. This is what diplomacy has come down to—spying, lying, and pretending."

"Maybe you *have* become a cynic, dear."

"Hard not to be. Did I mention that the Home Office is sending Lord Salisbury as special envoy to represent us at the conference? And he's bringing his wife, eldest son, and daughter. It gives the look of treating this assignment as a vacation for him to sign a document containing predetermined positions and leave with a hail-fellow-well-met to all."

"But surely Lord Salisbury will listen to your views."

"I can only hope. But he'll be arriving with a head full of anti-Turkish propaganda from the London press, and Russian Ambassador Ignatiev can be very persuasive. Ignatiev's already sent invitations for a private briefing with Lord Salisbury and for a dinner for him and his family. And he's calling for pre-conference meetings at the Russian Embassy where there will not even be an Ottoman observer. Obviously, he wants to reach an agreement behind closed doors before the conference even convenes."

"What about the new sultan, Abdülhamit?"

"I don't know what to expect. No one knows him. One thing for sure is that he'll remind me that he once met Stratford Channing."

"Sir Stratford de Redcliffe? The 'Great Ambassador' whose statue is in Westminster Abbey?"

"One and the same. Apparently, Abdülhamit is very proud that he met Sir Redcliffe as a young boy and that Sir Redcliffe remembered him when they met again in London, years later."

"Do I detect a note of jealousy?"

"I have the greatest respect for Sir Redcliffe, but I may have some envy that he served here at a time when Britain was welcomed as the Ottoman Empire's partner in reform. He was ambassador for 17 years. He had the ear of Abdülhamit's father, Abdülmecit, and he was trusted by the *Tanzimat* reformers. They're all gone now."

"What about Mithat Pasha? Isn't he a reformer?"

"Yes, and he hopes to save the empire by turning it into a constitutional monarchy."

"Would that work?"

"It could, but the same obstacles that reduced the reforms of his predecessors to grandiose edicts remain."

"Like what?"

"The reforms promise equality. Sounds good. But the Christians don't want to serve in the Ottoman army, and they don't want to give up their separate religious courts or economic concessions. As for the Muslims, they don't want to fight next to Christians and definitely don't want to fight under Christian officers."

"Many an English mother would like her sons exempt from Queen Victoria's endless wars, I'll say that. Anyway, surely the Christian complaints about unfair treatment are based on something?"

"Hard to say. For hundreds of years their treatment has been separate and largely privileged. But now, self-interested provocateurs tell them that, in the event they should suffer harm, foreign powers will step in and protect them—possibly give them their own country. So, this motivates some to allege mistreatment. I've been reading reports by an Englishman, Colonel Burnaby, traveling through eastern Anatolia. I met him when he was here, preparing for his travels. Everywhere he goes Armenians tell him that they are fine but that the Armenians in the next province are mistreated. But when he arrives in the next province, they assure him of mistreatment in the province beyond."

"So, is there no hope for Mithat's constitution?"

"There's always hope, of course, but I fear it may be too late. The Powers have lost patience. Gladstone has shamelessly exploited the cursed Bulgarian issue to embarrass Disraeli, hoping to replace him as Prime Minister. Then there's the bond collapse. Everything has conspired to turn public opinion against the Turks."

"Don't these things always blow over?"

"Unfortunately, no one expects the Russians to be patient. The one thing we can't have is Russian troops in Istanbul and Russian ships in the Golden Horn."

Ambassador Elliot concluded this remark by throwing off the covers, sliding his legs around and down onto the Turkish carpet, and standing erect as though to bar the way of a Russian advance.

TWENTY-ONE

"Long live our Padishah!" hailed the palace guards with raised swords as Abdülhamit, returning from the investiture ceremony at Eyüp, stepped from the royal *kayık* onto the landing pier at Dolmabahçe Palace. He hardly heard them. He was preoccupied with the statements of congratulations, admiration, and wishes for a long reign and life that were part of the ceremony. Preoccupied with the feeling that he would need to separate the sincere from the insincere among his well-wishers and that this would take time and guile.

He entered the palace and stared at the giant chandelier, the overwhelming opulence of everything. This palace had been the pride of his father. At a time when the empire had been eclipsed by Europe, the palace recalled when the empire had been superior to Europe. He found the sumptuousness disconcerting. The sultanate did not rest on luxury, but on power. Excess of any kind weakened power. That was the story of his father, his uncle, and his brother. Abdülhamit resolved that at this defining moment in the empire's history, when many feared and others plotted the empire's dissolution, grandeur would not define his reign.

As he had instructed, the room where he would work and receive guests contained a modest-sized desk and chair that he had built himself of mahogany with inlaid mother-of-pearl. He was a carpenter. The job of the carpenter was to take the wood of a tree that had been a source of beauty for hundreds of years and give it new life through furniture that would radiate beauty and function for hundreds' more years. He pivoted into the seat of the chair, which he kept without a cushion, to feel anew, each time he sat in it, the perfect execution of the chair's form. He opened and re-closed a desk drawer to enjoy its effortless and silent movement. In the empire's dying limbs and hollowed trunk, he could see a polished desk with drawers that opened easily and smoothly, waiting to be built, beautiful, and admired. The Empire needed to function as well as this chair and desk. It needed to be beautiful to behold and silent in its working, serving the people and striking awe in those who would consider challenging it.

The room also contained a western-style couch, two stuffed arm-chairs, and a divan. The walls bore several large paintings of pastoral scenes, reflecting Abdülhamit's love of the countryside, of his farm in Kağıthane. Nigar was living there now. She might be doing the things he loved to do. Feed and pet the many cats. Wander among the sheep. Brush the horses. Admire and pick the flowers. Select the vegetables for the evening meal.

He felt the urge to see her. She had seemed to love him—even as no one before had shown themselves to do—and she made her love known to him with the most simple of gestures, touches, facial expressions, and whispers of affection. It was powerful to feel loved. He missed it—all the more because he accepted that he could never go back, never wander among the flowerbeds, never pick a perfect tomato off a vine and eat it in the garden. Never spend a night with Nigar, never ask her to come to him. Because she might refuse. Unlike any other of his subjects, this woman, who was his wife, would not be afraid to say no. And if he asked, and she said no, everyone would know.

Principal Secretary Küçük Sait entered the room, interrupting his thoughts. Sait had a religious education, a conservative bent, and a loyal disposition. He was not yet comfortable in his job, one given to him as the trusted friend of Damat Mahmut, husband of one of Abdülhamit's sisters. A principal secretary could be powerful, but was also vulnerable.

"You have requests for audiences from the European Ambassadors who wish to present their credentials and to receive your formal recognition of existing treaties," Sait said. "And from your ministers and members of the Council of State, and from others, as well, including Messieurs Assani and Yorgo. Mithat Pasha says that his need for a meeting with you is particularly urgent. In what order do you wish to see them?"

"It's *Ramazan*. I will not meet with non-Muslims," he began. He did not want to feel hungry in the company of anyone who was not fasting. "I will meet first with Grand Vizier Rüşti, followed by Minister of War Redif, and with the remaining ministers and others in any order. As for Mithat, I will meet with him in two days." He was tempted to delay meeting with Mithat even longer, but two days was long enough to establish that he was the sovereign and not so long as to be a serious insult. "Schedule the ambassadors from Christian countries after *Şeker Bayramı*. Among them, I will see the British ambassador first."

"Yes, sir. Is there anything else?"

"Let it be known that I want everyone in the palace to keep the fast. No exceptions but those recognized under Sharia law."

"It shall be done, my sovereign."

"And bring me the telegrams and letters of congratulations on my investiture and translations of articles on my enthronement in the European press and in the local Greek, Armenian, and Jewish newspapers."

"Yes, sir."

It was propitious, if not providential, Abdülhamit thought, that his ascension to the throne occurred during *Ramazan*, the most holy of Muslim holidays. Muslims were focused on

159

religious observance and expressions of piety and self-pity for the discomforts of fasting, and non-Muslims were resigned that little could be accomplished, while everyone enjoyed the long afternoon siestas, the feasting that broke the fast each day, and the socializing and festivities late into the evening hours. *Ramazan* gave him what he wanted — time to delay decisions and a venue for sending a message that the empire and the Caliphate were in the hands of a faithful, practicing Muslim.

He read first the telegrams of congratulations from provincial governors. In addition to the obligatory language of approbation, most contained information about provincial conditions. From border provinces in the east and west, the information was of Russian troops gathering on the borders. The governors requested more troops and asked that the soldiers receive their pay, which was in arears by months to years, as well as arms, boots, and winter clothing. But in all cases, the governors stated with equal emphasis that despite their neglect and inadequate numbers, the sultan's troops were in good spirits and prepared to die for him in the name of Allah.

"I know the empire has many troubles, my sovereign," wrote one of the governors from an eastern province, "but I assure you that none is more urgent than the care of your troops. They have not been paid, and many of their families are too poor and too distant to provide for them. I do what I can personally and by cajoling local merchants, but in their destitution, the soldiers demand food even from the peasant farmers who struggle to feed their children. But be assured that if these soldiers are armed, fed, and clothed, the Russian swine will be forced to retreat with the name of Allah ringing in their ears."

"When your bureaucrats and the pashas of Istanbul talk of reforms," wrote another, "they mean freedom to run the government without interference from you. When the people speak of reform, they mean protection from unscrupulous tax collectors."

Many governors wrote that they were working diligently to stamp out corruption, an affirmation that caused Abdülhamit to smile. He was new to the sultanate, but not naïve.

He flipped through several spy reports, which affirmed the Powers' plan for a conference in Istanbul with the objective to give Russia enough to preclude war, but not so much as to impinge on the interests of the other Powers or to provoke him, Abdülhamit, to reject a peaceful settlement.

Abdülhamit put down the spy reports. A conference of the Powers in Istanbul. Possibly a war with Russia. He was as near to a chain smoker as is possible without lighting a cigarette with the butt of the previous one. Routinely, a half hour did not pass between cigarettes, and he never considered a weighty matter without the benefit of several. He had not had a cigarette since before dawn, as required by the *Ramazan* fast. From his desk drawer, he pulled out the small, flat cardboard box that contained his oval-shaped, Murat brand of cigarettes and removed one. He held it between his fingers as though preparing to put it in his mouth, but, instead, slowly passed it under his nose and inhaled deeply of the tobacco's bouquet. He closed his eyes and repeated the gesture, as though the aroma might be enough to steel him against the temptation to light it. He drew in the fragrance a third time, reached back into the desk drawer for his matches, and struck one on the underside of his chair. In the time of the Prophet Muhammed, there were no cigarettes. Cigarettes were not food or drink, not sustenance of any kind. They were not swallowed. Cigarette smoke was breathed, like air. How could smoking cigarettes be a part of fasting?

He would not smoke in front of guests, but he would not deny himself cigarettes from dawn to dusk. It was not possible, and he convinced himself that it also was not a deprivation necessary to comply with the *Ramazan* fast. He inhaled deeply and let the smoke roll slowly out of his nose. Inhaled again, and blew a series of rings, watching them rise slowly and dissipate. He was renewed and prepared to take on the Russians, the pashas, and even the Brits, if they continued to publish disparaging cartoons of Turks. He was sultan *and* Caliph.

******

Abdülhamit's conversation with Grand Vizier Rüşdi Pasha was short.

"I hear nothing that suggests the conference will deter Russia from invading, save that you agree to grant Russia everything that she might wish to gain through war," Rüşdi stated.

"And what might the Russians demand?"

"Minimally, dominion over the Danube Province and several provinces in the east."

"Would you advise that I accept this in lieu of war?"

"I cannot say, but I will support your decision to the best of my abilities, my sovereign."

The meeting confirmed what Abdülhamit had heard: Rüşdi was indecisive and conservative. Good characteristics for a grand vizier. He would not question decisions and would not advocate for reforms.

******

Waiting for the arrival of Minister of War Redif Pasha, Abdülhamit smoked two cigarettes back to back. "If Russia declares war, can we defeat her?" was his opening question to Redif.

"We defeated her in the Crimea," Redif answered hastily, without sounding convincing. "With the help of Britain and France, of course," he continued, searching for solid ground.

"Russia doesn't know that Britain and France would not join us against her. Perhaps she's bluffing?" Abdülhamit speculated, as though testing Redif.

"No one thinks so. They can conscript an unlimited supply of young men." Redif was unsure whether he wanted to leave the impression that the empire could win a war against Russia or that it would be ill-advised to give Russia a reason to go to war.

"They'll have an advantage in numbers of men, then, you think?"

"Yes, in regular troops. But our advantage is in the irregulars. They fight on territory that is their home, and they fight to save their homes," Redif responded with more confidence.

"In the east, the irregulars are Kurds. I have reports that the Russians are sending money to Kurdish tribes to fight on their side."

"Yes, I've heard this, but the Kurds know of the Russian atrocities against Muslims. The Kurds will take the Russians' money, but they won't fight on their side."

"Anything else?"

"The east also has many refugees that the Russians drove from the Caucasus Mountains: Tatars, Persians, Azeri Turks, Laz, Turkomans and Circassians. All of them suffered slaughter, rape, and pillage. They lost their homes and land. They are grateful for the refuge the empire has granted them, and they are eager for revenge."

"And in the west? I'm told that the Christians in the Danube Province will welcome and support the Russians."

"The Danube Province is also where many Circassians fled from the Crimea. The Russians drove them out—death marches, mass murder, rape, the slaughter of their women and children. And the Russians murdered wounded soldiers. The Circassians bleed hatred. No one will fight with greater loathing for the enemy."

"Do we have adequate guns and ammunition?"

"Our cavalry has the American rapid-fire Winchester rifle, and the infantry carries the American Peabody-Martini with long range accuracy. The rifles are arriving daily."

"So, you think we can win?"

Redif hesitated. "With the help of Allah, my sovereign," he said with a conviction he struggled to feel. Mothers might accept that Allah permitted their sons to be sacrificed, but a *serasker* knew that his decisions put them in their graves.

Abdülhamit did not find the answer satisfying. "Everyone knows that the British do not want the Russians to gain territory. And yet, what I hear is that, if we choose war, they will not help us. Have you heard anything different from this?"

"I hear many things. I hear Russia has delayed attacking because she believes Britain will help us. I hear the Russians are buying time to get more troops in place. I hear the British are using the conference to build support to enter the war on our side." Redif shifted his weight, eager for the meeting to be over.

"If we go to war, will the people support that decision?" Abdülhamit surprised himself with this question. The kings and queens of the countries he was expected to admire and emulate considered public opinion in their decisions. Should he?

Redif was equally surprised by the question, but he knew the city. "In the European cafes, performers sing of the bravery of Turkish soldiers, and the people cheer. In the markets, people talk of volunteering to fight. In the mosques, imams preach war against the infidels. In the coffeehouses, the men talk of victory, and the veterans of the Crimean War expose their wounds. If you choose to go to war, the people will support you."

Redif knew that he spoke the truth, but he also knew that Abdülhamit had no understanding of war. Had not watched colleagues die, never seen partial bodies writhing, never experienced shells explode and men screaming, never seen terror in the eyes of fleeing women and children. Even in victory, he, Redif, had seen these things, was awakened at night by the sounds of them, poured sweat from the reliving of them. He would lead an army into war if ordered to do so, but he would not advocate for it.

******

Abdülhamit dreaded his meeting with Mithat Pasha. He hardly knew him, but he instinctively disliked him, resented him. Reports Abdülhamit read suggested that everyone from foreign ambassadors to people in the streets admired Mithat and looked to him as a reformer who could save the country. But the man had deposed his uncle and brother. He did not trust him.

Seeing Mithat seated opposite him only confirmed his distaste for him. Mithat had a large head on a sturdy body taller than most and sat erect with an air of confidence that Abdülhamit perceived as arrogance. Surely Mithat was not without ambition. If only it were not *Ramazan*. Cigarettes and Turkish coffee could smooth pauses and add graciousness to a stilted atmosphere. A little smoke in the air. Demitasse cups on the coffee table. Instead, only space separated them in his stark office. Abdülhamit opened by asking Mithat what he had heard about the pre-conference meetings at the Russian embassy.

"I'm sure I know less than what is reported to you, my sovereign. I know only what is whispered everywhere. Russia's demands are harsh, and if we do not agree to them, she will declare war."

"What is your advice?" Abdülhamit regretted asking the question. He did not want Mithat to think that he needed his advice. But Mithat's aura of authority seemed to demand the question.

"Britain recognizes that Russia's territorial grab is a threat to them. I believe they'll oppose the Russians if we present a proposal that protects Christians without Russian intervention." Mithat stopped short of proposing his constitution. He wanted Abdülhamit to focus on its purpose, a proactive Ottoman alternative to what Ignatiev might be proposing and to war.

"And your proposal, I understand, is for me to issue a constitution that protects the rights of Christians, is that correct?" Abdülhamit asked.

"A constitution that protects the rights of all the citizens of the empire, my sovereign. Everyone would be equal under the law, pay the same taxes, be heard in the same courts, attend the same schools, and serve in the military together. A constitution guaranteeing equal treatment for all would give Britain what it has to have, without giving Russia what it wants."

Abdülhamit found the decisiveness with which Mithat spoke particularly distasteful, as though no other view could warrant consideration. "I read reports that suggest the Christians' demand for equality is insincere and would not be welcomed," Abdülhamit countered.

"People resist change, but as a provincial governor, I learned that even people from communities that have distrusted each other for generations will accept change and work together when they see it benefits them."

Abdülhamit resented Mithat's reference to his experience as a provincial governor to justify what he proposed. Nevertheless, he could see no other course. "I want you to convene a commission of notables. They are to prepare a constitution that protects and strengthens the empire and reflects its needs and those of its people for my review," he said with what Mithat found to be surprising conviction. But Abdülhamit's intent was not lost on Mithat. The constitution would not be Mithat's, but that of Abdülhamit's commission.

"I will be pleased to do so, my sovereign. The members of the commission and I will do our best to serve you and the country," Mithat said, rising from his chair. "With your permission, I will take my leave to pursue the noble and serious task that you have given me."

"Of course. May Allah be your guide."

Abdülhamit lit a cigarette as soon as Mithat left. On entering the room, Mithat would certainly have smelled fresh cigarette smoke and known that he, Abdülhamit, was cheating in this aspect of the fast. Abdülhamit was angry that he had given Mithat this opportunity to feel superior. Surely Mithat also desired a cigarette. Why didn't this insufferable pasha pull out a cigarette case and suggest they smoke? Abdülhamit inhaled deeply. Mithat be damned.

He had a large map of the world on the wall and was briefed each day on the affairs of state in the European countries, on the history of the empire's relations with them and their relations with each other, and on the personalities and known weaknesses of the Western and Russian leaders. On his accession, *Le Petit Journal* had written that he was of average intelligence with little education, a slight that ate him like an ulcer.

TWENTY-TWO

Ramazan, the month of fasting by which the faithful experience the hunger of the poor, is followed by *Şeker Bayramı*, the three-day holiday known in Arabic as *Eid el-Fitr*, which starts with the first day of the Muslim calendar month of *Shawwal*. A time of special prayer rituals and reconciliation with Allah, *Şeker Bayramı* in Turkish means Holiday of Sweets, which reflects the holiday's tradition of distributing candy and desserts, especially to children, but also to relatives, friends, neighbors, and the less fortunate, to whom those of means are also expected to give money. During *Şeker Bayramı*, everyone visits every relative possible, in hierarchical order, for the children to receive candy and for the adults to share something sweet, wish each other a happy and holy holiday, and through the unspoken gesture of the visit, sweeten any relations soured in the previous year.

The entire city rejoiced. Although the non-Muslims had not spent a month fasting, they had endured the inconvenience of secretive smoking, eating, and drinking so as not to offend or tempt their Muslim cohabitants in this city, where the holy days of each faith were cause for celebration by all. Non-Muslims adopted the customs of Muslim holidays. Muslims came out to watch Easter parades. Faiths were much practiced but little understood by many of those who practiced them, some attending mosque on Friday and church on Sunday — just in case. Istanbulites observed the Muslim holy day on Friday, the Jewish holy day on Saturday and the Christian holy day on Sunday. Everyone celebrated *Şeker Bayramı*.

Even a man like Mithat Pasha, obsessed with the details of his work, looked forward to *Şeker Bayramı* — three days with his family. Fifteen years earlier, Mithat had been sent to Van to investigate tax fraud. One of the purported offenders was a wealthy Kurdish tribal leader who, as a matter of courtesy, asked after Mithat's children, and Mithat acknowledged that, although he had been married for eight years, he and his wife had but one daughter. His wife had nearly died in the birthing and could have no more children.

The next day, the tribal leader returned with a girl—maybe 16. "She will make you a good wife," the Kurd said. "All the women from her village bear sons."

Mithat protested that he could not accept the girl as a gift, but the tribal leader insisted. "Her parents were intending to sell her to the palace in Istanbul. They're proud of her beauty and say she is unusually intelligent, as well. They're too poor to provide her with a dowry acceptable to a man of means, and they want a better life for her than the one they live. If you accept her, she'll not be sold."

Mithat assumed that the Kurd had paid the family what they expected to get from the palace, if selling her, indeed, had been their plan. But Mithat also knew that the girl represented an attempted bribe. Some of the Kurd's productive land had been recorded as unproductive to avoid taxes. But the tax official was the one who recorded the designations of land and almost certainly received payment from the Kurd in consideration thereof. The tax collector would lose his job. On the other hand, the records, of course, showed no such transaction, so the Kurd, however guilty, would be charged with nothing. And consequently, Mithat rationalized, the girl could not be viewed as a bribe. The girl was simply an available bride whose family wanted her to be the wife of a prominent official.

"Leave the girl here," he said. "I'll have her taken care of, and if I decide to marry her, I will pay her parents the bride price. If not, I'll return her untouched." Paying the bride price would remove any accusation that he had taken her as a gift. And he would be saving her from a life of slavery in the palace, he rationalized.

"It's not necessary for you to pay, my pasha. The family is pleased to have her live a comfortable life, which they know she'll have with you."

Mithat wanted to marry this girl. She had stunning eyes, a lithe body, and a warm smile. He was captured. But how could he do this? Would he divorce his wife? No. She was a loving mother and wife, whom he loved. Also, her parents had passed away. She would have nowhere to go. He wrote to her, asked her permission to bring a new wife into the house, and asked her to remain as his wife and to live with them. If she agreed, his conscience would be clear. If she did not, he would not marry this girl, even though he knew her smile would appear in the middle of writing a report, in the middle of thinking about everything and nothing.

Mithat paid to have the girl live in the home of a judge next door to where he was staying. It permitted him to see her often and check on her progress. She was a peasant girl and needed to learn how to live in a modern house, how to dress, how to present herself. He gave the judge's wife money to buy her suitable clothing. He hired a tutor to teach her Turkish, of which she knew little, and to teach her to read and write. His work often took him to the empire's distant provinces, and she would need to be able to read letters he sent her and to write letters to him. His first wife knew how to read and write. Jealousy was inevitable. He needed to do what he could to minimize it.

To Mithat's surprise and pleasure, the girl, to whom he gave the Persian name Şehriban, demonstrated a quick mind and excellent memory. After the first week, he began to leave work early in order to personally help her trace letters, form

170

words, and recognize words, both oral and written. She smiled when she made a mistake. She smiled when he complimented her. She made him smile. In his desire for this girl he felt weak, humbled. He prayed five times a day, every day, until the letter came from his wife.

> My loving husband. No woman could ask for a more considerate husband. You did not abandon me when I was told I could have no more children. I am deeply grateful that you will not divorce me. I would prefer to leave your household, but I have nowhere to go. I will be a loving aunt to your children, and I will not be unkind to their mother. Your loving wife, Fatma Naime.

On this *Şeker Bayramı*, as he passed the three days with his wives and children, these memories of 15 years earlier came flooding back to him. He had two daughters and a son with Şehriban. Mithat felt doubly blessed by the harmonious household he enjoyed. He could honestly say that he continued to love and admire his first wife, his first love. He could not imagine how someone could marry and love four wives, as allowed under Muslim law, but he knew absolutely that it was possible to love two.

******

For Nigar, *Şeker Bayramı* brought to mind the image of Gül, the girl with the branded arm. Throughout the city, even in the poorest neighborhoods, children would be given sweets. Nigar determined to take candy to Gül. It would be a small gesture, but she wanted to do it.

171

Arriving at Süleymaniye Mosque, Nigar was overwhelmed by the thousands of cheerless faces in the courtyard. Children too thin. Some obviously ill. Children with hopeless and fearful eyes. Few children with shoes or clothing that would be adequate for the coming winter. Children who should be alive with play were listless.

She kept the candy she had brought in her purse. The problem was not one girl with a branded arm, but hundreds of children, many of whom would die for no crime other than being born to Muslim parents in the Danube Province. Everyone said a war was coming. It would bring tens of thousands more refugees to Istanbul. If she went to Abdülhamit, could she convince him to avoid war?

But she knew that thought was driven by her fantasy that she could be a trusted advisor to him. And she knew what was said everywhere in the market. Even if the Russians received the territories they wanted without war, the Christians would still drive the non-Christian population from these places by death and worse, and the survivors would continue to come to Istanbul for protection.

She would not go to Abdülhamit, the man she had loved, the man who gave up love to be venerated as the Shadow of Allah on Earth, untainted by love for a woman. Instead, she would go to her friend Cristo. She would ask him to help her bring joy into the lives of these children, at least for one day.

Cristo was sitting outside his shop as always, when, to his delight and surprise, Nigar alighted from the carriage. A scarf covered her hair, but she was not veiled. Her dress appeared to be more conservative in cut than he remembered her wearing before, but perhaps it was only the distortion imagination works on desired objects that are absent, and even more so when unattainable. She looked beautiful. "Tea!"

172

he yelled down the street as he stood up to greet her. "You have come for tea, I hope, Madam. I'm honored by your visit. It's been too long."

"Yes, I would love tea, and it's a great pleasure to see you. I only hope you'll not be angry with me when I tell you my purpose in coming."

"If you have something to say that I may not want to hear, just warn me, and I'll cover my ears," Cristo said, laughing, and reached out to take her by her outstretched hands and escorted her to the curb and onto the sidewalk. "I have a fine stool inside. A beautiful woman used to sit on it and take tea with me twice each day."

"She was blessed to do so. How is your niece Athena doing with the store?" Flora asked to delay getting to the purpose of her visit.

"Thanks to you, she's doing well. You taught her everything. She's needed almost no help from me."

"She's a lovely girl and learned quickly."

"Her business is good. I think she even has the eye of a young Englishman. He comes much too often to the shop and comes at times when it's unlikely that other customers will be in the store. Initially, he made purchases, but now, rarely."

"I thought you said she would be unable to marry?"

"I meant my sister would be unable to find a husband for her. That's because my sister would be looking for a Greek husband, whose own mother would ask too many questions, know too much gossip. Gossip is a nasty business. Lives are ruined over nothing."

"Does Athena speak English?"

"No, and I'm sure the Englishman speaks no Greek. Probably they speak in French with some Turkish, as we do. Life is changing, especially in Istanbul."

The tea arrived, which helped Flora delay revealing the purpose of her visit, but finally she spoke of it. "Cristo, I came to ask you for help."

"Anything you want, of course."

"As you know, today is the first day of *Şeker Bayramı*. I want to collect candy and perhaps other sweets, as well, from the merchants here in the European quarter to take to the refugee children in the Süleymaniye Mosque compound. You know all the pastry shop owners. If you ask, they cannot say no. I can pay a small amount to each merchant."

"They'll ask who these children are, of course."

"I'm not ashamed of these children or embarrassed to seek charity for them."

"How many children are there?"

"Hundreds. They live in squalor. To give them candy from the finest pastry shops in the city will not change their lives, but for one day, they might smile, even laugh. It's a small thing, but I would like to do it for them."

"And I will help you. But first we'll have our tea." Excellent tea, he thought, as he took his first sip and watched Nigar take hers and smile at him. "You make me a better man. If I get to heaven, I'll tell St. Peter that you made me do it, and he must let you in when it's your turn."

"Thank you, Cristo. I'm very grateful for your help. You must come with me to the mosque compound to deliver the candy and see the children smile."

"First, we must collect the candy."

Nigar lost count of the pastry shops they went to. Not one of them would accept even a token of payment from her. Cristo made sure of that.

"Cristo, do you think you can get to heaven by giving candy to Muslim children?" asked one, laughing as he packaged a generous amount of multiple kinds of hard candies.

"No, I'm trying to get *you* into heaven. Not an easy task. A little candy won't do it, but at least God may count it for something, you old tightwad."

"Cristo," whispered another when Nigar was out of earshot, "you're a clever man, using good works to seduce a woman, and a beautiful one too."

"It's not like that," Cristo said sternly. "She's my friend and a good person. For that, you must give me another kilo of candy."

"The whole Greek community celebrates *Şeker Bayramı*," observed one of Cristo's closest friends. "It's good for the merchants and good for the people. Greeks don't even think of it as a religious holiday. I'm happy to give candy to the refugee children. No one who fears God should harm a child, Cristo, or deny a child joy. Take them lokum. I make the finest."

They spent the day collecting candy, and they arrived at Süleymaniye Mosque compound just after the Sundown Prayer.

******

Fatma first heard the news from one of the pastry shop owners near the mosque. He said that a Greek shopkeeper and a Western woman, reportedly the wife of the sultan, were collecting candy for the refugee children. He mentioned it as an excuse for why she should be less demanding of him.

"You tell me you've heard that sweets will come to us from Pera, but these children live by food, not by rumor," she said, pointing to the children waiting behind her.

Every pastry shop within a few kilometers of the mosque knew to expect Fatma and her band of rag-robed children during *Şeker Bayramı*. She organized the children into groups

175

that she took to one pastry shop each. The shopkeepers were easily moved to give generously when looking into the faces of the children. But she could not bring so many as to be overwhelming or burdensome to the merchant. She had learned to live overwhelmed without being crushed by it, but she understood that she could not expect the same of those outside the mosque compound.

Fatma's pitch was always the same. "*Şeker Bayramı* is a holy holiday. You have an obligation," she would say. "Look at these children and tell me they are less deserving than your own who eat sweets until they are ill during this holiday. Am I not right?"

"Fatma," she would hear, "you'll drive me into debt. I can't give away all the sweets I spent the entire month of *Ramazan* preparing for this holiday."

"No. And I do not ask that. I only ask that you look at these children and give what you can. May Allah bless you for your generosity."

And following the Sundown Prayer of the first day of *Şeker Bayramı* in this year of 1876, a carriage filled with sweets arrived at the Süleymaniye Mosque compound; the rumor was proved real; and Fatma was waiting for them.

"We've brought sweets for the children," Nigar said, addressing Fatma. "Can you organize the children to unload the carriage and distribute the candy?" Nigar could see that Fatma was quite elderly. Her face was weathered and wrinkled, but she stood erect, looked physically strong, and had a confident look in her uncovered face that was unusual among poor Muslim women.

"I can, Madam," Fatma responded. "The children do as I tell them." Fatma wanted to ask Nigar and Cristo why they had done this. Instead, "You're very generous, Madam. May Allah bless you," was all she could think to say.

"And you, as well, Auntie."

Under Fatma's directions, the children remained disciplined, but they smiled more broadly than she had seen in her 50 years of living as a refugee among refugees. She scrutinized Nigar. Rumor said she was a Muslim. Was that possible? It did not matter. She was generous. Allah would, indeed, bless her for it, Fatma thought, and she wished it so.

Gül ate more candy than she had ever dreamed she would have. On this night her mother cried tears of happiness, of gratitude, and fell asleep with her heart unburdened of revenge.

****

Abdülhamit welcomed Şeker Bayramı as eagerly as everyone else. He could smoke openly, and he could devote three days almost entirely to family life in the palace, a pleasure he looked forward to. He had the women of the harem play the instruments they were studying: piano, lute, oud, saz, and violin. He played his own repertoire of French tunes on the piano.

He had Karagöz puppet plays performed in the harem quarters. In other parts of the city, these performances were venues for satirizing high officials, including recent sultans, but for the palace performances, the objects of ridicule were popularly recognized and timeless: the greedy merchant out-witted by the common man or the lecherous imam beaten up by offended women and their husbands. On important holidays, such as Şeker Bayramı, French acting troops came to Istanbul, and Abdülhamit invited one of them to perform Tartuffe, a favorite of his, at the palace.

Wealthy families sent the finest sweets of the city to the palace with wishes for the blessings of Allah on the new sultan.

Abdülhamit also distributed pastries and generous alms to poor children, so that people were soon speaking of his largesse. He wished to be beloved by the common people, the people who were not pashas. He was *their* sultan.

Abdülhamit spent the holiday enjoying everything that brought him pleasure, comfort, and even happiness. Yes, he was happy, he thought. Not the same happiness he had known with Nigar, but satisfying, nonetheless. As sultan he was daily showered with admiration and acknowledged as without peer. His every need was anticipated and met beyond what he might think to express. No love from one person could equal that.

TWENTY-THREE

But by the end of the three-day holiday, Abdülhamit was ready to get back to work. Pursuing personal happiness did not seem natural. What he loved was being at his desk, reading reports, trying to determine the motives behind everything reported, requested, or advised. To get to truth, he needed to hear from multiple sources, each of whom would have a different motive. And with the threat of war, he had to know, in particular, what the non-Muslims were thinking.

He called his trusted Greek banker, Yorgo, whose motive in all things seemed to be solely to make money for both of them, to his office. "The Russians are threatening to cross the Danube, claiming they will do this to protect the Christian population. What do you hear in the Greek community?" he asked Yorgo, offering him a cigarette as he took one himself, struck a match, and extended it to light his friend's cigarette.

Yorgo was surprised that, as sultan, Abdülhamit had not changed his habit of lighting the cigarettes of his friends and guests. He took it as a good sign that their relationship would not change and that he could be honest in response to Abdülhamit's unexpected and politically charged question. "In the Greek community, we know the Russians are exploiting what happened in the Danube province." Yorgo exhaled slowly and reached for his coffee, buying time. He had hoped they would talk about interest rates.

"Would the Greek community welcome a Russian invasion?" Abdülhamit's tone was not accusatory or angry. It was simply enquiring, as though asking the price of baklava.

Yorgo took another drag on his cigarette and another sip of coffee. It was a fair question, but the answer needed context. "The Greeks are bound to the sea and to the commerce it makes possible," Yorgo began carefully, wanting to be honest but nuanced. "There are Greek fishing villages along every sea-coast, and Greek businessmen in every coastal city. We know everyone and they know us. We prosper by making friends, not enemies. War makes enemies."

"But the Russians are Christians."

"The Russians may be Christians, but we Greeks are loath to have Russian Orthodox overlords. Greeks pay taxes to the masters of many lands. In Greek we say, 'me kheiron beltiston,' the least bad is the best. We live by that, and each Greek village, each Greek community, will choose the least bad—some wisely, some not."

Abdülhamit studied Yorgo's face, the face of a trusted confidant and advisor for 20 years. This man was one of two who had made him rich—possibly the richest man in the empire. "If Russia crosses the Danube, will the local Greek population support the Russians?"

"They will wait to see who the victor is. If Russia wins, they'll expect favorable treatment. But their situation in the Danube Province is precarious. Greeks do not trust the Bulgarians or the Bulgarian Orthodox Church. Choosing the least bad will not be easy."

"What about Britain and France? If we go to war, will they join us?"

Yorgo's face relaxed. He was more comfortable talking about this. "Britain exports four times as much to us as they import from here. Even Gladstone knows that. If he succeeds in replacing Disraeli as prime minister, he'll have to put economics first, or rule only briefly. For France, it's the same. Look at the

180

market in Pera. Every window displays imports from France. And this is true in every major town and city of the empire."

"What about our failure to pay our debt?"

"I'm a banker. A banker does not wish for the death of a debtor. So long as the borrower remains alive, there's hope that he'll pay. Britain and France stand only to lose if the Ottoman Empire is destroyed. Owing them money may be a good thing."

Yorgo knew his answer was glib, but it sounded credible and was not untrue. What he knew to be true was that the empire was in danger, and it kept him up at night. His family lived well. But he worried about their future.

******

Assani, Abdülhamit's Armenian broker, hoped they would talk about the price of American cotton and its impact on Egyptian cotton, which was the buzz at the bourse, but he had heard that Abdülhamit was asking about the attitudes of his non-Muslim subjects. To his surprise, Abdülhamit began with an historical question. "People say that the Russians urged my uncle Abdülaziz to buy warships so that the empire would go in debt and undermine British and French support. Some even say that the Russians had a secret agreement with Abdülaziz to take over the ships. What do you know about that?"

"People speak badly of your uncle, because he became a puppet of the Russians. But I knew him when he was a vital ruler. I helped him get the financing for those ships, which he bought because he needed them. The Empire has thousands of miles of coast. The ships were a source of pride and security. He would never have given them up. Who knows if the Russians encouraged the purchase or what their motives might have been? Countries—both your enemies and your allies—do what's in their interests, and it's what *you* need to do."

Abdülhamit liked the answer. He could trust this man. "The Russians are preparing to invade. I receive reports that some Armenians in the east are asking for Russian passports, providing military intelligence, and constructing buildings that appear to be barracks for Russian soldiers. Can this be true?"

Assani knew that many Armenians in the east bought into Russian propaganda. He had not heard of the passports or the barracks. It was uncharacteristic. They should have been waiting to see who would win. "The Russians say they want only to protect Christians," he began, "even though everyone knows their goal is to control territory. But people who are afraid or poor are easily deceived by promises."

"Do the Armenians want to live under the Russians?"

"No. Most Armenians know that they benefit from a prosperous Ottoman Empire. But in the east, Armenians feel vulnerable. Armenian merchants and bankers make their money from the peasant farmers, who resent them. They send their children to the American missionary schools in the hope that a son in America will be a business connection or a safety net. But no one sends their sons to Russia."

Assani looked at Abdülhamit and paused, while inhaling deeply from his cigarette and exhaling before continuing. "They don't want to live under the Russians. They fear losing their language and their church. But they see the Russians on the border and position themselves to survive. The Armenians in the east need to see a strong Ottoman army to give them hope that they'll be protected." It was the truth, Assani thought, and he had no reservation about sharing the truth with his friend, the sultan of the Ottoman Empire.

Abdülhamit sent for Dr. Fonseca, a prominent physician in the Jewish community whose family had served as physicians to the Ottoman palace for generations. Although Jews were a significant non-Muslim presence in the empire, the Christian nations never spoke of the fact that the Jews had gone to the Ottoman Empire seeking refuge from Christian persecution.

Jewish merchants controlled specific markets and the import and export of goods as local agents for European businesses. They controlled the production of some products, such as leather. They were important in banking and in medicine. The Jewish *millet* was physically and politically divided in matters of Judaic practice and belief, and it was divided by country of origin and social class. But the Jewish community was united in considering themselves to be, and behaving as, a traditional Ottoman *millet*, internally governing themselves by Halacha, Jewish law. The Jewish *millet* had its own newspapers, hospitals, homes for the aged, orphanages, and welfare associations for the distribution of food and clothing for the poor.

"Your ancestors have served mine well," Abdülhamit said to Dr. Fonseca. "And my mother told me that when I appeared weak and unhealthy at birth, your father oversaw my care until I was strong. Now I'm the sultan, the Caliph of the Muslim world, thanks, in part perhaps, to a Jewish doctor."

"Yahweh—Allah, as you say—directs our affairs beyond our understanding. In Edinburgh, where I studied medicine, I had a liberal Rabbi friend who once postulated that the fractions among Jews, Muslims, Christians, and other religious faiths, as well as the fractions within each of the religious faiths, are fractions that exist, not because some of us are right, but because all of us are wrong, created imperfect."

The philosophic bent of the response took Abdülhamit by surprise. He was tempted to ask Dr. Fonseca to speak further on it, but he was not confident to discuss religious beliefs, certainly not with someone of another religion. He turned the conversation back to the mundane, asking, "Why did you return here to practice medicine?"

"I'm an only child, and I thought my parents needed me. Also, I missed Istanbul. It's my home." In fact, his parents urged him to stay in Scotland. They felt he would have a better future there than in the "sick man of Europe." The demise of even bad authority never bodes well for the people ruled, his father pointed out, especially for minorities.

Staying in Edinburgh had been tempting. The Jewish community there ranged from Zionist to Hasidic and Orthodox to Reform. There were capitalists, socialists, communists, and opportunists. In Edinburgh everything was possible, but nothing was settled. It felt vital to be a member of the educated Jewish community there.

"I'm told that my Christian subjects want to be treated the same as Muslim subjects," Abdülhamit continued. "Do Jews want the same? "

"Jews want to live as they choose, which varies greatly among them and has little to do with the form of government under which they live. Jews look to be protected, rather than ruled."

"But if they're protected, do they also want to be equal in all things with Muslims?"

"It's the fashion now to look to Britain, France, and America as models. People think that if everyone has a voice in their government, everyone will be treated the same, and the government will only do what they want. But, as we know, utopia exists for aspiration. As Jews, we are perhaps more skeptical—or should I say realistic—than the Christians."

Again, Abdülhamit felt the need to direct the conversation away from the philosophical. "You lived in Britain. Were the people happy with their government?"

"People are happy when they have what they want. The upper classes want to maintain their position. The religious want freedom for their religious practices and beliefs. The poor want the basics of food, shelter, and, now, even education for their children. If the people have these things, they support the government."

"Does the Jewish community feel it has these things here?"

"We have physical security, which is highly valued. Other than that, we do not attribute what we have to the government, and we do not look to the government for what we need. We've come here from many places, because the empire accepted us. Your own father welcomed Jews who escaped the Crimea when the war there began. In fear of war, some have begun to arrive from the Danube Province. If Russia invades, many will come. They'll have nowhere else to go."

"Would the Jewish community provide soldiers for a war with Russia?"

Dr. Fonseca had not expected such a question, but his answer was quick and unequivocal. "I'm sorry, my sovereign. The community will pay whatever tax you assess in lieu of service, as it does now, but it will not provide soldiers. Paying the tax has worked for centuries. That's why the tax has survived, despite the efforts of the reformers to eliminate it."

"I appreciate your frankness, Dr. Fonseca," Abdülhamit said, feeling grateful for this support of his instinct to resist the reformers, the self-important pashas who presented themselves as patriots more capable than any sultan to administer and lead the nation.

"I'm afraid I must beg your leave, my sovereign," Dr. Fonseca said. "I'm expected at the hospital, and there's an epidemic of cholera in the Balat community. If you permit, sir."

"Yes, of course. Thank you. Your observations have been very helpful."

TWENTY-FOUR

Abdülhamit was determined not to be duped by the pashas, not to be seen by foreign governments as a puppet of the pashas, not to be perceived by anyone as uninformed. He stood in front of his large map of the world at least once every day. He continued his tutorial sessions on history and the political environments and international policies of the major international players—even America, which no one thought to be important in world affairs, but where he had commercial interests in arms and cotton.

He brooded about Mithat Pasha, assiduously reading reports of every meeting Mithat had with anyone, his comings and goings, and what he said when he was overheard. Of course, some spies reported that Mithat was plotting to restore Murat to the throne. Not even Abdülhamit took this seriously. Annoyingly, however, even those who did not agree with Mithat about a constitution spoke of him with admiration, and British Ambassador Elliot was reported to have said that the Europeans trusted and respected him. Mithat could not be ignored.

But he could be reassigned. Perhaps as governor to the Bulgarians. Mithat was known for his personal interaction with the people in villages, towns, and cities. He spent a lot of time with Christians. In today's environment, he might be assassinated. But at the same time, Abdülhamit did not want to give Mithat opportunities for success. In the Danube Province, Mithat could seek Christian support to prevent war with Russia, and if he succeeded in this, everyone at home and abroad would fall at his pompous feet. Also, to retain any hope for European support against the Russians, Abdülhamit knew he had to appear to support Mithat, much as that galled him.

Abdülhamit did not accept that Mithat lacked ambition. This man had brought down two sultans. He might have ordered the assassination of one. And in announcing his, Abdülhamit's, own accession to the throne, Mithat issued a public pronouncement stating that under the new regime all citizens would have equal treatment and attend the same schools. He had taken advantage of the situation to state his own policy and make it difficult for him, Abdülhamit, to pursue any other. Mithat presented the constitution as a savior for the empire. Proclaim it, and Britain would accept that the empire was serious about protecting the Christians, and Russia's justification for intervention would be destroyed. But to Abdülhamit, the constitution was an ultimatum imposed by Mithat. What he, Abdülhamit, needed was a strategy to use Mithat's ambition against him and expose his ideas as ineffective.

Abdülhamit decided to make Mithat grand vizier and have him announce the constitution, as Mithat proposed, on the opening day of the official convening of the Istanbul conference, December 23. If Russia backed off its demands, the Powers might credit Mithat, but the people would credit their sultan. If Russia persisted in its position, it would be a rejection of Mithat and his constitution. Mithat would be forced to advocate against accepting whatever proposal might result from the conference, and Russia would be obliged to declare war. Everyone would see that the constitution and Mithat had failed. If the war went well, he, Abdülhamit, could take credit. If it went badly, he could blame Mithat and the failure of the constitution.

****

Returning from Dolmabahçe Palace in his carriage, Mithat rode silently. He sat square-shouldered and erect, clutching his heavy black cloak against the cold and cradling his worn leather briefcase, now without the copy of the constitution that Abdülhamit had requested be left with him. Abdülhamit had informed him that his appointment as grand vizier, along with the proclamation of the constitution, would be announced in four days' time on the opening of the Constantinople Conference. He should have been excited, but he was melancholy. Could he trust Abdülhamit? Maybe it was just the damp, cold December morning. The temperature was just above freezing, and Istanbul smelled of mildew, touched of slick, and looked of dew and mist.

Back at his office, he sent for his friend, Namık Kemal. "I need you to publish editorials and articles about constitutional government. We have four days until the conference opens. Abdülhamit said he'll introduce the constitution and announce my appointment as grand vizier on that day. I want the idea of constitutional government on everyone's mind, alive in the marketplace."

"Incredible, my friend," Namık said with excitement in his voice. "Congratulations! You're about to make history, about to change our country beyond the aspirations of its most progressive reformers. May Allah bless you and all of us that we've lived to see this day."

"Thank you. You're kind. Many have helped, you especially, but hard work lies ahead. We don't yet know this Abdülhamit. If Allah wills it, our country will be changed."

"But Abdülhamit's agreed to the constitution, and he's appointing you grand vizier. Doesn't that show he's committed to reform?"

"I hope so. Unfortunately, I sense that he's agreed to the constitution without believing in the need for it. He may have a head full of historic Ottoman glory. I understand he's getting history lessons," Mithat said with a tinge of derision.

"His father has an honored legacy for his support of the reformers. Surely he knows that," Namık said, hoping to change Mithat's mood.

"The people must be educated. I'm counting on you and your newspaper. We must convince the people to be with us. If we don't, the empire won't survive."

"With the help of Allah, I believe we cannot fail, my brother," Namık responded, feeling the need to inject optimism. Mithat was dour at a moment when Namık had expected to find his friend rejoicing.

"I hope you're right. We *must* succeed," Mithat finished with a look of determination. The battle to reform the empire was personal, life-defining, and worth risking his life.

******

That night, Abdülhamit surprised Principal Secretary Sait by stating that he did not wish to see any spy reports, telegrams, intercepted messages, or official communiques—documents he would normally spend hours skimming through after dinner. He would devote tonight to the constitution. The constitution would be *his*, not Mithat's.

A five-candle candelabrum in Abdülhamit's study illuminated his figure bent over the pages of the constitution. Little time passed between cigarettes. Coffee was delivered hourly. This night could determine his sultanate, his legacy, the future of the empire.

He was pleased to find no surprises in the document and little need for him to make changes. His advocate, Grand Vizier Rüşdi Pasha, had been successful in preserving near-absolute authority for the sultan in the debates of the Constitutional Council. Rüşdi had bested Mithat. Or, more likely, Mithat had been willing to compromise to secure a constitution for the empire. That was Mithat's weakness, his singular focus on having the constitution proclaimed.

Of particular interest to Abdülhamit was the article defining the position of grand vizier. Mithat had proposed to replace this office with that of a prime minister who would answer to parliament and not to the sultan. Abdülhamit was relieved to see that this change was not in the final document. If it had been, he would have struck it. If the highest officer in the government were not directly accountable to the sultan, the sultan could not rule. The constitution also left the hiring and firing of ministers to the sultan's prerogative, and each minister was directly answerable to the sultan, which left the grand vizier with little authority.

The parliament's Chamber of Deputies would be elected, but the members of the Chamber of Notables would be appointed by the government, which meant the sultan. Although the constitution protected freedom of the press, Abdülhamit decided to let that stand. He knew the press could be controlled by the government subsidies on which they depended. It would be useful to have the appearance of a free press. The sultan could dissolve parliament and abrogate the constitution by declaring a state of emergency. The constitution recognized the sultan as Caliph. He would be accountable only to Allah.

The parliament was to approve budgets submitted by each ministry, and a Council of Accounting would audit their accounts. In this, Abdülhamit agreed with Mithat. The empire would not be safe from foreign meddling so long as it was in debt to them.

All citizens would be called Ottomans, be treated the same, have the same obligations to the state, and be subject to the same laws, regardless of their religion. Only matters of religion would be referred to the religious courts. Abdülhamit thought this impracticable but accepted it as necessary to proclaim in principle to placate the Europeans.

Several articles of the constitution dealing with provincial governance reflected Mithat's principles of decentralization, which annoyed Abdülhamit, but he could not justify making a change. He needed to appease the Christian populations in the provinces to impress the Powers and hold off the Russians.

Only one thing was missing, and he added language as Article 113, authorizing him to exile persons he felt to be a danger to himself or the state. It was not essential language, since the constitution left him an autocrat. He could exile anyone without such a provision, but constitutional authority would insulate him from criticism when he used it.

As morning neared, he closed the document. He could live with this constitution. It did not fundamentally change his ability to rule or his position as ruler. He wanted to be known as a reformer and to be recognized as the force that made reform possible. But he would be no figurehead, no constitutional monarch. He lit a cigarette and ordered a final coffee to celebrate. The constitution left him no less powerful than the most famous of the sultans before him, but the first to have his authority codified in law. He applied his *tuğra* to the document and instructed Sait to deliver it to Mithat.

Throughout the night, his favorite cat, Hanımefendi, slept on an old robe of his next to his chair. Hanımefendi was a small-framed, short-haired, calico female that he found as a kitten among hay in the barn on his farm in Kağıthane twelve years earlier. She was a ferocious hunter, especially when she had kittens to feed. Abdülhamit loved cats, fed and petted the many that lived on his farm. But Hanımefendi was special to him. She was the only cat he brought with him to Dolmabahçe

Palace from Kağıthane. True to her feral roots, she was no lap cat, preferring to be at his feet on his robe, grateful for every stroke he reached down to administer. He loved this cat, and she reciprocated. Throughout the long night, he reached down often to stroke her and evoke the purring that reassured both of them that they were loved.

Now, he picked up Hanımefendi with the robe on which she rested and placed her at the foot of the divan in his study. Then he lay down and waited for her to shift herself up against his legs, as was her custom, and fell deeply asleep. He slept through the call to Morning Prayer, through his early morning routines, and long enough into the late morning that his personal eunuch and Principal Secretary Sait conferred as to whether they dared wake him or should call a doctor.

But when he sat up at the call to Noon Prayer, he looked refreshed. He looked, as he felt, vigorous and confident that he was now the sultan of a modern empire that all nations would have to respect. A sultan to be admired and loved by his subjects. To be desired even by beautiful women, women like Nigar, whose visual image in that moment was as if she were standing opposite him, her scent present as if his face were in her neck and hair near the spot behind each ear where she touched the drop of perfume that was unique to her, that he had not smelled since, and that stirred him as if in the heat of August in Tarabya. He wanted her and thought to order that she be brought to the palace. But he stopped. Desire was a weakness antithetical to the power he felt in this moment. A sultan's subjects praised him out of respect for his title and for what he did for them. It was not love, but it was enough.

TWENTY-FIVE

On December 23, 1876, Mithat awoke before the call to prayer. He slipped out of bed, performed his ablutions, and listened to the sound of heavy rainfall. This was *the* day. He had hoped for sunshine to bring people into the streets. Not to be.

And yet, he was energized. This was a day of which historians would write. With the help of Allah, he had made this day possible, a day that had the potential to turn the empire's previous 600 years into an historic anachronism. He waited in silence, listening to the noise of rain on roof, windows, and street, until, at last, the melodic invitation to prayer, "Allah is the greatest," rose from the throat of one, another, another, and yet another *muezzin* from the balconies of hundreds of minarets close and distant, loud and muffled in the syncopation of the rain. He was eager to thank Allah and to ask His help on this day that heralded the *new* Ottoman Empire. He stood at the end of his prayer rug, held his hands palms up, and began the prayer ritual that he had performed thousands of times before, but never with more gratitude.

A few hours later, he and other notables were on a platform outside the gate, called the Sublime Porte, to the Topkapı Palace, the complex of buildings that remained the symbol of the Ottoman government. Thousands of people crowded forward.

Principal Secretary Sait read the document from Abdülhamit, which announced Mithat's appointment as grand vizier, the promulgation of the constitution, and some of the constitution's primary features—phrases that spread via cables, newspapers, travelers, and the wind.

- The constitution would continue the reforms of Sultan Abdülmecit, Abdülhamit's father.
- The rights and duties of all would be the same as those of every civilized society.
- All subjects would enjoy liberty, justice, and equality.

The pronouncement declared that these principles conformed to the Sharia and that the sultan's utmost wish was for the happiness and prosperity of his subjects.

The words rights, liberty, justice, and equality tumbled from mouths that searched for what the words might mean, attributed meanings to the words, and expressed wonder at what the words might portend for the speakers' lives.

"Did you hear? Abdülhamit has proclaimed a constitution."

"What does a constitution do?"

"It makes us a modern country. Just like Europe."

"But Europe is Christian. Will we be Christians?"

"Liberty, justice, and equality have nothing to do with religion."

"There's no law but the Sharia. No constitution should be above the Sharia."

"But Abdülhamit said these words are in Sharia law."

"We've always known our duties. But rights? What rights will we have?"

"Your children will attend school."

"Like the Christians?"

"With the Christians."

"How is that allowed by the Sharia?"

"We'll all be equal."

"Will Christians be soldiers in the Ottoman army?"

"To be equal is just a principle. The army needs money more than men. Non-Muslims will pay a tax not to serve, just as before. Believe me. Nothing will change."

"This Abdülhamit is clever. Maybe the constitution is just a delaying tactic to give him more time to prepare for war."

"Ten Turkish soldiers can defeat a hundred Russians any day."

"He'll get the British to fight the Russians, and then all of this reform, rights, and freedom will be forgotten."

"But Mithat is grand vizier and a reformer. He won't allow that. They say he wrote this constitution."

"He's a great man and patriot. We owe liberty, freedom, and equality to *him*."

"And to the sultan. Don't be fooled. This is still the Ottoman Empire. Abdülhamit is no figurehead."

******

Mithat put in a brief appearance at the grand vizierate before taking his carriage in a large elliptical circle through the old city, out toward the original city walls, back along the southern side of the Golden Horn, and across the bridge to the new city of Galata and Pera. Everywhere, people were in the streets, shouting and celebrating the constitution and praising him and Sultan Abdülhamit II.

Most gratifying to Mithat was that the people in the streets were not just Muslims, but also Jews and Greek and Armenian Christians. He stopped first to see the Jewish Chief Rabbi. Then the Greek and Armenian Patriarchs, hoping to confirm that support emanated from the top. He was not disappointed. They expressed their best wishes for the success of the constitution and pledged him their support and that of their communities.

He was on an emotional high, relieved of a great burden. Reform had been achieved and the empire might well be saved.

As he approached his home, he saw a large crowd waving flags inscribed boldly with "liberty" and shouting, "Long live the country! Long live the constitution!" He stood up in his carriage and waved to them. "Thank you. Thank you. May Allah bless you," he shouted in response to their cheers, as he made his way through the crowd and entered his *konak*.

"You did it!" Şehriban said, as she rushed to meet him with a strong embrace. "The Ottoman Empire has a constitution! And I, a poor Kurdish village girl, have a great man for a husband!" She was smiling broadly and kissed him passionately, knocking his fez onto the floor.

Mithat held her by the shoulders, looking into her eyes, before embracing and kissing her again. Never had he felt so loved. "Allah has made it all possible. No man has been more blessed than I. He willed the country to have a constitution and made me His instrument. He put me in a remote place to find a beautiful and intelligent woman who has lost none of her beauty and has increased in wisdom." He held her tightly, as if grasping happiness.

"You lie with such facility!" she whispered. "You must intend to become sultan? If so, know that I will permit no other woman to enter the harem. A sultan with only one woman in his harem will command no respect and be deposed within days." She winked and pressed her right index finger lightly against his forehead.

Mithat laughed. "In our times, deposed Sultans live comfortably with their wives and children in a palace. I would make up for the time I spent away from you with my work. You have inspired me to become sultan! A sultan with only one woman in his harem, whose affection he would enjoy any time

197

of day or night!" Mithat moved his right arm from her waist down to her buttock and pulled her tightly against him.

"Oh, my love, not now. It's daylight. The servants," she said pushing against his chest in a feigned effort to free herself.

"The servants know to ignore us. Maybe they'll make love on the table while we are in bed. I have my suspicions of the footman and the cook. The cook is a fine looking woman," he said pulling her more tightly against him.

"Mithat! The cook? You've been eyeing the cook!" she said with genuine surprise.

"No, not eyeing, my dear, just observing. The eyes of this sultan rest on the only object in the world that he desires."

"Truly, your tongue is that of a sultan, and I will have you, my sultan, right now as the crowds cheer you, because by tonight you may be deposed."

Outside, the crowd, which included Mithat's first wife and his children, continued to praise liberty, freedom, and equality; continued to extol Mithat, Sultan Abdülhamit II, and the constitution; and continued to wonder what rights and duties would fall to them. The mood of the city warmed the cold night.

******

That same day, Friday, the 23rd of December, the Powers convened their Constantinople Conference, a sham venue for Russian Ambassador Ignatiev to announce the demands worked out over the previous weeks. Abdülhamit received confirmation of this from multiple sources. Christian nations that convened a conference on December 23rd could be expected to reach their agreement not later than noon on the 24th. On Christmas Day, they would celebrate the birth of Christ and their miraculous accord to protect the Ottoman Empire's Christian subjects.

Abdülhamit hoped that Britain would oppose Russia, but Britain's representative, Lord Salisbury, having arrived with no sympathy for the Turks, fell under Ignatiev's charm. Salisbury had been secretary of state to India twice and was reported to carry the Western colonialist attitude of burden, destiny, and superiority.

Within an hour of the conference's opening, Abdülhamit began to receive reports. His lead representative at the conference, Foreign Minister Safvet Pasha, whom the Powers granted only the status of "observer," deftly suggested that the constitution negated the purported purpose of the conference. The constitution provided for equal rights for the empire's Christians in all provinces, and the Ottoman government could not agree to any measures not stipulated in its constitution. Ignatiev was furious. Surprisingly, Austria did not support Ignatiev. And Salisbury was reported to equivocate, as well. Perhaps British Ambassador Elliot, whom Abdülhamit regarded as a friend, was having some influence on Salisbury after all. With only minor variations among the reports of the rancor and lack of consensus that characterized the day's session, Abdülhamit grew increasingly confident that he had won the first round.

Other reports were less comforting. Although the streets were filled with celebrants hailing the constitution and yelling, "Long live our Padishah," praise for Mithat Pasha also was reported everywhere. The people knew that the constitution was Mithat's. The reported large crowd waiting for Mithat at his home was proof of this. More galling still was the report of Mithat's visit to the Chief Rabbi and the Patriarchs of the Armenian and Greek churches and of their expressions of support for him and his constitution. This was unacceptable. Mithat should have invited the Rabbi and the Patriarchs to pay their respects to the sultan and express their thanks to *him* for the constitution. They *and* Mithat would have known that this was the correct protocol. Abdülhamit would not forget this.

One report had a friend of Mithat's telling a foreign reporter that the sultan would be the servant of the people under the constitution. Yet another cited Mithat as suggesting that the next step would be to transform the empire into a republic. And the informant in Mithat's house noted that his wife had called him "sultan" as the crowds were cheering him outside.

Abdülhamit was angry. Not only at his own powerlessness, but at Mithat's arrogance. He had appointed Mithat grand vizier and agreed to the constitution, because he felt he had no choice. There was too much momentum on the street and among the Powers to do otherwise. But now it was clear that he had to rid himself of Mithat. There could only be one sultan. Except this was not the time. Mithat was the center of adulation. "So, everyone cheers Mithat Pasha," he said to Principal Secretary Sait.

"They cheer you, as well, my lord. Mithat has the Europeans and the locals believing that he can defeat the Russians without going to war. But he has not yet delivered, and they will abandon him if he does not. Whereas, *you* are the sultan. The people will support you even if you call them to war, which is the only victory the Russians will honor. The British may venerate a constitution, but the Russians do not."

"So, is war inevitable?"

"Unless you give the Russians everything they want without war, yes. This is why Mithat is destined to fail. The Russians will not back down. They will insist on terms that Mithat will have to recommend that you reject. His adulation will be short-lived."

Abdülhamit accepted this as the obligatory posture for a principal secretary, but there was truth enough in it to give him both solace and unease. He did not feel prepared to lead his country in war. He had barely taken office. Decisions he would make would cause men to die, whether the decisions were right or wrong. The image of Azrael taking his mother as he sat helplessly next to her deathbed returned. Azrael would hover over the battlefield and take soldiers indiscriminately, and he, once again, would be helpless. If he ordered soldiers to die, would Allah hold him accountable? "What will happen if we give the Russians what they want without war?" he asked.

"You could be deposed. There would be little support for a sultan perceived to be weak in the face of crisis. When parliament is convened, it could revise the constitution to make the sultan a figurehead, as in Britain, or even to turn the empire into some kind of republic, as in France. Mithat could be sultan in all but name. In any case, no agreement will satisfy the Russians. Soon, they would demand Istanbul and the Bosphorus, Mesopotamia and the Persian Gulf. The British want Egypt and the Arabian Peninsula. France wants the Levant and North Africa. Italy wants a limb, as well. The Greeks, the Armenians, everyone. You could be left with but a small piece of Anatolia, if you survived."

Only a few months before, when Mithat asked him if he would accept to be sultan, he hesitated in responding—a show of humility and respect for the gravity of the responsibility. But he knew he was acting. He was eager to be sultan. Perhaps naïvely so, he thought now. He had not anticipated having to decide between wrong and potentially more wrong. He had not expected that his decisions could have unforeseen consequences. Day after day, he read the reports from his representatives at the conference and what purported to be intelligence from many sources. None of them offered hope for a resolution that he would be able to call a victory.

The Constantinople Conference held nine sessions over 29 days. The Powers presented their final offer on January 14,

1877. It provided that for five years, a commission of Western consular officers would oversee the administration of the Balkan provinces and also that the Powers would exercise prior approval of governors, who were to be Christian, appointed to the provinces of Bulgaria, Herzegovina, and Bosnia. Together with a copy of the demands, Lord Salisbury sent a message to Abdülhamit that said, "Accept or fight alone."

Abdülhamit hesitated. Faced with the potential—even likelihood—of losing a war, he turned to avoiding blame for accepting or rejecting the Powers' demands. He asked Mithat to hold a public meeting and make a recommendation.

Mithat convened 240 people, including 60 non-Muslims. The sentiment even among the non-Muslims was that the Russian position was an ultimatum. Some suggested that Russia might not be prepared for war after all, since they were continuing to negotiate. There were those who thought the reports from the western and eastern borders of massive troop buildup might be a ruse. Surely the Russians had not forgotten the Crimean War. Despite having Salisbury in their pocket, they had to know that Queen Victoria and Prime Minister Disraeli were pro-Turk and would not want Russian influence extended in the Balkans or eastern Anatolia. Salisbury could say accept or fight alone, but London, not he, would make that decision.

Abdülhamit was informed that the entire city was discussing the Russian demands and that the *softas* were marching in the streets and chanting "war." He read the local newspapers, which were also calling for war and hinting at a lack of patriotism among any with a counter viewpoint. Reports told him that Mithat was an outspoken advocate for war in the public meeting, arguing that capitulation would mean being a puppet of the Powers. Mithat was seen in the meeting and in the streets as the champion of the people and the empire, preserving both from Russian violation. Once again, Abdülhamit felt out-manuevered by Mithat. He seethed.

Principal Secretary Sait suggested that he make a gambit of promising reforms even greater than those provided for in the constitution. It would be a way to present himself as in charge of the empire's strategy and as the true champion of reforms. And it might prevent a war. But Abdülhamit could only see more reforms as another victory for Mithat.

The decision of the public meeting to reject the Conference proposal was unanimous, and on January 20, 1877, Abdülhamit stood on the terrace of the palace with a telescope, watching the ships carrying the participants of the conference home, along with their ambassadors. It was a diplomatic snub, but Abdülhamit felt no regret. He did not accept that he bore responsibility for what had happened.

On his farm in Kağıthane, he had watched Hanımefendi skillfully wait for the perfect moment when facing dangerous prey. Once, he saw a large rat scurry under a board, and he brought Hanımefendi and placed her next to it. She stared intently, sensing, perhaps smelling, what was under the board. He pushed the board aside with his foot and watched as cat and rat froze in place, face to face. The rat returned Hanımefendi's stare and hissed in the hope of frightening her. But Hanımefendi did not move, did not flinch, and showed no hint of fear as the rat bared its teeth, hissed and threatened. She wasted no energy. No move to intimidate, anticipate, or preempt her prey. She waited. She waited longer. Longer still. Waited until the rat made its inevitable and fateful move, spinning to run away and exposing the back of its neck, into which Hanımefendi, in one graceful leap, sank her teeth while simultaneously digging her claws into the flesh of the rat's back, holding the struggling creature to the ground until it writhed no more. Then, without easing the death-grip of her jaw, she released her claws from the rat's back and began to drag the warm, limp body to her kittens for their dinner.

Making the first move cost the rat his life. Success required patience and pouncing when the enemy exposed his neck. The constitution had failed. Mithat's adulation and support from Ambassador Elliot had been trumped by Lord Salisbury's opposition. If there were war, it would be on Mithat. Surely, everyone could see this. Mithat's neck was exposed, and Adülhamit would exile him under article 113 of the constitution.

TWENTY-SIX

"Well, it's over. The Turks have rejected the conference's latest humiliating offer. All of us, ambassadors and conference representatives, are being sent home," Ambassador Elliot morosely announced to his wife, as though pronouncing the death of a dear friend.

"What's the purpose in leaving Istanbul with no Western ambassadors?" asked Lady Elliot in disbelief. Her husband's demeanor surprised and concerned her. He was a slender man, just above average height with a slightly long and large nose made more prominent by his thin face. His shock of graying hair was well-groomed as always, and his suit still looked pressed at the end of the day. She always felt secure and fortunate when she looked at him, but for the first time, what she saw now was vulnerability, disappointment.

"It's a kind of protest. Ignatiev proposed the gesture, along with every other feature of the conference; Salisbury offered his support; and everyone fell in line." His tone had shifted to resignation.

"Lord Salisbury's wife spent almost all of her time here sight-seeing from Mrs. Ignatiev's carriage. I hoped to win her over, but she arrived with such an anti-Turk bias that she left no opening," Mrs. Elliot observed, feeling the need to share in the sense of failure.

"The Ignatievs' prattle about protecting Christians from barbarous Turks reinforced the Salisburys' prejudices. Lord Salisbury behaved as though his charge was to find out what the Russians wanted and make sure they got it, as though Britain were a Russian colony!"

Switching to indignation made Lord Elliot feel better, but Mrs. Elliot still heard failure in his voice. "What happened is not your fault. Disraeli made a mistake in sending Salisbury."

"I don't feel responsible for what happened. But I do regret that I was not appointed the Crown's representative. I think the Russians would have backed down, if they had seen us as resolved against them. And I think the Turks would have given more if they'd seen us as their ally. A compromise should have been possible. Thousands will die because it was not."

"What about us? Will we be coming back?" It suddenly struck her that they might be personally affected by the failure of the conference.

"It appears not. I think Salisbury's convinced London that a pro-Turk ambassador is a biased representative. Amusing, considering how he allowed his own anti-Turk view to make him a tool of London's enemy."

"Surely London will see that Salisbury failed?"

"I'm not sure London has decided what represents victory and what represents loss. I don't know whether I would be more favorably viewed in London if I had a role in the dissolution of the Ottoman Empire or in its survival!"

Lady Elliot was relieved to hear his tone change to the light irony so familiar to her. "Well, the empire's still standing, isn't it? So, you must be due *some* credit," she said.

"Not me. The Turks. They're tough and resilient, which the West acknowledges, but they're also smart, which the West doesn't see. And that's why I predict the empire will survive. Men like Mithat Pasha will find a way. Even the new sultan. I'm told he reads everything. The West would be wise not to underestimate him."

"Do you think they do?"

"Yes. The Western representatives experience the European atmosphere of Pera, Fener, and Galata, the *konaks* of the pashas in Beyoğlu, the *yalıs* on the Bosphorus, and the modern homes in Tarabya. They interact with well-educated Turkish pashas and with Greeks and Armenians, all of whom speak French. They see a population in Istanbul teeming with Christians. This is their world view of the Ottoman Empire. A sultan might be poorly educated and might never leave this city, but he knows Istanbul is not the Ottoman Empire."

"And if we don't return here, where might we be posted?"

"I've heard Vienna, but it's not confirmed. If so, it could be seen as a kind of poetic justice: the pro-Turk diplomat from London posted to the city that twice blocked the Turks' advance into Europe. Almost amusing."

"I can't believe we won't be coming back here," she responded, abstractly with a distinct note of disappointment.

"We'll be leaving in two days. I'll have a lot to set in order before we leave, but I couldn't make myself work late today. Have a servant bring our warmest coats and an extra blanket. I'll have the carriage readied. We're going for one last tour along the Bosphorus."

"It's dark and cold. No one goes sight-seeing at night in January."

"But I'm not no one, Madam. I am the famous British Ambassador Sir Henry Elliot. I will share the warmth of my body with yours in the January cold and dark of Istanbul, where you will feel unsafe to free yourself from my embrace and cannot but submit to my desire."

"And if the desire is mine?"

"I shall be your slave."

"Call the carriage then, you fool. You shall know the lot of a slave."

Despite the cold, he requested the open carriage. It was a clear night, and they rode pressed together as tightly as their heavy coats and warm clothing permitted. "I will miss Istanbul," he said. "Remember when we climbed the old wall? We could see the Bosphorus, the Golden Horn, the Marmara, the Princess Islands, and even Mt. Olympus faintly in the distance."

"I remember it well. We were told it was a dangerous part of the city. Too near the thieving gypsies' camp. But you ignored the warning, and we ended up having tea in the tent of a gypsy fortuneteller who claimed to have relatives in Bucharest and Budapest. "

"The gypsies claim home to many places and to none."

"Her fortunes were pretty accurate too. She said that I would enjoy my time here and that you would spend yours trying to prevent a war that was inevitable."

"No special prescience there. The gypsies are better informed than the palace, or London. They have to be, so they can move on before a disaster strikes, and they get blamed."

The moon was almost full, the sky alive with stars, the air crisp and dry. Sir Elliot had the driver turn around just before they reached the Albanian district.

"And what is my slave thinking now?" Lady Elliot asked at last.

"In the warmth of your body next to mine, my only thought is that all the world is your boudoir, where I hasten to take thee."

"I thought all the world was a stage?"

"To a literary genius, yes. Whereas I am but your slave whose highest aspiration is to make his entrances and exits, a poor player content to strut and fret his hour full of sound and fury, signifying nothing."

"Love sought is good, but given unsought is better."

"Too late, I fear, to be unsought. But love is blind, and lovers cannot see," he said burying his face in her neck.

"Imagine if Shakespeare had lived in Istanbul," she said, kissing him as the cold and Istanbul embraced them and they each other.

TWENTY-SEVEN

Mithat Pasha's agitation grew daily. Announcing the constitution had had no effect on the Constantinople Conference. The culmination of months of work, the signature reform in a life dedicated to changing his country, had been ignored by the Powers.

And Abdülhamit had been a bystander. If Abdülhamit had demanded to meet with the participants and expressed strong personal support for the egalitarian principles of the constitution, the British and the French could not have ignored him. He could have appealed for time to demonstrate his sincerity and the effectiveness of the constitution. But Abdülhamit sat in the palace, read reports, smoked, and drank coffee.

Mithat puzzled over Abdülhamit. He approved change but was unwilling to use it to his advantage. If Abdülhamit did not carry through on the constitution's provisions, it could only appear to have been a ruse to trick the Europeans.

And there were other priorities, as well, including the empire's finances. Mithat sent a message to Abdülhamit requesting that the finance minister be dismissed and that he, Mithat, be given permission to examine the ministry's management and the empire's financial structure. He promised a plan to get the empire out of debt. The Europeans could always dispute what represented fair treatment of Christians, but the language of economics was not subject to interpretation.

Education was another priority. A democracy needed an educated populace. Without education, the people could not even be proper Muslims or Christians. The religions, as the people practiced and professed them, were rife with centuries of superstition, myth, misapplied rules, prejudice, misinformation, and propaganda. But a sultan who was suspicious of democracy was unlikely to be persuaded by an argument that posited the need for educated, informed voters—much less the need for educated practitioners of their faiths.

Mithat had proposed to Abdülhamit that the first meeting of parliament occur under the eyes of the Constantinople Conference delegates—a bold statement that the conference was an affront to the sovereignty of the Ottoman nation and its people. But days passed without a response from Abdülhamit to this proposal, to several other of his suggested actions, and even to his request for a meeting to discuss these matters. Mithat grew impatient and wrote an uncharacteristically sharp memo to the sultan on January 29, 1877. He reminded Abdülhamit that one purpose of the constitution was to "abolish absolutism." He noted that Abdülhamit had not responded to his request of nine days earlier for authority to proceed with laws he had proposed. Perhaps, Mithat suggested, the sultan might want to entrust the position of grand vizier to someone else.

In his response, Abdülhamit requested that Mithat come to the palace. The orders authorizing his requests were being prepared, and Abdülhamit desired to give the documents to him personally. He would expect him just after the Sunset Prayer on February 5.

Mithat sent a quick message to his journalist friend, Namık Kemal. "Prepare, my friend. We are about to change our country."

On the morning of February 5, Mithat went to his office in the grand vizierate. He was preparing for the authorities the sultan had promised. Over the previous two days, he had met with many officials and even some merchants and bankers for their thoughts on lessening the burden on the state treasury, increasing the income of the treasury, and preventing waste and corruption. He asked Namık Kemal to meet with him, because Namık had an ear for the public mood. Namık reassured him that the people in the street still looked to him as a hero who was fighting to reform their country. He would have public support for his plans, particularly for ending corruption and foreign debt, and Namık promised to write supportive editorials as soon as Mithat was authorized to make his plans public.

They parted with an exceptionally long embrace that reflected their sense that this was a special time. Mithat might succeed in his reforms. Or the reforms could be shut down by a sultan who was showing his love of power. Or the country could be destroyed by war with Russia. But whatever happened, their embrace affirmed their resolve to do their part. The rest was up to Allah, to *kismet*. They accepted this.

The meeting with Namık buoyed Mithat's spirit, but he was too impatient to attend to work at the office and decided to stop at his *konak* to fill in some time before going to the palace. As his carriage approached his street, he noticed a contingent of soldiers standing and sitting on a bench in a small park not far from his home. He had never seen soldiers there before. It seemed odd, as though they were waiting for orders to conduct some kind of mission. Otherwise, the streets had only a few pedestrians hustling home or to get a loaf of bread, olive oil, a cabbage, or sugar before the neighborhood markets closed. So different from the afternoon only a month before, when he came home early and made love to his wife as the crowd cheered him and the constitution. That memory now seemed as if a dream.

"I'm not home to stay. I just stopped by on my way to the palace," he said to Şehriban, who met him at the door. "The sultan has agreed to meet with me and give me authorization for some of the reforms called for in the constitution."

"That's wonderful—except that I know you'll be working even harder," she said as they walked to their home's informal sitting room. "Shall we have tea or coffee?"

"Tea. The sultan always serves coffee." He paused for a moment. "I do regret having spent so much time away from you and the children," he said, as if to emphasize that he was sincere this time, as opposed to all the other times he had said the same thing, and as though he might not have a chance to say it again.

"Darling, from the day I met you, I knew that I shared you with the nation, and I've been proud to do so. More importantly, I understand that what you do for her you do also for me and for our children. And now, at last, it seems the nation appreciates what you're doing. I hear it every day. The children and I could not feel more proud, more loved or more valued as a result of the work you do." Despite herself, she put her head on his shoulder. "I'm sorry. I'm crying from happiness."

"The meeting with Abdülhamit will be short, I think," Mithat said after a brief silence.

"Good. We can have dinner together. The cook is preparing your favorite—lamb stew."

******

Riding to the palace, Mithat remembered every bad omen. From the accession speech Mithat had prepared for him, Abdülhamit had struck the language about common schools for all citizens and about abolishing the slave trade and freeing the palace slaves. He had opposed changing the office of grand vizier to prime minister. Abdülhamit's non-responsiveness to his requests felt more like a personal attack than a disagreement on whether to implement the constitution. He remembered the discussion among the ministers about deposing Murat and offering the sultanate to Abdülhamit. Grand Vizier Mehmet Rüşdi had expressed a fear that they were moving too quickly and hoped they would not live to regret the decision. Today, Mithat had regrets. Although he knew it was apocryphal, the folk curse, "May you be grand vizier to Selim the Grim," came to mind. Selim I, sultan in the early 16th century, had a number of his grand viziers executed. Abdülhamit was not likely to become another Selim the Grim. And yet, who Abdülhamit would be as sultan was hidden behind the walls of the palace, concealed among spy reports, and masked by his exterior gentility—shields against the outside world.

At the palace, Mithat was greeted by Principal Secretary Sait. "I've been asked to request the seal for the Office of Grand Vizier," he said.

"But of course," Mithat responded. The seal was always in his briefcase. "I'm being relieved of my office?" he asked almost with a sense of relief. He wanted to be grand vizier only if the office was empowered to make the changes he wanted to make.

"Yes."

"Does the sultan still wish to see me?" Relief was now replaced with fear. Abdülhamit had lied in saying his requests would be granted. Were the soldiers in his neighborhood related to this?

"No, you're to board the imperial yacht, which will take you into exile."

"I'd like to say goodbye to my family."

"I'm sorry. His majesty has instructed that you are to board the yacht directly. But he asked me to assure you that no harm will come to your family."

"That is kind. Thank him for me, please. And where will I be exiled?"

"I do not know. The captain has orders."

******

Mithat stood on the deck as the boarding plank was removed and the yacht pulled away. Two soldiers stood one on either side of him. Were they there to prevent him from jumping overboard? It amused him that the sultan would be concerned that he might attempt suicide in order to feed a rumor of his execution. The perfect plot for a Karagöz play with him as the hero and the sultan as the villain. An amusing thought that brought only momentary comic relief.

He considered the promise of no harm to his family. Abdülhamit had lied about why he was to come to the palace. Was he lying about not harming his family? He wondered what his family would be told and when he might be able to let them know where he was. He could not see the future for himself or his family. And obvious harm awaited his country.

He stared into the black water. He had never contemplated suicide. He would never be the one to silence his voice. From wherever he was exiled, he would make his voice heard. But he was disconsolate as he looked at the water, wondering how old his children would be when he next saw them and whether the empire would still be standing. He was a reformer, not a revolutionary. He wished no physical harm to Abdülhamit, but if Russia invaded and Britain stayed on the sidelines, Abdülhamit and the empire might not survive. And if they did not, what would be the future for him and his family?

In the fifth prayer of the day, he asked Allah to keep his family safe and for His help to continue the fight for his country from wherever he was exiled. He tried to sleep, but it was interrupted by regrets and second thoughts of things done and left undone, words said and unsaid, convictions acted on and not. The sleep of men who know their imperfections.

******

Abdülhamit wanted Mithat Pasha gone, and he was. His orders to the yacht captain were to go only as far as the Bay of Çekmece and wait. If there were a public demonstration against Mithat's exile, either in the streets or diplomatically from the Powers, Abdülhamit left himself the option to bring Mithat back.

But there was no reaction. Nothing. The cold night made harsh by the damp and wind invited no one into the streets; and the talk in the coffee houses, in the pashas' *konaks*, and in every ethnic neighborhood was of the coming war with Russia. Ambassador Elliot, Mithat's staunch advocate and admirer, was gone. The great reformer, the hero of the people and of the Western diplomats, was forgotten. Abdülhamit ordered the ship captain to take Mithat to the country of his choice in Europe.

Still, all was not as Abdülhamit wanted. The soldiers found no incriminating documents in their search of Mithat's home or of his office in the grand vizierate. No employees in the vizierate, nor any current minister, remembered Mithat proposing the overthrow of Abdülhamit or of Mithat ordering the murder of Abdülaziz. This was the man who made no secret of wanting to be a prime minister and reduce the sultan to a figurehead. Surely, he had not abandoned that ambition? Sooner or later he would turn and expose his neck, and Abdülhamit would pounce. But, for now at least, he could not send demanding requests and could not court the public's adulation. Abdülhamit was alone at the head of the empire, and he would act.

He directed that parliament be convened, hoping to show himself as the empire's true reformer. For expediency, the delegates to parliament were appointed by the provincial and district councils, rather than elected. The numbers of Christian and Jewish delegates appointed from areas where they resided in significant numbers were set to over-represent them. They were also over-represented among the total number of delegates so as to preclude any criticism from the West. Abdülhamit also appointed an Armenian Christian as vice-president of the assembly and two Jews as administrative aides. Even with this bias in representation, the Muslim delegates were in the strong majority, and Abdülhamit expected parliament to do as he instructed.

When parliament opened on March 4, 1877, he sent a speech that enumerated the laws that parliament would need to pass in order to implement the provisions of the constitution. He promised to open a new school to train civil servants to implement these laws and to select students without regard to religion. He even used Mithat's language of being citizens of one country. The speech was his public statement of support for the constitution.

That night, Abdülhamit read reports of how he had been praised in parliament, in the coffeehouses, and in the streets. Reportedly, even Christians were vowing to fight to defend the empire. He called for one of his favorites from the harem and slept soundly, but he rose early, feeling an urgency to attend to being sultan of the Ottoman Empire.

One change to which he gave priority was the palace. He abandoned Dolmabahçe and moved to Yıldız Palace. He was not comfortable in the opulence of Dolmabahçe or with its location on the shore of the Bosphorus. Dolmabahçe seemed vulnerable: any foreign warship could steam into the Bosphorus, any Ottoman force determined to depose him could attack from either land or sea. In contrast, Yıldız was a walled country estate in the hills overlooking the Bosphorus. It was easy to secure and had ample land to accommodate the rural trappings that he missed since leaving Kağıthane: a lake, a stable of horses, as many cats as wanted a home, dogs, a zoo, an aviary, flowers and flowering plants, and paths to walk in nature, unobserved, and in total security. The move symbolized his assumption of complete power. Even the palace he lived in was no longer inherited from previous sovereigns. The Ottoman Empire was his, and he would remake it.

Abdülhamit followed the European press, hoping for favorable reactions to his opening of parliament. Russian Ambassador Ignatiev, however, was the news. Leaving Istanbul, he had not returned to Moscow but had gone to Europe, where he continued to press leaders there for agreement on the Russian position at the Constantinople Conference. Abdülhamit disliked and resented Ignatiev, not only because he was attempting to destroy the Ottoman Empire, but because he was personally haughty, confident, and unafraid to use his power and position — everything Abdülhamit was not, but wished he were.

Still, there was some good news. Abdülhamit heard that Britain's response to Ignatiev was that she would continue to seek a peaceful resolution and was prepared to defend Istanbul, if necessary. Despite this caveat from the British, however, Ignatiev prevailed. The Powers signed what was effectively an ultimatum to the Turks.

"What's the news?" Abdülhamit asked, addressing Principal Secretary Sait, who had entered his study.

"The Powers have signed an agreement, your majesty. We've just received this translation of it."

Abdülhamit read the protocol. "So, the Powers have agreed to monitor how well we treat Christians and threaten unspecified measures, should we fall short of their expectations," Abdülhamit observed, on putting it down with an angry flourish.

"You noticed, I'm sure, my sovereign, the reference to their concern for peace. Apparently, there is still an interest in deterring a Russian invasion."

"An interest, possibly, but this protocol is an insult. They know that I pledged that all citizens would be treated equal. It's not for the Europeans to decide whether some of our citizens are faring well and others not. Reforms take time. The Christians, themselves, have to demonstrate that they desire equal treatment. That they will fight for their country."

"Do you wish to send a response?"

"Yes. Draft a response that notes their apparent concern for only some of our citizens, although the rights of all are equally protected by our constitution. We do not accept their right to monitor how we treat our citizens. And remind them that the alleged Bulgarian massacres were the reaction to Christian attacks on Muslims incited by foreign agents. If the Russians want war, they shall have it, but don't put that in the response."

As he read the spy reports, memoranda from governors throughout the country, and especially the news items from the European press, Abdülhamit felt powerless, morose, and angry. In approving the constitution and convening parliament, he had done the bidding of Mithat, who had led him to believe that these actions would deter war. But the public praise he received initially for these actions had dissipated, and the ultimatum from the Powers exposed him as without respect. No one in Europe feared him or his army.

Worst of all, reports he received from Europe were of European leaders conferring with Mithat, who was writing opinion pieces in the European press. One report had Disraeli promising Mithat that Britain would press Russia to accept peace if the empire were to show evidence of good will, as though Mithat were Abdülhamit's representative. In one article, Mithat wrote of being a patriot devoted wholly to the welfare of his country, willing to be poor and exiled rather than compromise his principles. To Abdülhamit, this confirmed that Mithat was not a sincere patriot, but a self-promoting enemy.

And talk in the coffeehouses now questioned why Mithat had been exiled and implied that Mithat would have been able to negotiate a peace.

"You have a cable from Mithat Pasha, your majesty," said the Principal Secretary, clearly uncomfortable, knowing that Abdülhamit despised Mithat. "He requests an urgent response."

Mithat's cable reported that he was in Vienna and had an invitation to meet with Emperor Francis Joseph. He asked to be advised of Abdülhamit's views in order to represent his position in the meeting.

Abdülhamit was livid. The arrogance of the man! Mithat was behaving, not as though exiled, but as if posted to Europe as the empire's special envoy! For Abdülhamit, this decided the matter. Mithat negotiate peace? Absolutely not! Abdülhamit would not give Mithat an opportunity to succeed in negotiating peace. His response to Mithat was that he would not accept peace and would not consider anyone who advocated it to be a true patriot.

*****

In London, Prime Minister Disraeli pondered how to respond to Abdülhamit's increasingly hard line. He was under great pressure from Gladstone and the liberal party to punish the Ottoman Empire, on the one hand, and to keep Russia from destroying it, on the other. Disraeli conferred with Queen Victoria, a staunch supporter of the Turks. They agreed that Russia was likely to declare war soon and that public opinion

220

would not allow them to join the Turks. Russia might quickly overrun large parts of the Ottoman Empire.

In the hope of exerting influence on Abdülhamit, Disraeli sent Sir Austen Henry Layard to Istanbul as Britain's new ambassador. Layard had worked in Mesopotamia in the 1840s for the "Great" Ambassador Stratford Canning. Disraeli knew of Abdülhamit's admiration for Canning. He might listen to Layard. Layard was well known and respected for his Mesopotamian archaeological excavations, from which many extraordinary Assyrian and Babylonian artworks were in the British Museum. He could engage Abdülhamit on many levels. It would be his job to convince Abdülhamit that a compromise for peace was in the joint interest of the Ottoman and British Empires.

But when Ambassador Layard arrived in Istanbul and presented his credentials to Abdülhamit, the meeting did not end well. Abdülhamit was, as always, warm and charming. They shared cigarettes and Turkish coffee. They spoke of Layard's archaeological digs, and Abdülhamit took the opportunity to speak of meeting Canning and to express his admiration for him. But these were the pleasantries of diplomatic training. Both of them knew the business of the meeting.

"Her Majesty's government feels that peace would be in both our countries' interests, you see," Layard said at last.

"Does Her Majesty's government believe that the peace Russia offers would be lasting? How long has it been since the Crimean War? Russia drove the Muslims from the Crimea. Why would they not drive the Muslims out of the Danube Province? Out of Ardahan, Kars, Erzurum, and Van?"

"If Russia were to violate the terms of a peace agreement, Her Majesty's government would be required to reconsider, of course."

"Russia has prepared its armies to invade my country. She is waiting for an opportunity. You know their methods. If Russian agents provoke an incident that violates the peace agreement, how can I trust that Her Majesty's government will believe the truth of what may happen?"

"I can offer no guarantees. I only regret to inform you that if you enter into war with Russia, my government will not join you."

"So, we must fight alone, either now, or after some future provocation that Her Majesty's government will be unable to prevent. Delay only gives Russia more time to prepare."

Layard sent a cable to London reporting that Abdülhamit had not agreed to compromise.

And in his palace, Abdülhamit listened to the reports of the eunuchs he had sent into the streets. News of the meeting with Layard had spread. Everyone expected war, was excited by the prospect of war, and declared their eagerness to fight. That the adversary would be the hated Russians raised the level of enthusiasm. The eighteenth century wars with the armies of Peter the Great and Catherine the Great were recent memory to the Turks, and veterans of the Crimean war were many. Boisterous men promised the gold and silver of their wives, the lives of their sons, and the conviction that Allah would keep the soldiers from harm.

Late that night on a bench in the gardens of Yıldız Palace, Abdülhamit watched the moon and stars, a few faintly visible lanterns of *kayıks* in the Bosphorus, and the dark masses of land in Asia and Europe that were his empire, the empire he would preserve by waging war.

******

In Europe, Mithat missed his family and longed to be at home, engaged in confronting his country's problems. As when he lived in Europe the first time, political intellectuals debated. Communism was in vogue. And although a colony of Turkish exiles welcomed him, Mithat had little in common with them. They thought of themselves as rebels in exile, revolutionaries. Whereas, Mithat was a practical man, a reformer. His vision was to demonstrate the efficacy of reform to the empire's people and its sultan. In the provinces, he had proved empirically that it could be done.

He read in the newspapers that Abdülhamit had opened parliament. Bittersweet. Mithat knew he should be happy that parliament had been convened, but he could not help but be disappointed that he was not there to witness it. And, although he knew it was vain, he had to acknowledge to himself that he was unhappy he was getting no credit for it. He took more pleasure in the event after reading a letter from his friend, Namık Kemal, who observed that in parliament the deputies were Ottomans, not Christians, Jews, or Muslims; not Greeks, Turks, or Arabs. Parliament had made their country the Ottoman country of Mithat's vision.

Mithat busied himself by writing for European newspapers and for Namık's paper in Istanbul. Despite his personal unhappiness at having been exiled, he refrained from direct criticism of Abdülhamit and continued to call for Europe to have patience.

Letters from his wives kept his spirits up. They wrote of the soldiers searching the house and his office. The soldiers had taken every paper they could find and some books. But there were no rumors that they had found anything that Abdülhamit found objectionable. They knew now that one of the servants was a spy for Abdülhamit.

That the soldiers had confiscated his papers and that one of his servants was a spy came as no surprise to Mithat, and yet it shocked him. What had Abdülhamit suspected? He thought that everyone knew he was as open and honest as he knew himself to be. Apparently not. For the first time in his life, he realized that Abdülhamit might see him as an enemy of his country, instead of its most fervent patriot. That everyone was suspect.

TWENTY-EIGHT

It was late April. A spring mist carried by a cool, seasonal zephyr found Cristo inside, instead of sitting on his stool on the sidewalk. Nigar walked in with her umbrella tilted down, so as to hide her face until she was well inside, where she tilted it back coquettishly to reveal who she was. "Madam Flora! What a wonderful surprise," Cristo shouted. He had not adjusted to calling her Nigar.

Nigar smiled broadly, enjoying Cristo's expression of pleasure at seeing her. It had been seven months since Abdülhamit had become sultan and she had left her shop next to Cristo's. So much had changed. Before, she would never have made a gesture that could be interpreted as flirtatious. When she left, she had no clear picture of her new life as an abandoned wife, a Christian turned Muslim, a young woman in Istanbul with means but nothing to do. But now, she had a plan, a mission. She felt in charge of her life, confident. Enough so that she could flirt with Cristo and know that she was completely in control.

"It's my pleasure to see you, as well, my friend," Nigar responded, extending her hand as he made an elaborate bow and reached to kiss it. "Shall we have tea?"

"Such a question! I'm sure the tea delivery boy spotted you and will be here in a moment. If not, I'll thrash him for neglecting his duty! How have you been? You look fabulous."

The tea arrived, and they exchanged the conversational courtesies of old friends.

"But you did not come here for tea or to see my grizzled face, though I wish that were true. How can I help you?" Cristo asked, sensing that she was searching for a way to open a serious subject.

"You know me too well. Yes, I came to ask your advice. I've decided to help the refugees coming from the Danube Province."

"Yes, we see them begging everywhere. More every day. What do you wish to do for them?"

"I want to grow food on Abdülhamit's farm, where I live. I can never grow enough, of course, but perhaps I can make a small difference."

"Does Abdülhamit know you wish to do this?"

"No. That's what I wanted to talk with you about. Do you think I should speak with him?"

"Would it make you uncomfortable to see him?"

That was the question, wasn't it, Nigar realized. "I don't think so," she answered carefully. "It's just something I would not initiate, if there were another way."

"If you go to see him, do you think he would ask you to live at Yıldız?"

Another direct question. "No. We settled that. He's a proud man. He would not ask again. But people will know I went to see him. They will say he asked and I said no or that I asked and he said no. I don't wish to cause him the embarrassment of such falsehoods."

"I see the problem."

"I could send a message, but I'm proposing to turn Abdülhamit's prized flower gardens into vegetable plots and to plough under most of his pasture where the finest Arabian horses that are now at Yıldız once grazed. I feel I should ask his approval personally."

"Abdülhamit will approve of what you propose. He's not loved by everyone, but he's known to feel responsible for the welfare of the refugees. You should go see him."

226

"And if there's gossip? Won't I have embarrassed him?"

"Wear a heavy veil like every other woman who petitions him. No one will know who you are."

"What a great idea," Nigar said, her eyes bright with pleasure.

******

Waiting for her turn to be shown into the sultan's audience chamber, Nigar was nervous. What would she feel when she saw Abdülhamit? What if he refused her request? At last, it was her turn. Entering Abdülhamit's chamber, she sat down in the chair opposite him as indicated, and as soon as the escort left the room, she removed her veil. "Thank you for receiving me, my sovereign," she said.

Abdülhamit was visibly shocked. His mind raced. Had she come to live in Yıldız? Palace intrigue had been a problem for many sultans. Caused the death of some. With his older brother Murat still alive and with two younger brothers, he had to be vigilant. Nothing would spark palace intrigue faster than to bring Nigar to Yıldız. "What is your petition, Madam?" he asked, attempting to gain control of the situation, but immediately feeling awkward at having addressed her as "madam."

Nigar had resolved that she would not permit herself a single thought of their former relationship during her time in his presence. But she failed. This man was still her husband. He had not renounced her, as he could have, to effect a divorce. Would he do so now? "You are aware, my sovereign, of the many destitute refugees in the city. More arrive daily. The mosque kitchens struggle to provide food. I would like your permission to turn much of your farm at Kağıthane into vegetable gardens."

Abdülhamit was not sure if he felt disappointed or relieved. "But, of course. The refugees are my subjects. I will spare nothing to assure their well-being. You'll need tools and workers. I'll increase your support."

"Your support is already generous, my sovereign," she responded, catching herself as she almost said, "my love." "I have enough money. The refugees will contribute their labor."

"I don't want war, you know," he said in a tone of desperation. "I want peace. No one comes to my aid. The British. My ministers. The pashas. No one gives me a way to avoid war without giving up domains entrusted to me. The Muslims in every territory I might give to Russia to avoid war would be killed and driven out. No one cares about them. Pawns of those who call themselves the Powers. I have no choice. And if I show any lack of resolve, the pashas will surely depose me. Perhaps assassinate me, as I believe they did Abdülaziz."

Nigar was momentarily shaken. He spoke to her directly about matters of state in the manner she had hoped he would if he had invited her, as his wife, to be his partner, to share the joys and stresses of being sultan. She wanted to offer an opinion or console him. He looked older. Tired. Beaten down. Without joy. So different from the man in love she had known the previous summer. Now, he was a man in fear. The former had been her husband, the latter was the sultan. "I know you will do everything you can to help your subjects," she said after an awkward pause. She shifted in her chair. The audience had gone on too long.

TWENTY-NINE

"Russia has declared war, my sovereign." The speaker was Minister of War Redif Pasha. It was April 1877, and this was the first of many staccato pieces of information Abdülhamit would receive from this day until the end of the war. News, exaggerations, and lies arrived hourly via multiple sources like rain through a screen, finely disbursed detail that felt refreshing but not satisfying. Abdülhamit wanted more. He feared that he did not know what he needed to know, and he was convinced that if he read just one more spy's report, he might know truth.

"Parliament has declared war on Russia." The speaker was Ahmet Vefik, the man Abdülhamit had appointed to preside over parliament. Once the empire's ambassador to the Court of Napoleon III, Ahmet was well educated and known to be an arrogant Francophile.

"Thank you. This is the gravest decision the people can make, to declare war. You made them see their duty," Abdülhamit responded.

"Thank you, my sovereign. The people's representatives are not of high intelligence, but they increased income, property, and animal taxes and authorized the sale of war bonds, which they required property owners and civil servants to purchase. They also conferred on you the title of *Gazi*, as the sultan of a nation at war."

"Well done. With the help of Allah, we will succeed on the battlefield, as well."

A telegram from Vienna noted that Austria had informed Russia that she would remain neutral, a signal that Austria did not support a Russian pan-Slav gambit in its back yard.

A telegram from Bucharest confirmed that Rumania agreed to permit the Russian army to pass through its territory, but that Russia had declined Rumania's offer to contribute troops. The Russians would cross the Pruth River, the border between Russia and Rumania, in order to gain access to the Danube from favorable terrain in Rumania.

A telegram from Athens stated that the Greeks had offered to enter the war on the side of the Russians, but that their offer was also rejected. They may have asked too high a price. The Russians were pro-Slav and well aware of the dislike of the Bulgarians for the Greeks and the Greek Orthodox Church.

A spy's report from Belgrade observed that the Russians refused the Serbs' offer to join the war. The Serbs' offer to fight particularly irritated Abdülhamit, since the empire's troops only the previous year defeated a rebellion by the Serbs and refrained from wiping out the entire Serb army out of humanitarian compassion.

A cable from an informant in St. Petersburg explained that Russia saw allies as complicating the division of the empire after the war and as unnecessary militarily.

In several meetings, British Ambassador Layard assured Abdülhamit that Britain absolutely would not tolerate Russia's concept of a "big Bulgaria" from Burgas on the Black Sea to Dedeağaç on the Aegean, but he acknowledged that Britain's current policy was not to join the Turks in the war. Nevertheless, Abdülhamit heard in his sympathetic voice an implication that she might, if the war were protracted and went badly for him.

A dispatch from Berlin said that Bismark expressed the view that partition of the Ottoman Empire might be the best solution for the so-called "Eastern Question." This sentiment infuriated Abdülhamit, who saw the Western obsession with his country as a problem for them to solve as a sham pretext for colonial expansion.

An article by a Western journalist reporting from St. Petersburg noted that the Russians anticipated an easy victory in both the west and the east. The Russians were counting on the pro-Slav and anti-Muslim feelings of the local population in Bulgaria and from the Armenians in the empire's eastern provinces to facilitate their victory.

An article from another Western journalist in St. Petersburg questioned whether Russia's weak economy could sustain its army in a prolonged engagement and suggested that this would drive Russia to seek a quick victory.

Another reporter observed that Russia's primary concern was London. A change in the political wind could sail a flotilla of British ships to Gallipoli.

A report from the governor of Ardahan asked urgently for more troops. Ardahan was expected to be one of the first targets of the Russians in the east. The population was nervous about the rumored assault. Some had begun to migrate.

The Governor of Batum expressed confidence that his Black Sea port's geological advantages would permit the sultan's troops to withstand an assault even of a significantly larger number of Russian troops. He asked for support from the sea.

Many officials from the east spoke of Armenian support for a Russian invasion. Some feared local fighting between Muslims and Christians in a war environment. With the army engaged with the Russians, local vendettas could get out of control.

The Governor of Erzurum wrote of meeting with representatives of the American mission schools. These schools mostly educated Armenian Christians, yet the missionaries' concern was of a Russian occupation. The Russians did not tolerate protestant missionaries. These Christians, at least, expressed their hope for a Muslim victory. The report was one of the few to make Abdülhamit smile.

Abdülhamit met daily with Minister of War Redif. "The Russians have crossed the Pruth River?" Abdülhamit stated as a question. He did not have troops in Rumania, only in fortifications south of the Danube River, the border between the Rumanian and Danube provinces.

"Yes, my sovereign. Our sources say they will attempt to cross the Danube between Nikopolis and Rusçuk."

"Will we not attempt to stop them from crossing the Danube?" The war was upon him, and Abdülhamit realized that he knew nothing of military strategy or tactics. He was completely dependent on Redif and his commanders in the field. The war had been rumored and anticipated for months, but Redif had initiated nothing to stop the Russians. Abdülhamit had appointed Redif for his loyalty and lack of ambition, but if the war went badly, he, not Redif, would be blamed.

"We would be at a disadvantage to engage the Russians north of the Danube. We would have to fight at the place of their choosing. Whereas our troops are in highly fortified positions south of the Danube, which is swollen from spring rains. The Russians will find it difficult to cross, and if they succeed, they have to engage us where we're dug in. They'll be fighting between the Danube, which will block an easy retreat, and our fortresses, which will block their forward progress. We also control the Balkan passes. My plan is to make their advance too costly to continue, to trap them between the Danube and the Balkans for as long as it takes to force their retreat."

"I have reports from St. Petersburg that the Russians intend even to occupy Istanbul."

"Their army has set out from Kişinev, a thousand-kilometer march to Istanbul. They will not cross the Balkans."

"Thank you. May Allah be with us." Abdülhamit's voice was not confident. He sent for Commander Abdülkerim, commander in chief of the armed forces. In military matters, this was the man he trusted.

Abdülkerim was 71 years old. He had fought in several wars, including the Crimean War. He was a corpulent man who looked more like the scholar who had studied in Vienna for five years than the veteran commander of war. He had a full mustache that had retained a hint of color and turned down to merge into his heavy white beard. Between them, they covered most of his mouth. His relatively large nose was crooked but ironically contributed to his appearance as scholarly, rather than pugilistic. He inspired confidence. "The Russians are marching through Rumania to cross the Danube. Are we ready?" Abdülhamit asked.

"Yes, my sovereign. We have troops in well-fortified positions. They're armed with the Peabody-Martini rifles that can reach the Russians well before they are within range for their Krupps and Berdan rifles. We have the American cartridges made from solid brass. Very reliable. The Russians will suffer heavy losses in an attack on any of our positions."

"Why would they not skirt our positions and advance directly to the Balkan passes?"

"They know we would pursue them, and they would be trapped. To successfully cross the Balkan Mountains, they must first defeat our forces north of the Balkans. We have troops in Vidin, Nikopolis, Sistova, Rusçuk, Tirnova, Şumla, and Silistria. The Russians will be looking to retreat across the Danube before they reach the Balkan Mountains."

"What about our troops in Bosnia, Herzegovina, Albania, Serbia? Will you call on them?"

"The local populations in those provinces could see a withdrawal of our troops as an opportunity to rebel—even to declare independence. We will protect all your domains."

"And in the east?"

"We can supply our troops via the Black Sea. The Russians will have to transport everything they need over mountainous terrain anywhere they wish to attack. As in the west, our troops are in well-fortified positions, against which the Russians will be fighting at a disadvantage. Also, the Kurdish irregulars will harass them wherever they go."

An optimistic prognosis from Abdülkerim was balm to Abdülhamit's worried mind, but he sent several eunuchs to the city's taverns and coffeehouses to gauge public sentiment, just to be sure. Their reports were exciting. People were volunteering to fight. Businessmen were outfitting troops. People were buying bonds and giving jewelry and money to the treasury in support of the war against the hated Russians. The taverns were filled with raucous patrons singing patriotic songs.

Abdülhamit would not lead them in battle, but almost 400,000 troops with the best rifles in the world were in his hands. A modern navy of 132 vessels, second only to Britain's, flew the Ottoman flag under the command of Hobart Pasha, a thirty-year veteran of the British navy. The fleet was almost entirely ironclad. What power could defeat him? This was his moment. Allah had willed it. He would become the sultan whom history books would declare to have saved the Ottoman Empire. Once again, Ottoman power would lie like oil on the waters of the Mediterranean and Black Seas, feared even when it could not be seen. Ottoman authority would be respected on the continents of Europe, Asia, and Africa. His name would be honored in the cities holy to Muslims and the city holy to Christians.

There would be war, and it was not his fault. Parliament had declared it. There would be war, and he would be the victorious *Gazi*. He felt emotionally and physically strong as he put down the last report and prepared to retire to his bedroom, the sanctuary where he was adored, where he submitted to comfort and pleasure, and where he was absolute in all things. The place where his will was anticipated more than obeyed.

Tonight, he would call for the girl he had spotted who was new in the harem, a beauty from the Caucasus. A gift from a wealthy Armenian baker in Kars, who sought to supply the army in the east with hardtack biscuits, the only food the Ottoman government centrally procured for its soldiers. The army was marching beneath the flag of the Prophet, and the *Gazi* would conquer this delicacy in the harem. He knew the fragrance she would wear, and he could smell it. He knew her skin would shock his touch with its softness.

THIRTY

The war was as war is. Decided upon by men who did not fight, who took credit for victory and assigned blame for defeat. Fought by men who died. Some quickly and mercifully, others slowly and unspeakably. By men who fought for what was right and died at the hands of wrongdoers. By officers who ordered men to die and prayed to live forever in the Kingdom of Heaven. By officers who led, running and riding tall at the fore, and fell as every other corpse among the dying. By men spared under heavy fire in the arms of angels. By men who, in battle, were at one with the earth—digging holes in it, piling it high, listening to it absorb the thuds of shells, thanking it for protecting them. By men who, in death, returned to the earth. By physically and spiritually wounded men who lived beyond the war but without relief from it.

The war came to land-holders and landless, moneylenders and borrowers, merchants and shepherds, children and parents—all of them terrified. All branded as enemy so as to be eligible for death, rape, maiming, and plunder by the righteous. The war pitted humans against inhuman enemies—soldiers *and* civilians.

The war was recorded by correspondents and artists and critiqued by military attaches and soldiers of fortune. Everything was observed. Numerous chronicles shared some facts and disputed others.

The soldiers were nursed by surgeons and nightingales and mourned by mothers, wives, and poets.

The war was fought in the name of God, in the name of Allah, in the conviction that faith would bring victory, and in the anxiety of doubt. In the hearts of men under fire, belief waged war with reality. Survival became victory and confirmed faith. Survivors gave thanks in disbelief, crying aloud and silently, as they buried friends, comrades, family, and unidentifiable remains. Bodies and pieces of bodies that once loved and were loved were transferred to the Almighty as the dead's last source of love and the only hope of forgiveness for the living.

Bayonets in face-on confrontations killed men sweating fear in sub-zero temperatures. Bayonets killed the wounded and maimed corpses. Rifles, pistols, and cannons killed at distance and close up. Hundreds of thousands of rifles and pistols and tons of ammunition were manufactured, shipped, and placed in the hands of soldiers—at a profit.

What each fighter knew was that the enemies were murderers. Muslims knew that Christians had killed Muslims. Christians knew that Muslims had killed Christians. Every witnessed act had an apocryphal exaggeration. Combatants acted on the fear that if they did not slaughter the opposing religious adherents, they would be slaughtered by them. The fighters engaged with the motivation of revenge, the conviction of rectitude, and the fearlessness of the righteous. The fighters vowed to give their lives, but at the moment of death, it came unexpected.

THIRTY-ONE

"The Russians have taken possession of the Barboş Bridge across the Sereth River." The speaker was Minister of War Redif. "It means the Russians intend to cross the Danube west of the mouth of the Sereth River."

"Why didn't we attempt to prevent them from taking the bridge?" Abdülhamit asked.

"It would only have slowed them. We're waiting on the other side of the Danube. In retreat, they'll regret having crossed it."

Abdülhamit willed himself to have confidence, but Redif did not inspire it. He seemed as passive in his person as his offered strategy was defensive. To Abdülhamit, the capture of the Barboş Bridge was his first loss of the war.

Bad news came daily. In the east the Russians advanced on Kars. The defense of the east depended on holding Kars. The Russians were also making a move for the port of Batum, a prized possession for Black Sea commerce and key to the Ottoman supply of troops in the east. To reach Batum, the Russians had to cross several mountain ranges, but by late April they had captured Muchaster, the main town on the route to Batum. Another loss.

In the west, Hobart Pasha, commander of the Turkish fleet, urgently requested permission to take control of the Danube River. He had ironclad monitors anchored at the Black Sea port of Sulina. But weeks passed before approval came. It was too late. The Russians were already in place all along the Danube's northern banks. Starting up the Danube, Hobart's ironclads

238

sustained heavy fire from shore and were forced to retreat. Within a few days the Russians had mined the river. Already an advantage Abdülhamit had been assured was his had been negated. He read reports long into the night, searching for some observation that would reassure him. In vain.

The Russians intersected the road to Ardahan en route to Kars, cutting off supplies and reinforcements to both cities. Also in the east, the Turkish defenders abandoned Doğubayazıt as the Russians approached to attack. How could his soldiers abandon their post?

Despite the grim news, Redif assured him that the Russians would not take Kars or Erzurum, the main defensive positions in the east, and that in the west the Russians would soon regret their ambition. "When they cross the Danube, we're ready for them," he said almost daily. But Abdülhamit was not reassured by strategic talk of losing battles to win a war.

The month of May did not begin well. A Russian mortar pierced the armored deck of Turkey's flagship *Luft-i-Celil* and sank it in the Danube, along with its 217 crew and four, 150-pounder guns. An intercepted dispatch from a Western military attaché at the front criticized the Turks' failure to use its naval fleet early on to prevent the Russians from reaching the shores of the Danube, an observation that fueled Abdülhamit's failing confidence in his military pashas.

To the fire of permitting the Russian army to cross its territory, the province of Rumania added fuel by declaring its independence from the Ottoman Empire on May 11. Abdülhamit was furious. If, as he was assured, his troops would drive the Russians back across the Danube, the Rumanians would be at his mercy, and he intended to show little. He envisioned armistice terms under which he would quadruple their annual payment.

And he would assign to Rumania the tax collectors about whom he received the most complaints of corruption.

In the east, the Russians reached the port of Batum and were shelling it from the hills. "We have an ironclad in the port," Redif reported. "It will make short work of the Russians above Batum. And we have sent ironclads north to bomb the Russian cities of Poti and Sukum. We will incite a revolt among the Muslim Abkhazians and force the Russians to return home to address it."

But on May 17, Redif was forced to report that the Russians had overrun Ardahan. "They shelled it with long range artillery."

"What were our casualties?"

"The report I have does not mention our losses, but those who escaped are on the road to Erzurum. The Russians will never take Erzurum."

"What about Kars?"

"It's our most heavily fortified city. Your troops will defend it to the last man."

The eastern and western war fronts had Western military attachés and reporters from the Western press following every Turkish and Russian unit. The next day Abdülhamit learned from one of their dispatches that, in capturing Ardahan, the Russians had taken at least 1,000 prisoners, almost 100 field guns, and a large quantity of ammunition and stores. The report estimated Turkish losses at 3,000 dead and wounded and the Russian dead and wounded at less than 600. It was simple math, and Abdülhamit again questioned the strategy of waiting to be attacked. It was not working in the east. Why would it work in the west?

On the same day, Abdülhamit received reports from several sources that the Russians were setting up siege batteries to the north, west, and east of Kars.

Even in Yıldız Palace, Abdülhamit felt under attack. First, a friend of Mithat's in parliament circulated a petition, requesting that Abdülhamit bring Mithat back from Europe, and 90 deputies signed it. Then, angry about the news from the east, the deputies voted unanimously that Abdülhamit bring Mahmut Nedim to trial for getting the empire into the war. Nedim had been grand vizier under Abdülaziz and had the nickname of "Nedimov" because of his fawning relationship with Russian Ambassador Ignatiev. Mithat had dismissed him on the deposition of Abdülaziz. Abdülhamit took umbrage that parliament thought it their prerogative to direct him to do either of these things. He did nothing.

Suddenly, everyone thought they knew how to win the war. The *softa*s, in protest of the loss of Ardahan, demanded Minister of War Redif's resignation and proposed that they take part in parliament's deliberations. Abdülhamit shared their reservations about his *serasker*, but he thought that the country definitely did not need *softa* voices added to the babble of parliament. He used a provision in the constitution to declare the constitution to be threatened and exiled the *softa*s from Istanbul.

From the east, more bad news. The strategy to cause an Abkhazian revolt had back-fired. The Russian troops retreated into the mountains out of range of the Turkish fleet's guns, and the civilian Muslim population poured onto the docks to be rescued. They knew that whenever the fleet left, the Russians would come for revenge. Over the course of the summer, 50,000 refugees were ferried from Abkhazia to Ottoman ports.

Abdülhamit was angry about the stupidity of the maneuver and chided Abdülkerim roundly for it, but at the same time he found comfort in the honor of rescuing Muslims. Anatolia was significantly depopulated from disease and drought. The

Empire needed people to return the land to productivity. The influx of refugees in Istanbul was a problem, but Anatolia needed them.

By the end of May, the Russians were in complete control of the Danube. They sank a second Turkish ironclad, torpedoed a monitor, and blocked passage of the river with small torpedo boats. No one any longer had the courage to tell Abdülhamit that this was not significant. Nor would he have believed them. He read the foreign press accounts translated for him daily. The empire had borrowed heavily to purchase its powerful fleet. Now, the fleet was useless.

Abdülhamit put down the last of the reports. Soon, he would know the efficacy of the strategy to trap the Russians between the Danube and the Balkans. He walked into the gardens of Yıldız Palace. All was quiet. Dark. He was alone but safe. That was the beauty of Yıldız Palace. He could be alone among trees, flowerbeds, a lake, and the sounds of birds and animals. Alone with the burden of being sultan, of being *Gazi* for a nation at war, of being Caliph to Muslims fleeing to his bosom. Alone with the burden of not knowing whom to trust to carry out his will. Unsure even of what his will should be.

THIRTY-TWO

The London newspapers provided Mithat a panoramic window on the war between his country and Russia. The papers had multiple reporters with the Russian and Turkish forces, reporting the movement of every army, division, and battalion. They reported on strategy and on tactical movements, beforehand and after the fact. They wrote details of the locations and geographic settings of strategic sites and battles, descriptions that were vivid to Mithat, having served as governor of the Danube Province. For each town mentioned, he could recall the names of some and the faces of many people he had met—Muslims, Jews, and Christians. War was surely ending the lives of many and changing the lives of everyone.

Mithat had known Britain as friend; Russia as enemy; and Austria-Hungary, Germany, and France as countries that could be influenced by Britain and reason. In Europe, he saw that reason had little impact and that Britain was politically divided. Queen Victoria and Prime Minister Disraeli wanted to intervene on the side of the Turks, but Foreign Minister Lord Derby and opposition leader Gladstone were strongly opposed, as was public opinion. Until June.

In June, the news of the war began to change public opinion as people read of Russia's military success and reports that the Russian army was inciting civilian carnage. They read of how in the east, in preparing to attack Doğubayazıt, the Russians armed the local Christian Armenians. The result was a massacre of Muslim civilians and Russia's capture of Doğubayazıt.

News quickly followed that Russia had crossed the Danube and captured fortified cities, partly with the help of their majority

Christian populations. Many of the Muslim residents who did not escape were killed. Accounts in the papers described refugees from the cities and surrounding Muslim villages filling the roads, fleeing the bear, fleeing their neighbors, fleeing the crimes of war. Walking with whatever they could carry or pile on an ox-cart without protector or certain destination.

By the end of the month, the papers reported the Russians in force south of the Danube. And in the east, the Russian army had Batum and Kars under siege. From London, as Russia overran Ottoman territory, she looked to be threatening British interests from Egypt to India.

"I promise you that Britain will not tolerate Russian occupation of Istanbul or the Gallipoli Peninsula. The Queen will not accept it. Public opinion will not," Prime Minister Disraeli assured Mithat. Disraeli knew that what he promised was little solace, but it was all he felt confident to pledge. "Our ambassador in Russia reports that the Russians cannot bear the cost of a long war," he added as consolation.

"My government intends to trap the Russians between the Balkans and the Danube. The Russians will be forced to withdraw if they cannot cross the Balkans before winter," Mithat reported, based on news from Istanbul. "I lived there. No army can march or be supplied during a Balkan winter." Mithat's tone lacked confidence.

"We'll pray that works—for you and for us." Disraeli's tone also did not reflect confidence in the strategy, but he did not say anything of the Russian military successes. That would serve no purpose, nor be news to Mithat.

"Our soldiers will bear whatever it takes to halt the Russian advance." Mithat struggled to be upbeat, but the meeting was disappointing. He had hoped that Disraeli would say Britain had decided to enter the war. It was the only way for Britain to secure with certainty an outcome that protected her interests. Surely she must know this.

Mithat took little comfort from the London press's pivot to pro-Turk editorials. Even though the Turks were winning some of the battles, most of the news was of Russian success, both in the west and the east. The reports of civilian massacres and of roads filling with Muslim refugees were particularly troubling. He knew what would happen. In other places where the Muslims had the advantage and the Turkish army looked to be the victor, Muslims would kill Christians. And, of course, that happened. A quick end to the war was essential. That could only happen if Britain were to enter the war or demand Russian withdrawal as the condition for remaining out of it.

As frustrating as it was for him to be in London, Mithat accepted that he might be in the only place where he could influence the war. Regardless of what happened on the battlefield, London could have a voice in the outcome of the war and of peace. She just had to say she was in. That's what Mithat urged in the editorial he wrote that night. A show of British resolve could bring peace and save tens of thousands from misery and death. And in his letter to his family, he expressed his sense of purpose. Surely his exile was Allah's will. He would do in London what he would have done at home. Devote himself to the cause of his country.

THIRTY-THREE

"Commander Muhtar has again engaged the Russian forces besieging Kars," Minister of War Redif reported to Abdülhamit. "The Russians suffered heavy casualties."

Redif's failure to mention Turkish casualties let Abdülhamit know that they were significant. But he did not ask about that. No point in diminishing good news.

Muhtar commanded his forces in the east. He was his youngest commander and his best. In contrast to the strategy in the west of waiting for the Russians to attack, Muhtar had begun taking the fight to the Russians. Successfully, for the most part. Muhtar knew the terrain and people of the eastern front well, having served as governor of Erzurum. He also was seasoned in the Montenegrin campaign of 1862, in Yemen a decade later, and most recently in suppressing the uprisings in Bosnia and Herzegovina. Abdülhamit welcomed Muhtar's cables. "Does Commander Muhtar have what he needs?" Abdülhamit asked.

"His troops have the American rifles and plenty of ammunition. He also has support from the Kurdish irregulars. The key cities of Kars, Batum, and Erzurum are well fortified. Our troops are massing to retake Doğubayazıt. The Russians will find it hard to hold. They're in a hostile environment. In addition to the Kurds, eastern Anatolia and the Black Sea coast have Muslims of many ethnic groups that the Russians brutally expelled from the Caucasus. They will harass supply convoys and take revenge where they can."

"And in the west? What word on the Russian movements there?" Abdülhamit knew this question made Redif uncomfortable.

246

"Abdülkerim reports that the Russians appear poised to cross the Danube near Galatz. He's waiting for them," Redif responded nervously, knowing Abdülhamit's skepticism.

"Yes, he's waiting," Abdülhamit reiterated with displeasure. "Perhaps tomorrow you'll report some success from this waiting."

Abdülkerim was in command of the forces on the western front. Aloof and secretive, he was known to ignore the military views of others, as well as requests for elucidation of his own. He did what he did, which, since the declaration of war more than a month ago, effectively had been nothing. Given his seniority and experience, he was the logical choice to command the forces on the western front. But Abdülhamit's doubts were reinforced by reports in the foreign press that cited foreign military attaches' criticisms of the Ottoman strategy. No one seemed to think it wise to wait for the Russians to cross the Danube River. Foreign reporters also commented on Abdülkerim's corpulence, saying that he was unable even to mount a horse and that he rarely left his quarters. His posture, one observed, was as though expecting victory in sheer deference to his age and stature.

Abdülhamit was growing impatient. Redif had been an adequate *serasker* when his job consisted of telling Abdülhamit what he wanted to hear. Now he was responsible to prevent the Russians from seizing large chunks of the Ottoman Empire, to conceive and execute a strategy to counter a determined enemy that was launching a two-front assault. Abdülhamit suspected that Redif was not up to his assignment, and yet, Abdülhamit hesitated to act. The battle in the west had not begun. Perhaps the Russians *would* regret crossing the Danube.

In the east, Muhtar continued to have success, though at a cost. His forces succeeded in retaking Doğubayazıt, but when the city surrendered, the Kurdish irregulars took no prisoners.

Many Russian soldiers and Armenian civilians died before the Turkish commander established order. Remnants of the Russian army fled into the mountains, followed by the Armenian civilian population of the area. This news disturbed Abdülhamit. The Armenians were members of his flock. He relied on Armenians personally. He was troubled by their alliance with the Russians but equally by the revenge taken on them as helpless civilians, now forced into the mountains as refugees. Imagining their plight, he saw the faces of children. Those of his children. Those of the children in the streets. Those of strangers' children who kissed his hand for sweets at Şeker Bayramı. Why had the pashas forced him into this war?

Throughout the month of June, Muhtar held off Russian assaults on Batum and Kars, taking and inflicting heavy casualties. And in Istanbul, the first session of parliament came to an end. Abdülhamit no longer had to endure reports of what was said there, particularly doubts expressed about the handling of the war. Much as he wished otherwise, he knew he would be held accountable for the war, and any expression of doubt about how it was conducted was an expression of doubt about him.

The last days of June foretold the disaster of July. "The Russians are crossing the Danube, my sovereign," Redif reported. "Abdülkerim has more than two hundred thousand of your heroic troops at his command. They will make the Russians regret the crossing," he said with forced conviction.

Abdülhamit listened politely. "The foreign press reports that our men on guard in the hills near where the Russians crossed withdrew without a fight," he observed dryly.

Redif felt challenged. "We did not expect the Russians to cross at that point. We had too few men there. But the Russians will not take our fortified positions."

"Let me know when Russian regret for crossing the river is based on defeats in battle," Abdülhamit responded with obvious sarcasm.

The Russians easily took the fortifications at Sistova, where its Bulgarian Christian population provided support and celebrated by killing most of the city's Muslim population before they could escape. To his surprise, Abdülhamit read reports of this slaughter in the British press. Perhaps the British would finally see that atrocities were as easily perpetrated by one side as by the other. He discussed this with British Ambassador Layard, with whom he met regularly. Layard offered condolences and once again promised to urge London to intervene.

The news quickly got worse. Russian engineers built a pontoon bridge over the river that facilitated easy crossing for troops and supplies. And on June 28, as if to taunt Abdülhamit, Tsar Alexander II crossed the river to congratulate his troops. No accidental symbolism. The Russian army and the leader of Russia were physically in the Ottoman Empire.

This news shocked Abdülhamit. He could hardly tolerate leaving the Yıldız Palace compound for the Friday Noon Prayer. A sultan at the site of war was the manner of the sultans of centuries before. He could not imagine going to a battlefield, even to rally troops from beyond the reach of enemy fire.

July brought unremitting losses. The Russians captured the city of Tirnovo, the ancient capital of Bulgaria, which gave them an open road to the Balkans. A concerted two-day attack on the heavily fortified city of Nikopolis netted victory, along with 7,000 Turkish prisoners, munitions, supplies, and arms. The foreign press was expressing surprise at the failure of the Ottoman army to coordinate. The Russians were picking off one position after another while substantial Turkish forces remained guarding positions not under attack or in danger of it.

"We have the passes guarded, my sovereign. The Russians will not cross the Balkans. They will be trapped," Redif assured Abdülhamit.

"Where will they try to cross?"

"Şıbka is the best pass. The road is wide and hardened. The heaviest guns can be pulled over Şıbka. We're waiting for them there."

It won't be a long wait, Abdülhamit thought, but said nothing. He had lost all faith in Redif.

But instead of attacking Şıbka directly from the north, as the Turks expected, the Russians sent one army across the Balkans over a narrow footpath that Russian engineers widened so that field cannon could be dragged over it. The Russians were able to attack the Şıbka defenses simultaneously from the north and the south. It was a two-day battle but not a serious contest. The Ottoman forces guarding the approaches to the pass were overrun on the first day and those guarding the fort at the top of the pass were forced to retreat after the second day.

From the foreign press, Abdülhamit learned that the Russians had lost only 14 men in taking the pass to heavy losses of his own men, including 400 taken prisoner. The Russians now seemed in possession of the very ground—that between the Danube and the Balkans—that Redif had assured him would be their graveyard. Abdülhamit stared at the large map on his wall. The road from Şıbka, over which military traffic could pass at speed and quantity, led directly to Sofia and on to Adrianople and Istanbul.

If the Russians could not be stopped before crossing the Balkans, how could they be stopped from marching into Istanbul? Abdülhamit resolved to act. He needed more troops, more money, and different military leadership. He rallied the public with the standard of the Prophet to raise volunteers and money. He appointed Rauf Pasha to replace Redif as *serasker*. And he replaced Abdülkerim with Mehmet Ali as commander for the western front. Mehmet Ali was a young commander in the mold of Muhtar in the east. Mehmet Ali had been born in France, was raised by Germans, and arrived in Istanbul as a teenage hand on a merchant ship. He became the protégé of a Turkish pasha and graduated from the military academy. Although he had converted to Islam, he was disliked by some of his officer colleagues, who viewed him as a foreigner. But Abdülhamit knew of his exemplary military record and liked him personally.

"I've sent word for Commander Osman Pasha to proceed as rapidly as possible to Plevna. We must stop the Russian army before they can advance to Sofia." The speaker was Rauf Pasha, Abdülhamit's new minister of war. "Plevna's geographic setting gives it natural fortifications, and Osman and his men can reach it in a few days."

Abdülhamit looked at the map. "So, Plevna will decide the war?"

"Yes. I believe so. Commander Osman will fight to the last man, and the last man will die to save him. And you, my sovereign."

******

Osman was of medium height with a large head. Bright eyes and a Roman nose marked a long, handsome face that was framed by a full beard and heavy mustache that grew into each other without evidence of where one began and the other ended. Despite the abundant facial hair, his face looked open, inviting—the face of a man that suggested a loquacious and convivial demeanor in complete contrast to his nature. Thick,

251

beautiful hair almost entirely hid ears so small as to appear without purpose—an after-thought on a man intended to be more listened to than listening. His red fez rested elegantly on his large head, increasing his physical stature. His large-boned structure, barrel chest, strong hands, and steel posture made his quietly articulated verbal directives law. He was Commander Osman Nuri Pasha.

As the Russians began crossing the Danube, Osman was stationed at Vidin in the Danube Province with approximately 20,000 troops under his command. The Russian strategy was obvious—cross the Balkans and march to the center of Bulgaria and on to Istanbul. Vidin was too far west to be a target in this strategy. And, as was a pattern, Istanbul was indecisive. By the time his orders to march to Plevna arrived, he knew that it would require an extraordinary effort for him to reach it before the Russians. He set out on July 13 under an intense sun.

The boots of 20,000 soldiers, the wheels and draft animals of several hundred carts, and the hooves of hundreds of cavalry horses and pack animals raised a cloud of dust that choked the nostrils and throats of the men marching in determined will to do their duty, to die, if that was their fate, on this road or in the battle at the end of it. Osman stopped his horse periodically, watched them pass, and urged them on in his understated tone that rested in the ears of his men more powerfully than the most demandingly shouted command. He loved these men. He asked nothing of them that he did not demand of himself. Resolve, endurance, discipline.

They were passing through rural countryside with numerous villages, whose residents saw the dust approaching long before the army passed their gardens, fields, and vineyards filled with produce. All the residents of the villages, regardless of religion or ethnicity, were the sultan's subjects. He, Commander

Osman Nuri Pasha, was responsible for their safety and the protection of their produce and property. The men, whose ration was two biscuits per day, understood this. Not a single grape was to be eaten from the vineyards passed. Not a single tomato plucked or ear of corn stripped from a stalk.

"Sergeant Ahmet," Osman called out in the heat of the fourth day. "Please step forward." A man distinguishable from the other dust-covered troops only by the sergeant's bars on his arms stepped forward. "Empty your pockets," Osman said in a quiet, almost fatherly tone, in response to which Ahmet pulled out a few tobacco leaves. "You stole those leaves from the field we just passed. You are a disgrace to the Ottoman army," Osman said as he ripped Ahmet's sergeant's bars from his arms. He raised the cane he carried and brought it down on Ahmet's left shoulder. Ahmet winced in pain and turned slightly just as the cane came down on his right shoulder and took him to his knees. Osman struck him several times on his back as he bent over, whispering, "Forgive me, my commander. I made a mistake. I ask for forgiveness in the name of Allah."

Osman swung his cane without anger. He did not curse the man as he struck him. He simply carried out his duty as commander to enforce his order and administer punishment. "Discipline," he said to his next in command, Tevfik Bey, "it's the only indispensable weapon in war, the one weapon that can decide a battle with certainty. If we lose discipline, we may as well surrender without wasting the lives of our soldiers."

The July sun was not relieved by even an occasional cloud. Each man carried 70-100 rounds, a rifle, a sword, and gear. To reach Plevna before the Russians, Osman determined that he needed to cover the 120 miles in six days. They rested little and only at noon. Less hydration was lost while walking between sunset and sunrise. They had adequate biscuits for the two-per-day-per-man ration he had set, but inadequate water. The men were allowed to supplement the rationed water from such sources as they could find. Most of the streams at this time of year did not run clean. Men got dysentery and could not keep up, fell from sunstroke, and died along the road.

Osman watched soldiers collapse. They were tough men who endured as long as they could and without complaint until they lost the battle against these unseen enemies. Soon, he would send these soldiers into battle, where some would die and some would be wounded fighting an enemy they could see and hear. But after the battle, he would have the wounded cared for. They would not be left on the side of the road. But just as the enemy on this march was different, so was the tactic of engagement. Osman could not wait or go back for the suffering. Reaching Plevna before the Russians would decide the fate of his country.

On July 19, Osman and his troops reached Plevna just ahead of the Russians. Plevna lay at the juncture of two rivers, the Grivitza and the Tutchenitza, and one creek with more raw sewage than water that had the presumptive name of Vid River. Osman assessed the defenses. There were rudimentary earthen defensive works guarding the approaches to the city from every direction. Extended ridges and hills covered in oak and beech trees provided natural obstruction from three sides. Numerous gardens, vineyards, and fields of corn met the eye in every direction. The fields showed the care of farmers who took pride in them. Men would die here, Osman thought. He might die here. And so would nature—the trees, the vineyards, the corn fields. In the course of armies fighting to destroy each other, this perfect vista would be destroyed. He would protect the citizens of the town, the territory of his sultan; he could not protect the natural beauty of this place or the produce and property of the sultan's subjects.

"I want three lines of defensive trenches on the slopes of the hills connecting the earthen dugouts," he said to Tevfik. "I'm going into the town to speak with the residents."

Plevna, a city of reportedly 17,000 people, was not different from many in Bulgaria with which Osman was familiar. It had narrow cobblestone streets in poor repair. Churches, mosques, a market, a school, small shops, one very large house, several other houses suggestive of affluence, but predominantly the small houses of residents of subsistence to modest means. Many of the houses also housed animals on the ground floor, as well as in pens next to the houses. No animals were left outside the city at night. The town smelled like the residential extension of the farming and animal husbandry on which it depended. In the Danube Province, even small cities were ethnically and religiously diverse: Bulgarian, Turkish, and other Muslims; Bulgarian, Greek, and other Christians; and sometimes gypsies, a few Jewish families, and the occasional European doctor or entrepreneur. Plevna was majority Bulgarian Christian.

Osman saw that the houses that suggested wealthy owners were empty. Residents of means had left the city, having heard that two armies were intent on it as the prize over which they would battle. Men of means could take their families and leave, expecting to return when the war was over to pledge allegiance to the winning side and reclaim what was theirs with the help of the victors. Ordinary men knew that their only hope of retaining what little they had was to stay next to it, to guard it until abandoning it was the only way to save their lives and those of their children, a reckoning each person knew would depend on which side won.

Outside the context of war, the diverse residents of the town played complementary roles in the economic life of the town. Each needed the other. Accepting each other was not a question of tolerance but of intercommunal dependence and mutual benefit. But the residents knew that war between Christian and Muslim armies would change centuries of accepted order. Profound disorder seemed certain. And yet, many stayed. Everything they had was here.

Osman walked the streets, greeted the people, and asked them to come to the square where he would address them. At the square, perhaps two hundred men gathered in front of where he stood. A few women and clusters of children stood further back. His message to them was that he was there to protect them as subjects of the sultan, regardless of their religion, and that his troops knew that he would tolerate no harm to civilians or pilfering of produce from their fields. He promised that the army would purchase what they needed from them and would hire them to use their draft animals and carts to bring the wounded from the battlefield. He wished them safety from the inevitable shells that would miss their targets and expressed his hope to speak to them again when there was peace.

As they set about preparing the defenses, Osman's soldiers gave thanks to Allah for the abundant supply of water here and drank deeply. They had no time to rest from their march and set about immediately unloading the pack horses that carried the picks and shovels. At least now they could spare the sweat extracted from throwing their backs into digging the trenches Osman ordered. Sweat rolled from their foreheads, burned their eyes and was absorbed by every piece of clothing. They tasted it and smelled it. Sweat was a part of war. Some from fear, some from exertion. A part of each man and groups of men, of the air, and of the memories and myths of the war that would follow them long after the war was over. Sweat unlike other sweat.

By midnight, the trenches were adequate, and the soldiers could turn to Mecca and pray before falling deeply asleep on biscuit-fed stomachs, too tired even to dread or feel excitement for the war awaiting them.

In his austere tent with its cot and small writing table, Osman ate his biscuit, drank water, and indulged himself afterwards with one cup of Turkish coffee, which he sipped as slowly as any he had savored in his life. Fifteen thousand of his soldiers had survived the march, and they had just barely arrived in time. They joined a few thousand soldiers who had been garrisoned here. Intelligence reports put the Russians at 13,000. What would be the Russian mode of attack? Tactics would matter. Resolve, fortitude, and discipline would matter. His troops were ready. He was ready. And like his soldiers, he fell deeply asleep.

The Russians began lobbing shells at 4:00 a.m. from a distant wooded slope. The Turkish command reveille sounded immediately, and Osman's soldiers responded as though rising from a good night's sleep. No disorder, no muttered discontent, no swearing. They took their positions and waited.

"Answer each volley," Osman ordered his gunners. "Fire as soon as an enemy gun gives away its position." The engagement did nothing more than state each side's intent to do battle. Neither side's guns could do effective damage from such distance. Eventually, the Russian troops began to advance, but the Turkish rifles pinned the Russians down beyond where they were a threat.

The day passed with almost no Turkish casualties. Russians had fallen quickly at first, until they retreated beyond the reach of the Peabody-Martini rifles. Both sides continued to lob shells with long range artillery to little effect.

Osman sat in his tent that night, sipping his one cup of coffee for the day. Obviously, the Russians would change tactics. Intelligence reports said reinforcements had been requested. He had sent out his own request for help. If the Russians waited for reinforcements, several days might pass with no action. He would have his troops expand and deepen the earthen defensive fortresses. And wait for the enemy to show his hand.

The wait was over on the following morning. The Russians formed closed ranks and charged the trenches with bayonets fixed. They did not even try to use their inferior rifles. They ran at the trenches while the Turks picked them off. Soldiers in the closed formations fell, but the majority kept running, coming for the trenches. Osman watched this suicidal attack with his field glasses from one of the hills where he had his command post. The Russian officers wore white uniforms and were as easy a target as you could wish for and fell one after the other, each replaced by another, until the Russians were at the first trench, clashing bayonet to bayonet with its defenders.

Osman marveled at the courage and discipline of the Russian soldiers and particularly of their officers. Without the officers taking the first bullets, falling before them and being replaced by others, no army's soldiers would have continued in closed formation to assault the Peabody-Martini lead. Russian officers and soldiers fell in multitudes, and yet the closed formations kept coming with some soldiers seemingly wrapped in the arms of angels, keeping them from harm, keeping them upright and shouting "hurrah, hurrah, hurrah," echoed by the Turks' cries of "Allah, Allah, Allah." The dueling shouts echoed in the hills even above the noise of the long guns, the rifles, and the steel on steel of bayonets. Cries of desperation, victory, or the common password to heaven and hell.

The Russians kept coming and prevailed in the bayonet to bayonet fighting in the first trench and then the second. But when they attempted to assault the third, there were too few left in the arms of those angels, too many bullets finding the mark

258

of those still standing, too few white officer uniforms without holes oozing red. The hearts of even the bravest men recognized suicide. Fear of death overtook the glory of death. Comrades fighting to save each other found themselves standing alone, their comrades lying beside them.

The remaining Russians retreated over the bodies of their comrades, the bodies of their enemy, the bodies of the dead and of those praying for death. They fled, thanking God, vowing never to be brave again, vowing to return to the mothers, wives, and lasses left behind in the villages of Mother Russia.

Osman watched. He issued no orders. None was needed. His men fought bayonet to bayonet and prevailed. With the Russians retreating, he considered giving the order for pursuit, but his men were exhausted from the march to Plevna, the shoveling, and the fighting. And his cavalry was inadequate in number and consisted of Circassian irregulars whom he did not trust. He would not have the reputation of his army sullied by what they might do if sent in pursuit. And if he succeeded in killing even a large number of the fleeing Russians, it would not end the war. To end the war, he had to stop the Russians at Plevna.

THIRTY-FOUR

"Have you met Commander Osman Pasha?" asked a moderately plump lady in the front row with pink cheeks and wearing a flowered green dress and a large white hat with a rose in the band. "From what I read in the papers, his stand at Plevna was an historic triumph of generalship and courage."

"Yes, Madam," Mithat responded. "I have met him. He is among the finest of our generals. The men believe in him."

Mithat was the guest at a benevolent society meeting in London. There were many of these societies of middle and upper class women devoted to helping the omnipresent poor of London. The society members raised money, but giving money to the poor was not their main mission, and many members considered giving money to be counterproductive. They braved filthy and dangerous streets to reach the hovels of the poor, advising them on health, sanitation, available services, and child rearing. And they read from the Bible, leaving copies as a witness to their Christian charity with people they knew could not read.

But the Turks' war with Russia provided a new platform for good works for some of these societies, particularly after the Turks' victory at Plevna, which raised public consciousness of the war and the prospect that the Turks might defeat the Russians. Politically, Britain might not be willing to enter the war on the Turks' side, but that did not mean the British people did not want the Turks to win. Some of the benevolent societies were raising money for the Turkish cause. Mithat was a guest at a meeting of one of these.

"We decided at our last meeting to contribute to the war effort of your country," said the president with an air of importance that implied their contribution would surely be the key to an Ottoman victory. Her husband was a member of the House of Lords. "We would like your thoughts on what and how we might contribute."

"Thank you very much. My country is grateful for any assistance you might provide. The need for medical supplies in particular is beyond what was anticipated."

Mithat knew that this appeal would be well received. The Ottoman army's medical corps was near to non-existent, and the number of doctors and facilities in cities and towns in or near battle zones was inadequate. At the outset of the war, the Ottoman government advertised for surgeons and hired them from all over the world. British physicians, in particular, answered the call, and London papers carried accounts from Plevna and other battle sites of doctors working under appalling conditions to administer to the wounded in makeshift hospitals, sometimes without anesthesia or means to sterilize instruments. A Dr. Sarell managed the ambulance services for the Ottoman Red Crescent Society. The work of doctors Gill, Heath and Crook was known. On the eastern front, doctors Stover and Striven walked 150 miles to Erzurum over a snow-drifted mountain road they could track only because a telegraph line ran along it. British doctors were on both the eastern and western fronts. The Ottoman troops and commanders held these physicians in high regard. Some physicians died. Some lived under enemy fire and amidst disease and filth, working as though unaware of the danger, because doing what could be done, no matter how little, was their oath and their constitutional makeup.

"I don't understand why we're not fighting with the Turks," exclaimed one of the women. "Did you read in today's *Daily Telegraph* of the massacres of Muslims by Christian Bulgarians? Surely Christians would not have done that without Russian provocation," said a thin woman in a red dress with skin so pale and perfect that she seemed a living portrait, waiting to be hung in a gallery.

"Did you see the photographs in *The Illustrated London News* that showed the desperate conditions of refugees along the roads in Bulgaria?" asked another.

"Yes, and the carts carrying the wounded from Plevna to Sofia, where beggars were lined up for alms," said the lady in the white hat.

"Yes, giving alms at a time when you might die is considered felicitous in Islam, I understand, and the beggars exploit this," observed the lady with the perfect skin.

"I read that the queen herself gave money to the Turkish Compassionate Fund," observed a plump woman from the back. "Surely, we can do something."

"There's an English woman, Lady Strong, who is running a hospital for the war wounded in Sofia. She wrote recently to our Lord Mayor, seeking donations. How much could we afford to send?" asked the president.

"I suggest we have a special fund-raising event," responded the woman who was the society's treasurer. "Mithat Pasha, might we count on you to address such an event?"

"Of course. It would be my honor and obligation to my country." It was not something he enjoyed, but he could not refuse. He reflected on that obligation in his letter to his family that night:

I believe that my role in raising awareness of the injustice of the war and eliciting sympathy and money may be more useful to the war effort than any newspaper editorial I have written. These Christian benevolent societies are remarkable in their willingness to raise money to help Muslim soldiers fighting a Christian enemy. I have given this much thought. Our own country's historic tolerance made it a safe haven for Jews and many other non-Muslims. They benefited from taking refuge, and we benefited from taking them in. My dream is for the Ottoman Empire to lead the world as the country in which men of diverse faiths live peacefully together. Unfortunately, in starting this war, Russia is exacerbating religious hatreds. Worse yet, I fear it will destroy any chance of our country becoming a constitutional monarchy with a sultan answerable to the people.

He put his pen down and looked at the letter. He was sure that Abdülhamit read every letter. Did it matter that the last sentence might displease Abdülhamit? He did not intend ever to work for the government again. If he were permitted to return home, he would retire and live out his years raising beautiful flowers, spending time with his wives and children, assuring they received the best education. Yes, he did want to return home. He obliterated the last sentence.

Tend beautiful flower gardens and spend time with his family. Yes, he would do that. But he would also continue to write and advocate for democracy. He knew he would never give up the dream, however remote it might become. And tonight he would write yet another editorial making the case for why Britain should join his country in the war. Perhaps with just the right turn of phrase... He would not sleep until it was finished. And tomorrow he would request another meeting with Prime Minister Disraeli. He had not seen him since the Russians' defeat at Plevna. Surely, that victory would help Disraeli to advocate that Britain join with the Turks.

THIRTY-FIVE

"You're the woman who brought candy to the children for Şeker Bayramı," Fatma said, looking at Nigar critically, questioningly. What was this Christian woman doing here again?

"Yes, my name is Nigar." She only used her Muslim name now. She was comfortable with it. Comfortable being a Muslim, even though she knew that Muslims did not accept her as Muslim and saw a Christian when they looked at her. They observed the superficial things. That she had blue eyes and auburn hair. That she did not carry herself like a Muslim woman. That she did not wear a veil, only a light scarf over her head that allowed some of her hair to show. She felt no need to camouflage what she was, a European who had adopted Islam. People stared at her even on those rare occasions when she wore a transparent veil in the manner of the wives of the pashas in order not to offend the pious, such as when entering a mosque.

"But you're a Christian?" Fatma stated with a questioning intonation.

"I *was* a Christian. I accepted Islam. I accept Allah as the sole deity and Muhammed as his Prophet," Nigar responded with the phraseology requisite to become a Muslim. "Your name is Fatma, isn't it?"

"Yes, but why are you here?" Fatma asked, not accusingly, just curiously.

"I'm here to ask for your help. I have gardens in Kağıthane. I'm raising vegetables for the food kitchen here."

"I'm an old woman. What do you need from me?"

"I'm a Muslim, but everyone sees me as a Christian. People are suspicious of Christians, especially now because of the war and the refugees coming from the Danube Province. I need someone here that people trust, someone who can prevent chaos when I deliver my produce and who can convince the refugees to eat what I bring."

"The people here will eat anything. More refugees are arriving every day."

"What will they do?"

"Beg. Eat from the soup kitchens. Sleep wherever they can." She paused. "And die. Many are dying every day. There's disease here. The grounds of this mosque, a holy place, have become hell."

"I understand that what I'm offering is a small thing. But, if you'll help me, I wish to do it."

"May Allah bless you," Fatma responded, instinctively.

"Thank you. Helping those in need was required of me as a Christian. It's required of me as a Muslim." Looking past Fatma, she noticed the little girl branded with a cross, whom she had met with her mother when they were begging on the day of Abdülhamit's girding of the sword ceremony. The girl was staring at her. Impulsively, she spoke to her. "Will you help me? There are many chores to do at the farm. And I can pay you."

She had not given a thought to connecting with this girl. But she remembered the scar and threw out a life-line, an alternative to begging, to a life of parrying with the diseases that thrive among close-quartered people. The little girl stood wide-eyed, and said nothing. But she smiled.

"Let me speak with her mother," said Fatma, who instantly grasped the potential for one of the many she regarded as in her care. Even as a 12-year-old, when she first arrived here, she comforted and fed younger children and did what she could to distract them from their memories of violence and fear. And she listened to their stories, the stories of children who, as she was, were lone survivors. The stories of children who had seen terror in the eyes of their parents, because they recognized that they could not do the one thing a parent must do—protect their children. The stories of children who had witnessed acts they knew must be forbidden, but for which they had no words. She listened to their crying and to their silence, with which they pressed their stories under the weight of time, hoping to forget.

The life she had known of helping her mother raise her younger siblings, making yogurt, baking bread, gathering firewood, and milking goats had ended when she was twelve. But at night, the screams from her village that reached her where she hid among brush in the hills above the village often woke her—the images of her parents and siblings, as if beside her.

A 12-year-old girl without parents who had escaped the massacre of a village was assumed to have been violated and unfit for marriage, though no one ever asked her. Once, she considered announcing that nothing had happened to her, that she was a suitable Muslim wife. But why? To have children? No, she was surrounded by them. To be someone's wife? No, her life was full, and it was hers. She was Fatma, a rock in a sea to which the vulnerable could cling, to which they could return as often as they needed, until they learned to swim.

Fatma understood the prejudice against the girls, like Gül, branded with Christian crosses. More had arrived. No one spoke of it, but these girls, as she had been, would be considered unsuitable Muslim wives, unsuitable even to enter heaven. Their fate was sealed in the scarred tissue that would never heal. The grandsons that Gül's mother wanted to avenge the deaths of her husband and son would never be. Fatma had not confronted Ayşe about this and never would. But she knew. In Nigar's request, Fatma saw an opportunity for Gül, a chance for her to escape the mosque compound, to escape her own fate of being a refugee for 50 years.

She looked around for Gül's mother. "Ayşe," she called. "Do you remember the woman who brought candy for the children during *Şeker Bayramı*?"

"The Christian?" Ayşe asked.

"She was a Christian, but now she's a Muslim. She has a farm and will be bringing fresh vegetables to us. She'd like Gül to help her."

"I will not have my daughter helping a Christian," Ayşe responded sharply.

"If you give Gül permission to work with this woman, she'll be in the country where the air and the ground are clean. And she will be paid for her work. I believe Allah has sent this woman to save Gül." The words shocked Fatma almost as much as Ayşe, but she said them with the conviction of belief. In her role of procuring necessities for the destitute, her contacts extended to each of the city's Muslim, Christian, and Jewish sects. Her life had stripped her of religious prejudice. She prayed to Allah for the well-being and eternal reward of everyone who offered aid to those in her world of misery, whatever their religion.

"Allah would send a Christian to help us? I don't believe it," stated Ayşe with a note of anger.

"Our experience has taught us to hate Christians. Allah gave us this hatred. But now He sees our need and sends this woman. Everything is Allah's will and our fate."

"You believe it's Allah's will?"

"I do."

268

THIRTY-SIX

Following their first victory, Osman and his men turned to the between-battle work, some of which was more distasteful than fighting. In fighting, the fear of death allowed killing. Between fighting, the wounded were dying slowly, and the dead were murdered corpses.

"Go into town and hire every available cart to take the wounded to the hospitals, and assign a soldier to each cart to make sure the wounded are not robbed or caused further harm," Osman directed Tevfik. "Have the men begin burying the dead at the break of dawn."

Osman mounted his horse and rode into town. It was after midnight. The school he had commandeered as a hospital was alive with lanterns. The wounded who could walk had arrived throughout the battle. They arrived without having received the simplest life-saving first aid. The surgeon was Charles Ryan, an Australian who looked too young to have finished medical school. He and Osman acknowledged each other, but there was no formal exchange. The surgeon was removing, at the shoulder, the mangled arm of a soldier who was smoking. There was no anesthesia. The soldier made no sound. Did not flinch or move, though the sweat rolling down his face and his tight facial muscles telegraphed extreme pain. He was willing himself through it, staring at the ceiling and smoking as though that cigarette brought him the greatest satisfaction— and might be his last.

Every bed in the hospital was occupied. And in every available space, the lesser wounded were squatting, waiting.

Some of the dying were on the floor, the surface of which was red with pooled blood and blood-soaked clothing. A few of the wounded were Russians. Soldiers providing care gave the wounded the water that their bodies craved but would not satisfy. Some of the soldiers certainly knew they were dying, but they wrung life from the water, as if to prepare for death.

Osman could see that the surgeon was doing reverse triage, treating first those who could definitely be saved, then those who might be saved, and not looking into the faces of those who would die regardless of what he did for them. Some would die because they refused amputation of legs or arms, fearing rejection from heaven if not whole.

The soldiers assigned to help the surgeon had no medical training. They cleaned and dressed wounds. Did whatever the surgeon asked of them, whatever he showed them how to do. They were strong men, but human, and executed some tasks while wiping eyes of the blur they accepted as sweat. The surgeon wiped *his* face. The wounded wiped theirs. The hot summer air did not move, even in the courtyard outside. Nature showed no compassion in any of the venues where the wounded and their caregivers faced down Azrael through moisture-burned eyes.

That night Osman slept for two hours and rose for prayer. He was a pious man and never missed a prayer that could be performed outside the demands of battle. He performed his ablutions, prayed, ate a biscuit with a glass of water, mounted his horse, and went to the market. As he feared, the spoils of war were abundant. Russian uniforms and boots. Hats, shirts, pants, and socks. Russian rifles, pistols, swords, and knives. Stacks of Russian rubles. Anything of value that could be taken from a corpse or wounded man. Pictures of wives, children, and village girls. Crosses and Bibles. Rings and medals. The market was crowded. Currency traders from as far away as Sofia were buying up the rubles for 10% of their value. Local residents bought clothes.

Osman returned to his tent. Many things demanded his attention between battles. There would be another attack and, if he prevailed, probably more after that. He did not expect the Russians to leave, at least not until winter. If he could hold out, the snow and cold of a Bulgarian winter might force the Russians to retreat. The Tsar might run out of will, or money, or public support to continue the losses he was suffering. Osman was determined to make Plevna a longer and more costly fight than the Tsar was prepared to endure.

He sent several battalions to Lofça to secure the roads to Sofia and Orhaniye. He gave orders to strengthen the earthen forts, to make the walls higher, to dig more subterranean rooms for stockpiling provisions and sheltering soldiers and horses. He ordered that the three lines of trenches in front of each fort be extended so that they connected all the forts to the extent the topography permitted. He increased the number of cannon emplacements on strategic hills. He ordered that carts be hired to transport to Sofia the wounded who would be unable to return to the battlefield. He needed to empty the makeshift hospital in Plevna of as many wounded as possible before the next battle.

He attended to his most important task, discipline. He ordered the first four soldiers caught robbing dead Russians to be executed. He ordered the Commander of the Egyptian military battalion to execute two soldiers from among those of his men who had presented themselves to the hospital with their trigger finger shot off. Osman demanded obedience and integrity. War was not about protecting soldiers from harm. It was about losing fewer men than the enemy. Men would be lost. Good men. Men who respected and trusted him as their commander. But he could not guarantee their life. They had given that to him. And though he did not hold it lightly, he held it, and when necessary to save the lives of many, he took the lives of some. "Lose control of a few and you lose control of all." Every officer under him had heard Osman say this.

"We're fighting a Christian army in an area with many Christian civilians, some of whom may hate us. They may see their friend in our enemy, but they are subjects of the sultan. We must protect them." Another Osman edict.

A few men with wounds so terrible they had been left for last by the surgeon were inexplicably still alive two days later. Some died when attended to. Some died on carts destined for Sofia. Men with trigger fingers precisely shot off ceased to appear at the hospital.

Robbing the dead continued. The Circassians hated the Russians and lived within the law only to the extent that it could be enforced. Four executions were not enough to change a culture in an environment where darkness and the many priorities of the enforcer were their friends. But within a few days, even the Russian dead had been buried. Most robbed of anything of value. Many beheaded.

Osman encouraged the men as they strengthened the fortifications, offered reassurance to the townspeople, filed his daily report to Istanbul, and enjoyed his daily cup of coffee. He refused to meet with journalists. Journalists at the front lines had occurred first in the Crimean War. Osman Pasha thought the concept a dangerous abomination. He ordered Tevfik to keep them away from him and to share nothing with them.

Osman and his soldiers ate better now. Their ration of biscuits could be supplemented with local vegetables, fruit, and even meat, so long as they paid for it. All of the soldiers were at least a year in arears in pay, but the families of many sent them small amounts of money. Osman purchased some food from funds he controlled for supplies. Everything was shared.

On July 17, a supply convoy arrived, confirming that the road was open. On July 18, scouts reported the Russians were massing forces for a new assault. Istanbul confirmed that the Russians asked the Rumanians for help and that Rumanian troops were headed for Plevna. Spy and journalist observations estimated 40,000 troops, with perhaps 200 cannon, mobilized for the attack. Osman, who had at most 20,000 troops, alerted them on July 30 to prepare for an assault.

On July 31, Osman had completed his Morning Prayer and breakfast when he heard the first cannon fire in the direction of Graviche Fort. His men were ready. No need for him to issue orders. He mounted his horse and rode through a heavy fog to a ridge to watch with his spyglass. From nearby hills, Russian guns were bombarding the fort with cannonballs and shrapnel casings. Osman could see the explosions from the cannon barrels, wait for the boom of sound a moment later, and follow the whistle of its trajectory until the shell burst. He knew the bombing from the cannon would be ineffective. Almost a ritual more than a military tactic. He waited for the inevitable infantry charge.

The fog was good cover for a charge, but the Russians delayed. Finally, at 9:00 a.m. the fog lifted and with it a sea of Russian uniforms rose with the noise of a tidal wave against a sea-cliff shore and advanced on the Turkish trenches below Graviche Fort. The Russians charged without regard to life. Young boys, who could not imagine dying and could not see life beyond the order to die, fell one upon the other, each fallen replaced by another scrambling over the body of his comrade, each hoping to reach the trench, to sink a bayonet into the enemy, and to emerge from hell alive. The first two battalions were cut down one upon another with barely a man left to stagger back beyond the reach of the Peabody-Martinis.

Simultaneously, Osman could hear attacks on three other forts. But they seemed less intense. Graviche Fort appeared to be the Russians' primary objective. Perhaps they thought it the most vulnerable or the most advantageous from which to attack other positions. Perhaps they thought they could instill panic in his forces if they could capture even one fort.

The front line stretched for 20 kilometers in a broad arc. Eighteen of the earthen forts defending the town were under concentrated infantry attacks. Osman trained his spyglass, looking through dust, smoke, and flames. Listening to explosions and the shots of rifles, pistols, and cannon; hearing screams of pain—shouted in agony, suppressed in honor, released in fear.

Every 10 minutes, the Russians made a new assault, the last around 4:00 p.m. At Graviche, they overran the trenches and reached the fort. Osman moved to within earshot of the sounds unique to hand to hand, bayonet to bayonet fighting. He had no orders to give. No men in reserve to call upon. He heard the grunts and shouts, the groans and cries of men prevailing over foes and others overcome by them. He could not discern who was prevailing until he saw the Russians scrambling back across the wall over which they had charged a short time before. The certainty of death chased the Russians, and the exhausted and grateful Turks did not pursue them.

Riding back to the highest ridge, Osman could see that the Russians had suffered a similar fate in the other two arenas of concentrated attack and were also retreating. They had not captured a single fort. Russian dead lay everywhere, one on top of the other in many places. Osman had begun the day outmanned more than two to one, but the dead were almost eight to one in his favor. In his Evening Prayer, he thanked Allah for the victory and asked that He heal the wounded and accept as martyrs his soldiers who had died. Then he mounted his horse and rode to the hospital.

In the makeshift hospital and the grounds outside them, the situation was worse than after the first battle. Additional houses and the principal mosque had been pressed into service as places for the wounded to await treatment and to recover. Wounded men and men who had already died were pressed tightly together. Men holding body parts, internal and external, who should have died and who were in pain so beyond a threshold that they did not cry or utter a sound, prayed for a miracle and for eternal life.

Everything associated with the wounded was contaminated. The surgeon was not performing surgeries in the designated hospital. He had set up a table next to the river under mulberry trees with lanterns hanging from the branches. It was cooler and possibly more hygienic, though he had abandoned hope for maintaining sterile conditions or instruments. He desperately needed sleep, relief. A drink. A woman. A cigarette. Tea or Turkish coffee. Osman watched him work. They again acknowledged each other but said nothing.

Osman inspected the city. Some houses had been damaged. A few had burned. One woman sobbed uncontrollably next to the bodies of three children outside a partially destroyed house. Her husband, consoling her, appeared wounded.

With the sounds of incoming shells threatening death, the residents of the city could do nothing except carry on with the minutia of life. Eat meals and sleep. Hug their children and each other. Love each other deeply in the fear of loss. Pray for life, forgiveness, salvation. Beg for the lives of their children, despite knowing what might befall children after a hate-fired war. They lived to survive the next exploding shell and the silence that followed.

It was after midnight when Osman rode out for a look at the battlefield. A clear night with a full moon. Osman remembered that this particular field had been a beautiful vineyard when they arrived. Not a single stake remained standing. Not a single vine was erect. Here and there the leaf of a vine could be seen between bodies. Russian dead lay scattered across many acres. Some with faces at peace. Others with faces frozen in agonizing pain. Carts were collecting the wounded. Soldiers were helping other wounded soldiers walk to the city.

Osman saw a frail, elderly woman who appeared to have gone mad, wandering among the dead Russians, cursing them, collecting their rifles and ammunition, and muttering exultations to the Padishah and Allah. She dragged her booty to where a group of Turkish soldiers were eating. "Auntie, we do not need their guns and ammunition. Go home and sleep," they told her. But she seemed unable to comprehend.

One of the soldiers took the rifles and ammunition from her. "Let's go home," he said. She looked at him blankly. "You are my aunt," he said. "I will take you home." She took a step but stumbled, and he lifted her into his arms. Osman watched. This soldier would have spent his day killing the men in this field. That was required of him. Carrying this elderly woman home was not. A soul's antidote to war.

A few furtive figures seen among the dead may have been robbing them. Osman could not be sure, but he knew it would happen. The dead were too many to be buried quickly. There would be time over the next several nights for robbery and mutilation. And motivation. The conditions of war easily justified hatred for the enemy, and the omnipresence of death diminished respect for it. He could not stop the looting. He was no longer the supreme force. War was.

Osman gave few orders. The subordinate officers and troops set about the between-battle tasks as ritual. No one needed to be told how to prepare for the next assault. Spy and news reports were that the Russian forces, together with local Bulgarian volunteers and the Rumanian army, were expected to be more than 100,000, possibly 150,000. With some recently arrived reinforcements, Osman had no more than 30,000.

Action resumed on the first of September when a large Russian force attacked Lofça to cut Osman's life-line, in which they succeeded despite losing 8,000 men. Osman lost only 2,000, but the remaining 1,500 were forced to flee to Plevna.

"The Russians are in position to attack at any time. If we prevail, we'll move on Lofça to re-open the road," Osman said to Tevfik, as though the loss of Lofça was unimportant. And at this moment, it was. Osman did not allow himself to mourn a loss or celebrate a victory. Each was only an episode that informed his next move, as it did that of the enemy.

For three days Russian cannon-fire turned hills along a now 25-kilometer, circular front into volcanoes spewing fire and smoke with the percussion exclusive to bombs, a noise no one would confuse with any other. The Turkish earthworks sustained some, but not critical damage.

On September 13, the Russians resumed their closed formation infantry assaults on five of the primary defensive forts with total disregard of casualties. Osman watched wave after wave fall before the deadly Peabody-Martini barrage until Russian reinforcements in overwhelming numbers surmounted the trenches and drove his men from three of the forts. But Osman had anticipated this and had his own cannon entrenchments overlooking the forts pour hellfire into the captured earthworks.

Osman watched the fighting from positions near enough that, in the course of the day, three horses were shot out from under him. Occasionally, he would point his spyglass into the distance where the Grand Duke Nicholas and Tsar Alexander II were watching the action from a platform well beyond the battlefield and the reach of armaments. The fields across which the Russians had attacked were a mass of dead Russian soldiers. Here and there among the dead, a few of the wounded moved. And whenever the noise of battle abated, Osman heard wounded Russian soldiers yelling the names of the Grand Duke and the Tsar in anger and see them shaking their fists in the direction of the platform.

And then the Russians withdrew. Osman had prevailed.

In war, a commander can abandon a hopeless battlefield, save those troops not lost, take them home or to a new battlefield where they might fight in triumph. But in victory, Osman could not save his troops. His orders were to win until defeated.

THIRTY-SEVEN

News of Osman Pasha's victory at Plevna brought only brief comfort to Abdülhamit. Süleyman Pasha, one of Abdülhamit's commanders in the Danube Province and an ambitious man, had attempted to recapture Şıbka Pass and been forced to withdraw. In three attacks, Süleyman's losses totaled 4,000 dead and 8,000 wounded. Russian losses were less than a tenth of that.

Among the reports Abdülhamit read of the botched attempt to retake Şıbka Pass was an account in the *Augsburger Zeitung* that praised the Turkish soldiers but noted derisively that only one among 800 wounded was an officer. It was true, Abdülhamit thought. Whether they were military pashas or pasha bureaucrats, they had all let him down, dragged him into war when he was barely in office, mismanaged the empire's finances, and made his job more difficult than that of any sultan in 600 years by raising unrealistic expectations with talk of a constitution, democracy, rights, freedom, and equality—all concepts that undermined his authority and the public's respect for authority. Concepts with consequences the pashas themselves did not understand and that his subjects certainly did not.

He had given the pashas every chance, and he had been patient with individuals until incompetence could not be ignored. He had established a military council, to which he took every decision related to the war, and its advice constituted his orders to the commanders in the field. He did everything he could to hold the pashas accountable. Yet spies throughout the city reported disgruntlement with the war in the markets and coffee shops of every neighborhood. And they laid the blame for failure on him!

"Do you have any good news for me?" Abdülhamit asked his friend, British Ambassador Layard.

"The queen is pressing even harder for my country's intervention in the war. Osman Pasha's stand at Plevna has given heart to the pro-Turkish forces in Britain."

"But she is not prevailing?" Abdülhamit stated as a question.

"Not yet, but I never lose hope, and you should not either." He took a sip of coffee and inhaled deeply from his cigarette, as he considered how much bad news to relay.

"Any news from your attachés on the front?" Abdülhamit pressed, fearing the answer.

"Unfortunately, I'm told by my attaché in Kars that large numbers of Russian reinforcements have arrived in the east. He estimates the Russian force there to be as many as 60,000, with 200 field guns."

He did not mention the other part of the report: Muhtar's army was demoralized by sickness, and soldiers were deserting out of fear of death from disease. Reports said Muhtar had less than half the Russian number of troops and guns. Layard also did not mention the attaché's description of inadequate food and clothing for the Turkish troops, particularly as winter was approaching. As always, Layard said he would send yet another cable to advocate that Britain's interests were threatened if Russia were not stopped.

Abdülhamit thanked him. Layard always made it seem as though at any moment London might reverse its course. Abdülhamit dared not resign himself to failure. It was a contest between his country and Russia. But it was also his personal struggle against the world.

Battle news see-sawed, particularly in the east. Russian attacks were repulsed, but when Muhtar went on the offensive, he had to retreat. The Russians were forced to give up some gains as indefensible. Briefly, Russian offensive moves ceased, and Muhtar sent an optimistic cable, suggesting that the Russians might be preparing to withdraw in anticipation of winter.

But the Russians were only waiting for reinforcements. When their assault resumed, they had advanced artillery guns that used shrapnel, which discharged fear as effectively as death. The Kurdish irregulars disappeared, significantly reducing the force at Muhtar's disposal.

News reports of two major battles devastated Abdülhamit. At Alacadağ, the Russians took 12,000 Turkish prisoners, after killing and wounding 5,600. At Deveboyun 3,000 were killed and wounded, 1,000 taken prisoner, and another 3,000 escaped into the hills over a broad area, effectively deserting. The Russians now occupied the plain surrounding Erzurum and had Kars under siege.

"The Russians are demanding surrender. Muhtar is asking for instructions." Principal Secretary Sait was reading from a cable.

"Tell him to defend all positions to the last man. Victory is always possible. And if not, at least an honorable death. As prisoners, the men die slowly and without dignity."

"He says the citizens of Kars and Erzurum are calling for surrender to preserve their lives and property."

"Only our victory can protect them. As we've seen elsewhere, my subjects suffer equally whether the Russians enter a city by victory or surrender."

The city of Kars was shelled day and night. Abdülhamit was bombarded with negative news. Soldiers were falling from disease as fast as from shells.

"Kars has fallen," Sait reported. "Only a few officers and cavalry escaped."

Over the next few days Abdülhamit saw the reports of his losses at Kars: 17,000 taken prisoner, 2,500 dead, and 5,000 wounded, most of whom were left untreated in the cold. Few could be expected to survive. As Abdülhamit expected, the reports described the city as plundered by the Christian militias that followed the Russian army and by the Cossack cavalry, whom the Russian officers could not control.

And then a spate of good news from the east. "Reinforcements from Batum have arrived at Erzurum."

"The citizens of Erzurum are now resolved to fight."

"A Russian attack on Erzurum's defenses has been beaten back."

"Disease and the harsh winter weather are crippling the Russian forces."

"Assaults have ceased, possibly until spring."

But in the west, the Russians had overrun the Turks' positions that kept roads open to Plevna. Only one Ottoman supply convoy had reached Plevna since the September victory. It was now late November.

"Please advise the members of the War Council that I have dissolved the Council. I no longer have use for their services," Abdülhamit said to Sait. If he was to be blamed for the outcome of the war, he would at least heed his own counsel.

It was after midnight. He walked into the garden of the palace along the path that ran to the lake. It was a brisk, late November night, too cold to sit on a bench by the water as he intended, so he continued walking. Around the man-made lake. Past his expanding zoo of exotic animals and pausing at the aviary that was being filled with birds from around the world. The night was bright enough that he could see many of them, most asleep except for a few nighttime hunters. A large horned owl watched him with the slightest turning of his regal head. The king of the night stared at the king of the empire, each admiring the other.

Several kilometers of paths wove through the palace grounds. Most were shaded by trees native to the grounds, but others were introduced from as far away as China and the new world. Abdülhamit controlled every aspect of the physical world of the palace. He was making it a beautiful and pleasing place in which to be. A sanctuary for animals, birds, plants. And for him. What he wanted was for the empire to be equally safe and prosperous, equally under his control. He knew what the empire needed. But enemies external and internal were thwarting his aspiration that the empire be a prosperous and peaceful sanctuary for its people.

He felt the chill of the on-coming winter. It would affect the war. His troops would endure the cold. Would the Russians?

THIRTY-EIGHT

"Your excellency, I believe you should have defensive bunkers, forts, and trenches built to protect Istanbul. A line from Durusu Gölü on the Black Sea to Büyükçekmece on the Sea of Marmara. The Russians show no intent to pause for winter. Preparing the city's defenses would be an advisable contingency." The speaker was Valentine Baker, known as Baker Pasha, a British soldier-of-fortune who had been dismissed from the British army after a clumsy attempt on a train to kiss a young woman who was affronted by his love-struck impulsiveness. He had a long, drooping mustache, close-set eyes, high cheek bones, and a small, neutral chin. His features presented a worried look and made him appear older than he was.

Baker Pasha had been hired by the Ottoman government to train a new gendarmerie force, but once the Russians crossed the Danube, Commander Mehmet Ali Pasha requested that Baker be assigned to serve as one of his subordinate officers. They shared a strategic vision for the war: consolidate the Turkish forces and go on the offensive.

Ambassador Layard knew that Baker had won Abdülhamit's admiration. In the early engagements with the Russians after they crossed the Danube, Baker repulsed their attack at Yeniköy, riding in the lead of three offensive charges that forced a significant Russian retreat. His fearless leadership in these battles was widely reported, praised by his subordinate officers, and admired by the Turkish soldiers who followed him into battle.

Baker was on leave in Istanbul for a few days, and, as Layard hoped, Abdülhamit requested a briefing from him.

Layard knew that Abdülhamit was receiving optimistic field reports from commanders who felt responsible to draw success even on a page of failure, reports that gave Abdülhamit little concern that the Russians might reach Istanbul. Perhaps Baker's opinion could provide balance.

"If this is the contingency plan, what do you propose as the plan of first order?" Abdülhamit asked with genuine interest.

"Your Excellency, Commander Mehmet Ali Pasha and I believe that Şibka Pass and Plevna are costing you many soldiers without strategic advantage. The Russians are crossing the Balkans via several passes. They no longer need Şibka. And Plevna is a defensive position of little use in deterring the Russians if they decide to march on Istanbul. We believe the forces at Şibka and Plevna should be withdrawn to Adrianople, along with our forces and those in other outposts, as well."

"You propose allowing the Russians free passage to Adrianople?" Abdülhamit asked, surprised.

"To lead them to believe we are unwilling to fight against their superior numbers. They would arrive at Adrianople after a long march, while our men would be dug in and rested. We believe we could force a retreat under the harsh conditions of winter and, in pursuit, destroy much of the Russian army. A decisive victory would destroy their will to resume the war next spring."

"So, the defensive positions you propose from Durusu Gölü to Büyük Çekmece would only be needed if you fail at Adrianople?" Abdülhamit stated as a question, reflecting that he was unsettled by the prospect that a last ditch stand might be needed.

Baker was aware of the optimistic reports Abdülhamit received from some of his commanders, who insisted that the Russians would not be able to continue their campaign through the winter. Abdülhamit could be told that his army had lost a battle, but not that he would lose the war. Not Istanbul. "I believe we'll succeed. But in war, you need a contingency plan. That's all," he responded.

"I understand. Please accept my thanks for the service you are rendering to my country," Abdülhamit said, by which Baker knew he was dismissed.

"It's an honor to lead your soldiers in battle. They fight with courage and skill," Baker responded as he rose to leave.

On November 27, Baker boarded the train for Sofia to rejoin Mehmet Ali, now commander of the western front. Despite Baker's counsel to Abdülhamit, their orders were to organize a force to go to the aid of Osman at Plevna and to leave Commander Süleyman free to pursue the prize of Şıbka Pass. Süleyman saw retaking Şıbka Pass as the means to winning Istanbul's approbation and being promoted to replace Mehmet Ali as commander of the western front. Baker and Mehmet Ali commiserated.

"I expect to be relieved of my command," Mehmet Ali confided. "I sent a telegram today advising Istanbul that I was not able to field an adequate number of battle-ready soldiers to send in relief of Osman. In Istanbul, they know how many battalions are assigned to me. I know that most of my battle-tested battalions have lost half their numbers and that the newly formed battalions sent out to me have no training and couldn't put down an uprising of palace eunuchs!"

The Istanbul strategy continued to be to defend every town, road, and mountain pass, regardless of strategic value or the fact that this allowed the Russians, with their superior numbers, to pick off Turkish positions sequentially. One of these positions was Kamarlı Pass. Baker joined Mehmet Ali in riding there to assess the situation of the troops guarding that pass.

THIRTY-NINE

Commander Osman Pasha, programmed by the ritual of Morning Prayer, stirred in his cot, though no call to prayer came from the minarets of Plevna's mosques. Every *muezzin* had left the city as part of a growing exodus of the Muslim population. They traveled to as-yet-unthreatened villages, towns, or cities, if they had relatives in such a place, or on to the home of the sultan, whose duty it was to protect and provide for them. They could see the end and did not wish to welcome the Russians or test the mercy of their Christian neighbors.

Osman also saw the end. He asked for permission to withdraw his troops from Plevna and make a stand at Orhaniye, but Istanbul said no. "It's because we've made Plevna a symbol of Turkish success," Tevfik said. "The foreign journalists tell me that in Europe they're cheering for us to defeat the Russians."

Osman had received telegrams of congratulations from all over Europe. Even from the United States. Abdülhamit had conferred the title of *Gazi* on him and given him gifts of a beautiful chestnut stallion and a bejeweled sword. But he was feeling more a failure than a success on this cold morning in early December. He slid out from between the two wool blankets under him and the two on top and placed his feet in his slippers. He took the few steps to the small table in the tent where a basin of water was ready for his ablutions. Since fighting had stopped, he never missed a prayer. Allah had brought him to this place at this time. It would be up to Him if he lived to leave here.

After Morning Prayer, Osman rolled up his prayer rug, put it on the end of his cot, and straightened out the blankets. He put on his uniform, great coat, and boots and waited for his aide to bring his morning glass of water and biscuit. He could no longer look forward to a cup of coffee at the end of the day. Really, there was nothing to look forward to on any day. He was hungry. He knew his troops were. No one was starving yet, but everyone was hungry. The townspeople no longer offered produce to sell, even if there were money to buy it.

From the beginning, his position at Plevna had been at the mercy of supply wagons—up to 1,000 every two weeks— and their safe passage depended on Turkish fortifications guarding the Lofça and Orhaniye roads, which the Russians now controlled.

He ate his biscuit and drank his water slowly, watching the sun at the crest of the hill and the cold mist from the valley rise to meet each other. At least it did not look as though it would rain today. The relentless rains of November had turned the entire area into a sea-bed of mud, almost impassable on horse or even on foot.

In heavy rains, the heads of decapitated Russian bodies in shallow graves rolled down hills. Long after the last battle, birds, animals, and humans scavenged. Stomachs full, the birds and animals skulked away from this unnatural feast. Human scavengers disavowed their shame in their urgency to salvage detritus of even the least value.

Osman knew that he could not hold out. Nature had become an enemy. The Russians were patient. His government, impotent. His soldiers, cold and hungry. He mounted his horse and rode the slippery trail into Plevna. Many houses showed damage. The Russians lobbed shells from 500 guns daily into the Turkish forts, subjecting the forts and the town to earthquakes of tremoring ground that spread terror among those relying on the earth to keep them safe. Some shells landed in the city—even hitting buildings with Red Crescent flags, possibly by accident. The shellings were a pointless and malicious exercise that angered Osman. Militarily, nothing was accomplished, but the shelling was laying waste to even Christian lives and property.

He rode through the market where no one any longer came to buy or sell, although he knew there was a black market where scarce items were sold for a hundred times their value. He dismounted outside the school, which was still the primary hospital. The weather no longer permitted the wounded to be in the yard. Nor did their condition. He had commandeered every available house and public building, mosque, and church to house the wounded. The road was no longer open to send the most seriously wounded to Sofia.

Despite the cold, the school's door and windows were open. The smell of the dying, of dead flesh, had been barely tolerable before. Now, the putrefaction met him even as he tied up his horse. He covered his mouth and nose with a scarf and entered, looking for the doctor.

He said nothing. Not a single man among the wounded showed life enough to recognize that he was there. Two of the soldiers providing care looked in his direction, saluted him, and resumed their work. The doctor had his back to him, kneeling over a patient on the floor, carefully removing maggots from an open wound. Every offensive smell that could associate itself with a human body was present, but the smell of gangrene dominated. It was eating soldiers who had refused amputation and others whose wounds had become infected. Osman could see efforts at cleanliness by the soldiers providing care, but it was a battle they were losing.

Osman waited until the doctor stood up from caring for the patient on the floor and indicated that he wished to speak with him outside. "I know you're doing what you can. I want to thank you. My government and I are grateful."

"We doctors and the soldiers who help us cannot do what is needed. But the dying wounded are not the main problem. I visited several forts yesterday. Your men are suffering from exposure and dysentery, but I also saw cases of smallpox, typhoid, and diphtheria."

"Thank you. No one told me of this," Osman said, in a tone as though informed he had lost every man in an assault of no strategic value. Illness among soldiers under the conditions here was expected, but smallpox, typhoid, and diphtheria could not be ignored.

Just a few weeks earlier, Grand Duke Nicholas had sent Osman a message, urging him to surrender. But Osman rejected the offer, saying that his troops, who cheered his response, would happily continue to shed their blood for their country and their faith, rather than surrender. But now, the wounded were dying, and 40,000 unwounded men under his command were threatened with deadly diseases, exposure, and starvation. In the battles he had won, his men had killed more than 30,000 enemy soldiers with a loss of 8,000. It was time for one last battle, one last chance for his men to die with honor. He called a council with his subordinate officers.

"Our men face starvation and disease," he addressed them. "As their officers, we must surrender or lead an escape."

"If we surrender, our men will die as prisoners," said Tevfik. "Better we should die attempting to escape."

"Does anyone disagree?" Osman asked and looked at each of them in turn. None disagreed. "Advise the men. We'll charge the blockade just before daybreak."

Osman rode from fort to fort to boost morale as soon as it was dark. The soldiers were eager to fight. Anything to get their minds off their stomachs.

December 10 was a typical morning. They had to wait for the fog to rise. Word of their plan had leaked. The remaining Muslims of the town had gathered with carts and animals, children and possessions, to follow them to Sofia, Istanbul, or anywhere the Turkish army would lead them. Plevna was certain death and worse. Tevfik argued that the civilians should be ordered to remain in the city. Osman said no. It would be cruel and pointless.

They attacked as soon as there was light enough through the lifting fog to see their targets. But the fire and smoke of the Russian guns that responded challenged their determination not to die as prisoners. Here, the Peabody-Martini rifles had no advantage. In the first assault, the Turks took one Russian position. The second wave took another. But the Russian guns from the forts rained shrapnel. Osman watched as officers fell dead and wounded and the ranks of his soldiers thinned and fell back into the rabble of carts, women, children, old men, and animals trying to follow them.

He was watching from the back of the big chestnut stallion that was a gift from Abdülhamit, seeing that everything would be lost or, perhaps, in one heroic gesture, be won. He spurred the chestnut and galloped to the fore, calling his men to another charge with the cry of "Allah," which echoed from the troops as they attacked the entrenched Russian positions. In minutes, Osman felt a sharp pain in his right calf and simultaneously felt the life of his horse slipping away as it fell beneath him. Two soldiers rushed to his side and yelled out that Osman had been shot. They carried him to the shelter of a mill nearby.

News spread quickly that Osman had been killed, demoralizing the troops, whose charge was dissolving among dead and wounded comrades.

"Sir, the soldiers are retreating and being cut down. They will all die. Should we surrender?" Tevfik asked on seeing that Osman was not seriously wounded.

"Raise the white flag," Osman said in a barely audible tone. He wished his wound had been mortal.

FORTY

Nigar sent her carriage for Gül every morning and rode back with her to the mosque late in the day, her carriage leading carts loaded with the late fall harvest of cabbage, kale, potatoes, root vegetables, and melons. Fatma had shamed several owners of carts to go to Kağıthane each afternoon and bring the day's harvest to the mosque kitchen. "But Auntie, if I don't use my cart for paying customers, how will I buy bread for my children?" one protested.

"I only ask what is necessary to save your soul from hell. It's too little, but I will ask Allah to accept it."

"You may kill me to save me, Auntie. May Allah reward you."

"May He have mercy on us all. I will leave some vegetables in your cart for your children."

Most of the work on Nigar's farm was done by refugee women and their children. Nigar allowed them to set up camp in the barn that had once housed Abdülhamit's prized horses.

"Do you know how to count?" Nigar asked Gül on one of their first days together helping with the harvesting.

"No. A few boys walked to a school in a neighboring village, but no girls."

"I'll teach you. It's easy."

The counting lessons helped to pass the time as they harvested vegetables. Gül repeated the number after Nigar each time she pulled a root vegetable from the ground, cut a cabbage from its stalk, or picked a melon. They put the harvested items in groups of one, two, three, and up to ten before loading them on a cart. By the end of the second day, Gül could count to 100, and the next day to 1,000. In the following weeks, she learned addition and subtraction, as well. Numbers were fascinating. She learned to draw the numbers with a stick in the dirt, but they also floated in her mind until called upon for the enumeration of things again and again. A kind of magic.

Gül did not tell her mother what she was learning for fear she might stop her from going to Kağıthane. She loved getting away from the mosque compound, doing the physical work of harvesting, being the object of Nigar's attention, and learning numbers.

Every evening Gül's mother and Fatma were waiting for them. Today, late in November, was no different, except that there was only one cart, and it was not full. "I'm sorry, Fatma," Nigar said. "The harvest is over. This is the last of what I have."

"May Allah bless you," Fatma responded and embraced her, which surprised Nigar. Fatma had always kept her distance from her, as if she continued to see her as a stranger, a Christian, an "other" not to be completely trusted. "Your produce has given strength to many. We'll survive, thanks to Allah."

"Next year's harvests will be greater and better, Allah willing," Nigar said. Sprinkling her speech with "Allah willing," "thanks be to Allah," "by the grace of Allah," was as natural a part of her speech as that of any Muslim in the city. The circumstances of the refugees reinforced the concept of fate. So many who had lived simple and believing lives were killed before they could escape, died on the road to Istanbul, died in the filth of their environment in the city. But not all. Allah picked and chose. A choosing beyond explanation.

"I've heard that the Padishah gives people land in Anatolia. Some refugee families have carts, a few animals, even some money," Fatma said, interrupting Nigar's thoughts. "In the city, they'll be beggars and die, but with land, they could raise their children to love Allah and the Padishah."

"I'll ask about it."

"Ask the Padishah. He must know."

"I'll do that," Nigar said unhesitatingly. But riding back to Kağıthane, she had reservations. What if Fatma's information was wrong? She did not want to ask Abdülhamit for something that was not possible for him to give. It would embarrass them both. She directed the driver to turn the carriage to Pera. Cristo knew everything.

"Tea!" Cristo called out to the delivery boy down the street as soon as he saw the carriage. The cold day had brought few potential customers to wander the Grand Rue de Pera. He was closing early. "Every day I hope you will stop for tea and stir my old blood. It's been too long," he said, as he extended his hand to help Nigar from the carriage.

"Cristo, my friend," Nigar said, smiling broadly and kissing him on both cheeks. "You should have been a poet, or a playwright."

"But I am. Poems pour from my heart as I drink tea alone, waiting for your next visit. And as your hapless lover, I can deny you nothing. Is that not the perfect plot for a love tragedy? Or perhaps you see me as a tragi-comedy?"

"I see you as my dearest friend and a man destined to go to heaven for sure, since he denies no good deed on being asked."

"It's not heaven a jilted lover seeks, but I'll do my best to earn it, if it pleases you."

"It does."

They drank tea and exchanged news. Nigar about the work at Kağıthane. Cristo about his children and his niece's success with Nigar's former shop. They spoke of the war, as everyone in the city did. In Istanbul, the war was the refugees. They were begging everywhere.

"How do the Greeks feel about the war?" Nigar asked.

"Greeks drink ouzo and re-live history. Some do nothing and ask God to do something. Others understand the world as it is and give money to arm and clothe the Turkish soldiers. If the Russian army enters Istanbul, it will not be liberation, as some fantasize. Children and families will die. Good men in other times become rapists and killers."

"And you?"

"I want the Turkish soldiers between me and chaos. But I think you did not come to ask me about the war."

"You know me too well, although I did come to ask you about something related to the war. Some refugees have heard that the government gives refugees land. Have you heard of this?"

"Yes, of course. It's called the Refugee Law, but I don't know the details."

"The refugees are mostly uneducated. They need someone to explain what they must do to benefit from this law."

"Abdülhamit could order the minister of interior to have men go to the mosque compounds to explain the law."

"That's a wonderful idea. I'll ask him to do it," Nigar responded with enthusiasm.

"Abdülhamit will welcome an opportunity to do something helpful. In the coffeehouses the people blame him for the war *and* the refugees."

Cristo was right. Abdülhamit could make things happen. And he would. He *was* a kind man. A kind man, who had allowed her to live on his farm and gave her a comfortable allowance that made her life of raising food for refugees possible. Or was it love? Did he allow her to live by her principles because he loved her? Suddenly, she was conflicted about going to see him. She was sure she did not have romantic interest in him, but she had feelings. And surely he did also. But she would go. She had to.

******

"I came to see you again, my sovereign," Nigar said, taking him by surprise as she lifted her veil as a supplicant, "because I wanted to thank you for allowing me to raise produce for the refugees. They are very grateful, as am I." She was surprised that on seeing him, she did not feel as if she were in the company of her former lover and husband, just the sultan of the empire, of whom she, like any other subject, had come to make a request. A sultan who did not look regal, who was aging quickly, already using *henna* in his hair and beard. The war was degrading even the sultan. Did she also look older?

"I've heard reports of what you're doing," Abdülhamit responded, "and I'm pleased to hear them."

Abdülhamit received daily reports of the migration of the refugees to the city and felt personally responsible for their plight. He made generous gifts from his personal account and the palace account to the mosques and to the Red Crescent Society for their care.

"I'll send an order immediately to the Ministry of Interior," he said in response to her request. "My father passed the Refugee Law. At that time, famine and disease had emptied villages everywhere, and Turkmen, Tatar, and Circassian Muslims came here to escape Russian oppression in the Caucasus. But even today, Anatolia still has empty villages. I would be happy to see refugee families settle there. And I'll send an order to the Ottoman Bank to make loans for their first plantings."

"Thank you my sovereign. May Allah bless you for your generosity," Nigar said. She no longer felt romantic love for him, but she wanted him to be a successful sultan, a sultan who was admired by his subjects. A sultan *she* could admire.

"And may He bless you, as well. We are all at His mercy with this terrible war. Today, I learned that Plevna has fallen. Even more refugees will come. I've done everything I could. I spared no cost in buying arms. I listened to the military pashas, but they gave me bad advice. How could I have known?"

Nigar was unable to respond. He looked in genuine distress, helpless. Once again, he seemed to be searching for the counsel she might have given him, had he allowed her. He regretted his fate in receiving bad advice. She regretted that they had not shared a fate. Remorse, but no longer love. "Your soldiers fight with valor, my sovereign," was all she could think to say, before requesting her leave.

FORTY-ONE

The cable telling Abdülhamit that Osman had been injured and surrendered at Plevna did not mention casualties, but reports in foreign journals the next day put the numbers at 6,000 dead and wounded to 1,200 Russians and Rumanians. This, in four hours of fighting. The estimated number of Turkish prisoners was particularly disturbing, 43,000.

"My friend," Abdülhamit began a few days later in a meeting with Ambassador Layard. "I no longer expect military help, but I'm asking your government to intercede with the Russians on behalf of my men who are prisoners and being forced to walk to Russia. It's winter. They don't have the boots and clothing necessary to survive. I beg of you. They are good men."

"I'll speak with the Russian ambassador, and I'll ask London to communicate with St. Petersburg. The Geneva Convention requires humane treatment," Layard said with as much conviction as he could muster, hoping to convey a sense that such an appeal would be heeded. But he knew better. A report from one of his military attaches in the field described the fate of the Turkish prisoners as certain death. And Russia had not signed the Geneva Convention.

Abdülhamit was preoccupied with the war. But the opening of the second session of parliament on December 13 was a distraction of potential use to him. Parliament had declared war. Perhaps now at least some of the coffeehouse talk might be about the role of the people's representatives in this unpopular war. The message he sent to be read at the opening session praised the courage of the soldiers and called attention to the non-Muslim units participating in the defense of the nation—a signal to the Europeans and Russians that his non-Muslim citizens were not seeking liberation but saw their future served by a Turkish victory.

In time of war, he expected a supportive parliament. Instead, the daily reports on the discourse in parliament described contentious charges of corruption against ministers and accusations that the war was being mishandled.

"I'm prepared to resign, if it pleases you, my sovereign," said Grand Vizier Rüşti Pasha in reporting the accusations in parliament of his own failings.

"No, I do not seek or accept your resignation," Abdülhamit said forcefully. "The accusations are baseless. The members of parliament are ignorant." Abdülhamit was furious. The members of parliament knew nothing of the advice he received, the intelligence reports, the strategic facts on the ground. He spent his days pouring over cables from his commanders, newspaper accounts, and spy reports. He met for hours with his ministers, officers, and military advisors, as well as with foreign ambassadors, foreign military attachés, and foreign journalists. He emptied the treasury to buy the best weapons. He worked daily to the point of exhaustion to give his troops a fighting chance. And the members of parliament? Apparently, they had heard some gossip in a coffeehouse!

He had reconvened parliament on the urging of Ambassador Layard. One more gesture to reassure Britain of his commitment to the constitution and to fair treatment of his Christian subjects. One more gesture to encourage Britain to come to his aid. To no avail.

Parliament made him angry, but the war bore down on him, encircled him, until he felt captured in a confined space where he could not breathe deeply. He sat at his desk, his head as though weighted in the reading position, a report open before him. A diminutive figure that resembled a prisoner more than a sovereign. The report was from Süleyman, who had directed the disastrous campaign at Şıbka Pass. He reported having withdrawn to Sofia, while absurdly announcing that he would defend the entire Balkan line. A report from Commander Mehmet Ali in Kamarlı observed that he was facing 30,000 Russians with a force of 13,000. He expected the Russian-Rumanian forces of 120,000 at Plevna to attack the scattered positions of the Turkish troops. He recommended a general withdrawal for a final stand at Adrianople.

Abdülhamit raised his head. Once again, he alone had to make the decision. Süleyman wanted to fight to preserve the Balkans. Mehmet Ali was ceding the Balkans in a gamble for victory in one great battle at Adrianople, just as Baker Pasha had advised.

He closed the last report and rose slowly from his desk. His knees complained, and his neck had a crick that did not pass by straightening his back and forcing his shoulders and head more erect than natural. He walked past the beautiful tiled coal stove that heated the room and toward the door, accepting as he went the coat a eunuch wrapped around his shoulders.

Outside, damp cold greeted him, and yet, the temperature was not below freezing, and no snow lay on the ground. He sat on a bench looking out across the Bosphorus, allowing himself to feel thoroughly cold, imagining what it must be like for his soldiers who were prisoners, walking with little protection through mud, snow, and ice on little, if any, food or water. Some wounded. Some with fever and dysentery. Many dying. He shivered but knew he was not experiencing what they were. He was not hungry. His extremities were not beyond feeling from frostbite. He was not faced with knowing he would never again feel the warmth of love, an embrace, shared nakedness. He was not waiting for death as the only hope of relief, for the love of Allah to be his last and only love.

He walked slowly back to his office. As always, Hanımefendi was waiting and purred when he stroked her. Tonight, he would not send for a wife or concubine to share his bed. He was physically and spiritually crushed. He wanted nothing but to sleep, to lose the burden of consciousness.

FORTY-TWO

Baker and Mehmet Ali's assessment of Kamarlı Pass was that the terrain could not be held. The Russians occupied the high ground, a fact not lost on the troops, among whom desertions by the reserves approached 1,000 a day until Mehmet had 14 executed. Desertions decreased but did not stop. Cold killed more soldiers than the Russians. As many as 40 sentries per night froze to death, despite frequent rotations. As he had predicted, Mehmet Ali was recalled to Istanbul, and he left Baker in charge of organizing the only course they felt reasonable, retreat.

First, the news of Plevna's fall arrived. Then, winter brought a three-day hurricane of snow, locally called a Krivitza, through which it was impossible to see. It buried buildings, camps, and the materiel and provisions of war. Soldiers, civilians, and animals froze. Frostbite spread as though a contagious disease.

Baker considered his situation. The storm left the roads for retreat a sheet of ice covered in drifts of snow. There were 13,000 men at Kamarlı, facing 30,000 Russians. Word came that the Russian force of 120,000 that had been at Plevna was headed their way. The Circassian cavalry had deserted. The telegraph line was down, a bit of news that Baker welcomed. Now, he could not inform Süleyman of his intent to retreat. In the absence of Mehmet Ali, Süleyman was his superior officer, but he did not trust him.

A soldier arrived from a mountain outpost. "A Russian force is moving toward Taşkesen Pass."

"Şakir," Baker called to his most trusted subordinate officer. "I'm going to scout Taşkesen Pass." He recognized the Russian move as a flanking maneuver to trap them at Kamarlı.

For the troops at Kamarlı to escape, that maneuver had to be impeded for at least one day. He wanted to see the size of the Russian force for himself.

Reaching the top of the pass, he surveyed the valley below with his spyglass. The plain was swarming with Russian troops. Black great coats on a field of white, slogging in deep snow. Three battalions in one line. A whole division of sixteen battalions in two other lines. A battalion of the Guard. A mass of cavalry. Three batteries of artillery. He felt his adrenaline surge. The corpus of soldiers approaching seemed not a frightening sight, but a magnificent one, as though he were a spectator about to witness an artistic performance of monumental scale. He was a soldier, a British officer, an Ottoman officer, trained in the conduct—nay the art—of war. He would orchestrate the performance of his life. At the cost of it, if necessary.

Leaving most of the troops at Kamarlı under Şakir, he took the 3,000 men under his immediate command to Taşkesen Pass to face an enemy he estimated at possibly 25,000. Taşkesen, which meant "cut through rock," was aptly named. One of the few passes that a grossly outmanned force might successfully defend. He positioned his men across the heights of the pass. At dawn, every soldier could see the mass approaching them, and yet, Baker Pasha saw no fear in their eyes. They had belief. And with it, a chance.

The Russian cavalry came straight up the mountain road into the Turkish guns that cut down men and horses in minutes. Blood spotted the snow and created red veins in the white where it ran. The remaining able men and horses turned sharply, some falling among the ice and snow.

Then, with its signature shouting roar of "hurrah," the Russian infantry broke into a run toward the Turkish positions, avoiding the road and scrambling rock to tree, crevasse to out-crop. The Turks met the roar with a thunderous cry of "Allah" that rose sequentially from each unit as though a drill to verify that they were in place and ready. In the thunder and lightning of rifle and artillery fire of the next hours, some men lost courage. More lost lives. The fighting was so intense and the numerical onslaught so formidable that Baker contemplated that they might all die. And yet, after seven hours of fierce assault and determined resistance, 2:00 p.m. arrived, and no ground had been lost, giving hope to Baker and his men, giving them a will not to remain forever on this mountain, a will to breathe air unburned with gun-fire and smoke.

Baker moved from position to position to urge courage, exposing himself frequently, watching the sky for a hint of the dense fog common on other days, waiting for sunset, scanning for anything that would bring relief to his soldiers, who were dropping wounded and dead at a rate he knew could not be sustained.

As the sun began to set, the Russians charged again. Instead of remaining hidden, the Turks rose up with a cry of "Allah" and counter-charged. Baker had not ordered this. He would not have. But he watched and then cheered to encourage what at that point could not be reversed. An act of valor by men who threw their fates to Allah. They would not remain hidden for another attack. They would make the enemy fear ever to charge them again. The shouts of "Allah" became shouts of victory as the Russians retreated in chaos among the rocks and trees, down the slopes, into the fear of the next order to attack.

Darkness delivered them after ten hours of brutal warfare that had fallen predominantly on the two battalions in the foremost positions. They had lost more than half their number.

Baker's men fired an average of 275 rounds each and lost 800 of their comrades, but the men in the positions that had to be held, held them. Baker Pasha was overwhelmed with pride. They had saved the army at Kamarlı. They had saved themselves. They had saved him.

There was no time to sleep or rest. The wounded were moved under the direction of Drs. Gil, Heath, and Leslie, who had provided emergency care fearlessly throughout the battle. They moved to wherever called to attend to the wounded, exposed themselves to shelling on many occasions, and blocked out the danger around them as though working in a sterile hospital.

"I want dummy sentries set up across the heights with campfires behind them. We must make the Russians believe we're preparing for battle at dawn," Baker ordered.

The ruse effected, they turned their backs on Taşkesen Pass, covering themselves in darkness and warming themselves with the memories of comrades left behind and the promise of life after war. The army at Kamarlı, under Şakir, was to have begun its retreat as soon as darkness fell. Retreat was slow on the treacherous road surface, but all semblance of a marching army was lost the next day when they reached the plain and joined up with Şakir's forces and with those of several other military units in the region. A throng of men under arms, field guns on carriages, and materiel and provisions on pack animals.

Progress would have been measured regardless, but a city of refugees from villages and towns everywhere south of the Danube joined the army. They came down paths from the hills as though a volcano were spewing the refuse of humanity from the depths of the earth. Thousands moved across the landscape, trusting their survival to the will of Allah and this remnant of the sultan's army.

Baker never forgot the images. A small child's face barely visible from inside a saddle bag on a bullock with the other side stuffed with pans and bread. Bullocks led by men, by women, by children. Bullocks and donkeys pulling hundreds of carts piled with household belongings, babies, chickens, and ducks. Women on the verge of birthing or just having given birth. The elderly and the sick. Horses and donkeys with pack saddles of possessions and provisions. A frail man carrying an even frailer woman on his back. Many small children holding the hands of younger ones. Some carrying baby siblings wrapped in scarves hanging from their backs. Pregnant women with small children at their feet, in their arms, and holding their hands. Children carrying household items. Children herding single or multiple calves, goats, sheep and donkeys. Elderly men and women walking with difficulty. Some falling and not struggling to stand again, resigned to freeze by the side of the road. Snow would bury them.

They were fleeing death from Cossacks and Christian Bulgarians. Some of the atrocities were in retaliation for violence perpetrated by the Circassians and by other Muslim irregulars. Some of the carnage was merely opportunistic. The armies were engaged in war. The civilians were engaged in the free expression of the accumulated hatreds of centuries and the opportunity to acquire the goods and lands of their neighbors.

The ethnic Bulgarian Muslims were the Muslims most despised by the Christian Bulgarians. Their ancestors might have converted to Islam centuries before, but they were still viewed as traitors, families without honor. They were still called apostates, families that had abandoned God for manna. Had become the enemy's representative among them to collect taxes, occupy the offices that performed the functions of government, and live in many of the better houses of the cities and towns. The stories of these people's perfidy were retold to each generation. Bulgarian Christians hated the Turks, real Muslims, for being what they were. They hated the Bulgarian Muslims doubly for willfully becoming what they were.

War and winter spared no creature. Baker saw countless animals accustomed to human care left behind in empty villages and fields. They would seek food and shelter, find none, and die in the snow and cold.

Baker was deeply disturbed by the condition of the refugees, but his task was to save the troops under his command. "What are the scouts reporting?" he asked Şakir.

"The Russian cavalry are following, as well as some infantry battalions, but they are a considerable distance back and do not appear intent on attacking us."

"Perhaps they're waiting to see if we'll surrender." Baker was puzzled, but grateful that he could concentrate on saving his troops from their immediate enemies of cold, hunger, and fatigue. A tired soldier could welcome the warmth of dead cold.

The next day Baker received a telegram from Abdülhamit, thanking him for his service at Taşkesen Pass and promoting him to lieutenant general. In light of his army's current circumstance, his pleasure was muted. He hoped for orders to join other units in the defense of Adrianople, but with Süleyman in charge, he dreaded what orders might come.

His fears were confirmed. "Sir, a dispatch has arrived from Süleyman. He surrendered Sofia, a truce has been reached, and his orders are for us to turn back and retake as much territory as we can for negotiating post-war boundaries."

Baker conferred with the Turkish officers. All objected to the order and agreed to do nothing. Subsequent news came that the war was *not* over, and Baker's army continued its retreat, ignoring another order from Süleyman to turn and engage the Russians, an order that the Turkish officers concluded was equivalent to treason, a suicide mission. The officers agreed, instead, to cross the Rhodope Mountains to the Aegean, the only route of retreat that appeared open to them. Their anger with Süleyman was only exacerbated by news that he had abandoned Philippoupolis without a fight and then Adrianople, which left them exposed from yet another undefended road.

Baker still held out hope of winning the war, if they could reach the Aegean. From there, ships could transport them for the last line of defense at Gallipoli and along the Terkos-Büyükçekmece line outside Istanbul. Ignoring yet another suicide order from Süleyman to rest the troops on an open plain, Baker decided on a night march across a narrow mountain path recommended by local villagers. But the path proved so narrow that he was forced to abandon the artillery carriages, and the refugees had to leave their carts behind. The path was also icy and covered with snow. They travelled single file in some places. Everyone fought exhaustion and the desire to sleep forever. But once over that mountain, the scouts reported that the Russians were no longer following them. The remaining enemy was starvation.

"How many days' ration of biscuit do we have," Baker asked Şakir, knowing it was not much. Ahead he could only see more dense forest and ridge after ridge of difficult topography.

"Three, sir."

"How many days' walk to the sea?"

"The local villagers estimate two to five days, but they've never done it."

"I sent word for supplies and ships to meet us."

"We'll walk until we drop, sir."

Local villagers—many joining them as refugees—directed them to paths through the mountains. One ravine was so icy that they had to throw the pack and riding horses onto their sides and slide them to the bottom. Then, marching on the third day, the final day of biscuit, the forward scouts reached a ridge and yelled, "The sea! The sea!"

When Baker Pasha reached the ridge, he expected to see the Royal Navy, the Union Jack. How could London not be coming to the aid of the Turks? Surely Britain would not give the Russians Istanbul? But that was a momentary thought. He was a soldier in service to the Ottoman Empire. His task was to save Gallipoli and Istanbul, regardless of London. Approximately 35,000 men had survived the retreat. Surely, as many had survived other retreats and were waiting in Istanbul. He requested and received permission to move his troops to Gallipoli, secure it, and proceed to Istanbul.

He loaded as many troops aboard the two ships waiting for them as the ships could carry and discharged them at Gallipoli. Baker, himself, continued on to Istanbul, where he learned that to stop the advance of the Russians, Abdülhamit had accepted all of Russia's demands. Baker was disgusted and asked for a leave of absence to return to London. He would not be a part of surrender.

Surrender, he felt, was to dishonor the heroism of the troops. He had watched them, surviving on biscuit and water, pass through Christian Bulgarian villages without pilfering abundant food, because their orders were not to do so. These men had wills of steel and believed in *kismet*. He could not disagree. *Kismet* had him dismissed from the Royal Army, which led to the opportunity commanders of men dream to have—leading the world's finest soldiers in a historic battle.

Baker knew that reporters and commanders recorded the number of dead and wounded soldiers and the number of prisoners after each battle. He also knew that no one would record the number of civilian deaths or the dehumanization of women and children that he had witnessed. He knew that historians would write multiple, differing, and even contrasting accounts of the many acts of war, some of which they would describe as brilliant, courageous, heroic. Some as foolish, cowardly, shameful. None as uplifting to man or a credit to his Faiths.

The war's end would reestablish killing as murder. A treaty would pronounce peace to people who loathed each other and wanted only to see those whom they hated dead in this life and damned to hell in the next. Baker saw the future. It was war.

FORTY-THREE

Dr. Fonseca stepped down from his carriage. "Rabbi Halevi is expecting you. Please go and bring him here. I'll be ready when you return," he said over his shoulder to his coachman and proceeded in haste through the gate that opened to the small garden enclosure that from early spring to late fall would be alive with vegetables, grapevines, and the colors of wisteria on the walls and flowers in neat beds. The aroma of baking bread greeted him.

"I'm going to Adrianople," he said to his wife, Hannah. "Rabbi Halevi is coming with me."

"Why? What's happening in Adrianople?" she asked, surprised to see him home so soon after having left for his morning rounds at the hospitals.

"The Turkish army abandoned the city to the Russians. The Jewish community there is at risk."

"Many Jews have come from other cities. We'll welcome those from Adrianople too," Hannah stated with resolution.

"Of course, but we know what happens. Some will be killed before they can leave. Others will die on the roads."

"If the Turkish army has abandoned the city, why would there be fighting?" she asked.

"War changes people. You heard the stories from the Jews who arrived from Karlovo, Sistova, Kazanlık, and Eski Zağra."

"So why are you going to Adrianople?"

"Rabbi Halevi and I will propose that all the religious leaders stand together and appeal to the Russians for a peaceful occupation."

"What if the Muslims and Christians don't agree to your plan?"

"I believe they will. But if there's no agreement, we'll urge the Jewish community to follow us here."

"I'll prepare food. It's a long journey."

"Thank you, my love." he said, as he kissed her and held her tightly for a moment. They had been married for 25 years, and yet, whenever he held her, he felt stirred by physical attraction. "You're the blessing of my life," he said, smiling. "I already look forward to returning."

"Please be careful, my love," she said. "I'll pray for you and for the people of Adrianople."

They did not have children, which was a sadness for them, but they compensated by parenting the Jewish community. Hannah worked with several Jewish welfare associations that provided help to the disabled, the poor, widows, orphans, and the elderly. She baked bread for the beggars who came every day. When her garden was producing, she distributed vegetables. She counted every hungry child as her own. They could have lived in a better neighborhood among the bankers and merchants, but neither of them ever suggested this.

"How long will you be gone?" Hannah asked as he turned to leave.

"I expect to return in a week. We'll know quickly if our proposal is accepted."

They heard the carriage return, and Hannah handed him a basket with food and a scarf in which she had wrapped two loaves of bread. He exchanged greetings with Rabbi Halevi and addressed the coachman. "Thank you. I'll take the reins from here."

The coachman would be extra weight. Dr. Fonseca knew he would have to push the horses to their limit. His goal was to arrive in Adrianople in time to convene a meeting of religious leaders before nightfall the next day. Even in his light-weight, two-horse carriage, the journey would require twenty hours, plus time to feed, water, and rest the horses. If the weather held and the road were in reasonably good condition, they could arrive before the Russian army did.

"We're facing a new world," Dr. Fonseca said. "Our ancestors came here for security and the right to remain a separate community, the Jewish *millet*. The Turks accepted us. But now the empire's constitution calls for all citizens to be equal, and people—even the youth in our own community— are talking about nationalism, about loyalty to a nation and its government, rather than to their *millet*."

"The Jewish *millet* is their mother. She teaches them language, customs, and history; provides food and health care, education and welfare; celebrates festivals and ceremonies; builds synagogues, schools, and hospitals. The state does none of these for them," Rabbi Halevi said with emphasis.

"But this war has changed even the Jewish community, even you. I was at the Ahrida Synagogue when you held prayers for the success of the Ottoman army. You spoke of how the Turks had rescued us and asked that we now come to the defense of the Ottoman Empire. Was this not a new message?"

"Yes. I believe the success of the Turks against the Russians is vital to the lives of our people. The war threatens us even more than it does the Turks. Jewish men have formed several volunteer fighting units, and I gave them a dispensation on eating kosher. But I confess that I have grave reservations about Jews fighting in wars."

"But you asked them to fight."

"I asked them to support the Ottoman army. Some are choosing to fight. Fortunately, the 'soldier tax' is still accepted in lieu of service, and the community has shown its support in other ways. Many wealthy families have given generously to the state's war chest. Jewish notables have joined the Red Crescent Society and contribute money. Jewish women—your wife among them, as you know—have formed a society to nurse the sick and wounded soldiers returning to Istanbul. And I gave a dispensation to the dock workers to unload arms on the Sabbath. Abdülhamit knows we support the Ottoman war effort."

"The Jewish refugees arriving from the Danube Province are evidence enough that our *millet* will not be safe under Russian rule."

"The *millet* system has worked for centuries."

"Some argue that nationalism is only another form of the *millet* system, a means for peoples of different religions and languages to live by their own laws, to have their own countries. The Greeks want to live in Greece, Armenians in an Armenia, Albanians in an Albania, even the Arabs in an Arabia."

"Jews in a Jewish state?" asked Rabbi Halevi. The concept seemed incredulous to him.

"Yes."

"This nationalism you speak of would tear the Ottoman Empire apart even more completely than the Russians intend to do."

"Yes, I believe it would."

"Could this happen without war?"

"No. The world is not of one mind about religion, and it will not be of one mind about forming new countries," Dr. Fonseca said.

The journey was long. Dr. Fonseca set his horses on a pace that allowed them to continue with little extended rest but frequent short stops. As the sun set and the road emptied of other travelers, they heard two horsemen approaching fast from the rear. Dr. Fonseca's carriage had just passed through a particularly bad stretch of road, a bog of slick mud, and he encouraged the horses with a light flick of the reins as they found solid footing. They could just make out that the men might be carrying rifles. Bandits were an ever-present hazard of travel, particularly at night. There was the threat of the loss of their horses and carriage and also of death.

But when their pursuers reached the mud at a full gallop, one of the men's horses appeared to slip and fall. They heard the men yelling, but they quickly left them behind. The road led into darkness, and they neither heard nor saw any evidence that the men were in pursuit.

They stopped briefly in *hans* for travelers but did not sleep. Not everyone appeared friendly. It was safer to stay awake and simply rest and feed the horses. Twenty-six hours after leaving Istanbul, they arrived in Adrianople.

Rabbi Halevi had been to Adrianople once before and remembered the home of one of the two chief Rabbis of the Jewish community there. They explained to the Rabbi their proposal for preventing bloodshed.

"I know everyone," the Rabbi responded. "The Muslims will cooperate. They know the stories of Cossack atrocities against Muslims. And the Armenian Archbishop complains that the Russians have not kept their promises in the Caucasus. He does not trust the Russian Orthodox Church. As for the Greeks, they fear both the Russian and the Bulgarian churches. Everyone will listen to what you propose."

******

The next morning, when the dust raised by hundreds of horses and thousands of men became visible in the distance from the main Adrianople gate, the representatives of the *millets* were waiting to greet the Russian army.

Leading the army was Field Marshall Gurko, a man who cultivated a singular appearance by the cut and care of his facial hair. His sideburns, his mustache, and his beard on the sides of his face formed two long, v-shaped tapering points of hair that went almost to his chest. These points of beard were separated by an inverted "v" of open space between them up to his mouth via a clean-shaven chin, as though a trough for eating. His striking visage drew the eyes of others to his own, which were large and looked at once both fearsome and fearful. He had a lean, muscular build and an erect posture that conveyed authority.

Gurko had led the Russian invasion, capturing Tirnovo, Kazanlık, and three Balkan passes, including Şıbka, within 16 days of crossing the Danube. He captured Eski Zağra and Yeni Zağra, sealed off Plevna from the south and east, occupied Sofia, and routed Süleyman at Philippoupolis. Adrianople was his last obstacle to Istanbul.

He had received word that Süleyman had abandoned Adrianople, so he was not expecting a fight. He also was not expecting the delegation that he saw waiting. He signaled for the army to halt and proceeded alone.

"There are no soldiers here to resist your occupation of the city," stated the Greek Archbishop. "We ask only that you come in peace. Our communities are committed to peace."

Gurko had been fighting for seven months. He had seen every foul aspect of war, the atrocities spurred by cherished hatreds. War was not revenge, and hatred was not the emotion of a professional soldier. The war as military engagements was over. He would march to Istanbul unimpeded, and peace would be on Russia's terms.

"You have my word," he said. "I will bivouac my army well outside the city. I expect to receive orders to proceed to Istanbul, and I will leave my most trusted subordinate officer in charge of a small force to protect your city and to maintain peace among you."

FORTY-FOUR

In London, Mithat's emotions mirrored the news of the war and the vacillating debate among British political forces on whether to come to the aid of the Turks. He expected Queen Victoria's public call for Britain to join the war to be decisive. But it was not.

Nevertheless, Mithat continued to be buoyed by the frequent leaks of Queen Victoria's correspondence and conversations with Prime Minister Disraeli. She openly expressed the view that the Russian invasion of the Ottoman Empire threatened British interests and was initiated under false premises. Writing to Disraeli, she expressed her exasperation. "…it was not for the Christians (and they are quite as cruel as the Turks) but for conquest, that this cruel wicked war was waged."

Russia's success in selling its fabricated war motive was frustrating to Mithat. Surely this deceit had been obvious even to Gladstone, as well as to the leaders of Austria-Hungary, Germany, France, and Italy. No one trusted or believed the Russians. It should have been possible to turn this distrust into support for his country.

Still, Mithat continued to see signs for hope. From Istanbul, Ambassador Layard warned that the Ottoman Empire could be forced into an armistice contrary to Britain's interests. In London, the cabinet discussed sending British warships to the Dardanelles and Istanbul. The London press carried stories of heroic Turkish fighting and reported Cossack and Christian Bulgarian atrocities against Muslim civilians. The queen even pressed Foreign Secretary Darby, unsuccessfully, to protest these atrocities to his Russian counterpart in St. Petersburg. Editorials warned of Russian imperialism as a threat to the Middle East, East Africa, and India. Commentators cited Russia's provocations among Christians in the Danube Province and in the Ottoman Empire's eastern provinces and reminded readers of every historic Russian act of aggression in the Caucasus and the Crimea, against the Hungarians and Poles, and against the Polish Catholic Church. Poles and Hungarians had fled to the Ottoman Empire to escape persecution. Polish volunteers were fighting with the Ottoman army.

And yet, Britain did nothing, and when Mithat received the news of Osman's defeat at Plevna in early December, he felt hopeless.

A leaked cable from Ambassador Layard warning that Russia might occupy the Straits and Istanbul and destroy the Ottoman Empire seemed an answer to Mithat's prayers. Surely Britain could not ignore this warning. Nevertheless, an emergency cabinet meeting could only agree to advise Russia that were she to enter Istanbul and not agree to withdraw immediately, Britain would declare war.

Once again, Mithat found only the Queen to be adequately outraged. A note to Disraeli threatened that she would not remain sovereign of a country "…that is letting itself down to kiss the feet of the great barbarians, the retarders of all civilization and liberty that exist. Oh, if the Queen were a man, she would like to go and give these Russians, whose word one cannot believe, such a beating." And in a note to the cabinet, she reminded them that they had previously decided that even a threat of Russian occupation of Istanbul would free Britain from its commitment to neutrality. "If those were empty words," she wrote, "Britain would sink to a third-rate power."

"But for the queen," Mithat wrote to his family, "we might stand friendless in the world. I fear for your safety. You must make plans for leaving Istanbul should the Russians enter the city. Our home in Crete will be safe. If our government falls, I will join you there."

Britain continued to delay, even as the first month of 1878 brought more bad news. The Turkish troops that reached the Aegean were in such condition as to be almost indistinguishable from the tens of thousands of refugees who arrived with them. Adrianople was lost. The Russians were marching on Istanbul and Gallipoli without opposition. Belatedly, the British cabinet decided to send the fleet to Istanbul, but after entering the Dardanelles, the fleet was recalled when a cable from Ambassador Layard reported that Turkey had sued for peace and agreed to the terms offered.

Mithat could hardly believe that the British would be so trusting of Russia's intentions. And his concern was justified. The Russian army continued on toward Istanbul, despite the terms of the armistice. In London, word on the street was that the Russians had not expected Abdülhamit to agree to the harsh terms they proposed, so they were ignoring the terms they had set in order to continue expanding their occupation of Ottoman territory.

"What were the terms of the armistice?" Mithat asked a friend of his among the exiles.

"The Russians demanded secrecy. They fear the terms might prompt the British to demand changes or even to send its fleet. Austria-Hungary might also object. All we know is that the Russian troops are now right outside Istanbul at San Stefano."

"The terms of the armistice will not remain secret long," Mithat observed.

And they were not. The British cabinet objected to many of the terms, particularly the establishment of a greater Bulgaria and

Russia's unrestricted use of the Straits. Meanwhile, Abdülhamit asked Queen Victoria to intervene with Tsar Alexander II, but she had more faith in a show of force than in a diplomatic appeal. She continued to urge intervention, and the cabinet acted. The British fleet passed through the Dardanelles and anchored just outside the Golden Horn.

The question in London's expatriate Turkish community was whether Abdülhamit had asked for the fleet, had given permission when requested, or had simply been a bystander once Britain made her decision.

"Everyone underestimates Abdülhamit. I did also," Mithat observed to one of his colleagues in exile.

"My guess is that he asked the British to send its fleet but didn't put it in writing."

"That's possible." Mithat responded. "He might fear being deposed. If he keeps the people guessing, some will think he asked and Britain responded. This shows him as a leader who is respected."

"But if he doesn't acknowledge this, many will think Britain came without being asked, which would make him appear weak, if not irrelevant in the game of international power."

"True, but this scenario serves his narrative that the empire has no friends and that he's the only impediment to foreign domination," Mithat observed. "Abdülhamit would like to be seen as the empire's only hope."

"A useful façade to rally people behind him, perhaps, but it runs counter to his need to have Russia think that Britain came to our aid as our ally."

"Probably he also wants Russia to think that Britain is asserting her own interests against those of Russia," Mithat said. "It's a stronger message than simply defending an ally."

"Seems to me that defending the Ottoman Empire and protecting her own interests are one and the same thing for Britain."

"Of course. But that wouldn't change Abdülhamit's position or his preference for keeping both ally and enemy guessing. It's his only weapon."

"I heard that he's proposing to mount a horse and personally lead the troops under the banner of the Prophet, may he rest in peace, if the Russians attempt to enter Istanbul."

"A rumor he surely fed himself. It would serve him. But it would be out of character for him to risk his life."

"I heard he's preparing to escape to Bursa and restore it as the historic capital of the empire."

"Save himself and blame everyone but himself for the war and its outcome. He might do that," Mithat said, expressing his inner musings.

To Mithat, the only thing that mattered was that the British fleet was protecting his beloved country and city. Surely, he would be able to return to his homeland soon.

FORTY-FIVE

The war was ending or it had ended. There were too many reports on the status of the war circulating in the city and changing from day to day for Nigar to feel confident that she knew what was happening. But, in any case, she was too absorbed with helping the refugees, who were the war's most visible consequence in Istanbul, to trouble herself with attempting to learn what the truth about the war might be. The refugees had doubled the population of the city, and twice that many more were reported on the roads, in camps along the Aegean and Black Seas, in many cities in the east, and even in cities, smaller towns and villages in the Danube Province that were outside the war zone and had majority Muslim populations. The Ottoman navy was transporting the tens of thousands who had reached the Aegean across the Rhodope Mountains to Anatolia, Cyprus, and Syria.

Istanbul was a virtual refugee camp of misery, poor hygiene, illness, and death. Typhus wandered freely, struck randomly, and had no enemy. No one could ignore the refugees. Nigar heard that Abdülhamit opened unused palaces for them and gave generously from his palace, and even personal, funds to assure that none of his subjects would starve. He also kept his word and sent representatives from the Ministry of Interior to facilitate the able-bodied in homesteading unused land in Anatolia. Nigar and Fatma helped the families prepare for the journey.

Nigar started each day going over the work that was to be done with the families that lived with her at Kağıthane. Winter work—preparing the fields for the spring planting of vegetables, caring for the few sheep, chickens, and ducks she kept. Preparing seed beds, nurturing seedlings. And she continued to go to Süleymaniye mosque for Gül and bring her to Kağıthane. Sometimes they went to the market for food and supplies. Because the harvest was over, they had time to enjoy tea in the afternoons. Sometimes they went for long walks. They practiced math. Late in the afternoon, she returned Gül to the mosque compound to spend the night with her mother. And she gave her coins for her work, as she had promised. Her mother still begged, but not as much and without urgency.

"Gül should no longer spend nights here with her mother," Fatma said to Nigar one day. "The threat of this illness they call typhus is too great."

"I would be pleased to have Gül live with me, but will her mother agree?"

"Leave that to me. We watch many die here. Her mother will want to save her daughter."

From that day Gül and Nigar were inseparable. They made occasional trips to the mosque for Gül to see her mother, but stayed for only short periods. It was not difficult for Gül to understand the danger. She saw the bodies.

Gül's mother, Ayşe, died early one evening, and Fatma had her buried before morning so that Gül would have no opportunity or temptation to touch her. So many were dying that it took special intervention to get Ayşe buried so quickly. But everyone knew Fatma and everyone was indebted to her in small and large ways. So when she wanted something, it was done.

"I can never be your mother, but I will be as good a substitute mother as I know how to be," Nigar said to Gül, comforting her as she sobbed for her mother.

"My mother died in the village when my father and brother were killed and because of what the men did to her," Gül said when she stopped crying.

"You suffered, as well," Nigar said hesitantly, unsure if she should mention the scar.

"You mean the cross," Gül said. "The first night, I felt I would die from the pain," Gül said, touching her arm where the scar was.

"The world is full of pain. I'll do everything I can to help you."

"I know it sounds bad, but I'm more sad about my mother's life than about her death," Gül said in a remarkably calm voice.

"What's important now is *your* life. Would you like to learn to read and write? I would. We can learn together." Nigar had been thinking about hiring a tutor to teach her to read and write Ottoman Turkish for some time. She spoke Turkish well enough for business transactions and for social and personal exchanges. But, except for numbers, she did not know how to read and write Ottoman Turkish, which was written in the Arabic script. She would spend the rest of her life in Istanbul. She needed to be able to read and write Ottoman Turkish. And because of her scar, Gül would never marry. She needed to be able to function independently, which meant being educated in more than numbers.

"My mother only wanted me to raise sons and grandsons to kill Christians because of what happened," Gül said. She could not yet see herself freed from her mother's hatred.

"What happened that day was avenged by the Ottoman army. The perpetrators and many more were killed and any who escaped will face the retribution of Allah and suffer more than the death your sons and grandsons could inflict," Nigar said. "In heaven, your mother knows this."

Gül looked relieved, and her voice expressed resolve. "I'd like to learn to read and write."

FORTY-SIX

Abdülhamit felt frustrated and powerless. The Russian army was at San Stefano, just a few miles outside the walls of Istanbul. His navy failed early, unable to take control of the Danube. His army was routed in the west and lost significant territory in the east. His diplomatic efforts to bring Britain into the war failed. Many thousands of his soldiers died fighting, and thousands more were dying as prisoners. The war had driven the country into debt. The refugees had turned life in many areas of the city back to medieval standards of hygiene and living conditions. And everyone was blaming him. His effort to place the blame on Mithat and parliament had failed as profoundly as his army. No one spoke of the role of either Mithat or parliament in the disaster of the war. Worst of all, reports from London continued to say that Mithat was being treated as a hero, heralded for the constitution and parliament, even though neither would have been possible, but that he, Abdülhamit, had authorized them.

And parliament proved a complete failure. Instead of making decisions for which the people might hold them accountable, the delegates criticized ministers, strategic and tactical war decisions, the actions of commanders in the field, and him, sultan of the empire! They discussed whether there should be an independent Armenia, an independent Kurdistan, and even a Pontus! A Pontus! A territory not mentioned since its defeat by the Romans 2,000 years earlier! No one even knew where it was! The delegates were more dangerous than the Powers. At least the Powers had to worry that if one carved off a piece of the empire, another might eye a bigger piece and set off a war. But parliament could propose such nonsense without regard for the consequences. Parliament was a glorified coffeehouse!

Nevertheless, he held his wrath and took one last gambit to use it. He had already arranged in secret with Layard for the British fleet to arrive, but it seemed useful to get parliament on record in support of it. Surely parliament would agree to have the British fleet waiting to block the Russians from entering the city. But when the question was put to parliament, an uneducated delegate, a baker, responded by saying that he, Abdülhamit, had waited until it was too late to consult with them, and they could take no responsibility for the failure of the war.

Abdülhamit was furious when he heard this from Ahmet Vefik, the president of parliament. "I want every delegate who spoke out against me arrested."

"If they're arrested," Ahmet counseled, "it will attract sympathy for them. Their arrest will be all that people talk about. No one will discuss parliament's failings."

"I'll not listen to another delegate speak, and I will not read another report on what's been said!"

"You don't need to. You are in your constitutional right to suspend parliament, and I advise you to do so. I merely suggest that you order the delegates to return to their homes immediately, rather than arresting any of them. Life in the city is difficult. Your subjects face daily hardships. No one will call for the return of parliament."

That night, Abdülhamit brooded over the map. Which territories might be lost and which might be given independence in governance but remain formally a part of his empire and pay tribute? Everything beyond the walls of Yıldız and some within were potential threats to his rule. Sultans had been brought down by mobs, by military insurrection, by jealous and power-hungry harem women, and by bureaucrats and religious men.

The empire was strong when its sultan was. Sultans like his grandfather, who ruled with an iron hand, were revered, and the empire prospered under them. Sultans, like his father, who made accommodations with reformist bureaucrats, were bullied by foreign governments and internal interest groups. His uncle Abdülaziz was deposed by the very reformers he partnered with. And surely he was killed by them. And Murat was mad. Was he driven so by the fear he must have had of those who brought him to power? Or did they slip him some potion that induces madness!

Mithat presented representative government as a means of uniting the people as equal citizens. But everyone could see that they were not capable of responsible participation in the decisions of state. For the well-being of the empire, its sultan had to be absolute. He would rule in the manner of his grandfather.

******

The British navy passed through the Dardanelles, crossed the Marmara Sea, and anchored just outside the Golden Horn. "The British fleet has arrived, my sovereign," reported an advisor to Abdülhamit, known as İngiliz Sait (Sait, the Englishman), because he had graduated from Edinburgh University and was fluent in English.

"Let's have a look," Abdülhamit said.

They walked into the garden along the path that took them to the kiosk closest to the southern wall of the compound. On its veranda, you could see over the wall and to the Golden Horn in the distance. He pulled out his spyglass and saw the Union Jacks.

"The sailors are singing a song popular in London. It's a boisterous song confrontational to the Russians," Sait said. "The

329

lyrics go like this: 'We don't want to fight, but by jingo if we do, we've got the men, we've got the ships, we've got the money too. The Russians shall not have Constantinople'."

Abdülhamit smiled broadly, something that took Sait by surprise. He did not remember ever seeing Abdülhamit so pleased.

"We lost the war, Sait, but we'll not lose Istanbul. And we may still win the peace. In peace, we'll have the Europeans as our allies against the Russians. I will make sure of it."

Abdülhamit had leaked the secret terms of the San Stefano agreement to the European ambassadors, knowing that Britain would not be able to live with its terms. Even Germany and Austria-Hungary, which had a formal alliance with Russia, would not want their partner's role and power so significantly enhanced. The terms, of course, were completely unacceptable to him, as well, but he accepted them in order to halt the fighting and keep Russia out of Istanbul. He gambled that the Powers would insist on renegotiating the treaty.

******

"My sovereign, Ali Suavi was killed trying to break into Çırağan Palace with a band of refugees. They intended to kidnap Murat and declare him sultan." The speaker was Principal Secretary Sait.

"Ali Suavi?" Abdülhamit questioned with some incredulity. "I allowed him to return from exile. He was the only Young Ottoman who wrote pieces critical of Mithat."

"Yes, one and the same."

"And I gave him a job. Is no one to be trusted? Can I trust you, Sait? "

"May Allah be my witness. I am and will remain your loyal servant. But not everyone knows you as I do. People look for someone to blame for the hardships of the war."

Abdülhamit studied Sait's face. He knew Sait was speaking the truth, but the disloyalty of Ali Suavi was disturbing. Even someone beholden to you could rebel against you. No one could be known except by his acts. He needed more spies.

"Did Murat know they intended to make him sultan?"

"There's no evidence of that. He remains emotionally unstable."

"Yes, anyone planning to have him declared sultan would be doing so to have him as a puppet."

******

A second attempt to rescue and reinstate Murat was foiled soon after Suavi's. The conspirators were reported to be Masons sponsored by the International Society of Masons. International collusion was not proved, but the accusation hardened Abdülhamit's fear and suspicion.

Abdülhamit was also learning not to trust allies. Although the Powers agreed to renegotiate the San Stefano treaty at a peace conference to be held in Berlin, a proposal from Britain confirmed his growing skepticism of this professed ally.

"My government is proposing an alliance against Russian military aggression in Asia," Ambassador Layard began. "We're concerned about Russian designs on the Persian Gulf. Our alliance would assure that she acquires no further Ottoman territory in Asia."

"Why not put such a guarantee in the treaty to be negotiated in Berlin?" Abdülhamit asked.

"We will try, but there won't be a military deterrent to back up such an agreement. Russia could be in Baghdad in days and in the Persian Gulf before we could mount a serious counter offensive to come to your aid."

"How would our military alliance solve this?"

"By stationing British troops in the theater. My government proposes a base on Cyprus. We would administer Cyprus, but it would remain an Ottoman province. You would receive all revenue in excess of our costs, and you would retain control of non-administrative matters, such as, education, religion, and judicial proceedings." Layard watched Abdülhamit's face. The remaining provisions would not be to Abdülhamit's liking.

But Abdülhamit—no longer a novice in the politics of the Powers—knew to expect more. "What additional conditions would be attached to this alliance?" he asked.

"The Russian pretext for aggression will be an assertion of mistreatment of the Armenians. My government will request your agreement to conditions designed to preclude such a pretext."

"And what would those conditions be?" Abdülhamit asked, showing none of the irritation he felt at the insinuation that the Armenians needed British protection.

"Certain reforms in the administration of the eastern provinces."

"Our constitution provides for equal treatment of all of my subjects."

"We understand this in principle. But my government believes certain rights and responsibilities should be specified in our alliance, so that it's clear to the Armenians and to the Russians. The intent is to protect you from false allegations."

"I assume you have a proposed text for this alliance. My ministers and I will review it. You'll hear from me in one week," Abdülhamit said to indicate that the meeting was over.

Now it was clear. It was him against the world. Abdülhamit was frustrated with Britain. Nevertheless, he signed the agreement. The one thing he could not risk was another war with Russia—certainly not one in which he was fighting alone. A British base on Cyprus was distasteful, but security from a Russian invasion was essential. Neither he nor the empire could survive another war, and he never considered the survival of one without the other.

He and Ambassador Layard, with whom he had a warm relationship, continued to meet frequently, to share coffee and cigarettes, and to exchange news. Ambassador and Mrs. Layard were frequent dinner guests. Abdülhamit considered Layard a staunch friend of the Turks, but the positions London chose frequently did not reflect Layard's recommendations.

******

Abdülhamit read the last sentence of the Treaty of Berlin. He placed it on his desk in front of him, signaled for coffee, lit a cigarette, reached down to stroke Hanımefendi, and checked the large German pendulum clock that stood against the wall— 1:50 a.m.

"Do you wish to cable Ambassador Sadrullah Bey to sign it, my sovereign?" asked Reşit Bey, Abdülhamit's private secretary for diplomatic correspondence.

Abdülhamit felt that he had no choice in the matter and said, "Yes," with resignation. He took a long drag on his cigarette and exhaled with deliberate slowness, raising his head to follow the smoke as it drifted toward the ceiling, as though it might lead him to some revelation.

"I know the British feel I should be grateful. They take credit for saving Istanbul. The terms of this treaty are more favorable to us than were those of the Treaty of San Stefano. But the British do not seek to diminish our losses, but to limit Russia's gains." He did not say it, but he knew that the British feared Russia, not him, and that Russia feared Britain, not him. This was the state to which his empire had fallen—feared by no one.

He was bitter. Ambassador Layard had assured him throughout the war that Britain would join in the fight. He felt that the arrival of the British fleet at the end had been a calculated gesture. One that Britain knew she could make without losing a life—almost as though Britain had lured him into war, assuming he would be defeated and leave them an opportunity for gains at the cost of not a single British soldier.

"The British navy arrived knowing that if the Russians attempted to move on Istanbul, the Turkish army would be their ground forces. They're not challenging Russian interests in places where they would have to fight her alone," Reşit volunteered as though reading Abdülhamit's mind.

"And now Russia knows that we cannot fight her alone. And that Britain will not fight with us unless her own interests are challenged. This is the fault of Mithat, who took us into this war. Now he sits in London, claiming that everything he does is in support of me and his country with no thought of benefit to himself! Probably he takes credit for the British fleet arriving to save me!" Abdülhamit was indignant.

"Russia has no friends. Britain cannot allow her the Bosphorus and the Dardanelles, over which she salivates. Austria-Hungary does not want Slav domination in the Balkans. The Greeks only support Russia when they think they can secure more territory. They don't want a large Bulgarian neighbor. Our enemies fear our enemies," Reşit said, hoping to divert Abdülhamit from his preoccupation with Mithat.

"Mithat was proud of the reforms he carried out as governor of the Danube Province," Abdülhamit continued. "He wanted me to implement his reforms throughout the empire.

But the beneficiaries of his reforms were the Christians, not the Muslims, and the result was a war in which Muslims have been murdered, violated, and driven from their homes."

"I will send the cable to Sadrullah," Reşit said. "By your leave, sir." He bowed and backed out of the room, leaving Abdülhamit alone with Hanımefendi and his coffee and cigarette.

Under the Treaty of Berlin, Abdülhamit lost geography—in the east and the west. But most of the shuffled and re-bordered Balkan territories continued to be tribute-paying Ottoman provinces. What he lost was his enemies' fear.

And sovereignty. The Treaty called for the Powers to appoint or approve Christian governors; for Europeans to be appointed to positions within the Ottoman judiciary, tax administration, and gendarmerie; and for unspecified reforms affecting his Christian subjects. Abdülhamit's strongest objection was on this latter point. He insisted that he would only agree to reforms that strengthened Ottoman independence. Fortunately, the Europeans and Russians signed the treaty without coming to agreement on the specifics of the reforms directed toward the Christians, and this gave Abdülhamit the fig leaf he needed to sign it as well.

The sultan of lands that were home to the world's major religions, their multiple sects, and adherents of rare religious beliefs familiar to few, sipped his coffee, smoked his cigarette, smoothed the hair of Hanımefendi, and contemplated the territory and lives he ruled. He could not compete with the Powers militarily, and the Powers would only defend their own interests, which could overlap with his sometimes in some geographic areas, but would be in conflict in others.

It angered him that the Powers, particularly Britain and Russia, demanded privileges for his Christian subjects that they did not grant their own Muslim subjects. But he had to be a realist. The Christians represented a ready wedge for interference, anywhere, any time. The Powers were relentlessly self-righteous and watchful. He could not allow a pretext of Christian mistreatment. The Christians would require not equal treatment but the continuation of their existing, favorable concessions. He could not challenge Britain in Egypt; France in Tunis or Lebanon; Italy in Libya; Russia in the Balkans; or Austria-Hungary in Bosnia-Herzegovina. These parts of his empire nominally remained under his protection and paid tribute, but he knew the Powers could use even the least of pretexts to pick them off. In addition, Austria-Hungary wanted access to the Aegean at Salonika, and Italy wanted Albania.

Spies reported that, in both St. Petersburg and London, voices predicted that the empire would soon collapse on its own and counseled patience. This suited Abdülhamit. He was still sultan and Caliph, a position from which he wielded extensive power and which counted for more among his subjects than the Europeans might appreciate. He could outwait them. Wait for the rat to make the first move.

Nor was all well domestically. Spies reported malcontent in the capital. Everyone sympathized with the refugees, but their presence and needs overwhelmed every aspect of life in the city. They were camped everywhere, begged everywhere, and spread disease and the stench of human desperation everywhere. To fund the war, Abdülhamit had issued paper money, which the people did not value, and the result was inflation and public discontent. The wealthy felt less wealthy. Ordinary people felt impoverished. The poor felt hopeless. Rumors of plots to restore Murat passed in the market as casually as the exchange of news about the weather.

The most crippling provision of the Treaty of Berlin was the large war indemnity granted to Russia. It represented economic interference by the Powers. Nevertheless, he remained sultan, and he would fulfill that role. He vowed to eliminate the foreign debt. He would resettle the refugees in Anatolia. He would bring peace and prosperity to his people. His Christian subjects had their own schools and many missionary schools that their children could attend. He would build schools for Muslims. He would build a university, a medical school, telegraph lines, and railroads throughout Anatolia. He would give *all* his subjects reason to credit him for a better life.

But these were long-term goals. His immediate action would be to bring Mithat back from exile. Exiling him had absolved Mithat of responsibility for the disasters he had brought upon his country—the incompetence and uselessness of parliament and the decision to go to war. Abdülhamit would not allow Mithat to remain a hero in London.

FORTY-SEVEN

"Don't come near me," Fatma said, as Nigar stepped down from her carriage. "I have the disease. I came out only to say goodbye to you."

"Are you sure?" Nigar asked, reaching toward her.

But Fatma stepped back. "Yes, I'm sure. I'm an old woman. Allah is taking me in His mercy."

Nigar returned early the next morning and hurried to where the dead were washed for burial. Because of the volume of deaths and the fear associated with the disease, mass graves into which lime was tossed were the norm. Befitting her reputation in the compound, Fatma's body was lying slightly apart from the rest. "I will pay to have Fatma buried on the hill above the mosque," Nigar said, putting her hand in her purse.

"It will be done Madam," said the imam, using the form of address for a Christian, rather than for a Muslim woman, which annoyed Nigar, particularly since the Imam knew her to be a Muslim. But she let it pass. Fatma would lie among the wealthy and religiously honored in the shade of the cypress trees, a place she deserved. "I'll arrange for a headstone for the grave, as well," she added.

Silently, Nigar thanked Fatma. Fatma had intervened with Gül's mother, and in Gül, Nigar experienced joy and love in measure beyond what she expected. She looked at this young girl and marveled that this detritus of war was her daughter, her raison d'être.

Being a mother was one more phase in her life, one more experience that she could not share with her own mother. She wished that she could tell her mother about Gül, about her joy in having a daughter, and perhaps to ask for advice on how to raise her. She did the next best thing: she raised Gül as she had been. Education was what she remembered as the most important part of growing up. Doing her homework at the kitchen table while her mother cooked. Not something she and her mother ever spoke of. Education was assumed. Central to growing up.

As a scarred young woman, Gül needed an education. No one would give her anything. She might have to stand toe to toe with men, as Nigar did, as Fatma had. She needed a better education than the men with whom she might do business. She would need to extract concessions, while allowing them to feel they granted them in magnanimity.

Nigar had learned much in living and working in Istanbul, and she wanted Gül to benefit from it. No one would exploit this damaged village child who was her daughter. The population literate in Ottoman Turkish, even in Istanbul, was small. Nigar needed to find a tutor willing to teach them to read and write Ottoman Turkish.

She found Hasan Hoca in Kağıthane at the Bektashi *cemevi*, around which refugees were seeking shelter. Nigar liked Hasan immediately. He did not look at her as though she were anything but the Muslim she presented herself as. He listened to her request respectfully. He would accept no money to be their tutor, but he asked that she donate produce for the small village of refugees around the *cemevi*, which had a soup kitchen.

For Gül, reading and writing were completely new. Speaking on a page, hearing from a page was beyond imagining. But her mind absorbed it naturally, as though a field accepting a gentle rain. For Nigar, it was more difficult. She had to unlearn and relearn. The Arabic alphabet was very different from the Latin one she knew. Ottoman Turkish was written from right to left. Many vowels were not written, although they could be. Turkish had sounds that the Arabic script did not convey. A group of consonants could represent different words, depending on the missing vowels, so only the context of the sentence could reveal the meaning. Ottoman texts had more Arabic and Persian words than were common in speech.

"The scar on my arm. Will it affect my life?" Gül asked one night as they worked on handwriting.

The question surprised Nigar. Of course the scar was omnipresent in spite of never being visually displayed, but she had naïvely assumed that the scar was not something Gül thought of as defining her. "If *we* live as though it doesn't, no one else will be able to make it so. That's what I believe."

"I like that. I want to live as though it's not there."

"And I'll do everything I can to make that possible," Nigar said, embracing Gül as though she were too precious and too vulnerable to ever set free and, at the same time, a pillar that would hold her up whenever she questioned how to be her mother.

As her mother had done with her, Nigar taught Gül to sew in the evenings after their lessons were finished and their homework complete. They started with the simple stitches for hems, seams, and button holes, the stitches for making clothing. They made pretty dresses to wear in the house and to go to Pera, where Nigar thought she would take Gül to meet Cristo one day soon. They made baggy pants for working in the fields and common dresses to wear over slacks for going to the market. They made clothes for the children of the refugee families working on the farm and living in the makeshift village by the *cemevi*. Gül had skillful hands and enjoyed the work.

On this particular night, Nigar and Gül had finished tracing their letters, copying sentences, and reading passages to each

340

other when the guard announced the arrival of a woman who wished to speak with Nigar. "She says she knows you and that she comes from Yıldız Palace."

"Mela!" Nigar exclaimed. "What brings you here?" Mela looked little changed, and Nigar recognized her immediately. She still had the pale complexion and perfect skin of a young woman. Even without makeup, her face was beautiful, her eyes blue stars. She was dressed as a peasant woman with baggy pants and a generous dress over the top with a scarf on her head, pulled down and tied under her chin.

"I hope you don't mind," Mela said. "I need help. Even on that day in the hamam, your wedding day to Abdülhamit, I found you to be kind. And I admired your decision not to come to the harem. You're a strong woman."

"I'm pleased that you thought well of me on the day of my marriage. I was naïve, but I had no animosity towards you or the young girls. Please come in. How are you?" Nigar stepped back, signaling for Mela to step inside the door.

"Abdülhamit has not asked for me since he became sultan. I didn't want to wait until the palace decided to be rid of me. I wanted to leave while I can still do more than wait for death."

"How can I help you?"

"Even in the harem, we heard of your work to feed the refugees. I'd like to help you grow food. I feel it's my last chance to do something with my life, to be something other than a sultan's pleasure. I was a peasant girl. I know the soil. I don't ask to live in the house with you. I'll live with the workers."

"The workers are families who stay here for a few weeks or months while they make arrangements to resettle in Anatolia. You'll live in the house with me and Gül, whom I'm caring for as my daughter. She's a refugee from the Danube Province. We have plenty of room. And you can work in the fields as much or as little as you want."

"Thank you. You're very kind."

Nigar laughed. "Mela, the kindness is Abdülhamit's. This is his farm. We live here only so long as he agrees that we may. But you know that he owes you much and that you owe him nothing. And we both know that he would not deny our living here. It's not in his character. He has faults that do harm mostly to himself. Cruelty to women and children is not one of them. Gül and I will be pleased to have you share his kindness with us."

FORTY-EIGHT

In the summer of 1878, with the crises of the war's aftermath lessened, Abdülhamit turned to what he considered to be the remaining threat to his rule, Mithat. In London Mithat was the revered Turk, the champion of constitutional government, a voice for the restoration of parliament. In Istanbul, parliament lay buried under the squalor of refugees and the bodies of the typhus dead. No one spoke of it. Any pressure to recall parliament would come from London. No one would hear Mithat's voice from a remote province. Abdülhamit had his principal secretary write to Mithat to express the sultan's willingness to bring him home and appoint him to a governorship.

Mithat accepted Abdülhamit's invitation to return, but he declined a post as governor. Mithat requested, instead, to retire to Crete, where he had a house. The tone of Mithat's acceptance was deferential but contained no expression of regret or apology. The response annoyed Abdülhamit, but he decided that Mithat's capacity for influence from Crete was less than from London.

******

"Foreign fleets fired their cannons in salute when Mithat arrived?" Abdülhamit asked incredulously, when informed of the action by Principal Secretary Sait. "I sent him to Crete by military cruiser as a courtesy to show my good will!"

"I regret to report, as well, that many from the Christian and Muslim communities came to the wharf to cheer him." Sait was uncomfortable, knowing that this news would anger Abdülhamit.

"How would they do that if not put up to it by the British?" Abdülhamit stated as a question, still smarting from Britain's failure to help him in the war.

"Enemies win through victory in war. Allies gain by exploiting friendships, my sovereign."

"Mithat was responsible for the war!"

"The people are ignorant. They've made him a hero, when he's done nothing for his country," Sait responded, searching for a soothing message.

Welcome words, but Abdülhamit was not mollified. Why did the people not give him the adulation they gave Mithat? It was he, Abdülhamit, who had suffered from the war, who was misled by his generals, his allies, and even his spies. And yet his subjects as distant as Crete would heap praise on an exile who wrote treasonous editorials in support of democracy, a political system intended to emasculate their sultan! A system so ineffective that, under it, Queen Victoria could not have her will obeyed!

Mithat's retirement in Crete did not sit well with Abdülhamit. Mithat would have access to the people for his ideas of governance but no responsibility to govern. Abdülhamit decided to put Mithat where he could make a mistake and sent a cable appointing him as governor of the province of Syria, noting that the province faced serious challenges that required his experienced hand. Abdülhamit counted on Mithat's ego to entice him to take the assignment. He would go, and Abdülhamit would have his spies waiting.

******

"Sultan Abdülhamit has appointed me governor of Syria," Mithat said to Şehriban.

"We've barely been in Crete for a month. I thought you didn't want another position. You would become a gardener, remember, my love?" Şehriban said in a light, teasing tone that, nevertheless, revealed her underlying concern and disappointment.

"It's a meaningful appointment."

"Will you accept?"

"I feel I must. My country needs me. Syria is a province with people of many religions and sects of religions. It's exactly the environment in which we must show that they can live together in peace. I'm sorry, my love. This is the purpose of my life."

"The children and I are proud of you. We support you in whatever you feel you must do."

"And we'll go as a family. Damascus is a beautiful city. There are good schools for the children. I owe my country to do what I can, and I owe it to my children to see their father serving his country."

"If Abdülhamit had nine more men like you, or even two more, the empire would be strong," she said, throwing her arms around him and kissing him.

Mithat held his wife for a long time. "So, I'm not adequate? The empire needs at least two, maybe even nine more men like me?" he teased.

"It needs thousands. Tens of thousands. But only one you. One you is enough for the empire and for me."

******

It had been more than a year and a half since Mithat had experienced what, for him, was the joy of being a provincial governor. Long lines of petitioners waited for him on his first day in Damascus—personal requests, accusations of injustices and corruption, complaints of brigandry and lawlessness, and allegations of fighting among religious communities. He was exhilarated.

"The world is watching," Mithat admonished his chief tax collector. "The French have an interest in the Lebanese, the British in the Druze. The Americans build schools for protestant Christians. The Germans support emigrants to Palestine. The Spanish have a school and a Catholic church in Jaffa."

"How does Abdülhamit permit this?"

Mithat understood that he was being baited. Obviously the man reported everything he said to Abdülhamit. "All the people are the sultan's subjects, and it's our duty to protect his honor by treating them equally, as required by the constitution that Abdülhamit promulgated."

The spies were an annoyance, but Mithat focused on the personal welfare of the citizens, which required integrity in officials, efficiency in administration, and security in the streets and roads. Honest tax collection brought in funds for the repair and construction of roads, a School of Arts and Crafts, an orphanage, and a tramway connecting Tripoli to the port of Mina. He paid the troops and sent them in a show of force to dissuade the Hawrans and the Druze from an internecine war. Peace filled in wherever anarchy was driven out.

******

For Abdülhamit, the reports from Damascus were among the many from every part of the empire that he read late into the night. But he read those from Damascus with more care. Despite a large volume of reports on what Mithat was doing and saying, most contained inconsequential minutia or speculative and hyperbolic observations of no use to him.

346

He also received reports from Mithat, who had the audacity to request permission to initiate reforms and to recommend that he reopen parliament. Abdülhamit ignored these requests. Mithat was already implementing changes for which he did not need Abdülhamit's concurrence, and Abdülhamit was not about to enhance his power. Mithat also sent requests to retire, but Abdülhamit chose to ignore those as well. He would not have admitted it to anyone, but Mithat's success in a province that had been rife with trouble was helpful.

"Ambassador Layard has gone to visit Mithat in Damascus," reported Sait, watching Abdülhamit's reaction carefully. This was not news Abdülhamit would like.

"Do we know why? What's his purpose?"

"The British Embassy only confirmed his travel."

"What do you think?"

"Perhaps he's merely taking an opportunity to explore the markets in Damascus. He's taken his wife with him. I hear they have excellent gold and silversmiths there, as well as fine carpets and spices from around the world."

"More so than here in Istanbul?"

"No. It would be an excuse. The British could be up to mischief. He knows Mithat is a friend of the British. Perhaps he hopes to get information from him."

"We'll see what's reported when the two of them meet."

Abdülhamit could not help but feel betrayed. He regarded Ambassador Layard as a personal friend. Lady Layard had helped nurse wounded soldiers during the war. Ambassador Layard and his wife were favorites of everyone in the palace. Abdülhamit felt let down by Britain's stand during the war, but throughout, Layard had been his advocate. Now, he was in Syria conferring with a man Abdülhamit regarded as an enemy.

Many reports came from Syria about Layard's visit. A meeting with the military commander. Meetings with religious leaders. Several sight-seeing trips and trips to the central market with his wife. Reports on what they bought and how much they paid. Nothing was too trivial. Only a report from a servant in Mithat's home contained a sentence that suggested a sinister motive. "I overheard Ambassador Layard and Mithat Pasha speak of an 'independent country' and something about an 'Arab uprising'."

Abdülhamit knew this could mean anything. Layard might have shared a harmless rumor reported by one of his own spies. The most sinister interpretation would be that Layard was speaking of a British plot in which they wanted Mithat's collusion. Given the mix of interests among the religious and ethnic groups in the province, Britain could easily provoke an incident that would be a pretext to send in troops from Cyprus and declare Syria an independent protectorate. With Mithat as its governor? Abdülhamit was prepared to believe this of Mithat, but less so of Layard.

The matter was cleared up with Mithat's own report on Layard's visit, which included the information that Layard had reported the existence of a secret society plotting to establish an independent Arab state. Mithat promised to rout out the members. And when Layard returned and called on Abdülhamit to report on his visit, he confirmed what Mithat had written. Abdülhamit was relieved and disappointed. Mithat had escaped another trap.

Abdülhamit decided to transfer Mithat to the governorship of Smyrna, another troublesome province, but one closer to Istanbul. His spy network in Smyrna was more sophisticated and included many Christians, in whose presence Mithat might be less careful. Surely, the rat would expose his neck soon.

FORTY-NINE

"What a blessing you are to this farm," Nigar said to Mela, as she approached her in the field where she was overseeing the harvest of August vegetables. "I've never seen plants so bent with produce. They look like they know how desperately the refugees need food."

Mela stood up from where she had been picking tomatoes, and Nigar put her arm around her. They stood looking over the fields. "The farm is a blessing to me," Mela said. "It's taken me back to before I was kidnapped. I never forgot my life in our village. I remembered it, but it was like a dream. This farm has made it real. I remember everything we did to raise vegetables, wheat, sunflowers, melons. Caring for cattle, sheep, and goats. This farm has returned me to life as a happy young girl," she said smiling.

"It's wonderful. You deserve to be happy. Are you practicing your counting?"

"Oh, yes. I love knowing how to count. And I can do addition and subtraction in my head. I practice all the time."

"With Allah's help, one day we'll no longer need to grow food for refugees. Then, we'll set up a market, and you'll be a businesswoman, selling what you grow. You must join Gül and me in our Ottoman Turkish lessons. A businesswoman needs to read and write. And I'll teach you French. I'm teaching Gül. We'll have a market in Pera and sell your produce to the Greek and Armenian businessmen, the bankers and investors, the diplomats and spies. You'll be famous. Men will flirt with you. You're still an attractive woman."

Mela laughed. "In my life as a concubine for Abdülhamit, the sun didn't parch my skin. The wind didn't dry my hair. I had no work to callous my hands. My mother's skin was dry; her hair was brittle; and her hands were leather. But she had a beautiful smile and a loving touch. I would rather be like her than have men flirt with me."

Mela was such an effective manager of the farm that Nigar spent most of her time at the refugee camp around the Alevi *Cemevi*. The refugees needed everything. The environment fostered by the Alevis was very different from that around the Süleymaniye Mosque, particularly toward the women. For the first time, Nigar saw that Islam did not mean the same thing for all Muslims, and she began to think about what it meant to be a Muslim.

The imam of the *cemevi* invited her to use the building as a space to teach mathematics to the refugee boys and girls. Even a few adults attended her classes. Some fathers objected to their daughters' being educated, but as refugees, dependent on strangers, they were susceptible to influence. Most had never heard of Alevi Muslims or Sufi mysticism. They had not come to this camp because it was supported by the Alevi community. They were here by fate. Allah had brought them here, and they were at His mercy, at the mercy of the Alevi imam who spoke of Allah differently than had the imams in the villages they had fled.

Many things were new to the refugees. In the *cemevi* that served as the Alevis' mosque, the women and men were not separated for prayer. Consequently, most of the refugee women did not go to the mosque, even for Friday prayer. They were not comfortable praying among men. And the women of the neighborhood did not cover their faces and only loosely covered their hair, even when they came to the mosque to pray. These were Muslims unfamiliar to the Danube refugees.

But it was a community in which Nigar, at last, felt at home as a Muslim, accepted as a Muslim. No one looked at her as though she were a Christian. She felt no regret in having accepted Islam, and she was delighted that, in this Alevi community, she was experiencing the diversity of Islam. She knew broadly that Muslims divided themselves into Sunni and Shia and that they mutually considered each other heretics. Abdülhamit was a Sunni, so he surely assumed that she had agreed to be Sunni, as well. But she had given it no thought, and she never heard Muslims discuss differences among themselves.

She raised the question with Hasan Hoca. "I know you are Alevi. What does that mean? How do your beliefs differ from Sunni and Shia Muslims?"

"We Alevis are Shia. The Shia/Sunni split occurred over a dispute about the qualifications to become Caliph. To a Shia, Abdülhamit has no claim to be Caliph. For us, the Caliph has to be a descendant of the Prophet Muhammed, may he rest in peace. The split was not about belief."

"So you are Shia but Alevi. What does that mean?"

"We follow the Sufi tradition, which some call mysticism. We believe that the faithful's purpose is to live a life of striving for the unattainable goal of being perfect in our love of Allah."

"Can I be an Alevi?"

"Of course. It's a way of living. Your help to the refugees is an Alevi way of life. An Alevi expresses his love of Allah in what he does, in living in accord with the Quran's injunction: 'The best of men is he who makes himself useful to his fellow creatures'."

Nigar was not sure that she could spend her life trying to achieve perfect love of Allah. But she could live a life devoted to loving others, to helping others.

In the afternoons, she taught the basics of sewing, showing the women and girls how to repair damaged clothing that came to the camp through donations. They disassembled some that were too damaged and made new clothing from the pieces. Nigar demonstrated to the young girls and their mothers how they could match up complementary colors and patterns, and they accepted her, accepted the hands she extended to them, hands that sewed, that created useful from useless, beautiful from ugly.

Nigar wanted new cloth for them. She went to see Cristo.

"I know you come to take advantage of me, and I'll permit it. But only after we have tea," he said in greeting her.

"I won't pretend I've come only to see you, though it's always a pleasure to do so. I use my need for your help as a pretext. But I can only reveal my request after tea."

"I hear you are teaching refugees math and sewing," Cristo said as they drank their tea.

"Yes. And I'm learning to read and write Ottoman Turkish from an Alevi *hoca*. He's made me think about what I believe."

"In Istanbul everyone is a believer, but much of what they believe is not in the canon of their faith. And yet, they call those who differ with them unbelievers and heretics. A tolerant believer is a gift from God."

"A thoughtful observation, my friend. You should have been a priest."

Cristo laughed hard, spilling some of his tea. "I'm sure God is laughing with me. Not that I would be the first sinner among priests, but I might strive to be the most prolific one!"

"Do you believe God will punish us for our sins?"

"He created us as sinners, did He not? This is what my faith teaches. That all men are born sinners. So, if He did not forgive us, His creation of us would be cruel. How's that? Maybe I should be the Patriarch?"

"You have my vote."

"And you have whatever it is you came to ask for, my friend. What's your wish?"

"It's not an easy request."

"I'd be a fool to expect otherwise, and I'll do whatever is required to meet your need, a penance for my sins. God forgives, but it helps to give Him a reason, don't you think?"

"Yes, and I hope you have enjoyed your sins, so that the trouble of this request will seem worthy to have them forgiven," Nigar laughed, but then grew serious. "Many of the refugees arrive with no clothing worthy of the name. The camp receives donated clothing. Some in bad condition. I'm teaching the women and girls to repair clothing and to make clothing from pieces of clothing that can't be repaired and from new cloth. I buy cloth with what money I can spare. But I need more. When the women and girls put on a pair of pantaloons or a blouse they've made themselves, their faces change. They see an end to being hopeless. I'd like you to collect cloth from the cloth merchants. They have ends of rolls they cannot sell, even at discount. They have patterns and colors that are not selling. Even small pieces of no value to them can complement other pieces and make a new piece of clothing. I'm teaching patchwork clothing as art. The young girls love it. And we know the merchants are sinners who need God's grace. They cannot refuse."

"You have anointed me Patriarch. I will go to them in that capacity. But you must promise to meet me in heaven," Cristo said in a sincere and solemn tone.

"I'll be there. But first, I want a second glass of tea."

Cristo made the merchants feel obliged to save their souls, and Nigar soon had stacks of new material. Her sewing sessions provided physical and emotional renewal, an end to destitution in a new piece of clothing.

In the evenings, Nigar taught French to Gül and Mela. And the three of them studied the reading and writing of Ottoman Turkish with Hasan. Hasan demonstrated the graceful lines of Arabic letters which they copied again and again until he was satisfied that they had mastered them. He taught them how to join the letters together and how they changed when in the initial, medial, or final position of a word. He demonstrated how Arabic calligraphy became art, rather than communication, in decorative inscriptions, and for the *tuğra* of a sultan. He showed them how to draw the *tuğras* of the most famous sultans, such as Süleyman the Magnificent, and, of course, of Abdülhamit II.

Nigar's life was full, and she was happy. But despite Hasan's assurances that she was accepted as an Alevi if she chose to be, she felt spiritually unfulfilled. She prayed, but she knew she was not devoted to achieving perfect love of Allah. She was a practical person, not a mystic.

Maybe she was still a Christian? She resolved to go to Hagia Sophia, the once great Christian basilica, now a mosque. Perhaps inside this edifice with its duality as a Christian and Muslim holy place she could find inspiration or even the resolve to love Allah or God perfectly.

She arrived at Hagia Sophia for the Friday Noon Prayer and was surprised to see that no one was entering the mosque. Stepping inside, she understood why. The edifice looked more like a giant holding pen for livestock than a place of worship. Thousands of refugees were sitting, lying, standing with no apparent space among them. Anyone who lived or worked nearby knew that there was literally no space inside to perform ritual prayers. Only a few of the refugees were praying. She thought to leave, but her purpose in being here was not to pray, but to contemplate, possibly to hear the voice of the Almighty.

She made her way to where she could look up to the dome and watched the shafts of light from the 40 small windows at the base of the dome merge to illuminate the massive interior of the basilica. Light falling on the destitute. Nowhere had she seen more perfectly depicted the Christian image of the sheep under the protection of the divine shepherd.

Even the steps ascending to the gallery were encumbered by refugees, but she reached the top and stepped around people to reach the gallery's railing, from where she could take in the full grandeur of this place, holy and symbolic for both Christians and Muslims. A physical place of this world that was of another world. A place where it was possible to commune with the Almighty and know that He had no concern for your religious affiliation or the name you called Him. His one requirement was that you be kind and loving to all.

From the gallery, even the several thousand refugees crowded in Hagia Sophia could not obliterate or even distract from the awe and holiness of this place. She knelt and prayed. She felt her sprit filled. She stood and walked tall down the stairs and out into the street, removing her scarf, free to be whoever she was or would be.

And who was she? She was the little girl who was raised by a loving mother to be kind and honest, the core of Christianity and of Islam that was too little practiced by the adherents of both in the world in which she lived.

And who would she be? She would be a believer who did not judge those unlike her in religion or lifestyle, and she would ignore the judgment of those who saw her as less than they. Maybe that was one way to love Allah perfectly. At least the Alevis would not think her a heretic.

FIFTY

"My government wishes to express its deepest sympathy for what's happening in Bulgaria," said Ambassador Layard.

Abdülhamit had seen copies of some reports from British consuls in the Balkans and been told of many others. The reports described property confiscation, murder, rape, humiliation, and expulsion of Muslims throughout the territory, as well as the similar treatment of Jews.

They had just finished their ritual Turkish coffee. Abdülhamit swirled the small amount of liquid heavy with grounds at the bottom of the demitasse in the ritual motion that would precede having his fortune read. But he did not put the saucer on top of the cup and turn it over for the grounds to run down the sides of the cup and leave a pattern to be interpreted. Reading these patterns was a kind of national entertainment— often the preserve of the eldest woman in the household. In the palace, it was the function of the official fortuneteller and a ritual Abdülhamit looked forward to whenever Ambassador Layard and his wife were palace guests for dinner. For the sultan and his foreign guests, the patterns always showed positive events: long life, wealth, many children, an enjoyable journey. And the palace fortuneteller frequently knew gossip that could embellish his predictions to the amazement and delight of the guests.

But Abdülhamit was frustrated with his British friend and with the country he represented and was not in the mood for light conversation or humor. He set the cup back upright on the saucer. Layard was not here to commiserate over the refugees.

Layard got the message and followed suit in placing his coffee cup upright. He shifted his position. "My government wishes to convey its distress over the misrule of the Khedive Ismail in Egypt, your majesty."

"Misrule?" Abdülhamit responded. Misrule was a euphemism that might be applicable, but Layard would not have called for this meeting simply to complain of it.

"The Khedive has shown no willingness, despite our repeated warnings, to curb his lavish spending. He's driven Egypt deeply into debt. A strong hand is needed on Egypt's finances. We propose Ismail's son, Tevfik. He's well educated and progressive. He's committed to leading Egypt to fiscal health. My government is asking that you depose Ismail and appoint Tevfik as governor."

A commitment to being Britain's vassal, Abdülhamit thought. He knew of the Khedive Ismail's love of luxury. Ismail and many of the wealthy and powerful in Egypt had *yalıs* along the Bosphorus, where they escaped the heat of Cairo in summer. Despite his personal frugality, Abdülhamit enjoyed being in the company of those who lived well. He counted Ismail a friend.

What bothered Abdülhamit was the concept of deposing a leader. Any leader. If the British could arrange to have the Khedive of Egypt deposed, might they conspire to have him deposed? "I'll give you my answer after I consult with my ministers."

Two days later he sent the order deposing Ismail and installing Tevfik. The word from spies in Egypt, in London, and in the expatriate community in Istanbul was that Britain was resolved, and he would only look without authority if Britain, rather than he, made the change of governor. Despite his personal affection for Layard, Abdülhamit accepted that Britain was, at best, a self-interested ally—and might be a predator.

This assessment was reinforced a few months later. Abdülhamit was once again entertaining Ambassador Layard at his request. The Ambassador's customary social niceties went beyond what was usual, which indicated to Abdülhamit that the message was not one he would like. "And what message do you bring from London, my friend," Abdülhamit said.

"My government wants you to implement the reforms you promised that affect the Christians in the eastern provinces."

Abdülhamit inhaled deeply from his cigarette and paused before exhaling. "Christians are protected under our constitution, the same one for which you and your government have professed support. The Russians invaded on the pretext of protecting Christians. Is your government using the same pretext? To threaten what?"

"My government negotiated at Berlin to protect your empire, and we provide guarantees under the Cyprus agreement. In return, you were to appoint Christian governors and Christian inspectors."

"If your government is contemplating some kind of confrontation, I wonder whether the Russians will stand by as idly as you did when they invaded? I repeat that Christians are protected, and we will both find out what the Russians choose to do if your government decides they are not."

Abdülhamit waited. Britain did nothing. When it was clear that he had prevailed in the standoff, Abdülhamit appointed one Christian governor to the eastern province of Erzurum; appointed his ally, Baker Pasha, to a gendarmerie command in Anatolia; and sent word that he would receive one British judicial inspector for the eastern provinces. The concessions of a victor.

This proved to be the last diplomatic confrontation Abdülhamit would face with the man he considered his friend, Ambassador Layard. In Britain the Liberal Party won the election of 1880, and Gladstone, the leading anti-Turk voice in London, became Prime Minister. Gladstone's harsh view of the Turks was reflected in the man he sent to Istanbul to replace Layard. Goschen was an arrogant religious chauvinist. Abdülhamit was particularly offended by Goschen's open manifestations of prejudice against Turks and Muslims. And Goschen's barely disguised disrespect for Abdülhamit precluded an alliance on any matter. So when he delivered, as an ultimatum, his government's proposal to modify a boundary for Macedonia that had been set as part of the Treaty of Berlin, Abdülhamit rejected it without discussion. Had the vehicle for the message been Ambassador Layard, Abdülhamit would have heard him out. Layard would have relayed messages back and forth to London. Time would have passed. Several meetings. Perhaps a dinner with the palace favorite, Mrs. Layard. Cigarettes smoked. Coffee consumed. Fortunes told. Anger and humiliation abated. Perhaps a compromise reached. Instead, Goschen threatened that the British fleet would occupy an unnamed Ottoman port unless and until Abdülhamit agreed. The ultimatum was a dagger in British-Ottoman relations. Abdülhamit caved, angry and humiliated.

But Abdülhamit had avoided invasion, and he remained the sultan of an empire that was mostly recovered from the effects of the war. Fewer beggars plagued the conscience of those who passed them in the streets. Many refugees had left for Anatolia, although some continued to arrive in Istanbul from Bulgaria and from Russian-controlled areas in the Caucasus.

Abdülhamit recalled the paper money, halting inflation and restoring confidence in the marketplace. He paid the back salaries owed to the civil servants, who had not been paid during the war. He established a debt commission to pay off the empire's foreign loans and bond interest. Twenty-five percent of the empire's revenues went directly to the commission for this purpose. He imposed strict austerity on the palace and demanded the same of every ministry to keep within the spending permissible with the remaining seventy-five percent. Pet projects were delayed. He cut military spending deeply, although he paid the soldiers, including back pay. Eunuchs reported less discontent in the Istanbul coffeehouses.

He was in control and unthreatened from within or without. He took more walks in the garden. Petted and fed the many cats that roamed there. Spent more time listening to his children demonstrate their musical accomplishments. Sometimes even retired before midnight with extra thought as to who would share his bed.

But he could not will himself to feel safe. The world outside Yıldız was hostile. He could look out across its walls and imagine his empire, but he had no desire to risk seeing it. And events invariably reinforced his fear. In March 1881, Russian Tsar Alexander II was assassinated. This was the man who had defeated him. This man, who went to the battlefield and observed the fighting, who exhibited the boldness Abdülhamit envied, now lay dead. He had been Tsar of Russia, King of Poland, and Grand Duke of Finland. He was respected and feared among the Powers and was one of the emperors in the League of Three Emperors with Germany and Austria-Hungary. He had done much for his people: freed the serfs, promoted education, abolished capital punishment, promoted local government, and built more than 20,000 kilometers of railways. His suzerainty benefitted the people. And their gratitude was his assassination. His extensive and ruthless cadres of secret police had not kept him safe. If Alexander II could be assassinated, surely he, Abdülhamit, was vulnerable.

"Inform the newspapers that they are to report Alexander's death as from typhus. There's to be no mention or hint of assassination," Abdülhamit said to Sait, formerly his principal secretary and now grand vizier, who had brought him the news of Alexander's death. No one was to think assassination possible.

One month later, Abdülhamit received the news of Benjamin Disraeli's death. The most pro-Turk voice in Europe was gone from the stage. Increasingly, Europe seemed more an enemy than an ally. France invaded and occupied Tunis in response to an incident that was likely stirred up as a pretext. They demanded that the ruling *Bey* sign a treaty of protection. Tunis was a long way from Istanbul. Abdülhamit had no armed forces anywhere nearby. A naval expedition ran the risk of exposing his navy as ineffective. He protested and was ignored. Not a single Power joined in his protest. And yet, the province remained formally a part of his empire.

He did not have the military power to preclude any of the Powers from colonial encroachments. The threat of joint action by the Powers against him might be negligible, but the threat to his survival in power from losing bits and pieces of the empire was real. Would history remember that he did everything he could to save the empire or that everything he did failed? He added spies to the payroll and scrutinized everyone for loyalty.

Seeking loyal men, Abdülhamit turned to Mahmut Nedim, the former grand vizier under Sultan Abdülaziz, who was known as "Nedimov" for his pro-Russian stance. Mithat had dismissed him after desposing Abdülaziz, and parliament voted to have him tried as responsible for the war. But in Nedim, Abdülhamit saw a man who, if rehabilitated, would be indebted to him and be loyal. Abdülhamit appointed him minister of interior.

Mahmut Nedim understood Abdülhamit. He knew whom Abdülhamit feared, and he shared Abdülhamit's desire to be rid of Mithat. "Your majesty, I am pleased to serve you," he observed in their first meeting. "I've never ceased to suffer from the pain of knowing that your uncle was assassinated and that the perpetrators remain free."

"Abdülaziz committed suicide. More than 20 doctors confirmed this."

"Do you believe that? As Allah is my witness, I confess that I do not."

"What evidence do you have that it was not suicide?" Abdülhamit asked, leaning in.

"The evidence of logic. Who deposed Abdülaziz? And seeing that Murat was incompetent, who would have feared the restoration of Abdülaziz?"

"Mithat, of course. But we have no evidence against him."

"He would not personally have carried out the deed. He would have ordered others to perform it, and they can be found."

"How?"

"Through inquiries. Your secret police would have no difficulty in finding them."

"And they would confess?" Abdülhamit asked with excitement in his voice.

"But of course! The confessions of those asked to make them are not in doubt."

Abdülhamit strode into the garden, walked the path around the artificial lake, and sat on the kiosk veranda with the best views of his domains. He looked toward Asia and Europe and imagined the empire, all of which, except Istanbul, he had seen only on a map. Mithat would have no sympathizers or defenders. His principal advocates were off the stage. Disraeli had passed away; Ambassador Layard had retired from political life; and the fate of the Turkish constitutionalist once feted in London would not demand the attention of Queen Victoria.

He asked for coffee and lit a cigarette. Neither quite satiated his excitement. He walked to his zoo of animals from around the world and spoke with the zookeepers about the geographic home of several of them. He walked to the aviary and spoke with the keepers about colorful birds he had not seen before. Animals and birds came as gifts from rulers throughout the world. If he read about or saw a picture of an animal or bird of interest to him, he let his desire be known, and one or a pair would arrive.

Now that he saw a path for eliminating Mithat, time seemed to pass too slowly. He wanted Mithat dispensed with now. He rarely had time to enjoy the features of the Yıldız Palace complex. But now there was too much time. Even those things that he loved most about the complex could not distract him long enough to make the prosecution of Mithat for murder happen soon enough. He was a child anticipating gifts.

FIFTY-ONE

Gül had become a beautiful young woman who could read and write Ottoman Turkish and French and spoke both as an educated person. She sat and stood erect. She looked at others directly with her brown eyes from under dark lashes and eyebrows. Exposed, her long brown hair had natural waves that gave her the appearance of having been to a stylist. In another setting, every marriage broker would be telling their clients of this young woman.

Gül was 16 years old. Six years had passed since she had been branded. Three years since she had come to live with Nigar, who watched this shy village girl grow confident, taller than girls her age, and better educated than many daughters of pashas. Yes, she was a remarkable young woman, and Nigar knew that she could not remain only as her daughter on the farm in Kağıthane. Nigar wanted the best life possible for Gül. But what could that life be? No Muslim family would accept her as a bride. Even Alevi mothers would not see her as a bride for their sons.

That Gül was also considering her future came out as a question to Hasan Hoca over tea after one of their lessons. "Hasan Hoca," Gül began, "do Alevis believe in revenge?"

"What do you have in mind?"

"My father and brother were killed by Christians who also violated my mother and branded me," she said, pushing up the sleeve of her dress to expose the wound. "My mother admonished me over and over that I was to raise sons and grandsons to kill Christians. To my mother all Christians were guilty."

"Is that how you feel?"

"No. I don't want to raise sons and grandsons to kill Christians."

"In her anger, your mother forgot that the Quran explicitly forbids the taking of another person's life. Your mother is in heaven. She wants you to remember her kindnesses and love for you, not her anger," Hasan counseled.

"Thank you, Hasan Hoca. Thank you," Gül said, her voice reflecting that a huge burden had been lifted from her.

"There's no need to thank me. Give thanks to Allah."

Nigar listened to the exchange in awe. Yes, Gül was a grown young woman. How would she help her find a place in the ravaged world of post-war Istanbul?

The answer arrived the next afternoon in a carriage amid the dust of horses at pace. Nigar was in a cabbage patch near the house, in front of which the driver stopped the horses and the passenger alighted.

"Cristo!" Nigar called, "What a surprise!"

"A surprise? How is it that you have enjoyed tea with me these many years and never expected I would one day come to have tea with you?"

"You've slighted me by your absence!"

"The fault is mine. I accept it," Cristo said as he executed an elaborate bow.

"Come inside. Tea will be served, and you can tell me your real reason for this visit now or after tea. I prefer after, because it will keep you longer."

"I must look very old, if you think I would seek a quick departure from your company."

"You look not a day older than the day I first met you, nor any the less reduced in charm, which I resist only to preserve it."

"Well then, I thank you for thinking of my better self, which I do possess and occasionally attempt to display. What a lovely vista of vegetables."

"We grow everything. One of Abdülhamit's former concubines, who was raised in a village, oversees the workers, and I pretend to supervise her."

"Your pretense works wonders, I see."

"Equal, I hope, to yours in saying you have come to have tea."

"My niece, Athena," Cristo began after they had finished tea and cookies, "has eloped to London with the young Englishman I told you about. Comes from a good family, I'm told. He was representing several companies that sold British woolen goods. Athena has done well, even if my sister is distraught. Secretly, I think she's happy. Athena spared her the gossip and expense of a wedding here."

"Who will manage the shop?" Nigar asked, knowing the answer had brought Cristo to Kağıthane.

"*You* will, of course. You will, won't you? Just until I find someone."

"I have one condition."

"You expect to have tea with me every day."

"That too, of course. But my condition is that you allow me to bring my daughter with me and teach her the business. She's only 16, but, as you will see, she looks older and is more mature than most young women of 20. She speaks French, knows mathematics, and reads and writes both French and Turkish. Plus, she's beautiful, and she drinks tea."

"If she has you to teach her the business, it will flourish. Thank you. I'm delighted that the shop will remain open, but even more so that we will have tea, just as before."

"But, of course."

FIFTY-TWO

Mithat stepped off the royal yacht *İzzettin* at the port of Jeddah, along with the other prisoners from the trial for the alleged murder of Sultan Abdülaziz. The prisoners included the three confessed killers and their accomplices and two of Abdülhamit's brothers-in-law, Mahmut and Nuri, who, along with Mithat, had been convicted of ordering the murder. Also among them was Sheikh Ul-Islam Hasan Hayrullah, banished for life for issuing the *fetva* of deposition.

Many days had passed since they sailed from the dock below Yıldız Palace on the Bosphorus and across the seas of Marmara, the Aegean and the Mediterranean; through the Suez Canal; and up the Red Sea to this port where the cloudless sky greeted them with 100% humidity and 140 F degree temperature.

Mithat comforted himself in knowing that Jeddah was not their destination. They were to be imprisoned in the castle in Taif, several more days' journey overland. Taif was in the Sarawat Mountains, where the temperature was cooler. Desert tribes summered there. The climate permitted the cultivation of figs, grapes, and pomegranates. Taif was the transit point for Yemen's coffee beans, the basis for a perfect cup of Turkish coffee.

Taif was also the historic home of the Banu Thaqif tribe, against whom Muhammad won an important battle in his conversion of the Arab tribes to Islam, an historic event familiar to every educated Muslim. Mithat saw his secular service to his country as a religious duty, the duty of a good Muslim to provide honest government to those governed, even to those who were not Muslims. In prison, he would have time to pray five times a day, to do his religious duty for his spiritual life in a city important to the birth of Islam. The spiritual and secular semi-circles of his life were coming together to form his whole in the land of the Prophet, may he rest in peace.

To reach Taif, they would pass through Mecca. He would ask to stop there, so that he might pray in the compound of the sacred Kaaba. This would not fulfill the tenant of Islam that required Muslims of sufficient means to make the haj, but to be within the vicinity of the Kaaba and not perform a prayer there, would feel profane. Surely, his request would be honored.

Throughout the long journey to Jeddah, Mithat could not stop going over and over again the events that had brought him here. He heard the rumors over the years that Abdülhamit was jealous of his accomplishments and of the admiration and support he enjoyed from political figures in the West. Also the gossip that Abdülhamit was told that his deceased uncle had not committed suicide but had been murdered. Nevertheless, Mithat never entertained the possibility of what happened to him. He never wrote a word critical of Abdülhamit or blamed him for any of the empire's difficulties, not even over the war with Russia, not even when he was writing in exile.

And he never thought that anyone could take the allegation of Abdülaziz's murder seriously. The report of Abdülaziz's death as suicide was signed by 22 doctors, including foreign doctors. Idle people talked. Those hoping to benefit conspired. But no facts existed to give him reason to anticipate what happened. Yet here he was.

His most recent assignment had been as governor of Smyrna Province, a troublesome outpost that suffered physical insecurity. Murders and thefts were common, which instilled fear and harmed the commerce on which the city depended as a port for the transit of goods and people. The city had large Greek

Christian and foreign populations and hosted an underworld of sex, drugs, crime, bribery, and commercial chicanery that made some streets unsafe at any time of day. A late nineteenth century port that every sailor recognized, knew how to navigate, and saw no need to change.

But Mithat set about changing it with a visible, civilian police force to impede man's basest impulses. He opened an orphanage to care for some of the indigent children from the streets. He opened schools. As in other provinces where he had served as governor, many citizens expressed their gratitude for his attention to their welfare.

He was aware, of course, that spies reported to Abdülhamit on everything he said and did, as well as on things he did not say and do, but he had become accustomed to this and felt almost immune to it. Surely, even Abdülhamit would recognize false allegations. He believed that lies would be naked before truth. But events had rolled one after the other through the past month as boulders down a mountain, gathering speed, dislodging others as they tumbled, crashing to the bottom that was Jeddah. Sentenced for the rest of his life to a cell in the historic fortress of Taif. Sweat rolled down his face and among the hair on his chest, down the back of his neck, and along the sides of his spine.

The scenario of murder presented at the trial was based on the confessions of three people. One, a secretary to Abdülaziz for many years, claimed to have held Abdülaziz in his chair by wrapping his arms around Abdülaziz's shoulders from behind while the other two each sat on one of Abdülaziz's knees and held one of his arms as they cut first his left wrist and then his right. They claimed to have held him for approximately 20 minutes until they were confident that he had died.

This scenario was absurd. Abdülaziz was a large man, proud of his physical strength. The man who claimed to have held him in his chair was of small build, a clerk with the physical strength commensurate with shuffling papers and writing official pronouncements. The confessed murderers described no resistance from Abdülaziz, and the doctors' report described neat wounds that suggested no struggle.

Adding to the implausibility of what they described was the fact that Abdülaziz died in mid-day. At the time of his death, no one reported seeing anyone from outside entering the palace, and at the trial, no one testified to seeing the murderers enter. Nor did anyone testify to seeing them once inside, other than the guards who confessed to having posted watch for the murderers. No one testified to hearing calls for help or cries of pain. This, in a palace where Abdülaziz's mother was known to be always in close proximity to him. At the time of his death, his mother was the one who saw him slouched over in his chair from right outside his room through a window in the door. How would no one have seen the murderers enter or leave? Why would Abdülaziz not have called for help? Anyone could see that these confessions were wrung from torture.

But the trial was not held in the chambers of the Department of Justice, but in Yıldız Palace. The judges were selected by the palace. The marionette defense lawyers were appointed by the palace, challenged no questions, and offered no defense against allegations.

And how was he, Mithat, supposedly culpable? At the time of the alleged murder, he was President of the Council of State. The charge was that Sultan Murat and his mother desired to have Abdülaziz killed to prevent his return to the throne, but that they could not have him executed without the approval of the Council of State! Therefore, he, Mithat, and Abdülhamit's brothers-in-law, Mahmut and Nuri, who were also members of the Council, must have approved the murder!

370

And Mithat was accused of further demonstrating his guilt by taking sanctuary in the French Consulate in Smyrna upon hearing that he was to be arrested for Abdülaziz's murder. Only a guilty person would seek foreign asylum. Mithat wished that he had not done that, but the commander reportedly coming to arrest him had a reputation for brutality and was reported not to be in uniform. Mithat feared that the commander might be under orders to make him disappear, or kill him and claim he had resisted arrest. Abdülhamit was known to dislike ordering harm to his enemies but to relish its implementation. At the trial, Mithat could not allege these things, of course. He could only point out that the information he received initially caused him to fear for his life, but that he surrendered as soon as he was assured that he would receive a fair trial. Nevertheless, his initial action was taken as proof of guilt.

Other "proof" offered was the accusation that he would have feared for the fate of his reforms if Abdülaziz were returned to the throne. And why had he failed to insist on a thorough examination of the body in his presence, he was asked? Was it because the deed had been done at his behest? And why had he not launched an investigation of the death? The report signed by 22 doctors attesting to the death as suicide was noted as an inadequate defense.

And there were allegations Mithat had never heard before: a wound on the body above the left breast that not a single doctor had reported seeing, and the testimony of one witness that he had reported to Mithat that Abdülaziz showed signs of life as his body was transported from the palace. Why had Mithat not followed up on these two significant matters? Mithat was sure that someone could fabricate these things only under torture.

Found guilty, the defendants were sentenced to death. And yet, Abdülhamit, true to his nature, did not want to be held accountable for death sentences. He wanted to trick even Allah, Mithat thought, into thinking that he was a good man who implemented naught but justice on his subjects. He did not order the sentences carried out. Instead, he asked a commission of *ulema* to review the case, hoping to have them take responsibility for the death sentences. But the Sheik Ul-Islam rejected the request, saying that the case involved a civil action against the state, so the state needed to rule on it, as it had. For him to issue a *fetva*, there would have to be a new trial before a religious court. No fool the Sheik Ul-Islam, Mithat concluded.

But Abdülhamit persisted in seeking to escape responsibility. He delayed further. The trial became a matter of discussion in the British parliament, and Britain asked that the sentences of those who were not accused of carrying out the murder be reduced to life in prison. Several Western ambassadors wrote a joint appeal for clemency. Several doctors who had signed the original death report as suicide wrote a letter saying that the allegation of murder was baseless.

Again, Abdülhamit sought cover. He convened a Grand Council of dignitaries and *ulema* to advise him on whether to reduce the sentences. The majority of the council members voted not to reduce the sentences, but a significant minority voted for commutation to life in prison. It was enough. Abdülhamit had what he wanted: a minority opinion of dignitaries, complemented by the intervention of foreign governments. He commuted the sentences to life in prison. Allah could not judge him with the sin of murder.

Small comfort to Mithat. The empire was a different place from what it had been in 1876. The excitement of reform was gone. Everyone was hunkered down in their old ways, seeking to hold on to what they had. The trial and convictions had solidified Abdülhamit as an absolute dictator. At the edge of the Arabian

Desert, Mithat's parliamentary democracy was a mirage, an oasis mirrored by the sun through waves of heat, offering water to the near-death traveler who would never reach it.

FIFTY-THREE

"The prisoners have reached Taif, my sovereign," reported Grand Vizier Sait. "The world will soon forget them."

"Thank you," Abdülhamit replied, taking a deep breath and exhaling forcefully, as though shedding himself of a burden. Mithat was gone, finished. Now it was legally established that Abdülaziz had been murdered at the order of Mithat. He, Abdülhamit, had done but what the law required—brought Mithat to justice. As for the accusation that the confessions were obtained through torture, the people cherished the right to speculate on the truth more than they desired to know what it was.

Looking at the great map on the wall of his office chamber, Abdülhamit saw no external or internal threat. Britain's and Russia's mutual fear permitted him to remain neutral. Britain had what it needed—control of the Suez and no Russian warships in the Mediterranean. Austria-Hungary and Russia continued to eye the Balkan Peninsula as territory to be further divided, but neither wanted war. The human and financial cost of the 1878 victory rested heavy on Tsar Alexander III.

Nevertheless, Abdülhamit did not permit himself to relax. With rare exceptions, from before dawn until late into the night, he scanned the local and foreign press. He read reports from governors, dignitaries, and spies. He met with his ministers, with members of the *ulema*, and with foreign representatives and foreigners in the employ of his government. Enemies would plot against him, but he would be watching, informed, prepared.

But he allowed himself more evenings with his family, laughing at the antics of Karagöz and Hacivat in shadow puppet shows, and enjoying performances of Moliere and other plays by the palace troop or troops from France. Unlike the world beyond the Yıldız walls, within them, Abdülhamit created a happy world, where the people he loved were denied nothing and feared nothing. If a play or opera had a sad ending, he had it changed to a happy one. It was the world he wanted for all his subjects.

Yıldız was a world unto itself, reputedly with more than one underground escape route, of which Abdhülhamit was the only person who knew their number and how to access them. He wandered this world alone, seldom in the company of anyone else. He trusted a few of the men with whom he worked closely and some of his slaves. He had to. And they rewarded that trust.

But he had no one with whom he shared his thoughts or confidences or from whom he sought advice, as he walked or rode or sipped his coffee in the gardens. The empire was his. He would keep it in his control, out of the hands of the many who coveted it in whole and part, the foreigners *and* his subjects.

******

In the summer of 1882, however, revolution in Egypt disrupted Abdülhamit's illusion of peace. "British Ambassador Lord Dufferin requests an audience," announced Grand Vizier Sait. "He wishes to discuss the situation in Egypt."

For three years, Abdülhamit had read reports from Cairo about Ahmed Urabi, an upstart colonel whose "Egypt for Egyptians" movement was becoming a serious threat to the Khedive Tevfik's government and the British substructure that propped it up. Tevfik tried to buy Urabi off with appointment as minister of war, but this did not restrain him. Urabi's movement was supported by Egyptians of all classes. They chaffed at high taxation and foreign domination of their country, where the military officers were mostly Turks, and where senior officials throughout the government and the private sector were mostly British and French.

Abdülhamit sent an emissary to Urabi to see if he could use Urabi as a means of ridding Egypt of the British and French. But Urabi was as opposed to paying homage to Istanbul as he was to the Europeans. As minister of war, he began purging the army of Turkish officers.

Today's news was that the British fleet in the harbor had bombarded the city of Alexandria in response to an earlier protest riot, during which approximately 50 Europeans had been killed. Today's bombardment killed at least 250 of the local population. Surely, this would be the purpose of the Ambassador's request to meet. Was he coming to apologize for the bombardment? More likely to demand an inquiry into the deaths of the Europeans or to propose another change in khedive. The French fleet, which had been in the harbor earlier, had withdrawn. What agreement lay behind that? Were the French ceding interests in Egypt for assets elsewhere?

"I will see the Ambassador tomorrow afternoon," Abdülhamit responded. "Do you know what he wants?" Abdülhamit had yet to form a strong opinion of the newest British Ambassador, Lord Dufferin, but the subject of Egypt was a source of irritation.

"He will ask you to send troops to help the British suppress the Urabi movement and maintain order in Egypt," responded Grand Vezir Sait.

As was Abdülhamit's manner with all who came to see him, he received Lord Dufferin graciously and went through the

376

formalities, but sincerity and warmth were absent. "I understand you wish to speak with me about the situation in Egypt," he said as soon as courtesy permitted.

"Yes. My government feels that it would be in your interest and ours for you to send troops to help us secure civil order in Egypt. Urabi has declared your representative, the Khedive Tevfik, to be a traitor. There are demonstrations in the streets. We fear a popularly supported military uprising that could result in the assassination of Tevfik. There could be chaos that would cost many lives and the loss of Egypt to you as a province. I have two documents that my government wishes you to sign. They specify the provision of troops and the conditions of their service," Lord Dufferin said, extending them to Abdülhamit.

"I see. The Khedive Tevfik desires that I send troops?"

"You will see that he has signed the documents."

"I will review the documents and discuss them with my ministers and advisors," Abdülhamit said to indicate that the meeting was over.

"I hope to hear from you soon. The situation in Egypt could deteriorate rapidly," were Lord Dufferin's parting words.

The official request was worse than Abdülhamit expected. London wanted him to denounce Urabi, to send troops to help them suppress Urabi, and to guarantee that the Turkish troops would not ally with Urabi and would not remain in Egypt after security was restored. Effectively, a short-term Anglo-Turkish occupation would be used to guarantee long-term British rule. His instinct was to reject the request outright. But he delayed.

Weeks passed. Lord Dufferin pressed for a decision. Abdülhamit kept putting him off. His close advisors now included a well-respected Arab religious figure, Abu Huda, who pronounced his bona fides by wearing a green turban to indicate that he was a descendant of the Prophet. Disillusioned with his Western allies and the Western-influenced pashas, Abdülhamit was sympathetic to counsel that advised him to turn eastward, to emphasize his role as Caliph, leader of the Muslim world, protector of Muslims from Christian imperialism. Among his advisors, Abu Huda was this view's principal proponent. "Urabi is supported by all segments of Egyptian society. Their revolt is against Christian rule. If you send troops to put down a popular Muslim leader, the Arab population throughout your empire may see you more as villain than as Caliph," he advised.

Abdülhamit ordered the Council of Ministers to discuss the language of the documents. They held numerous sessions for this purpose. On several occasions, Lord Dufferin was kept waiting for hours on the promise that signature was imminent. But it did not come.

"The Khedive Tevfik fears for his life and has asked for our protection. The Egyptian government effectively is in the hands of Urabi. It's imperative that you send troops immediately," Lord Dufferin blustered.

"The British are bringing in more troops from Britain—20-25,000," reported Abdülhamit's minister of war.

"The British are sending troops to Egypt from India—possibly 10,000. They were seen boarding ships yesterday," observed a report from Calcutta.

"British warships are approaching the Suez from the Red Sea," read another report.

"British warships are approaching the Suez from the Mediterranean," read yet another.

"I believe you should send troops, my sovereign," Grand Vizier Sait said. Sait had waited until now to express his opinion. Abdülhamit trusted him, and he guarded that trust by rarely calling on it. "If the British army confronts and defeats the Egyptian army, Britain could declare Egypt an independent country. Such a move could be seen as a precedent by our enemies and by aspiring nationalists."

"I need the language of the documents to reflect our sovereignty. I will not have the British dictating how long my troops will remain in Egypt, nor under what conditions."

"I will make that clear to those reviewing the language, my sovereign."

******

Abdülhamit and Lord Dufferin received the news almost simultaneously. The British had attacked and scattered the Egyptian army at Tel El-Kabir and arrested Urabi in Cairo. Tevfik was restored as khedive. Egypt was a British colony that would continue the façade of remaining in the empire, recognizing Abdülhamit as sultan, and paying nominal tribute.

Abdülhamit received this as good news. He had not sent troops to suppress a Muslim uprising against a colonial power. He did not have the blood of Egyptian soldiers or the loss of any Turkish troops on his hands. He would not have a decision on his conscience about what to do with Urabi. Britain bore full responsibility. Also, Egypt was debt-ridden, and its population resented British rule and its daily manifestations. A headache Abdülhamit did not need. He continued in possession of what he wanted, Egypt as a part of his empire. No further loss of empire under his suzerainty.

But reports from spies everywhere gave Abdülhamit no peace. Spies conjured up revolt, assassination plots, independence movements, and even the specter of Mithat being smuggled out of the garrison in Taif. A powerful religious rebel, the Mahdi of Sudan, was in revolt against the British. One scenario had the Mahdi crossing the Red Sea, invading the Hijaz, capturing Mecca, and declaring himself Caliph.

The Mahdi frightened Abdülhamit less than the speculation about a British expedition to confront the Mahdi. Reportedly, it would make a stop at the Red Sea port of Suakin. This news was spun to him with a hypothetical chain of events, postulating that from Suakin, a small band of men could quickly reach Taif and rescue Mithat. The British had Egypt, but they were unpopular, as was the Khedive Tevfik. What if they brought Mithat to Egypt as prime minister of a constitutional monarchy? Would he not be the perfect antidote for anti-British sentiment? A respected Muslim leader to give legitimacy to the British model of government and its administration of Egypt. It was sinisterly brilliant.

Abdülhamit could not sleep. He called for no concubine. He smoked and drank coffee throughout the night, the last part of which he spent on the veranda of a kiosk from where he could see beyond the Yıldız walls down to the Bosphorus and along it to the Golden Horn. With the call to Morning Prayer, he signaled for his prayer rug and prayed for Allah to administer just punishment to Mithat—perhaps a fatal disease.

He considered ordering Mithat killed. He had the authority to do that. Mithat had been sentenced to death. He had given him leniency. Why? Because of Surah 4:93 of the Quran: "He who kills a believing soul intentionally Allah makes the Fire of Hell his abode." Being sultan gave him the power to order men killed, but not absolution for their deaths.

Abdülhamit went back to his office, where a stack of reports waited on his desk next to his morning glass of milk. Everything was in order, as it always was. The disorder was Mithat, who persisted in challenging the order Abdülhamit worked so hard to establish. As sultan, he made decisions and issued instructions grand and petty. But some things were done that he did not order—especially when it was known that he desired them to be done. Subjects wished to please their sultan. Surely it was Allah's will that a murderer suffer the same fate as the man he murdered. But how to assure that Allah's will prevailed? If he did not order Mithat's execution, but made his desire for Mithat's death known, would Allah not determine Mithat's fate, as he did the fate of every man?

FIFTY-FOUR

"My name is David," the young man said, smiling and extending his hand. This was the third day in a row that he had come to the shop. He purchased soap on his first visit and candles on his second. Today, he arrived the moment Gül opened the shop. In fact, she saw him waiting across the street for her to open, and she felt a rush of excitement that embarrassed her. He was among the most handsome, if not *the* most handsome, of the men to come to the shop. Tall, with dark hair that he did not cover with a hat in the style common among her customers, hair that he combed straight back without a part. His face was clean shaven without even a fine line of mustache that many European young men sported in Istanbul, as though required in the land of the Turk. She was embarrassed to think she would like to be kissed by him. He had what she thought were unusual eyes—blue, green or even brown, depending on how the light struck them.

He lingered in his first two visits, finding pretexts through questions about her merchandise to look into her eyes. And she did not focus her gaze below his eyes, as Nigar had taught her, but returned it directly, while also returning his smile. Beyond his mouth, his forehead, eyes, cheeks, and chin—every aspect of his face smiled. She could not help but smile at him, warm to him. Yes, that was the quality. He was warm. She felt warm standing face to face with him as soon as she opened the door, even though it was early in the morning and cool inside the shop. She knew her face was flushed, but she could not think what to do to take control of herself. Or of him.

"I'm from New York," he continued. "I'm making purchases for the family's businesses. May I ask your name?"

"My name is Gül," she responded and paused. "It means rose," she said, seeking to make the exchange something more than that of a name. But then she felt embarrassed that she might be suggesting that she was beautiful and added, "It's a common Turkish name for girls."

"Rose is also a woman's name in English. It may be a common name, but it's a flower of uncommon beauty. Many women are roses, but a few are special."

That was how it began. He waited every morning for her to open the shop, and after the day he introduced himself, he made no pretense to be interested in anything in the shop, other than Gül. She learned that his mother was a French Catholic and his father a French Jew. They had met at the university in Paris and eloped to New York. Their parents did not approve of their marriage. They spoke French at home.

He attended Catholic services with his mother and synagogue with his father. They told him that he should know both faiths and make his own choice. He never made a choice, continuing to attend the services of both faiths. He was baptized and circumcised. He loved the ceremonies of both faiths. "I grew up feeling I was the luckiest child in New York," he said, "because we celebrated the Jewish holidays *and* the Christian holidays. Choosing a faith never made sense to me. I feel a part of both. And I've never felt unfaithful to either faith by not being exclusively of one. I assume you're Muslim."

"Yes."

"Sunni or Shia?"

Gül was surprised at the question, not expecting an American to know the difference. The surprise showed on her face.

"I took a course at university where we studied Islam," David continued in response to her surprise, "including the difference between Sunni and Shia, as well as about Hinduism, Buddhism, Taoism—even atheism, that is, the arguments for and against the existence of God."

"I'm Alevi," Gül replied, surprising herself in her answer. She had not considered what kind of Muslim she was. She had never heard the word Alevi until she began taking lessons from the Alevi *hoca*, Hasan. "Did you study it also?"

"Not in my class, but I've read about Alevi practices and about Sufi mysticism. And I've read some of the poetry of Rumi. I know Alevis are not common here. Where did you grow up?"

"I live with my mother in Kağıthane, outside the city." It was true, she thought. Not the full truth, but true.

Gül was terrified to tell him much about her background. She never mentioned her real mother, but spoke of Nigar as her mother and of their raising food for refugees, and, truthfully, of her father having died when she was young. She decided to tell him that her mother, Nigar, was from Belgium. A Belgian mother explained her fluent French. She told him that Nigar had remained in Istanbul after the death of her husband, which, of course, by implication would mean her, Gül's, father. This was a lie, but it had elements of truth. Her father *had* died. Nigar *was* her mother now. Nigar *was* from Belgium and had remained in Istanbul. And although Nigar's real husband, Abdülhamit, had not died, their marriage had. He was dead to their lives. She did not want to say anything that might drive David from her life.

Almost three years had passed since Gül began helping Nigar run the shop. After the first few months, Nigar stopped coming with her in the carriage to open the shop in the mornings, but she continued for a while longer to join her toward the end of the day. They would go over the accounts and inventory.

Now, when she came, it was only to have tea with Cristo before they went home, and often Gül joined them. She called Cristo "uncle." He was almost a foster father and looked out for her. "If any of these young men who come to the shop give you trouble, you just call, and I'll embarrass them such that they'll never show themselves again," he said on the first day she tended the shop alone.

Gül was attentive to how Nigar handled the men who came to the store, offering just enough openness that the enjoyment of her presence brought them back, but never enough encouragement to think she would respond to interest in her personally. Some of the men flirted, but did not persist when she did not reciprocate, which she learned to do without offending them or making them feel rejected. They were customers.

Now, Gül was nineteen with long dark hair, somewhere between black and mahogany. She was tall and stood and walked gracefully and with confidence. Her dark eyes, long lashes, and dark eyebrows competed with her lips and mouth for the attention of every man who came into the store. Her clothing exposed little, but could not hide the proportions covered.

David waited for her every morning. They talked about life in New York and Istanbul. How the streets of both cities were filled with people who spoke many languages, attended different houses of worship, often spoke ill of each other, and yet accepted to live together. "When a man wants the finest suit available," David said, "he comes to my father's shop, and when a woman wants a distinctive and fashionable dress, she goes to my mother's shop, regardless of their personal feelings about Jews or Catholics. In New York, commerce transcends emotions. It's a beautiful city, like Istanbul. You'd feel at home there."

Feel at home in New York? Gül looked at him and then immediately looked away. What did he mean? "Are there

Muslims in New York?" she asked, failing in her attempt to ignore his implication in saying she would feel at home there.

"Of course. From many countries, including from parts of the Ottoman Empire. From India and Persia. From all over the world."

They talked about his formal education and about her education from her mother and the *hoca*. He was particularly interested in how she and her mother used their land to produce food for refugees. He knew about the war, but had not read accounts that described the devastating effect of the war on the civilian Muslim population of Bulgaria.

"My mother and I also make clothes for refugees from used clothing and sometimes from new cloth that merchants give us," Gül said. Gül appreciated that he seemed aware of her sensitivity about talking about her family. He never asked how her father had died, for example. And he never asked why she had not been enrolled in a school.

He came every morning for three weeks, never mentioning how long he would remain in Istanbul, and she was afraid to ask. How could she go back to life before him?

"I'm leaving for Bursa this afternoon," he said one morning. "I'll be buying silk. I have letters of introduction from a Greek friend of my father in New York. He knows many of the Bursa silk factory owners. I'll be gone about a week, I think. But you'll know the moment I'm back, because I'll be here, waiting for you to open your shop."

"I'll miss you. It won't be the same," Gül said before she could stop herself.

"I hope you'll miss me as much as I will you," David said as he reached around her waist and drew her to him, which required but a light touch to guide her where she was eagerly waiting to meet his lips.

"When I return from Bursa, I'll only be able to remain in Istanbul for a few days. My father has cabled, asking why I've been so long. I said I was having trouble finding the quality of fabrics that we need. But that was not true. I delayed because of you. I love you. I want you to come to New York with me as my wife. I've spoken with the ship's captain. He'll marry us. You don't have to answer now, if you wish to have time to think about it, but I'll need your answer when I return from Bursa. If your answer is yes, I want to meet your mother and ask her permission."

"No," Gül blurted out. "I mean, yes, I want to marry you, but I mean, no, you don't know who I am, and when you learn, you won't want to marry me." She began to cry as she rolled up her sleeve, thankful that she was wearing a blouse with billowy sleeves that made it possible to completely expose her arm up to the shoulder without removing her blouse. "I've always kept this hidden since I was little and my real mother and I were beggars. Nigar is my mother, but she's not." Gül was crying almost silently, and gripped David tightly around his waist. "I'm so ashamed. No one wants to marry a liar, but some of what I said was true." With her head buried against his chest, she told him the full story. She stopped sobbing and waited for David to apologize for withdrawing his offer of marriage.

David lifted her head and kissed her again. This time much longer. "The scar is nothing. New York is filled with scarred people. They come to New York to ignore their scars, to be valued for what they are beyond their scars, as you will be. You will be accepted. And loved. By me. By my parents. By everyone who comes to know you. And by our children, who will celebrate Christian, Muslim, and Jewish holidays and be envied by all their friends."

Gül started crying again. This time from joy, holding onto David as though she would collapse if she did not. "Are you sure you want to marry me?"

"More sure than before you told me your story."

"What about your parents? Will they accept me?"

"My parents married in spite of the disapproval of their parents. They would never disapprove. They will welcome you, and once they know you, they'll think me a worthy son and a lucky man. They'll see that I'm happy, and that's all they want for me. They'll only want for you to be equally happy in your marriage to me."

"I won't lie to them, ever. Or to you again, ever. Will you forgive me?"

"Only if you marry me."

"I will."

FIFTY-FIVE

Three years Mithat had spent in this miserable cell with its dirt floor, flies, bare stone walls, narrow slit of glassless barred window high up on the wall through which nothing was visible but the sky. Initially, he was allowed to have a servant, who cooked for him and did his laundry. The servant purchased vegetables, fruit, and meat. He was allowed to receive fresh clothing, money, tobacco, soap, and food from his family, though he knew from his family's letters that not all of what they sent reached him.

He was here on a life sentence, so there was no reason to have hope, but at the beginning, he could not help but feel that he might be released. He was innocent. Surely one of the men who had lied at the trial would recant his testimony to restore his soul before facing his Maker. Even Abdülhamit, who knew the truth, would have to consider the judgment of Allah. But when he sent an appeal to Abdülhamit, asking that his sentence be commuted, he did not receive a reply.

Nevertheless, in his letters to his family, he remained positive, expressing gratitude that as a ten-year-old he had memorized the Quran, so that now he could pass four or five days' time reciting it and feeling spiritually fulfilled. Remembering the rich events of his life also helped him to pass the time. He knew that their letters were read by several levels of officials and that some of their letters to him and his to them did not reach their destinations. But with the help of sympathizers, they managed to send a few letters outside of the official route.

Both of his wives and his married daughter from his first wife wrote to him, sent him pictures of the children and grandchildren, and reported on their health and progress in school. The letters covered practical matters about the family's properties and finances and asked about his food, comfort, and health. His letters also concerned matters of property and finances, expressed concern for their welfare, and reassured them that he was healthy and in good spirits, while acknowledging in one letter that he was conscious of his 60 years, a long life with many blessings. Perhaps he would die of old age, and if so, he would have no regrets. He frequently mentioned his pleasure in praying five times a day and Allah's mercy in forgiving him for having failed to do so most of his life. He reassured them that he was at peace with his *kismet*.

In one of her letters, Şehriban reminded him that when they had gone to Crete, he had promised to retire and tend a garden of flowers. She hoped that when he was released this time, he would keep that promise. But Mithat knew well why he had left Crete. As much as he enjoyed caring for flowers, it did not fulfill him. His real passion was the garden that was the Ottoman Empire. There was no more captivating garden, nor one that needed him more. He saw that its many varieties of roses, hibiscus, and tulips needed watering, pruning, and mulching, and he saw potential to enhance its beauty with new varieties, changes in landscaping, and new arrangements among its beds. Flowers with bent stems and shriveled petals asked for water and care. How could he not respond?

He knew that the empire offered its flowers to whoever bought the worthless bonds she proffered, promised her a future trinket for a current concession of mining or railroad track, fed her ego with the basest of flattery, or frightened her with threats of dismemberment—all the while stealing her archeological treasures. But he worked in the garden without regard to its profligate masters and ungrateful predators. There was no more beautiful garden, nor one that needed his care more.

But in the end, he had been cast out of the garden, thrown into this cell in this remote corner of the empire, where even the Ottoman army was not feared and where the tribes owed fealty to no overlord, had no interest in or respect for the Ottoman or any other worldly empire, and acknowledged not even the passage of centuries.

Now, almost three years had passed. The prisoners were not allowed to talk with each other except under guard during the brief periods of their two daily meals—also the only times they were allowed outside their cells. Each prisoner had a guard assigned 24-hours-a-day, every day. They heard that their increasingly severe conditions were due to persistent reports to Abdülhamit that they had escaped or attempted to escape and that others were plotting to free them. Because they knew these reports to be baseless, they could only conclude that the reports were fabricated to set the stage for their executions.

After the first year, Mithat received no more provisions from his family, and he told them they should stop sending any, as they were not reaching him. By the third year, even the prison food rations were reduced. One meal might be a light "soup" of water and flour and the second a small portion of boiled beet greens. He became thin, weak, and sick. He had an infected carbuncle and dysentery, and it seemed possible that the food was poisoned, which was a fear the prisoners shared. He no longer held any hope of being released and speculated as to the most preferable death: strangulation, hanging, poisoning, shooting, or illness?

He would die without seeing his empire become a nurturing mother to her subjects. But he would not die without hope. He would not see it, but he believed that the model for provincial administration that he had developed and that was in the Law of the Provinces would bring about national reform. What some called idealistic, he had proved practical. There were now multi-ethnic, multi-religious representative councils in small towns, district centers, and provincial capitals throughout the empire, venues in which Christians, Jews, and Muslims met together, had open discussions, and made decisions. If any democratic movement were to succeed at the national level, it would be because of the experience of these people. Citizens engaged in issues of fair taxes, equal justice, education, health care, and infrastructure would overpower the inter-tribal, inter-religious fights for which the empire paid a high price in lives, money, and international criticism.

Surely, the people would not accept to be ruled by an autocrat from Istanbul once they experienced representative government locally. They would no longer need a reformer in Istanbul to be their champion. They could become their own reformers. That was how it should be. His duty completed, he could be content even to die in this cell. Allah would surely bless him as a martyr in a holy cause. He asked Allah only that he die peacefully of the aging that he felt in every joint of his body, and he thanked Him for His compassion in forgiving his sins.

On a day when the breeze through his glassless window told Mithat that it must be late April or early May, his cell door opened. Two men wearing balalaika masks stepped into the cell, one with a silk chord stretched between his gloved hands — assassins. He greeted them in a calm voice and asked that he be allowed to perform his ablutions, pray, and recite the thirty-sixth sura of the Quran, the sura he had recited often on the deaths of others. But the larger man wrapped his arms around him from in front, and the second man tightened the chord around his neck from behind. Only his eyes could voice a prayer for mercy and forgiveness before all went black.

FIFTY-SIX

Gül was eager to tell her mother and Cristo the news. She hoped no one would be in the shop when her mother's carriage arrived, so that she could close early. Would her mother approve? Think her impetuous, naïve? Even driven by lust? Of course, even though she did not wish to acknowledge it, she knew that all of those things existed in some measure. But they were not behind her decision. David had become her friend, her confidant. He could never be only someone she had met in her shop and found physically attractive. She had shared her most intimate secrets with him. If he disappeared from her life, her heart would stop.

She would ask her mother to come with them to New York. Everything David said about New York made it sound like a natural home for a Belgian woman who had fitted dresses for princesses and concubines, married an Ottoman prince, been a shopkeeper in the most up-scale district of Istanbul, and raised produce to feed refugees. A still vibrant woman who might marry again in a place like New York. A woman who would walk her grandchildren in the garden David called Central Park.

When her mother arrived, no one was in the shop, and Gül immediately pulled the shades and locked the door. Cristo was waiting for them. Tea was on its way.

"You closed early," Cristo said as Gül approached.

"Yes, I wanted to have tea with you and mother," Gül responded, attempting to sound casual, as though this were just another day of closing up, having tea, and riding home to Kağıthane, where, after today, nothing would be the same.

"You want to marry an American?" Nigar said with an inflection of complete surprise. "When can I meet him?"

394

"He's gone to Bursa, but he'll be back in a week. You'll meet him as soon as he returns."

"It's the young man who wears no hat and has been waiting in the mornings for you to open your shop, I assume," said Cristo.

"You knew about him!" Nigar questioned incredulously. "And you didn't tell me? I feel betrayed by my best friend. Why do we have tea except to share what we know, especially gossip about lovers in Pera. I may never come for tea again," she said but with a light tone to indicate that she meant none of it.

"Well, I couldn't be sure. Gossiping about others passes time, but gossiping about the family of a friend is not wise. Do you not think me a wise man? If I'd told you of my suspicion, you wouldn't have looked surprised just now, and Gül would have thought me no more than a common street gossip. I'm your friend, but I'm also her uncle. Here comes our tea. If you wish to stand on being offended, you don't have to drink yours."

"I'll drink only not to be rude," Nigar said and smiled at him. "But now we need to hear everything about the man you propose to marry," she continued, turning toward Gül and embracing her.

Gül shared what she knew, which she realized was not a great deal. She wasn't marrying him because of who he was and what she knew of him but because of the kind of person he was, which was more difficult to express. "He talks to me about everything, and I feel I can tell him what I know and what I feel. When he asked me to marry him, I told him about what happened in my village, about the long walk to Istanbul, begging, being hungry sometimes, and feeling dirty most of the time. I showed him my scar. I was sure he wouldn't want to marry me after he knew the truth about me, but he only smiled and said something about everyone in New York having scars."

"He's right," said Cristo. "People take the hatreds of their homelands with them to America, but once there, they cannot kill each other for the grievances of their ancestors. They make accommodations."

"I even told him that my mother wanted me to raise children to kill Christians," Gül continued. "But I told him I didn't have that emotion in me, that if he married me, I would teach our children to love everyone. I love the mother I had before what happened, and I love the mother I have now," she said, starting to cry, and holding onto Nigar.

"In heaven your mother is a loving soul. She wants you to raise loving children," Nigar said as she stroked her hair.

"That's right," said Cristo. "Has anyone heard of an angel spreading hatred? Today's papers report that Mithat Pasha died of typhoid in the Taif prison. Mithat's dream that the *millets* of the Ottoman Empire would live in harmony will never happen. There's too much history. But America is new; its *millets* are new. Mithat's dream has a chance there. And you can be a part of it. If I were young, *I* would go."

"Will you come with us, Mother?" Gül asked.

The question sent Nigar's mind racing. She knew her answer would be no, but the question took her back to the day when she had arrived in Istanbul. Yes, she could make yet another new life in yet another country. But she had no desire to do so. "No, I will not join you. I came to Istanbul when I was young, a romantic idealist. It was exciting that Abdülhamit wanted to marry me, and I felt I could help him. But he didn't want my help."

"His mistake," interjected Cristo. "Your mother is a very smart woman."

"You're very kind, Cristo. Unfortunately, I fear history will not remember Abdülhamit well. Nothing I can do will change that. But I committed myself to his country. I'm happy here," Nigar said and continued, turning to Gül. "But I'll come to see you in New York when you have children, and you must bring them to see me, to see the land of their grandparents."

"Yes, and don't wait too long," Cristo added. "I'm getting old. We need more tea. Tea!" he yelled down the street.

"Thank you. Both of you. I don't know how I will find such good people as you in New York."

"I'll give you the name of a cousin of mine who lives there," Cristo said. "He's well connected in the Greek community. And the Greeks know the Turks. They hate each other in their living rooms, but in a new world it's easier for a Greek to do business with a Turk than with an Italian. Enemies know each other."

"You should have been a philosopher, Uncle Cristo."

"I am one. And a Patriarch too, thanks to your mother. I only open this shop to feed my family."

"We have so much to do," Nigar said, suddenly feeling as though they had no time to be having tea. "When are you leaving? Are you getting married before you leave?"

"I forgot to ask the day the ship leaves, but David said it leaves a few days after he returns from Bursa. We're getting married on the ship."

"We'll close the shop until you leave," Nigar said. "We have to get you ready. We have clothes to make, shopping to do. I'm so happy for you."

"I forgot to tell you. David's mother has a dress shop in New York. I'll be helping her. I'll be able to make my own designs. I told David about how we make clothes from rags. He's very eager to meet you."

"And I him. I do wish I could be on the ship for the wedding."

"Please, change your mind and come with us."

Nigar was tempted, but her life was here. Gül needed a new life. She did not. She was proud to be an Istanbulite, an Alevi Muslim citizen of the Ottoman Empire, a subject of Abdülhamit II, a sultan who welcomed the refugees she worked with. She no longer felt love for him as her husband, but she felt empathy for him and still wanted to help him. The Powers were directly and indirectly working to destroy his empire. Even though an autocrat, he was powerless, able to do but little. And what could she do? Nothing that would affect the international power struggle. Everything that would give her life meaning.

FIFTY-SEVEN

The cable informed Abdülhamit that Mithat Pasha had died of typhoid. The local newspapers reported the same, as did the international press over the next several days. Abdülhamit hoped that Mithat's death would not warrant mention by the European press, but all of the papers carried the notice. Also the *New York Times*. Not one varied from the official line of death by illness, and yet Abdülhamit was annoyed at the importance attributed to Mithat. The famous constitutionalist! And what had the constitution achieved? Nothing. It was hardly ever mentioned in the coffeehouses any more. And no one called for the restoration of parliament. The famous constitutionalist had given Abdülhamit his last indigestion. The empire and Abdülhamit's rule of it were safe.

Even the thunderheads of ethnic, religious, and nationalist politics poised to descend on him from beyond every mountain range no longer seemed ominous—mere showers with light wind. Not one of his informants reported signs of a threat. And his many personal connections to the non-Muslim *millets* and the non-Turkish members of the Muslim *millet* reinforced his perception that they were loyal to him and the empire and would remain so.

Few Greeks emigrated from the Ottoman Empire to Greece. Athens held historic mystique, but Istanbul, Bursa, Salonika, and Smyrna were bustling commercial centers. Hundreds of the empire's coastal towns and villages were home to Greeks, whose ancestors knew no other land. Abdülhamit had a Greek foreign affairs advisor to whom he delegated international negotiations.

The man he appointed as grand vizier, after dismissing Mithat, was of Greek origin. His ambassador to London was Greek, as was his cook, whom he trusted to prepare his food. His personal physician was Greek. A Greek banker managed his money.

His Armenian broker had made him rich, and many Armenians served his government. Armenian merchants negotiated the purchase of the American guns for the war with Russia. Armenians performed the Karagöz puppet shows and theater performances throughout the country and in Yıldız. The Armenian community's centuries of trusted service to the empire earned them the approbation, "the loyal millet." Their prosperity rested on fealty, not revolt. Some of Abdülhamit's advisors counseled him to punish the Armenians for their traitorous behavior in the east during the war. But Abdülhamit knew that any retribution, however justified, could provoke European intervention. Anyway, they had paid a heavy price. Many Armenians died during the war in the east.

Armenians were educating their children in American mission schools and sending them to America, not to the Armenian communities in Russia. Abdülhamit knew that Russia encouraged Armenian nationalism only as a weapon to further its interest for territory. Many reports confirmed that Russia feared that an independent Armenia could spur its Muslim minorities to aspire to national autonomy.

And Britain? Abdülhamit understood now that its base on Cyprus was not to protect his empire against Russian incursion in the east or even to protect the Christians there, but to defend British interests in Egypt, India, and East Africa. British interests did not include a war to establish an Armenia.

To save the empire, Abdülhamit relied on the interdependence of the empire and its Christian minorities.

The Greeks and Armenians managed and benefitted from the commercial and financial life of the empire and their favorable concessions for business. The Greeks and Armenians were the source of money for loans and owned most of the stores in the cities and towns. In even the smallest Turkish or Kurdish village, if there was a general store, it was owned by a Greek or an Armenian. The Agriculture Bank that provided loans to farmers throughout the empire had mostly Greek and Armenian staff. To prosper, the Greek and Armenian communities needed peace and stability in the empire, and this is what Abdülhamit wanted, as well.

The briefly rebellious Albanians were quiet again. They were Muslims and called him Caliph. The Palace Guards were Albanians. Abdülhamit praised them, thanked them, provided them with good quarters and food, and gave them gifts on holidays. They had centuries of history as fighters trusted to guard the sultan and Caliph. They benefitted from being a part of the empire. Their homeland was surrounded by Christian neighbors. Alone, they would be vulnerable.

And the Jews? The Jewish *millet* was grateful for the empire's protection. They would not rebel. Where could they go?

Arab gentry had palaces on the Bosphorus. Arab religious men paid him obeisance, called him Caliph, brought him gifts, and counseled him. Arab nationalism looked to be another British straw man to justify imperialism.

Abdülhamit was confident that he knew his subjects. The *millet* system gave everyone their independence within the structure of the state, a kind of federation of *millets*. Without the foreign agitation of false promises, the *millets* would remain allied with him. It was in their interest, and most of their members knew it.

And he deserved their loyalty. Everything he did was for the good of the people. Worthy even of praise, when, in his humility, he sought only allegiance. Yes, he was safe. Free to enjoy being sultan. But he could not. Mithat remained alive in his thoughts. He sat down at his piano and played a few bars, an activity that usually took his mind off troubling matters. But not tonight. He played only briefly.

How would Mithat have been murdered? Not publicly by hanging or a firing squad. Not with a knife or sword. Any of these means would be obvious to the imam who would wash the body. Strangulation was the obvious method. Many sultans and princes had been strangled. He held his breath, simulating the cessation of oxygen and gasping for air within seconds. A frightening way to die, unable to breathe, but with time and mind enough to think ever so briefly before death blanked out everything that was you.

Abdülhamit was disconcerted. He sat down to read spy reports but found himself disinterested in their contents—even in ones reporting that Mithat had not died but had escaped and was hiding in Istanbul or in London. Spies lied. He paid them, knowing they would lie, but knowing also that among the lies he could find truth. Divining veracity was his prerogative, the skill by which he kept himself safe. Tsar Alexander II of Russia, American President Garfield, and Sultan Abdülaziz had been assassinated. Queen Victoria had been the target of an assassination. Nationalists, irredentists, and religious zealots could achieve their objectives only with the consent of many. An assassin, however, needed no collaborators. No amount of diligence was too much. Every person representing a threat, as Mithat had, would be found out and eliminated—as a service to the nation.

402

Well into the middle of the night, he finally went to bed and was sleeping—though lightly—when he awoke to see Mithat standing erect at the end of the bed, staring at him, not judgmentally, not angrily, just directly, as though to say, "I am here. Day and night. In this world and the next."

"But I did not kill you," Abdülhamit whispered in a pleading tone, as though one more utterance of the lie might make it true.

Drenched in sweat, Abdülhamit flipped over and grabbed the pistol he kept under his pillow, but when he turned, prepared to fire, the image was gone. Despite foreign exile, internal exile, imprisonment, death, Mithat had prevailed. "Allah damn you to hell," he muttered, quietly, as though fearing Allah might hear him. But Mithat was a murderer. This was proved in court. A murderer must suffer eternal punishment in hell. Surely Allah would not favor a murderer over the sultan who brought him to justice?

He looked to the foot of the bed where Hanımefendi lay on the robe he had given her, undisturbed in her sleep, and he knew that he would never know what he saw in her perfect serenity—the peace of being loved.

EPILOGUE

Sultan Abdülhamit II ruled from 1876 to 1909 and was the last sultan to wield power. The novel ends in 1883 with the death of his nemesis, Mithat Pasha. Abdülhamit II, the sultan who wished to be blamed for nothing, was left accountable for everything. Despite some success, his vision was narrow and his administration a traditional dictatorship. He walked a tight-wire of censorship, spies on spies, loyalty obsession, religious exploitation, and diplomatic concessions for a surprisingly long time before being deposed by the Young Turks (not to be confused with the earlier movement of Young Ottomans).

Abdülhamit is a controversial figure, both in the West and in Turkey, and is often called "the red sultan," implying that he had blood on his hands. During the Russo-Turkish war, many Armenians in the east were killed and driven from their homes when the Russians, to whom they were providing support, lost battles and territory. But Muslims in the east suffered the same fate at the hands of Armenians in battle sites when the Russians were victorious. Historians do not represent these incidents as official Russian or Ottoman policy, but as the result of local ethnic animosities and opportunism. The same was true in the west between Bulgarian Christians and Muslims. But the blood was spilled during Abdülhamit's reign.

Also, the first bloodshed of the revolutionary activity of the Armenians began during Abdülhamit's rule. (These events were subsequent to the period covered in this novel.) Armenian revolutionaries armed Armenian peasants and provoked them to acts against their Muslim neighbors that today would be called terrorism. Armenian farmers in eastern Anatolia were oppressed by the Ottoman tax collectors and the Kurdish landlords and warlords. Provoking them to rise up was easy, but they had no chance when Abdülhamit authorized the irregular forces to restore order—a euphemism for taking revenge, in which they were joined by Muslim civilians. (This was not the uprising and subsequent violence and forced exile against the Armenians, which is characterized by some as genocide. That occurred later under the Young Turks.)

The revolutionary Armenian intellectuals assumed that the Ottoman government's inevitable harsh response to terror and treason would result in European armies coming to rescue them and secure for them an Armenian homeland from some of the Ottoman Empire's eastern provinces. But none came. Russia feared the nationalist aspirations of her own minorities and worried that Western intervention would strengthen British influence in the area. The Europeans, for their part, with no compelling national interests at stake, also were not eager for war. The Armenians were a minority population even in the eastern provinces. In all but one of those provinces, they were a small minority, living among an overwhelming majority of Muslims— Kurds, Turks, Circassians, Tatars, and Laz.

In addition to the peasants, many Armenians in several cities were killed at the hands of mobs. These attacks are laid at Abdülhamit's feet, because some attacks appeared orchestrated and ceased when Abdülhamit so ordered. Historians report vastly disparate numbers of Armenians killed in the uprisings in the east and the mob actions in cities. (A credible number may be up to 15,000.) But whatever the number may have been, the deaths, whether ordered or tolerated by Abdülhamit, painted him red. And he had Mithat's blood on his hands, as well.

But he also showed restraint. He did not order reprisals or prosecutions of Armenians for their acts of treason leading up to and during the Russo-Turkish war in the east. These acts were reported not just by Turkish officials but by the British Consul, a British traveler, and Western newsmen and military observers.

Armenian separatists openly incited revolution and treason. They bombed and occupied the Ottoman Bank in Istanbul, killed employees and police, and held bank employees, including Europeans, hostage. Their surrender was negotiated by European embassies on the promise of free escort out of the country with no punishment, a condition Abdülhamit honored.

When Armenian terrorists detonated a bomb intended to assassinate him, at least 20 guards were killed and many people injured. Abdülhamit did not order reprisals on Armenian citizens.

The characterization of Abdülhamit as a sultan with blood on his hands is juxtaposed by others as a "great" sultan because of his civil and diplomatic accomplishments. He initiated many civil public works projects that demonstrate the sincerity of his frequent expressions of concern for his citizenry and his commitment to improving their lives and the well-being of his empire. He modernized the dockyards of port cities and extended telegraph and railroad lines for thousands of miles throughout the empire. He completed a railroad to the Holy cities and lines in the European provinces to connect Istanbul to Paris. He improved life in the cities with gas lighting, water and sewer lines, and a tramway in Istanbul. He built the Museum of Constantinople as part of a policy to keep the empire's archeological treasures at home. He established a forestry department to preserve, restore, and regulate the cutting of forests.

He promoted education. To supplement the existing religious school network, he built primary and secondary schools for general education throughout the provinces and higher education technical schools to train his subjects in the modern skills of engineering, medicine, civil administration, and civil law. He recognized that without these skills, his Muslim citizens—and he as their sovereign—were at a disadvantage, not only relative to Europe and Russia but relative to the non-Muslim citizens of his empire, who had their own schools and educated many of their children in foreign, Christian-run schools at home and abroad. The Ottoman schools, primary through university, were open to non-Muslims, and there were separate primary and secondary schools for girls, as well as a women's teacher training university and a school of arts and trades, one for girls and one for boys.

He opened schools to train technocrats to staff the Ottoman bureaucracy, including the Royal Academy of Administration and a language school for diplomats. Abdülhamit had a passion for information as a tool of power, and he established statistical bureaus to provide a ready supply of data, including socioeconomic census information. Book publication thrived, and the vast majority of books published were on science, law, and literature.

Fiscally, Abdülhamit brought economic stability. He inherited a collapsed economy that was made worse by the cost of the war with Russia and the war indemnity to Russia stipulated in the Treaty of Berlin. Abdülhamit took measures to reduce spending and pay down the debt. He encouraged commerce by eliminating the tax on the internal transport of goods and set up chambers of commerce throughout the empire in provincial capitals and even in smaller cities. Manufacturing increased, particularly of clothing, cement, thread, glass, and tobacco products, improving the Ottoman trade imbalance and keeping the Ottoman currency stable relative to European currencies. The silk industry prospered, and mining—especially of coal—significantly expanded. One historian has credited the Abdülhamit era as the period when Muslims became entrepreneurs—much of the formal commercial activity prior to this having been conducted by Christians and Jews. Also helpful to commerce was the success of the Agriculture Bank network that provided credit and undermined the exploitive money-lenders.

Most historical accounts do not represent Abdülhamit as rigorous in religious observance, although he stressed his role as Caliph to a degree beyond what had been the tradition of his predecessors. Among his overt gestures was his personal financial support of and energetic promotion for the railway to Mecca, which assured safe passage for pilgrims and supported the perception he cultivated of himself as a devout person. He did not, however, perform the haj to Mecca, one of the requirements of a Muslim of adequate means to do so. Interestingly, there is no record of any Ottoman sultan performing the haj. In addition to the railway project, he is reported to have been generous in his personal philanthropy.

Some historians interpret Abdülhamit's emphasis on Islam and himself as Caliph in the later years of his reign as an attempt to strengthen the attachment of his Arab provinces to his empire. But the Arabs were less attentive to this appeal than the Europeans were. The Arabs ignored it. The Europeans feared it.

Culturally, the admiration for and pursuit of all things European, particularly French, were strengthened during Abdülhamit's reign, both by him and by the educated elite, despite his political support for Pan-Islam.

That the Ottoman Empire did not collapse during his reign is attributed by historians to the fear of his adversaries of each other and to Abdülhamit's astute foreign policy decisions. He recognized his military weakness and chose to solve disputes by negotiation. He compromised on the terms under which territories would remain loosely a part of his domain, and the Russians and Europeans accepted this as the quid pro quo for having effective control over resources and geography, while recognizing his suzerainty and paying nominal tribute.

The Ottoman *millet* system, under which its ethnically diverse communities enjoyed cultural, religious, linguistic, and judicial autonomy, was the hallmark of the empire's successful administration of its extensively diverse population for centuries. But it encouraged separateness of identity that the Russians and Europeans exploited for their territorial ambitions and that easily evolved into nationalism based on language, religion, and culture.

Commander Süleyman Pasha was blamed for the loss of the Russo-Turkish war, charged with treason, and sentenced to 15 years in a military prison.

Commander Osman Nuri Pasha, the hero of Plevna, remains a hero. Every schoolchild in Turkey knows the military marching tune, "The Osman Pasha March." He was highly respected by the Russians, who permitted him to bear his sword at the surrender signing ceremony, where he was saluted on entry. Even as a prisoner, he was not asked to relinquish his sword. After the war, he became Marshal of Yıldız Palace.

Baker Pasha returned to Istanbul after the armistice and was made Military Advisor to the Ottoman Army. But after their military victory over Urabi's Egyptian army at Tel-el-Kabir, the British decided to reorganize the Egyptian military under British command, and they offered this position to Valentine Baker Pasha. Once again he demonstrated exceptional bravery under fire in several engagements, but he died peacefully in bed.

Istanbul Sites

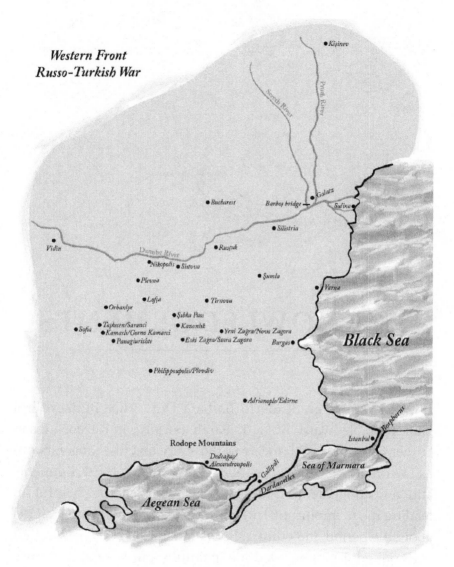

Western Front
Russo-Turkish War

Kişinev

Seveth River

Prut River

Bucharest

Barboş bridge — Galatz

Sulina

Silistria

Danube River

Ruşçuk

Vidin

Nikopolis • Sistova

Plevna

Şumla

Varna

Lofça

Tirnova

Orhaniye

Şibka Pass

Tujkesen/Saranci • Kazanlık

Kamarlı/Gorno Kamatci • Yeni Zagra/Nova Zagora

Sofia • Panagiurishte • Eski Zagra/Stara Zagora

Burgas

Black Sea

Philippoupolis/Plovdiv

Adrianople/Edirne

Bosphorus

Rodope Mountains

Istanbul

Dedeagaç/ Alexandroupolis

Gallipoli

Sea of Marmara

Aegean Sea

Dardanelles

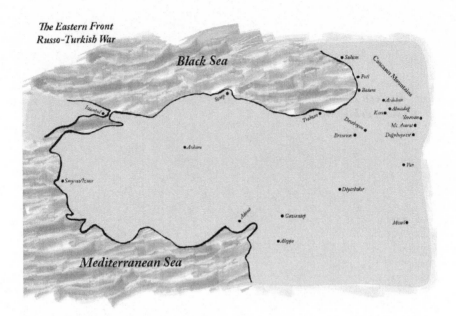

The Eastern Front
Russo-Turkish War

Black Sea

Caucasus Mountains

• Sukum

• Poti

• Batum

Sinop •

• Ardahan

Istanbul •

Trabzon •

• Almadağ

Kars •

Yerevan •

Mt. Ararat •

Dereköyün •

Erzurum •

Dağnbuyazıt •

• Ankara

• Van

• Smyrna/Izmir

• Diyarbakır

Adana •

• Gaziantep

Mosul •

• Aleppo

Mediterranean Sea

ACKNOWLEDGEMENTS

My thanks and gratitude to Barbara Day, Alice Bunker, Erol Hatipoğlu, Howard Roland, Sarah Sorkin, and Denis Ihsan Sumer who stuck with me, read the entire text (the long version) as I wrote it over several years, and provided helpful comments and encouragement. Denis was also particularly helpful in leading me to important Turkish sources and giving me insights about the period and culture. Special thanks to Nina Selz for her editorial advice, which led me, painfully but wisely, to reduce the text significantly in length and for her final copy edit and proofreading. Charles Rogers made my rough-drawn maps look professional and made a great cover from my amateur photo.

412

My wife, Carmel, read the manuscript in three edited versions, which was sacrifice enough, but forfeited many days and nights to my research and writing that might otherwise have been shared in travel and over movies, concerts, dinners, and wine tastings.

AUTHOR'S NOTES

This novel grew out of living in Turkey for eight years where I experienced a modern culture steeped in history. Turks still referenced the Crusades as defining the attitude and politics of Western Christian countries toward Muslim ones. They spoke of repeated wars with Russia from the 17th century on—but particularly of the Crimean War, the Russo-Turkish War of 1877-78, and World War I. I met descendants of refugees from those wars. Among the historic Turkish figures often mentioned, Sultan Abdülhamit II and Mithat Pasha, the primary protagonists in my novel, were unusual in that their names were as likely to be mentioned in derision as in praise. I felt that their story needed to be told through an accessible vehicle, a novel that remained true to the history of these characters and might inspire the novel's readers to explore this rich history further through the many well-written volumes by historians. And in particular I felt that this story was compelling because it is current. The human emotions, historic events, and conflicts in the novel continue to be experienced by the people of the region and are reflected in today's headlines.

While the events portrayed in the novel are of historical record, the thoughts and conversations of the characters are imagined, though they reflect the essence of what is reported in the sources I consulted. The direct quotes attributed to Queen Victoria, the *fetvas*, and the first sura of the Quran are cited in many sources.

The primary characters in the novel, Abdülhamit, Mithat Pasha, Hüseyin Avni, Osman Nuri Pasha, and Baker Pasha, as well as most of the minor characters, are historic figures who experienced the events recounted in this novel. The character of Flora, later called Nigar, is real as I present her up through Abdülhamit's investiture as sultan and her refusal to enter the harem. After this she is lost in historical record so far as I could find, other than some contradictory speculations. So, what I have written of her life following Abdülhamit's accession to the throne is from my imagination. The characters of Ayşe, Fatma, Gül, and Cristo are fictional composites of people who surely lived and whose experiences would have been those reflected in the novel's narrative.

I based the novel as closely as I could on the historical record, but the available accounts are not of a single narrative. Contradictions of fact and nuance abound. Some readers may disagree with my characterizations. I accept that, as I accept sole responsibility for what I present. The primary sources on which I relied for my narrative are provided below.

Place names and Turkish words. I used Istanbul throughout, although at the time of the novel the city was called some variation of "Constantinople" by speakers of many languages and even by the Turks in official documents. For other sites I used place names current at the time. I used the Turkish alphabet in spelling most of the Turkish words, except for those common in English, such as, pasha, Sheikh Ul-Islam, haj, etc.

Abdülhamit, *Abdülhamid'in Hatıra Defteri* (Memoir Notebook) (Ankara 2012).

Achtermeier, William O., 'The Turkish Connection: The Saga of the Peabody-Martini Rifle', *Man at Arms Magazine* Vol. 1, Number 2, pp. 12-21, 5557, March/April 1979.

An American Observer (anonymous), *A Few Facts About Turkey Under the Reign of Abdul Hamid II* (New York 1895).

Baker, Valentine, *War in Bulgaria: A Narrative of Personal Experiences*, Volumes 1 & 2 (London 1879).

Barry, Quinton, *War in the East, A Military History of the Russo-Turkish War 1877-78* (Solihull 2012).

Burnaby, Frederick, *On Horseback Through Asia Minor* (Oxford 1996 [originally published in 1878])

Çulcu, Murat, *Şu Bizim '93 Harbi', Osmanlı'da Büyük Kırılma* (This '93 war' of ours, a great Ottoman collapse ['93 refers to 1293 in the Muslim calendar—1877 in the Christian Calendar]) (Istanbul 2014).

Davey, Richard, *The Sultan and His Subjects*, Volumes I & II (London 1897).

Deringil, Selim, *The Well-Protected Domains* (London 2011).

Devereaux, Robert, *The First Ottoman Constitutional Period, A Study of the Midhat Constitution and Parliament* (Baltimore 1963).

Engin, Vahdettin, *II. Abdülhamid ve Dış Politika* (Abdülhamid II and Foreign Policy) (Istanbul 2011).

Fife-Cookson, John, *With the Armies of the Balkans and at Gallipoli in 1877-1878, etc. With plates and maps* (London 1880).

Findley, Carter Vaughn, *Turkey, Islam, and Modernity, A History, 1789-2007* (New Haven & London 2010).

Gay, J. Drew, *Plevna, the Sultan, and the Porte: Reminiscences of the War in Turkey* (London 1878).

Greene, Frances V., *Report on the Russian Army and its Campaign in Turkey 1877-78* (New York 1879).

Hanioğlu, M. Şükrü, *A Brief History of the Late Ottoman Empire* (Princeton 2008).

Haslip, Joan, *The Sultan* (London 1958).

Herbert, William V., Charles Ryan, and John Sandes, *Conflict at Plevna: Two Accounts of the Russo-Turkish War of 1877-78* (Driffield 2013).

McCarthy, Justin, *Death and Exile: The Ethnic Cleansing of Ottoman Muslims, 1821-1922* (Princeton 2004).

Mithat, Ali Haydar, *The Life of Midhat Pasha* (London 1903)

Müftüoğlu, Mustafa, *Abdülhamid Ulu Hakan Mı?Kızıl Sultan Mı?, Vol. I & II* (Abdulhamid, Great Emperor or Red Sultan?) (Istanbul 2007)

Osmanoğlu, Ayşe, *Babam Sultan Abdülhamid* (My Father, Sultan Abdülhamid) (Istanbul 2013).

Pears, Sir Edwin, *Life of Abdul Hamid* (London 1917).

Shaw, Stanford and Ezel, *History of the Ottoman Empire and Modern Turkey, Vol. II* (Cambridge 1977).

St. Aubyn, Giles, *Queen Victoria, a Portrait* (New York 1992)

Uzunçarşılı, İsmail Hakkı, *Midhat Paşa ve Taif Mahkumları* (Mithat Pasha and the Prisoners in Taif) (Ankara 1992).

_____. *Midhat Paşa ve Yıldız Mahkemesi* (Mithat Pasha and the Yıldız Trial) (Ankara 2000).

Yasamee, F.A.K., *Ottoman Diplomacy: Abdülhamid II and the Great Powers, 1878-1888* (Istanbul 1996).

PRONUNCIATION GUIDE AND GLOSSARY

Turkish pronunciation is regular. That is, letters have only one pronunciation, regardless of the word or position within a word in which the letter appears, with the exception of a few rare words that must be learned as such. Most letters of the Turkish alphabet are close enough to English to be acceptably pronounced as in English, and I do not include them here. I include the pronunciation of vowels in Turkish that in English have several pronunciations. 'A' as in arm. 'E' as in emerald. 'İ/i' as in eat. 'I/ı' as in comic. 'C' as in jam. 'Ç' is 'ch'. 'Ş' is 'sh'. 'Ğ' is a silent letter that lengthens the preceding vowel, like a diphthong. 'G' as in go. 'J' as in the French bon jour. 'O' as in sofa. 'U' as in uber. 'Ö' and 'Ü' as in German.

Alevi: A Muslim Shiite sect whose original followers ascribed to Sufi mysticism.

Ayran: A drink made by diluting plain yogurt with water.

Bey: historically a title equivalent to provincial or territorial governor. In modern Turkish, equivalent to "Mr." but used after a first name, e.g., Mithat Bey.

Cemevi: Alevi community building used as a mosque and for other community purposes.

Elif: First letter of the Arabic alphabet. Also a Turkish girls' name.

Fetva: A religious legal ruling made by the Sheikh Ul-Islam. May be a ruling on a matter of religious law or it may be a religious ruling on a secular matter.

418

Gazi: Honorary title given to military heroes of high rank.

Göbektaşı: Central, raised, round heated marble stone area in the "hot" room of the Turkish bath.

Hacivat: Supporting character in a popular type of shadow puppet show of social and political ridicule.

Hanımefendi: Polite title of address for a woman equivalent to "madam" when the woman's name is not used. In the novel, it is Abdülhamit's name for his favorite cat.

Han: A free waystation beside a road where travelers and their animals could take shelter. Also a Turkish variant on "Khan" to mean sultan, as in Abülhamit Han.

Henna: Red Ochre used by women for decorating their hands for celebratory occasions and by both men and women to dye their hair.

Hararat: The "hot" room in a public Turkish bathhouse.

Hoca: A teacher. Historically, connoting a religious teacher.

Karagöz: The lead character in a popular type of shadow puppet show of social and political ridicule.

Kayık: A narrow rowboat in common use in the Golden Horn and the Bosphorus. It could have as few as one oarsman or multiples of them. The word is the origin of the English word kayak.

Kismet: Fate.

Kızlar Ağa: The chief eunuch of the harem, always an African.

Konak: A term used for large houses, usually within walled gardens, occupied by families of wealth and position.

Kuruş: A unit of currency. In the period of the novel, there was a smaller unit, called a "para." Forty para equaled one kuruş, and one hundred Kuruş equaled one lira. The para no longer exists, but 100 kuruş continues to constitute one lira in today's currency.

Menemen: A dish of sautéed vegetables with eggs.

Millet: Communities in the Ottoman Empire based on religion, language and culture. Each millet had its own laws and courts based on its religion. There were several Christian millets, e.g., the Greek Orthodox millet was separate from the Armenian Orthodox millet.

Misvak: A twig from the *salvadora persica* tree, used to clean one's teeth.

Müezzin: Historically, the person who cried out the call to prayer from the balcony of a mosque's minaret. Today, the minarets have loudspeakers.

Ouzo: Greek anise-flavored spirit, equivalent to Turkish rakı.

Padishah: One of the titles of the Sultan, a Persian title, meaning Shah of Shahs or King of Kings.

Pasha: A title conferred on men of status in both civilian and military service. Used after the first name, pasha is similar to "sir" as an address of respect. Turks did not have last names until 1934.

Peştemal: Light-weight towels given to patrons in the public baths.

Pilav: Rice prepared in the Middle Eastern style that leaves the rice loose and not sticky.

Rakı: An anise-flavored, clear alcoholic beverage that turns a milky white color when water is added, giving it the sobriquet "lion's milk." Similar to ouzo in Greece and arak in Arab countries.

Ramazan: The ninth month in the Muslim lunar calendar which commemorates the revelation of the Quran to Muhammed. Muslims fast during this month from dawn to sunset.

Şeker Bayramı: Turkish three-day holiday celebrated at the end of the Muslim holy month of Ramazan.

Serasker: Literally, "chief soldier." Ottoman title for the Minister of War.

Softa: Student in the advanced religious schools.

Tanzimat: Term used generically for a series of administrative and judicial reforms implemented in the Ottoman Empire in the nineteenth century.

Tuğra: The calligraphic monogram or seal affixed to public documents, representing the signature of a sultan.

Ulema: Religious scholars who served as teachers in the religious schools and as judges in the religious courts.

Valide sultan: Title given to the mother of the sultan.

Yalı: A style of wooden house built on the shore of the Bosphorus, usually multi-storied with a dock to access the water from the shore level of the house and typically with at least one upper story that jutted out toward the water.

ABOUT THE AUTHOR

Allan R. Gall lived in Turkey for eight years as a Peace Corps English teacher, as a grants administrator for the Ford Foundation, and as a Fulbright-Hays research fellow. He has a Ph.D. in Near East Studies from the University of Michigan, and his dissertation examined the themes of Aziz Nesin's prodigious literary output. He translated Aziz Nesin's play, *Çiçu*, for *Ibrahim the Mad and Other Plays, An Anthology of Modern Turkish Drama*, edited by Talat S. Halman and Jayne L. Warner (Syracuse University Press, 2008). He authored *Of Mouse and Magic* (Two Harbors Press, 2011), a growing up novel for 7-12 year-old readers. "This book is not only great for children but for parents and grandparents also. Recommended for your child's home library," misslynnsbooks-n-more.blogspot.com. Listed among the 2011 Top Books Designed for Our Youth on thebestbookclub.com.

Allan grew up on a farm in South Dakota, taught high school English, and lived in The Yemen Arab Republic for three years as Peace Corps Country Director. He worked as Director of the Division of Operations for the federal Office of Refugee Resettlement, as the refugee policy expert on Barbara Jordan's Federal Commission for Immigration Reform and as the Deputy Inspector General and the Inspector General for the Peace Corps. He dabbles in carpentry and yard work, plays tennis, and spends time with his youngest grandson. He enjoys Doc Martin, theater, the occasional movie, Turkish food, and performances by the National Symphony Orchestra.

CPSIA information can be obtained
at www.ICGtesting.com
Printed in the USA
BVOW08s0502280318
511799BV00001B/2/P